HOW TO BE PERFECT

HOLLY WAINWRIGHT

Legend Press Ltd, 51 Gower Street, London, WC1E 6HJ
info@legend-paperbooks.co.uk | www.legendpress.co.uk

First published in 2018 by Allen & Unwin, 83 Alexander St, Crows Nest NSW 2065, Australia | www.allenandunwin.com
 British Library Cataloguing in Publication Data available.

Print ISBN 978-1-78955-0-559
Ebook ISBN 978-1-78955-0-566
Set in Times. Printing managed by Jellyfish Solutions Ltd.
Cover design by Kari Brownlie | www.karibrownlie.co.uk

Holly Wainwright is a writer, editor and broadcaster. Originally from Manchester in the north of England, she's been living in Sydney for more than twenty years and has built a career there in print and digital publishing, most recently as Head of Entertainment at Mamamia Women's Network. Holly also hosts a podcast about family called This Glorious Mess, has two small children, a partner called Brent and wishes there were four more hours in every day.

The Mummy Bloggers, Holly's debut novel and prequel to *How To Be Perfect,* was published by Legend Press in 2019.

Follow Holly
@hollycwain

CHAPTER 1

FRANCES

Frances had been aiming for an Elle Campbell kind of morning but, frankly, things had turned to shit. So far, her day bore very little resemblance to Elle's latest blog.

> Good morning, Goddesses.
>
> Let's begin where everything does—with the purest possible start to your day.
>
> Here's what works for me.
>
> I wake with the sun. Strangely enough, so does Alma. This tiny old soul seems to know when the world is ready for her. She starts the day with stretches. It's as if every morning she remembers she has arms and she throws them over her head in delight. And now, so do I.
>
> The light on Gurva farm is at its most dazzling at dawn, so after I mimic baby's stretches she and I head out onto the deck to watch the sun roll towards us up the hill. Then I lay her down on her pure wool rug while I do 15 minutes of

my mindful Elle-ness Moves™. Alma is always so peaceful watching me—she just lies there, cooing and giggling.

Then, me and my little shadow head to the kitchen. I throw back a shot-glass of bee pollen dissolved in warm, filtered water. Then I whizz up a Pure Start smoothie™—activated tree nuts blended in (filtered) organic coconut water with kale, organic blueberries, lady-finger bananas from the farm's plantation, psyllium, a teaspoon of raw cacao nibs, a sprinkle of gold-leaf powder (for that inner glow), a dash of milk thistle and a twist of bush-lime leaf.

I blend it thoroughly in my new Nutrimullet, which we had modified to run silently so it doesn't break into the peaceful early-morning energy of the farm, or disturb BB's meditation practice (gosh, he can be a grumpy bear without his morning med!). I whizz it for 90 seconds until it's ready to pop into my bamboo tumbler and be sipped through my copper straw, while I nurse Alma and quietly set my intention for the day.

Today's intention: Forgive those who have caused me pain.

Wishing you a beautiful, pure start, too. It really is the secret to moving through your day in a state of productive grace.

E xxxxx

PS: If that sounds like a lot for breakfast, you'll be relieved to know that I sip it slowly throughout the morning, loosening it with a gentle shake and a splash more coconut water. xx

If Frances was being honest, that didn't sound like a lot for breakfast.

As she re-read Elle's smoothie recipe, Frances was standing in front of the blender with baby Denny squalling on one hip, her phone in her other hand. She only had half the ingredients, and she'd still spent eighty-nine dollars at the health-food shop.

'Good job I'll be back at work soon, right, Den?' she said. 'Although I don't think this is quite what your dad has in mind.'

Frances put the phone down to scrape out the last of the psyllium—whatever the hell that was—from the tub with a plastic baby spoon, the only clean, dry implement she could find, one-handed, at this very moment. And it had to be this very moment, because she was so hungry she wasn't sure she could stay upright for as long as it was going to take for her very non-silent blender to chop through all this stuff.

'Shhhhh, Denny, shhhhh...' Frances gave him the plastic spoon to gum on as she tried to slice a supermarket banana with a butter knife. 'What's the matter with you, anyway? You just had a feed...'

Frances's morning wasn't as pure as she'd hoped. Denny had woken at five, which wasn't unusual, and he seemed even more 'unsettled' than yesterday. He hadn't let her put him down for three hours now.

Tipping the remains of the tub into her cracked old blender and muttering under her breath, Frances wondered whether it qualified as a 'pure start' if you'd been cursing solidly since you woke up.

She'd tried. Frances had taken Denny out to the sunroom after his first boob-feed and laid him on her Jmart 'sheepskin' rug in the hope of getting some yoga stretches in, her old work laptop open to one of Elle's videos.

But Frances couldn't touch her toes anymore, her insides hurt, and Denny just kept on whining. She'd thrown him the teething giraffe her sister-in-law had given her, then started chanting her mantra, the one she'd promised herself she'd use every day as she stretched.

'I am in love with my life. I am in love with my life. I am in love with my...'

But the morning trucks outside her window were drowning out her inner monologue, and she couldn't help being conscious of the sensation of her stomach rolls bulging every time she bent towards her toes.

Frances switched mantras, to one of Elle's. 'I am a work in progress, I am an unfinished masterpiece, I am a work in progress...'

The smell that hit her nostrils as she tried to get her nose to her knees cut things short. Denny needed changing.

Now Frances was standing at the fridge door, scouring for that six-dollar coconut water she'd bought yesterday. And still she forgot the psyllium. Perhaps if she could have sprung for the gold leaf, she'd be feeling better by now. Or if she just had the discipline to make it through those bloody stretches.

No wonder she and Denny weren't moving through this day with positive grace.

'Did you drink that coconut water I bought yesterday?' she found herself yelling from the fridge towards the bedroom. 'Troy?'

Frances pictured him coming home from work last night, tired and hot and possibly a little bit drunk, grabbing the cold bottle from the fridge door and sculling, before pulling away and looking at the label like, 'bleurgh'. She closed the fridge, Denny still whining in her right arm, and went to peer into the bin. Sure enough, there was the half-finished bottle of Orgococo Gold.

'You didn't even put it in the recycling!' Frances yelled again towards the closed bedroom door, then went back to the blender. 'Well, Denny,' she kissed her baby on his head as he rhythmically whacked her shoulder with the teething giraffe, 'no coconut water, no gold, no blueberries. What would Elle do?' She grabbed the blender and stuck it under the running tap for a moment. 'Sydney water's finest will have to do, Den.'

After ramming on the cracked lid, she flipped the switch

to high. Whirring and crunching filled the kitchen, the blades stalling and screeching against the raw nuts. What Frances wouldn't do for a Nutrimullet.

Denny started screaming in time with the blender. Frances held the lid on with one hand and jiggled him with the other.

'For fuck's sake, Frank!' Troy's voice broke through the racket. He was standing in the kitchen doorway, distractingly naked, bleary, rubbing his head. 'Can't you just have toast like a normal person?'

Frances flicked off the blender and poured some of the sludgy green-brown mixture into a wineglass—the only clean vessel within easy reach. 'Cheers, Troy,' she said, taking a swig and trying not to flinch: it tasted like bin. Denny's pudgy little arms reached towards the smoothie. She put it down and handed the baby to her partner as she pushed past him. 'I'm going to the gym.'

'Seriously?' he asked. 'But I only got in at two.'

'I am a work in progress,' she called back to him from the corridor. 'And I am going to the gym.'

I've got to get to Gurva, Frances thought, as she smashed down the stairs, flicking bits of smoothie from her shirt. *One of Elle Campbell's retreats will sort this rubbish out.*

CHAPTER 2

ELLE

It was truly great sex that brought Elle back from the dead. As she wrote:

> This is the kind of intimacy, Goddesses, that can only come from true honesty. From a partnership without secrets. From a love that can make a broken woman whole again.

Sex, and money. Somebody else's money. The 'About' page of her new blog read:

> If you have found me here, after everything we have been through together. I am going to take you by the hand and help you understand how you can build a better self, one deserving of this level of love, just as I have done. All we're going to need from you is your trust. Your trust, and a small donation.

Funds secured, Elle's 'trust barrier' came down, and the door was opened to her new blog, and her new world: The Goddess Project.

Once there, you'll find that the biggest seller in Elle Campbell's new online shop is one long piece of fake black hair twisted into a thick, glossy braid. Elle's disciples like to clip it into their own skinny ponytails when they are exercising—copying the guru's 'do gives them something to swing around while they squat.

Other popular purchases are Elle's trademarked 'gold dust' energy/vitality/libido powders for sprinkling into smoothies. There's a teeth-whitening powder made of a particular non-toxic chalk, patented push-up active-wear sports crop tops, and her all-natural fake tan, Glimmer, which produces the darkest shade of chestnut with a generous dusting of quartz-based glitter.

But it's the braid that's become the trademark of Elle's second act. Her hair-whipping work-outs and yoga sessions are followed by hundreds of thousands online. After being snared by her hypnotic butt-dips on YouTube, the hardcore have ponied up the cash to make it behind a paywall designed to keep out the haters and trolls, to a place where all of Elle's body wisdom is on offer to her tribe of plait-wearing true believers.

These people spin their arms in tiny circles in front of open laptops in spare bedrooms and sunrooms and lounges, furniture pushed aside, yoga mats unfurled. They sit cross-legged, iPads before them, to follow her meditation workshops, and they anoint themselves with her powders and potions and chant her trademarked mantras. And they spend up big to follow the complex 'pure' diet that, Elle says, cleansed her of negativity.

These people—the Elle-ness Army—believe that their guru is in exile. And some of them, a lucky few with the necessary disposable income, get to make the pilgrimage to Gurva, the northern New South Wales hinterland farm where the reborn guru conducts her Elle-ness workshops.

Five days at Gurva will set you back thousands—but, if

your commitment is true and your wallet is deep, you can leave the place a different person. With a resilience workshop from Elle, yes, but also intense twice-daily work-outs. Injectables. Microdermabrasion. Implants, if you take that package. A new diet plan, designed especially for you, a commitment to a month of packaged, organic, 'negative-calorie' pre-prepped meals, if you choose. A mantra of positive affirmations, voiced by Elle, sent directly to your phone daily, for an extra charge.

Yes, at Gurva you can choose your own adventure, set in the most photogenic pocket of the most Instagrammable valley on the coast.

Just don't photograph the guru—or 'gurvi' as Elle's followers like to tag her. Before they're allowed to get off the airport shuttle bus and onto the farm, every guest has to sign a strict 'no-selfies' policy.

These days Elle's appearances on social media are rare and heavily curated. Her feed is all emerald-green paddocks and sapphire-blue ocean, muted wood brown, pleasing plates of pickled vegetables and sprouting grains, warming bowls of clear, petal-peppered tea, rustic sheds and rolling hills, glimpses of golden sand. It says: paradise.

And every now and then, there's a hint at the identity of the man who, the origin story goes, resurrected Elle with one remarkable night—and his patronage.

A distinctive, tattooed arm draped over a tiny, tanned shoulder. A man's toned stomach; a capable hand gripping a tractor wheel.

And then the torso of a naked man lying in a field of yellow daisies. A tiny baby curled in the crook of an arm. The edge of a dark head resting on a shoulder. A long black plait snaking down alongside the baby's smooth body.

And a one-word caption:

Home.

CHAPTER 3

ABI

The last time Abi Black was a bride, she was twenty-seven and doing it for her dad. She was in the early days of pregnancy with her eldest daughter, Arden, and desperately trying to hide her growing belly in an empire-line gown, tipping a succession of champagne flutes into pot plants.

Now she couldn't imagine who she'd been trying to kid—she might as well have worn the positive pee-stick around her neck on a velvet ribbon.

Adrian, her groom, had been in his element, presiding over a riverside crowd of his old rowing team, uni mates, his finance friends, his family, her family. He'd been talking loudly, slapping backs, beaming at Abi over frothing bottles.

She knew that hindsight was all-seeing, but when she remembered that day now, what she recalled was an overwhelming feeling that she was in the wrong place, in the wrong dress. These were not her people. There had been some kind of mistake. She and Adrian were never meant to be so deeply predictable, and had promised each other over and over that they would never get married. But here they were, saying the vows, posing for the photographs.

Very few of those pictures had survived Abi's sharp scissors when Adrian had announced he was leaving her, five years ago. It had been an enormous shock and completely predictable all at the same time. She was 'destroyed and reborn at once', as she had written on her blog, The Green Diva.

The old, conservative part of her hoped the children hadn't read that.

Soon, she would be getting married again, at forty-three. And it was going to be different, immeasurably perfect. In three months' time, on New Year's Eve, she was going to marry the love of her life under the angel's trumpet tree in their farmhouse garden—and this time, *this* time, the stars would be aligned.

'You,' Grace whispered in her ear as Abi was banging out another stern email to the ethical diamond specialist who was making their rings, 'are turning into a bridezilla. I don't know why, but I never saw this coming...'

Abi threw her phone to the floor and rolled over, taking Grace's face in her hands. 'This is going to be the fucking Wedding of the Century, Gracey. And everything is going to be perfect, perfect, completely fucking perfect.' With every 'perfect', Abi kissed Grace on the eye. The other eye. Her cheek, her mouth. 'Like us.'

'I have no idea what you're talking about.' Grace laughed. 'There isn't much perfection happening around here right now.'

'What you're talking about, my bride, is what's going on behind that—' Abi pulled back from their kiss long enough to nod towards the bare wood of the closed bedroom door. 'In here, in this big brass bed,' she gave a little wiggle to make the old springs creak, 'everything is exactly as it should be...'

Abi looked to Grace for a smile of agreement, but it wasn't there. Her fiancée just gave a little shrug and hopped off the bed.

What was going on behind that door was the chaos of a falling-down farmhouse stuffed with six children, ranging in age from three to sixteen. Adrian—the man Abi had married the first time around—was living across the yard above the shed, mostly brooding on what he called his 'third act'. As far as Abi could tell, it involved him dashing out posts for his new-age financial blog, Manifesting Money, and endlessly emailing publishing houses with his book proposal of the same name; so far, none had bitten.

Their sixteen-year-old daughter Arden was busy building an online empire of her own from the bedroom she shared with her fourteen-year-old sister Alex. Arden and her boyfriend River made seemingly endless videos of her putting on and taking off make-up for Arden's YouTube channel, much to Alex's eye-rolling disapproval. River, serving as both cameraman and creative adviser, was now perpetually around at the farm, shirtless at breakfast, squeezing orange juice with his headphones in. Parcels of 'product' arrived daily, marked for Arden's dutiful application.

'It's all your fault,' Grace reminded Abi. 'Everyone thinks they're going to be internet-famous, just like you.'

'Then they've missed the point.' Abi laughed. 'I'm a cautionary tale.'

Abi had cemented her position as an alt-culture superstar when she'd landed a spot as a finalist in the most controversial blogging awards the industry had ever seen, the Blog-ahhs. She hadn't won, wasn't even runner-up, but that had been eighteen months ago and the experience had changed everything. These days a small team of writers based in different outposts around the country wrote for Abi's site—rebranded The GD. She was still the boss, the face who popped up on TV and radio to talk all things eco-warrior. And her interview podcast was more popular than ever. But since she had 'gone mainstream' as Arden called it, admiringly, Abi felt like her wings had been clipped, like the thrill of the old outlaw blogging days were gone. 'I'm a fucking performing seal in tie-dye,' she would grumble to Grace.

Yep, a lot had changed since the awards.

Outside their window, in the weakening afternoon sun, two little boys played in the veggie garden's muddy puddles, poking sticks deep into the dirt and flicking it at each other, their half-sister Alex keeping one eye on them, one eye on her phone.

'Muuuuuum!' she yelled up at the house. 'Are you two going to come out and look after these boys? I've got to go into town for my trapeze class!'

'Just what we needed,' Abi groaned, sitting up in bed and running a hand through her curly mop of hair. 'An actual circus.'

'If we're not careful,' said Grace, 'that's what this wedding will be.'

'*This* wedding? You mean *our* wedding? Your enthusiasm is underwhelming, babe.'

'I'm just not convinced, Abi, that us putting our frocks on and making a mountain of hummus is going to solve some of the...' Grace, always calm, always considered, searched for the right word.

'Fuckwittery?' Abi suggested, smiling.

'Challenges,' Grace corrected, not smiling, 'that we're dealing with right now. We've got some pretty big fish to fry, Abi.'

She moved to the chair by the window to pick up some discarded pants, and Abi followed, looking out at the boys. Teddy and Freddie were as dirty and wild-looking as any kids with unfettered access to the outdoors, mud and climbing-trees could be, but you could still tell, only just, that the outfits they were rapidly growing out of were a cut above the local farm kids', even in Daylesford. The designer labels were still faintly visible.

'We've got to get those little fish some new clothes,' Abi said to Grace.

'No, their *father* has to buy them some new clothes,' Grace replied, pulling on a pair of floaty trousers. 'Adrian has to take some responsibility for his choices about those two.'

'You're right, babe. I promise I'll get all this sorted out before the wedding.'

'That,' Grace looked Abi straight in the eye, 'would make me *much* more comfortable with the whole thing. Anyway,' she glanced down, stepping into sandals, 'I'm going to Skype Leisel.'

Grace's sister Leisel and her husband and three kids were on a year-long campervan odyssey around Australia. She was writing about it on a new blog, The Van Family, and her Skype calls into the farm when reception allowed were a rare treat that Grace hated to miss.

'Say hello from the madhouse,' Abi said, smiling again. She knew how much Grace missed her sister, and she couldn't help but feel that her beloved would be much more relaxed about their wedding if Leisel were here, cheerleading.

The little boys suddenly dropped their sticks and ran towards Alex with outstretched, muddy hands. The teenager sprinted towards the house. 'Muuuuuum!'

Where the hell was Adrian, anyway?

CHAPTER 4

ELLE

Elle's new kitchen had come equipped with a silent chef.

Mauna only cooked with organic ingredients. She had taken a vow of daylight silence as part of her commitment to Vipassanā meditation, and every morning she arrived, smiling, to whip up smoothies and snacks that fitted perfectly with Elle's posting schedule. It was part of Mauna's brief to ensure that each one was presented ever-so-slightly differently—a jewel-toned bowl here, an artful sprinkle of dried kelp there—to keep Elle's aesthetic interesting.

One of the many things Elle had learnt in the past fifteen months was that living in the country is different when you have money.

The small rural town of Talwyn where she grew up had been drying up on itself from the outskirts in, like a slowly fading scab. At the very first opportunity Elle had climbed on a bus out of there and, after a brief flirtation with her rural backstory, had barely returned.

Life at Gurva was different.

The homestead surely had original bones, but it had been meticulously renovated to suit the country-life fantasies of fancy city folk—all dark wooden floors and rough-hewn whitewashed walls. The low ceilings had been lifted and the traditional wraparound veranda now housed a yoga deck, a skinny lap pool and a couple of ivy-shrouded meditation nooks. Inside, huge picture windows framed views that were uninterrupted down the valley to the ocean. The master bedroom was drenched with sunlight but stayed at a perfect year-round temperature, like the rest of the house. Fresh flowers were placed in every room, including the cellar gym, and no two arrangements were the same, with Elle's preferences (all white, lots of fragrance, but *NO LILIES*, not ever) programmed into every staff member's phone.

Of course, since Alma, the homestead also boasted an all-white nursery. And a pale-pink-and-grey playroom. And a 'mudroom', something that had never featured in any rural home of Elle's youth but was, Ben told her, a traditional country touch: a space that existed solely to house rainjackets, gumboots and shaggy dogs' leads. The Gurva mudroom was a tasteful grey with a polished concrete floor; mostly, it housed yoga mats and the on- and off-road Bugaboo Donkeys.

It was not a home that Elle had built. But she was lady of this house now.

***

Gurva wasn't exactly where she had seen herself going when she'd walked away from the Blog-ahh Awards across Sydney's Pyrmont Bridge fifteen months ago—but it's exactly where she knew she was going twenty-four hours after she'd met Ben Bont.

The morning after the Blog-ahhs, every news site in the country ran an above-the-fold splash about dastardly Elle Campbell and her plot to win half a million dollars by lying and cheating, faking illness and death.

For about forty-eight hours, she was the most talked about woman in the country, trending on every form of social media and roundly sledged on every breakfast radio segment.

The morning shows tore up their rundowns and went deep on interviews with anyone who'd been anywhere near the awards. The footage from the night that showed Elle being escorted from the stage seemed to be on a loop on every screen in the land, but to Elle's surprise none of the main players—her husband Adrian, rival Abi Black or even her sister Zoe—were anywhere to be seen.

Only The Working Mum's Leisel Adams, as the eventual winner of the Best Parenting Blog, was live in studio on *Breakfast!* and *After Breakfast!* holding tight to her award and trying, in Elle's opinion, not to sound bitter about being the winner by default. 'Look, I'm delighted, of course,' she was saying to Simon Hedley, the breakfast host who, by the looks of him, was delighted to have had his worldview validated by this group of women who apparently couldn't compete for an accolade without drama and treachery.

'But isn't it true that you only won this award because the real winner was disqualified? Doesn't that make you the Steven Bradbury of mummy blogging?' he asked Leisel, a shit-eating grin almost cracking his pancake make-up.

'Simon, I said all I had to say on that matter last night, at the awards.' Leisel's smile was tight. 'All I have to say this morning is that all of the votes The Working Mum received are validation for the women out there who are always told they're not the *real* mums. I'm their voice...'

'Scintillating TV,' Elle said to no one in particular, since she was watching this unfold alone, from the bed of the beige-and-brown room of a highway SleepaLodge in western Sydney. It was the kind of suburban hotel frequented by salesmen and middle management away on a conference. It was not where one would expect to find The Stylish Mumma.

Elle hadn't needed advice on how to disappear: she instinctively knew that the media wouldn't stray past the limits of their metropolitan imaginations. That night, she'd walked over the Pyrmont Bridge to an ATM, swallowing her sobs. With the cards in her tiny evening clutch she'd withdrawn as much cash from each account as her limits would allow and headed down into the train station where she got on the first train west, west, west.

By the time she got off the train at a suitably unfashionable station, her tears were dry. She knew that in this transit suburb, the TarMart would be open late to service shift workers, so she went straight in and bought the most unflattering pair of 'mum jeans' she could find, a Tweety Bird T-shirt and a pair of imitation uggs. Elle scrubbed off her make-up in the mall bathroom and tied up her hair, then outside she flagged down a taxi to take her to the nearest SleepaLodge.

Close to midnight, she called the all-female ride-sharing company she knew bleeding hearts like Abi Black used when they were in the city. Elle paid the driver to take her room key to the five-star city hotel where she and Adrian had been staying and bring back her things. Elle instinctively knew that her husband wouldn't be there—she was certain he'd still be drinking and crying on his ex-wife's shoulder, and that even in his confused fury at Elle's betrayal, the last thing he would want would be to see her.

And she was right: the driver's coast was clear. By two a.m. Elle was considerably lighter in cash but in possession of the basics that would carry her to her next life.

She had started her last one with less.

In that beige hotel room, she clicked off the morning TV and opened her laptop.

It was time to make a new plan.

***

From where Elle stood now, at the pool's edge on the deck of Gurva's homestead, she could survey the boundaries of her new empire.

This morning—like almost every morning—Elle had spent sunrise in the windowless, underground gym while Lucille the baby nurse gave Alma her morning bottle.

The first thing Elle did every day down there was an hour of straight-up, fat-blasting cardio, pounding the silent running machine, pushing and pulling herself on the rower until sweat pooled on the floor. For all that her new 'brand' was about being kind to yourself, in actual fact speedily erasing all the signs of having given birth for the third time required you to be absolutely brutal with yourself. And it wasn't easy. Not even for Elle.

But it had to look effortless to Ben. Especially, perhaps, to Ben.

Ben was one of the few people she'd ever met whose discipline approached hers: a man who'd crafted his physicality with almost obsessive attention to detail. He'd mastered hapkido for strength and speed, took private one-on-one Pilates masterclasses for flexibility and lengthening, did sprint-training, boxing sessions with a former world welterweight, and so on. Ben was a man who, like Elle, knew that seemingly natural gifts sprang from unnatural commitment. But it mattered to him that all this effort was never complained or boasted about. It was all just part of what successful people did. It was all just part of being perfect.

Yes, Elle thought, you could say the two of them really got each other.

To her, that first hour of the day in the basement gym was a secret ceremony. Everything that came after, she believed, must be serene and calm, and as graceful as you'd expect from a wellness goddess. She showered down in the gym, blasting the air-con to plunge her into a dry, icy state, and then she went upstairs and started her day for the second time, with yoga on the deck and—when Ben was in residence—a family meditation session.

Today, like most days, Ben wasn't there. He was in Sydney, dealing with his many, many dealings. And that suited Elle. He'd made it clear to the staff—and across the farm there were around thirty of them—that she was now in charge when he was away.

That had been Elle's biggest challenge when she'd arrived here over twelve months ago—understanding the dynamics of this strange little fiefdom, and asserting her place at the top of the pecking order.

Not that there had been thirty employees then.

When Ben first told Elle about Gurva, it was called The Plantation, and it was his own personal retreat.

She would never tell him this, but she thought what he'd been doing with the property before she came to it was really rather beneath him. A few B&B guests in the cottages by the creek, some live-in cooking courses through high season. A fledgling spa to service the weekenders with facials and pedis and massages.

'It's my nirvana,' he'd told her. 'Where I go to drift and recharge. It's not a business up there—it's where I go to escape business.'

Why would you want to do that? Elle wanted to ask him. But she still hadn't—not yet. She had to bide her time.

Now, a little over a year later, the farm was a small satellite empire within Ben's global business. And if she could stick it out for three years, it would be hers too.

This morning, from where Elle stood on the deck, she could look down through the valley over the sprinkling of picturesque old barns that hid gleaming stainless-steel interiors: a state of the art spa-clinic, a commercial kitchen, a hall that housed a speaking space, and a gym with three different studios and a sprung yoga floor of native wood. At the heart of it all was the office: a control centre that allowed Ben to run his own hotel empire from the curve of a green hill, a twelve-hour commute from Sydney for people without private planes.

The guest cottages, still exclusive in number, were gathered by the creek at the bottom of the hill, and each had a morning meditation deck that faced the sunrise. Sixteen people at a time would come to do the five-day Elle-ness retreat, and while in residence they were looked after by a small army of fresh-faced young staff, experts in everything from tea ceremonies to aerial yoga.

None of the thirty people who worked here, nor the paying guests, were allowed near the homestead without express permission from Ben or Elle. 'We're not the main attraction at Disneyland,' Ben would say.

But there was another reason: to keep Elle scarce. Her notoriety wasn't always a bonus.

'Hey, boss. Good session today?'

Elle turned towards Matt, Gurva's head of operations. She'd personally hand-picked him to deliver on her vision for Gurva, so he *was* allowed up to the homestead whenever he liked.

'Not bad, Matt,' she said. 'Yours?'

'I ran around the dam,' he said, and she watched him push back his tattooed shoulders and suck in his already impressive sixpack as if by reflex. Matt looked like the personal trainer he'd once been, tight all over and groomed to within an inch of his life. The north coast's hippie vibe hadn't touched him one bit.

In the mornings, Matt would talk to Elle about guests who were arriving or leaving and whether she had any personal sessions with platinum visitors. Matt and Elle would also discuss any big decisions which needed to be made that day. Sometimes Elle would put Alma in a sling or in the Bugaboo and do a lap of the grounds with Matt—but not if they had guests in the cottages, or Elle would never make it back before dark.

Lucille appeared on the deck from the door to the main house, carrying a freshly fed little Alma. 'She's about ready for her morning sleep,' the nurse said, passing the baby to Elle.

'Then come back and get her in five.' Elle looked down at her baby girl. She had her dad's dark hair and eyes. She was looking up at her mum with the beginnings of a smile around her mouth. Elle felt her stomach clench, her throat catch. 'Time to sleep, baby girl,' she said. She knew the importance of routines with babies. That was how she'd trained Teddy and Freddie. That was how she got shit done. Routine above all else. Discipline.

Elle blinked quickly and lifted Alma. She held her close, her little head under Elle's chin.

Matt was bent over to shuffle a wooden slat in a dividing blind. 'We've finished the bar,' he told her. 'Should be ready for the next round of guests.'

'Great,' said Elle. 'I don't want it on socials, though. I want word to get out about it without word getting out about it, if you know what I mean.'

'I know what you mean.' Matt finished straightening the blind, and then himself. 'I think it's going to give us the edge. When's Ben back? I reckon he'll like it.'

'He's coming for the weekend, and I'm sure he will.'

'Well, I'll make sure it's all stocked and ready then.'

When Elle had first arrived, some of the Gurva team had been a little slow to understand that she wasn't just Ben Bont's latest fling. She wouldn't just stay a few days before running back to the city. What they came to know was that, actually, Elle had come to Gurva to remake it in her image.

Matt got this. And she could trust him because she knew his secrets, just as he knew hers.

'You can go, Matt,' she said. 'I'll come down for that class in an hour.'

He nodded, patted Alma on the head and went back through the house.

Fear, Elle knew, was the strongest bond of all.

CHAPTER 5

ABI

Adrian was hanging upside down from the beams of Abi's barn.

The conversion housed the studio where she recorded her podcast The GD's Shed, and it also housed an ensuite guestroom, where Adrian had been staying for well over a year.

As Abi shoved open the door, she wasn't even that surprised to see Adrian shirtless in faded rugby shorts, or that he was suspended by his knees, arms crossed over his tanned body, now-shaggy hair hanging down. Eyes closed.

'Watch it,' she said. 'You're beyond middle-aged. You could pull something.'

Adrian opened his eyes. 'Hi.' He folded at the waist, reaching up to grab the beam and throw his legs to the floor. 'Just a bit of practice. Getting in the zone.'

'For what?' Abi moved through the shed, picking up kids' clothes and tiny toys. 'Not child care. Alex has been watching the boys hit each other with sticks for most of the afternoon.'

'They will have loved that,' said Adrian, rubbing his head. Deliberately missing Abi's point, she was sure.

'Yes.'

Abi was at a loss when it came to The Adrian Problem. He'd been living with them—across the yard, but basically with them—ever since the Blog-ahh Awards.

When she'd invited Adrian to come home with her and Grace after the high drama of the Blog-ahhs, it had been a genuine gesture from the heart. He was broken, physically and mentally, and he needed her. There was no way Abi was going to leave the father of her girls flailing, no matter how much of a dickhead he'd been. This dickhead was coming home with her and Grace to get strong.

Abi was convinced—and Grace was counting on it, too—that he would send for Teddy and Freddie and they'd all stay for a few days, regroup, gather strength, and then bugger off back to Melbourne. Back to his fancy finance job. She thought he'd most likely file for divorce and sell the glass-and-white box-shaped house that Elle had designed. Maybe the boys would go and live with their psycho mother, maybe they'd share custody, maybe Adrian would find another young woman to stroke his ego and drain his bank account. Whatever.

What Abi hadn't imagined was that her ex-husband would move into her barn for good, and that she and Grace and their ragtag gaggle of tweens and teens would be helping to raise his boys.

It wasn't like they'd never talked about it. But every time she pushed Adrian on just how long he was planning to stay, what his plan was, or what he was imagining for the boys, he would tell her the time wasn't right, that he couldn't face the city, the judgement, the house.

He hadn't been able to face it for fifteen months. He hadn't even been to Melbourne in that time to visit his mother, and Abi knew from her own recent visits to the girls' grandma that Bonnie wasn't in the best shape.

Still, Abi realised, she would have to try again. He certainly looked strong enough to face anything, in that wiry way that middle-aged men got ripped—a touch of white chest hair, a weather-beaten smile. And Abi could sense that Grace might just wash her hands of the whole wedding idea if there wasn't some resolution to The Adrian Problem on the horizon. And that could not happen. There was no way he was going to screw her happily ever after. Again.

'Adrian,' she turned and leant on the desk, in front of where he was stretching, 'what the hell are you doing?'

'I'm stretching, Abi,' he replied, dodging the point again. 'What are you doing?'

'I'm wondering if you're ever going to move out of my fucking shed.' She made sure he couldn't miss this one.

There was an energy between people who used to be married, Abi knew. When you'd been together as long as she and Adrian had—almost twenty years, all up—you'd had every fight you were ever going to have, you knew each other's stories, you knew where all the bodies were buried. You were intimate without touching; you were always a little bit inside each other's heads. It was uncomfortable to have someone around like that.

Between Grace and Adrian, Abi had way too many people on the farm who could call her on her shit, and that was before considering that she also had two teenage daughters.

'Abi... I'm getting really close with this book thing.' Adrian used his soft voice, the one he'd always used when he was trying to reel in a client. 'I think going back to the city would be a negative choice right now...'

'The city isn't your only option, Adrian. It's not here or there, you know. There are other places in this big, wide world.'

'But the boys love being here with their sisters and Grace's boys. I couldn't give them that family anywhere else. I just feel...'

And this was where every conversation about Adrian's living situation stalled: the boys. One of the things Abi knew without asking was that Adrian had never expected to be raising two preschoolers alone in his fifties.

It embarrassed Abi to consider that when she and Elle's

sister Zoe had been plotting to expose Elle's treachery, they hadn't thought the melodrama through to its natural conclusion.

Of course, she hadn't known that Elle would blow up her marriage so spectacularly that night; it was perfectly possible that she and Adrian and their boys might have gone underground together. But knowing what she knew about the way Elle operated, she could have taken an educated guess that games of happy families were not in the Campbell clan's future plans.

The unfamiliar sensation Abi felt as she stood in front of a stuttering Adrian was guilt. And that was why this conversation always stopped here. If she hadn't been so consumed with 'winning' over Elle, she might have paused to think about what would happen to two little shaggy-haired boys once their mother was publicly humiliated.

That was the shit Adrian was calling her on without even saying a word about it.

'And the girls...' he said. 'You know, I think it's good for them to have their dad around, don't you? I think this Manifesting Money thing is going to be big, and then I'll be on the road promoting it, and it will be a real fresh start, you know. Like, a true rebirth.'

'And, um...' Abi wasn't sure what to say next, or when exactly Adrian had gone from being mister stock-market-suit-and-tie to being the guy who hung upside down in barns and talked about rebirth, but it was quite the transformation. 'If... I mean, when, that happens, where will the boys be? Are you thinking of seeing if Elle—?'

'No.' Adrian couldn't have jumped in faster. Her name was very rarely mentioned on the Daylesford farm, and especially not in front of Adrian. He flinched as Abi said it, as if hearing it caused him physical discomfort. 'No way.'

'Adrian...' Abi's guilt didn't stop her from seeing one truth quite clearly here. She put her hand on his; it was her turn to use her soft voice. 'I know what she is. But, she was there for most of their lives. We can wrap them up in this crazy house and give them lots of love, but sooner or later they'll wonder who she is. They'll need to know who all their people are.'

'We're their people, Abi. You, me, Grace, the kids.'

Abi's laugh was big, broad. 'I'll give you something, Adrian,' she said, 'you're as fucking crazy as I am. Every inch. You are the guy who just last year was telling me our girls couldn't live here, needed a fancy private school, deserved the best education money could buy and Melbourne society and all that BS. Now, that guy has joined the fucking circus and thrown his kids into the lion's mouth. Is this a mid-life crisis? Really?'

'I had one of those already,' Adrian answered. 'This is mid-life clarity.'

'Fuck.'

'Are you saying you don't want the boys here, Abi?' It sounded like a dangerous question, but Adrian was clearly confident of the answer.

'No, no. The boys are great.' Abi gave up for now and started moving towards the door, toys and dirty T-shirts back in her hands. 'Just buy them some new fucking clothes, will you?' She got to the door, turned around. 'You know, don't you, that if you're not ready to face it, I'm going to have to.' Adrian looked up at her, confused. But Abi felt a familiar expectation settling on her—for all those years they'd been together, she had been the fixer, smoothing over messes so that Adrian could glide right past them. Here they were again.

***

Blended family bullshit

There's a lot people don't tell you about blended families, GDs. I know you know that. Many of you have made one, live in one, came from one.

But even after nine years of living in a home

with kids who are 'mine' and kids who aren't, I still get surprised.

I get surprised by things like today.

My girls are the eldest of our tribe. They are at that very particular, tenuous time between being on Team Kids and on Team Adult. Being in that moment, they hate me writing about them, and so, I will make this as infuriatingly vague as they demand.

They've lived through a lot of change. My girls are resilient, which is what we say now when we mean tough. But last year, we thought most of our change was done. G and I were settled. My girls, her boys. A lot of us, but do-able.

Then, two new babies joined our tribe. They're not mine, not G's. Let's just say they're in the family ;). And like all of us women do, GDs, G and I just opened up and said, 'Sure, there's space for more, come in, cuddle on up.'

But some days, that's tough on our kids. Because my girls are the eldest, they end up taking a big role in looking after these little souls, while G's boys race around being free. Is that, even in our house, because they are girls? I hope not.

But we yell at them about it. 'What the fuck do you mean you didn't make them a sandwich when you made your own?' or 'What's this fucking mess about?' when we walk into a room that looks like we've been burgled or 'Why didn't you see that they were about to pick up a real-life snake?' (True story.)

And what no one tells you about all this expectation and pressure and yelling is that, truly, your kids might just rise to it.

Because one of the things no one tells you

about blended families is the never-ending, overflowing shitty bucket full of messy, smelly love that just keeps refilling. My girls love their little charges. They don't love making sandwiches for them, they're not saints, but they haven't missed an opportunity to make those little buggers feel like part of our tribe.

And I love them for it. Annoying teenage girls, even though I don't understand what you're doing up there on YouTube all day, I love you for your kindness and generosity to the tiny interlopers.

And look, it's just as well. Because I think we're stuck with them.

A x

PS: The other thing no one tells you about blended families is that for every one child you add to your household, the mess multiplies by exactly their age. It's science. Honestly.

Grace read Abi's latest blog post when she got back from the private tutoring class she'd started teaching in town.

After two years of home-schooling, she'd lost Abi's girls to the local high school this year, and for Grace, clearly, teaching eleven-year-old Sol and looking out for Freddie and Teddy wasn't enough of a challenge. Or maybe, Abi suspected, she just needed to get off the farm sometimes.

'So you spoke to Adrian today?' Grace asked Abi as she stood up from the kitchen table laptop and began unravelling her long floaty scarf situation.

'Yup.'

'And that's the upshot? That we're "stuck with" the boys?' Grace employed the air-quote bunny ears. She would never say something like that with a straight face—she believed that all words had intention, and consequences.

'He says we're their family—their people. What am I going to do? Kick them out?'

That night, Abi had made a big meal of her 'mush', as she called it: lentils and veggies and rice that had all bubbled on the stove for much too long, its blandness disguised with copious soy sauce and chilli.

She and Adrian had sat at either end of this same kitchen table, as big kids came and went, ladling blobs of mush into their bowls, sitting down or carrying them away to other rooms. Sol told them all about a frog that had been at the bottom of his gumboot that morning when he went to feed the chooks; how he decided to see if the chickens would eat it—and they did. Vegan Alex accused him of animal cruelty and threatened to dob him in to PETA. The little boys had swerved the chilli and found a hundred uses for the mush that didn't involve eating it: hair gel, play dough, missiles. Arden's ever-present boyfriend River made a polite attempt at doing the dishes.

There was mayhem and yelling and laughs and mess. Abi had kind of loved it. 'It was great, tonight, Grace. I think everyone's finally at home.'

'That's good.' Grace was hanging her scarves near the door. She went over to the giant pot on the stove and peered in for leftover mush. 'But Abi, those boys have a mother. A mother who raised them—'

'A mother who hasn't called them in six months.' Abi wasn't privy to everything that had gone down between Adrian and Elle over the boys, but she knew what he'd told her, that the calls had stopped. That Elle, by every conventional measure, had disappeared.

'I don't care, Abi.' Grace sat down with her dish and looked Abi in the eye. 'She's their mother. I'm a mother. So are you. If Adrian's thinking this is a long-term situation, she needs to know. He needs her blessing. Hell,' she blew on her mush and put it in her mouth, 'we need her blessing, too.' Grace was talking through a mouthful of lentils now. Still Abi could tell she was serious.

'He won't call her. It's pathological. He acts like she's dead.'

'Then, you're going to have to.'

That was exactly what Abi had been afraid Grace was going to say.

'Abi, I mean it. There has been too much change for our kids. Your post is lovely, but you'd be blind not to see that Arden is retreating from all the chaos.' Grace's spoon was down. 'The last thing we need is for those boys to settle in here full-time and that to blow up in our faces—and crush them—all over again when Elle changes her mind.'

'Custody shit is serious, G. I don't think Adrian wants to face it.'

'Well, being a grown-up sucks,' said Grace. 'But someone's got to be an adult for those little boys.'

One of things Abi loved the most about Grace was that she was always fucking right. She affirmed the niggling, uncomfortable truths that Abi pushed away.

'Sure, I'll track down that lying monster,' she said, standing up and stretching. 'Tomorrow.'

'I think,' Grace said, scraping the last mush from her bowl, 'that Arden might know exactly where Elle is.'

CHAPTER 6
FRANCES

> I gave Eddie some water and now I'm worried I've poisoned him. He keeps doing these really sad little burps.
>
> Isiah has a rash. Although it could be a graze. Or a mozzie bite. What do you think? Pic attached.
>
> It's three a.m. and Bette hasn't woken up yet. Should I wake her for a feed?... Sorry, it's three a.m.
>
> I've taken a picture of Ely's poo. I know, I know it's TMI, but have any of you seen this colour before?

Frances's mothers' group WhatsApp conversation had been saving her life and stressing her out in equal measure.

Before Denny, Frances would never have imagined that she would look at a picture of another human being's shit on her phone, but now it seemed like a perfectly reasonable thing to do.

And no, she hadn't seen that shade of green before.

But some days the relentless *ping-ping-ping* felt like a niggling stress headache. A persistent signal that connecting with these women was just another thing she wasn't doing quickly or well enough. And a reminder that there was an outside world, and she was soon meant to rejoin it. Lying on the lounge scrolling through Instagram and trying to feed her colicky baby was not, it turned out, the only thing expected of her.

That quiet panic had started when Denny was about six weeks old, when texts from her sisters-in-law about being kind to herself and 'cocooning' with her newborn suddenly changed. They became links to 'get your body back' gym sessions and ever-more-pressing invites to playdates and coffees and 'walk 'n' talks'.

For years, Frances had watched motherhood happen to other people. Real people in her life—like her sisters-in-law—and 'unreal' people on her social feeds—like Elle Campbell.

Now it was Frances's turn to parent publicly, and all she could think was: *How did they do that?* The post-birth photos, with these beautiful pudgy, clean babies curled up on bountiful chests. The outings: 'Took little Elvis for his first ever splash at the beach today!' when the beach was fifty minutes' drive if the traffic was kind. And then, of course, the exercise and the dieting, the mass reclamation of the bodies.

Frances realised she had watched all this happening without question or comment, but now that it was her turn, it seemed like science fiction.

How could she become one of them? One of the women who had it all together?

***

Frances had followed Elle since Before.

Since before Elle had been betrayed by her husband and sister. Since before she'd lost her beautiful little boys.

For a while, in the early days of Frances's own pregnancy, when she'd been feeling too ill to do much but lie on her bed and scroll through her phone, she had spent a lot of time venting about this injustice in closed Facebook groups, swapping conspiracy theories and clues about where Elle was, where Adrian was, how all this had happened and how justice would be restored.

Some of Frances's real-life friends, who had once followed The Stylish Mumma's every post, mimicking Elle's everything—from maternity wear to birthday party décor to manicure tips—didn't feel the same way. After the Blog-ahhs, they enjoyed watching the fallout on their Facebook feeds and the tabloid sites, and then they'd washed their hands of Elle Campbell.

'That psycho bitch,' as Frances's best friend and 'work wife' Linley called her.

Frances and Linley were nurses. They'd qualified together, and then worked in the same general ward at a small private hospital, dealing with middle-aged men's heart problems and bringing fiftyish women back from hysterectomies.

During that time after the Blog-ahhs, their lunchtime walks in search of Vietnamese rolls had become impassioned arguments about Elle.

'Imagine,' Linley had said once, 'telling everyone that your husband's got cancer and that your dad's dead, just to get more followers. Some people have no shame. And I can't believe I fell for those bloody hair extensions she was pushing for a while. They made my hair look like a disaster at a basket-weaving class.'

As they walked the few hundred metres to the Vietnamese street food cafe, Frances tried to make Linley see that Elle had been hoodwinked by a powerful man, that guys like Adrian had been taking advantage of young women like Elle since the dawn of time.

'He's like Dr Darling,' Frances told Linley, allowing herself an inner shudder. 'He has a Master of the Universe complex and thinks women exist solely to serve him.'

It was up to them, she went on, and every woman who had ever been betrayed by a man to stand by Elle Campbell. She knew Linley was one of those women.

'No one can handle seeing a beautiful woman do well, Lin. They want to tear her down. It's fucking Adrian who's the villain here. And Elle's sister. Jealous, jealous, jealous. And Abi Black and the American idiots who ran that awards show. They should be ashamed of themselves for letting that con man take everything from her.'

But Linley, like the *Daily Trail* and *An Evening Affair* and the women's websites Frances had always followed, remained unconvinced. 'Really, Frank?' she'd asked, looking up from her phone as they walked. 'It seems like a lot of trouble to go to just to stop someone winning an award...'

'Exactly. And way too much trouble to make all that stuff up to win one.'

'I don't know,' Linley huffed. 'I never trusted her. Too perfect.'

***

It was Elle's perfection that Frances had loved.

As a follower of The Stylish Mumma since way before she was a mother of any kind, Frances had been mentally filing away images of what life would be like when she had her own beautiful little kids to spoil and dress up. The blog became a template for the world she wanted to live in, and the woman she wanted to be in that world.

Beautiful, successful, thin. With a husband who adored her,

and gorgeous, loving kids, and a home that never embarrassed her—even if people just popped around unannounced.

Because her life—before or after Denny—didn't look much like that.

Frances's life looked like a small apartment in a newish block in Rockdale in southern Sydney. It was starting a new diet every Monday, four shifts a week at the hospital, a job she'd always wanted and studied hard to get—but now, after only a few years, it was becoming routine. It was the gym and coffee with girlfriends and dinner out on special occasions and Sunday lunches at her mum's. And it was a husband she'd married at twenty-two after three years of dating.

Troy Graham had been exactly her type when she'd met him. He was working at the club that she and her friends frequented every Saturday night. Popular, happy, tall with just a hint of the dork about him, he was cute enough, with his curly black hair, and funny enough, with his mother's Irish sense of humour. They'd got along so well from the very beginning, laughing at each other's jokes, bonding over their sprawling, loud Catholic families: hers Italian, his from Dublin. They were a no-brainer—'The Barman' and Frances quickly became the Couple Most Likely among their friends.

But a part of Frances was always pushing away the expectation that the love of her life would be... more. It wasn't just the Friday-night rom-coms that had led her to think that, but also her Facebook and Instagram feeds, full of women's birthday and anniversary messages about their partners, gushing about 'best friends' and 'lovers' and 'soul mates' and 'supporters'.

Sometimes Frances looked at Troy, who came home from work and played *Fallout 4* on the lounge for hours at a time, and wondered what she could say about him on the occasion of a special day.

Still.

After they'd got married, they lived with his parents for two years while she finished her studies, and saved madly for a deposit on a unit. Frances was one of four—the only girl—and her family home had been full of her brothers and their wives and their babies. If she was honest, she'd had enough of the chaos and noise, and grabbed at the chance to escape. With Troy's mum, they lived in the converted garage, and worked and worked and worked, nights and weekends, putting away the overtime until they could get their place: suburbs away from the families, a little piece of independence, a little room to move—things that Frances had always craved.

When they got the keys, she had never felt more Elle-like, more in control of her destiny. Maybe it *was* true; maybe anything was possible.

They moved in, started putting their hand-me-down furniture in the right places. And then, almost immediately, Frances found out she was pregnant. If she was honest—which she wasn't with anyone in her family, god no—it was a bit too soon.

Hands up, it was her and Troy's own fault. The Pill hadn't been agreeing with her for a while and they had been lax with the condoms. But another year would have been perfect. She could have moved up one more grade at the hospital. Troy could have stayed on day shifts. They would have had a bit more in the bank, been a little more sorted.

Still. She'd always wanted a family. A picture-perfect family.

And just as the nausea had lifted and she'd begun to feel better, Elle had reappeared in Frances's life, with a new blog and a new message, and a pregnancy of her own.

***

Frances obsessively followed The Goddess Project's pregnancy posts.

> The last thing your body needs while it's growing a tiny human is more fat to carry around that slows you down, inside and out. Keep moving,

Friends, and don't give in to the 'comfort' eating myth. There's no comfort in bad health.

Frances had read that one while demolishing a plate of her mother's cannoli on the lounge after a shift, having given in to exhaustion and sugar cravings. She'd put down her spoon and made one of a hundred vows to herself to be better.

Then, when Denny was just a few days old, when she was still arguing with Troy over their baby boy's name—he wanted Dennis for his dad; she would rather set her hair on fire—Frances was delighted when, scrolling through her phone while she was trying to breastfeed, an alert popped up to a new, members-only blog post from Elle.

One for all the mummas

The kitten's out of the bag, Ladies. I have been blessed with a daughter.

We have called her Alma. Because what she brings is love and kindness. A healing.

And her arrival was healing, Warriors.

She took 16 hours to find her way to our world but there was no pain, only joy.

There was no medicine. Only breath. No hospital. Only nature.

Yes, Alma was born in the open air, down by the water. Clearly, walls couldn't contain the love that was bursting from me when my girl broke through.

Remember, Warriors, what hurts us is fear. It's also what holds us back from being everything our loved ones need us to be.

If you are a new mumma too, and I know many, many of you are, maybe you're struggling right now.

Maybe you're struggling with why you don't

instinctively know what to do with the little person who's sent to teach you something you're not sure of yet.

Maybe you feel like you don't know how best to love and care for them.

You do know. You just aren't listening.

If you are wondering how you will ever summon the energy to give all that you have to give, look inside yourself.

Can you honestly say you are your best self right now? That you are giving yourself all the love and care that your baby needs from you?

Look hard at yourself, Warriors. What aren't you doing?

What are you feeling incapable of giving?

I say this to you because I am a new mother all over again, and I refuse to carry the toxic lessons of the past into this beautiful little girl's pure heart. She deserves better.

Can you do the same? Be the woman you were created to be, the best guide your baby deserves?

Listen to yourself. Listen to your baby. Listen to the goddess whispering in your ear. You can do it. You can do it.

E xxx

Frances burst into tears.

There had been plenty of medicine involved in Denny's arrival, and Frances was still smarting from the shame.

She'd told her doctor, her midwife, Troy and everyone who would listen that she wanted a 'natural' birth.

Her sisters-in-law, of course, had let her know what they thought: 'But Frankie, this is why God invented painkillers.' 'No one needs to feel that, sister. And no one needs to see you feeling that, either.'

But Frances was determined. Plenty of other things in her life were beyond her control right now: this wasn't going to be one of them. She was going to take this experience and own it, Elle Campbell-style.

It didn't turn out that way. With Denny overdue and an induction ordered, with the pain beginning and Troy looking nauseated at the edge of the bed, she sensed this was not the moment to take control. She had never been so out of control in her life.

This pain did not *hurt*. This pain took her to another place. A place so dark, so brutal and searing, she no longer cared what she was there for. She just wanted out.

As one contraction finished, she was filled only by the dread that another would come.

She bared her teeth at Troy. 'Make. It. Stop.'

'I can't...' He looked around at the birth centre for someone, anyone. But the midwife had 'popped out' for a moment, calm as a Buddha.

Frances looked around, too, with what felt like fresh eyes. As per the order of no-intervention, there was a birthing pool filled in the corner of the room. A fit-ball by the door. A shower big enough for two. There were candles, for fuck's sake. And were those fairy lights?

This was a public hospital. And she was a nurse. How had she conned herself into thinking fairy lights were the answer? If Frances hadn't been trapped in the bed by ferocious, gut-slashing agony, she would have leapt up and trashed it all—the candles and the lights and the inflatable pool. WHAT WAS THIS SHIT? WAS IT A JOKE? DIDN'T THEY KNOW WHAT HAPPENED IN HERE? DIDN'T THEY KNOW HOW BABIES CAME OUT?

'YOU *CAN*!' she screamed at Troy. 'Go and GET SOMEONE!'

The pain was coming back for her.

Troy ran out to find the doctor. And for a moment Frances was alone with the jagged knives and the blackness.

It hadn't been too late for a trip down the corridor to the place where the drugs lived. *The place*, Frances remembered thinking, *for people who'd been through this before. I bet everyone ends up here eventually*.

Please, peace, come. And, it did.

But afterwards, when the bleeding had become a trickle rather than a flood, and the adrenalin had faded, and she could no longer conjure up the sharp edge of that slicing pain, Frances felt foolish. Cowardly, even. Embarrassed. Her friends and sisters-in-law looked at her with 'I told you so' in their eyes. They smiled and told her it was okay: no one knew how bad it was until they were there.

Denny—at that time known only as 'The Baby'—was a beautiful, squalling bundle, but she couldn't help feeling that somehow she had failed him before they'd even begun.

There was no pain. Only joy.

Had Frances been doing it wrong?

***

Now she was typing into the mothers' group WhatsApp conversation:

> Is five months too young to put Denny in the crèche at the gym? He'll be asleep.

The little writing-in-progress bubbles popped up. Disappeared. Silence.

Nobody wanted to say yes. Nobody wanted to be the one who said no.

She knew she'd come a long way since she was the mum of a six-week-old—a mum who would never get off the lounge. Now she was working on her nutrition, going to the gym, and all-day trackie pants were a distant memory.

And she had Elle to thank for that. For pushing her off the comfort cliff, as she called it. For showing her that she could handle this motherhood business if only she took herself in hand and toughened up.

But Frances still had so much to learn. Still so many ways to be better. A better mother and better wife, a better woman. One of those women who really did have it all together. There was still so much a trip to Gurva could teach her.

She threw her phone down.

'I am a work in progress,' Frances whispered as she shoved the nearest damp towel into her gym bag. 'I am in love with my life.'

She was going to the gym. Again.

CHAPTER 7

ELLE

Ben Bont had installed a yoga swing in the bedroom.

Elle got back from her afternoon gym session to find a workman finishing the job.

'I think that hook will hold,' the man said. 'Go easy,' he added, and winked at Elle as he packed up his tools.

Fuck you, thought Elle when he left, making a mental note to tell the housekeeper never to use that firm again. They had to be locals—there was no way a farm employee would talk to her like that.

She looked at the swing. Not a challenge, she decided, but clearly some kind of hint from Ben. So tiresome to be in this stage of a relationship, she thought, as she went to shower in the ensuite. The time when the power balance was always shifting.

Ben would be here in an hour or so. When she'd first moved into the farm, his visits had been sporadic, short and passionate. Since Alma, of course, they'd been more regular, and lately he was flying in every weekend and sometimes popping up midweek unannounced.

Elle never knew which Ben she was going to get when he stepped off that plane: the one who scooped her up and took her to bed, or the one who was stressed and distracted and barely looked up from his phone. The one full of praise for any progress made on the farm, or the one who was searching for something, anything, to be furious about.

But there was something she could control: Elle resisted leaving the farm as much as possible.

'I'm hosting some potential investors at Shamara this week,' he'd told her, just a few weeks after she'd first arrived at the farm, and was eye-deep in plans. 'And I want you with me.'

Shamara was Ben's Sydney harbourside house. It was, like all the other homes within a five-kilometre radius, a hulking Spanish-style pile that filled every inch of its prestigious block and where every room, every window strained towards the epic view. It was imposing and beautiful in its way, but Elle had no interest in spending time there. It was a place that had nothing to do with her, or her plans.

'I can't, Ben. I'm much too busy here,' she'd said, stroking his floppy, fair hair out of his face as if he were a needy child. 'There's just so much to do. You'll have fun without me.'

He'd rolled his much-reported baby-blue eyes, but smiled at her. 'Such dedication,' he'd said, moving in to kiss her.

After that, every time he asked her to come to Sydney with him, Elle said the same. And then there was the pregnancy excuse. And then there was Alma.

'But I *need* you with me,' he'd say now. 'And Alma. I miss Alma so much.'

'Alma needs her routine—and Gurva needs me,' Elle would reply. Which was true. But also, the right tactic for dealing with a man like Ben Bont was to leave him wanting more.

Ben was a high-risk strategy. She'd known from the minute she'd sat down next to him on the plane. Managing this shifting power dynamic, keeping it in her favour for as long as she could to get what she needed—that wasn't a simple game to play. In fact, it was harder than she'd imagined.

Three years, she needed. Three years until whatever they built at Gurva would be forty per cent hers. That was the agreement she and Ben had made, back when she first set eyes on the place and shared her plan with him. Give me three years here and I'll build you a new business, she'd pitched. And Ben, remarkably, giddily, had agreed.

In Elle's head, that was also the deadline on their relationship. And they were fifteen months down already.

Not that it was always hard work to be around Ben Bont: as long as you were on your game, it could be intoxicating. He was a man who gave himself to everything in his life completely—whether it was his health, his sex life or his work. His staff called him Mister 110 Per Cent; as in, 'That won't be good enough for Mister 110 Per Cent.'

The three-year plan was the deal Elle had made with herself within a few days of meeting Ben. But it had taken her much longer again to get his measure, to learn his borders and limits. She was still testing them, gingerly. This latest project she and Matt had cooked up might do just that.

Still, her motivation was solid. Ben moved in a different stratosphere and had lifted her there, too. A world with staff, private planes—and high expectations. Being with him had pushed her clear of having to make grubby media deals to court public approval. She no longer had to roll around in the mud with her dumb sister Zoe and the Abi Blacks of the world. Ben Bont's kind of wealth bought you privacy. Non-disclosure agreements. Hush money.

Also—for now, at least—Ben adored her. Having a partner he could talk business with was a novelty for him. He seemed to love her ambition, encouraging her to think big. Basically, Elle knew, he loved seeing himself reflected back.

Oh, and Alma. The baby had probably bought them another eighteen months.

Baby Alma had also bought them the permission to go

public. And now the big reveal was in the works. It gave Elle butterflies to think about everyone—especially those who had abandoned her, abused her and declared her finished—seeing what she'd built. What *they'd* built.

***

Elle put on a white silk kimono and went to check that Alma was down for the night.

She'd had live-in help back in Brighton, but compared to a qualified baby nurse, a housekeeper and a chef, her au pair/ personal assistant Cate had been no assistance at all. Now, Elle thought, if she'd only had proper staff back when she was juggling the boys with The Stylish Mumma, think how much she could have achieved.

Her boys. She shook her head to dislodge the thought. But she must send Arden another email tonight.

Lucille had Alma all ready for Elle to cuddle before she went off to sleep.

This is the way to parent, she thought. It was how everyone expected it would be to have a baby before they actually had one—just love and cuddles and the smell of clean baby scalp. No sleep deprivation, no wondering what the hell was wrong *now*, no fear of impending disaster.

Elle knew she was living a strange fantasy life. It was so far from any reality she had known, either as a child or in her life in Melbourne. She had thought she and Adrian were 'rich' in that Brighton house. But there were different levels of success, and this one was as far from Brighton as the glass-box house had been from her father's final fibro shack on the edge of Thalwyn.

She kissed Alma on the head. 'Night-night, darling.'

She'd probably spent about forty-five minutes with her baby today. Forty-five good minutes. *Better than twelve stressful hours*, she thought.

'I can hear Ben's plane,' Lucille said, as Alma started to whimper.

'Better go,' Elle said to her baby. 'Daddy's here!'

***

Elle knew that part of what attracted Ben to her was her reputation.

'Did you really do it?' he'd asked on that second night, the night they'd had the sex she later described on her blog as 'restorative, transporting, healing, hot'.

'Do what?' she asked, head on his chest. Of course, she knew.

'Lie about your husband being sick. Lie about your dad. All of it?'

Elle had been wondering what she would say when he asked her. She'd planned a denial, of course, but something about Ben Bont changed her mind.

'Some of it,' she said, in the smallest voice she could muster. 'I did some of it.'

'Good,' was all he said. And he'd never asked her again.

Ben Bont wasn't really interested in truth: he was interested in maximising potential. In himself, in his businesses, in the people around him.

He was thirty-two and, she could tell, he felt like he'd lived his life already. He'd taken his not inconsiderable family fortune, and doubled it, tripled it, creating bars and clubs that attracted the kind of people who would go anywhere and spend anything as long as it looked sensational on Instagram. There were enough of these people, obviously, for Ben Bont's hotels to instantly become guest-list-only wherever they were opened.

By the time he met her—Elle knew from her diligent trawling of his social accounts, the business press and the social pages—Ben had already begun to shift away from the traditional tools of workaholic productivity that he had employed for decades—no sleep, coffee, cocaine, impatience, fury—and towards less conventional means to the same end.

For example, was a meditated mind really, as many suggested, sharper, more productive—super-charged, even? Could 'positive' nutrition fundamentally change your energy levels, without the inevitable crash offered by his favourite stimulants? If you pulled an hour from your work schedule to exercise powerfully, would you end up getting more out of the remaining hours? If you were religious about your sleep, could you literally fit more living into the hours you were awake?

Slowly his posse had changed, along with his physique. Out went the three-phone-wielding sharp-suiters, the 'guys' who would always encourage him to indulge in another espresso, another deal, another line. In came the laid-back yogic millionaires—Ben's new tribe. At first sight they resembled surfer bums—all height, broad shoulders, tousled hair and baggy boardies—until you got close enough to notice their watches were Rolexes.

Ben had been looking around for a business venture with meaning—something that might actually improve people's lives, from the inside.

And then, he'd met Elle. A woman headed down the path of spiritual reinvention herself. She was, he told her, the perfect partner for this phase of his life.

What a coincidence that was.

CHAPTER 8

ABI

'No, I am not wearing a fucking tux.'

'Well, I'm sorry, I just thought that at gay weddings one of the—'

'Adrian. Did you grow up in a different fucking time?'

'No. Just a different fucking world, obviously.'

Adrian and Abi were side by side in the veggie patch. Helping in the garden was out of character for her ex, but he had volunteered, buoyed by the news that a publisher was finally interested in his Manifesting Money book.

'Oh, yes,' Abi said, 'a world where middle-aged men marry gym bunnies half their age, but same-sex weddings are a no-no.'

'Ouch. I never said a no-no, Abi. You know I'm very happy for you, I just... thought you might wear the pants.'

'Then clearly,' Abi yanked out a particularly stubborn creeper, 'all this time you've spent living with Grace has been wasted.' She stood up. 'And no one is wearing fucking pants.'

Actually, Abi had no idea what her bride would be wearing. Grace had gone strangely silent on the subject.

Of the two of them, Abi had turned out to be the wedding enthusiast. Almost the moment that the result of that damned plebiscite had been announced, she'd been gripped by an immediate need to propose. Grace, on the other hand, thought it was a little beneath them.

'I don't care, babe,' she'd said, when Abi had been asking her 'if ' and 'when' during the campaign for marriage equality. 'If I was straight I wouldn't care about getting married and I don't care about getting married now either.'

'But don't you want to just because *WE CAN*?' Abi demanded.

'That is never a very good reason for doing anything,' Grace replied. 'Give me a better one.'

'Because I love you and I want the entire world to know.'

'Um, I think everyone who matters already knows.'

'Because I want the kids to be part of the kind of family that our families could never have conceived of.'

That was getting warmer; Abi could tell from Grace's smile. 'I have to tell you though, babe,' she said, 'if you're proposing, you suck at it.'

'Ahh...' Abi had figured it out: Grace wanted romance. She wanted a gesture. This, Abi could do.

But right now, in the veggie patch with Adrian, Abi's wedding thoughts weren't about their dresses. She was thinking about a call she'd got this morning, and how to approach it with Grace.

Maybe Adrian would be a good place to start.

'I got a call from *All-Australian Yarns*,' she said, kneeling up and squinting against the building sun. 'About the wedding.'

'Really? Tell me.'

'They want to cover it. Stop eye-rolling! Not in a tacky way. They want to tell our story, from, you know... all angles. And have the wedding be the end piece. Like, a parable about being who you are, a same-sex marriage love-in, a positive family story...' she felt a little foolish under Adrian's look. 'I don't know. It's not like me not to know, but I don't.'

He seemed unimpressed. 'All angles?'

'They want to interview the family. The kids. And you. Maybe even Edie, Grace's ex. You know,' Abi got back to the weeds, 'the evolution of a modern family.'

Adrian, too, turned his attention to rummaging in the soil. 'Don't do it, Abigail.'

Abigail? 'What?'

'Don't do it. I think we've both had plenty of experience with the media and how they fuck things over. It's not like they want to tell a genuine, nuanced story about us all—they just want drama. They'll make us all look like a soap opera. And you know what else they're going to want to talk about, don't you?'

'I think you mean *who* else, don't you, Adrian?' Abi couldn't hide the irritation in her voice. 'But thank you for mansplaining the media's motivation to me. It's lucky you're here to save me from myself. Jesus!' She stood up, brushed off her shorts, pulled off her bandana. 'I'm only thinking about it.'

'Don't think about it.'

'That's easy for you to say,' Abi said, 'from where you sit, hiding from the world. But some of us are out there in it, trying to build something. And... I know you might not be comfortable with this idea, but it could be really... important, for other LGBT people to see this. To see that everything can be fine. That you can have a family. You can have a wedding. You can have a fucking civilised relationship with your ex.'

'Very fucking civilised right now,' said a girl's voice, and Abi looked up.

It was Arden. She and River were back from taking Teddy and Freddie into town to a drum class.

'Can you two try not to kill each other in front of the children?' she asked Abi and Adrian.

The way that Arden clearly no longer included herself in 'the children' made Abi's heart twinge a little bit. 'You're making me feel really, really old, girl,' she said, pulling her daughter towards her with one arm and kissing the top of her head.

'Mum. You're sweaty. Get off me!' Arden jerked away, but she was smiling a little bit.

The boys came charging down the garden towards them, ubiquitous sticks in hand. Teddy threw his arms around Abi's legs as Adrian stood to sweep Freddie up in a hug.

'Are you really thinking of letting a TV crew film the wedding?' Arden asked, as disinterestedly as she could manage.

'Jesus, how long have you been there?' Abi yelled over Teddy's yelps—he had taken to pretending he was a puppy lately. 'No idea. I just got a call. We'll talk about it.'

'I think you should totally do it,' Arden shouted back. 'Be great for my followers.'

Fuck me, Abi thought. *They're all at it*. But out loud she just said, 'Don't mention it to Grace yet, I haven't talked to her about it.'

'Talking to Dad first?' Like any sixteen-year-old girl, Arden could smell an opportunity to stir. 'That's dangerous.'

'Shut up, you.' Abi bent to untangle Teddy. 'Come on, let's get you some food, puppy.'

***

Arden was getting more complicated by the day, Abi was learning.

After Grace had suggested that she talk to Arden about Elle, she'd engineered a way to get her alone—harder than it should have been, in her opinion—by offering her a lift out to River's after dinner the next night.

Usually, if River hadn't come to their place in his banged-up ute, Arden would have ridden her bike over to see him. But she hated getting sweaty doing that now the weather was getting warm, so she'd clearly weighed up the cost of a 'mum conversation' in the car.

While Adrian struggled outwardly with Arden's relationship with River—a boy two years older, of no discernible ambition, who'd rarely left town—Abi had found it kind of beautiful watching her teenage daughter fall in love. But as Arden became more and more herself, and less and less Abi, mother–daughter relations had become increasingly fraught. As Arden had slowly shaken off her alternative affectations—the clumpy boots, the rags, the heavy black eyeliner—and become much straighter, more *normal*, Abi had fought a near-constant urge to criticise.

Her daughter spent countless hours in her room, putting on and taking off make-up in front of a tiny camera, as far as Abi could see, and spending all her Saturday job money on the parcels of cosmetics that arrived daily. Of course, Abi knew that now many of them came for free, just so Arden would use their stuff in her videos: packages were starting to arrive via Paris, via Korea... Abi understood the online world. But to her, a teenager being plied with these expensive products was crazy. For a start, a sixteen-year-old didn't need twenty-five creams to look young.

At Grace's wise urging, Abi had never let loose on Arden about this. They'd simply set up boundaries around the YouTube channel and her blog, and let her find her way.

For a while, it was Abi's favourite meditation to run through all the things she would love to say to Arden, silently, in the shower, every morning:

A teenage girl who likes make-up? How original.

Why would you choose to look like a brainless bimbo?

Do you know how many piglets died for your lip gloss?

Every minute you waste staring in that fucking mirror is a win for the patriarchy.

You are just a cog in the machine that keeps women feeling terrible about themselves.

You know you look a little bit slutty with that much bronzer, right?

And, of course:

Darling, you are so much more beautiful without all that shit on your face.

But she kept the comments in her head. And, slowly, she was seeing Arden come around to a more interesting aesthetic with her 'art', as she insisted on calling it, branching out into fantasy and experimenting with transformations, instead of another 'Fourteen Ways to Cover a Pimple'. Now, it wasn't uncommon for the family to be breakfasting across from an elf, or an orc, or a mermaid. Often, River would be there, too, squeezing oranges with a pair of twisted horns glued to his forehead.

But Abi kept an eye on that YouTube channel.

In her darker moments, she took comfort in the fact she still had sway over Alex—who, at fourteen, appeared to be becoming more feminist by the day. Yesterday she'd come home wearing a ripped homemade T-shirt with the slogan 'Riots Not Diets'. Abi had nearly wept with pride.

But when it came to River, Abi was unperturbed. He treated Arden well. They didn't seem to fight. Abi heard them laughing a lot. He was pleasant to have around: at least pretending to be interested in their family and weighing in on chores when he was at the farm.

'But they're having *sex*!' Adrian had exclaimed, eyes bulging, six months ago when Arden had first asked if River could stay over on Friday nights.

Grace and Abi had exchanged a look.

'Yes, Adrian, they're teenagers,' Abi had counselled. 'That's what teenagers do. And I for one would rather they did it here where there are bountiful condoms and everyone is safe and warm, than out in the back of his ute in a paddock where god knows what might happen.'

'I'm sure they've done that, too,' Grace had added, helpfully.

Abi had won that round, and now River was at their place a few nights a week, sharing a pull-out sofa in the farm's front room with her daughter. Those mornings, Adrian avoided coming in to put the coffee on.

'So, Arden, I'm going to ask you something,' Abi started, eyes on the road as they drove to River's place.

'I knew there was going to be a price to this ride, Mum.'

'It's about Elle.'

That had taken Arden by surprise. She blinked quickly, breathed in. 'Uh-oh.'

'Gracey tells me that you... know something about her.'

'Well, Mum, to be fair, anyone with an internet connection can know something about her right now.'

'I thought she was...' Abi searched for the right word. 'Underground.'

Arden snorted with laughter. 'Underground? Mum. Where have you been?'

'I don't know what you're talking about.'

'I can't believe no one's asked you about it, to be honest, Mum.' Arden's tone was packed with condescension. One of Abi's least favourite things about having teenagers was your instant relegation to village idiot when they were around.

She swallowed, trying to keep it together. 'Okay. I'm a fool, I get it. Just humour me.'

'She's running a big wellness thing up in Byron,' Arden said like this was no big deal, putting her feet up on the dashboard. It was dusk; the light on the trees outside the car was beautiful. 'She's hooked up with Ben Bont.'

'Ben Bont?' Abi wasn't exactly keeping up with the social pages, but the name rang a bell. 'The guy who owns all those hotels? The playboy guy?'

'Not so much of a playboy now, apparently. He's gone all Zen. Since the baby, I guess.'

'The... baby?' Abi looked left at Arden, sharply. Adrian's face flashed in her mind. 'For fuck's sake, Arden. Who knows about this? Why isn't it all over the press?'

'It will be, I'm sure, Mum. But they've been keeping it on

the down-low. You have to pay to follow her site, and I just don't think that many people have caught on yet.'

Abi pulled the car over. She was feeling dizzy and suddenly aware of her heart pumping quickly.

'What are you doing, Mum? Why are you stopping?'

'Arden. I need a minute. Do you have any idea what this information will do to your dad?'

'Dad?' Arden sounded like she had never even considered that. She might be having sex, thought Abi, but Arden was as self-absorbed and immature as any kid.

'Yes. Your dad, Adrian. The man who's raising Elle's *other* babies, you know, without a word from her—'

'Well, I'd hardly say that *he's* raising them—'

'*ARDEN!* Not the fucking time.'

They sat in silence for a minute. Then something struck Abi. 'How do you know all about this? Have you been following her or...?'

'She emailed me.' Arden said this quickly, in the same offhand tone, but her eyes suggested it was beginning to dawn on her that this was a bigger deal than she'd thought.

'*ARDEN!*'

'She likes my videos. She mailed me to see if I'd go up there and do a special thing about this product she's making, a fake tan or something—'

'You are fucking kidding me now, right? She hasn't called her sons in six months but she's emailing you, *my daughter*, about fake tan? And you didn't think this was important information for me or your dad?' Abi's cool-mum mask had completely slipped. She found that she was tugging at her hair.

'Mum! Calm *DOWN*. I didn't think...' Arden went quiet. 'Anyway, all this "me and your dad" stuff is deeply weird. After everything that went down with you guys, your happy families stuff is bullshit.'

'Is that what this is about? You're talking to Elle Campbell and keeping it a secret from us because you're shitty about your dad living here?'

I need to get a grip, Abi thought. *Grace would tell me right now, I need to get a grip and listen.*

'I don't know.' Arden shrugged. To Abi, her daughter suddenly looked twelve years old again, not sixteen and being driven to her boyfriend's to stay the night.

'Arden. Baby.' *Channel Grace, channel Grace*. 'The reason I was asking you about Elle is because I have to get in touch with her...' *Deep breath*. 'About your dad and the boys. All this is really hard for him. And Grace and I want to talk to her to see if we can make a plan for everything to be... a bit more sane.'

Abi put her hand out to Arden, who had her knees pulled up to her chest in the passenger seat, arms wrapped tightly around herself. She had about three inches of foundation on, but her mascara was beginning to run.

'Would you like that? If we made some proper plans for the family?'

Arden batted Abi's hand away with her knees, but she nodded.

'Good. Okay then. Just let me process all this.' Abi took a literal deep breath, turned on the ignition. 'A baby? Shit.'

'It's been a while, Mum.'

'Has it? Fuck, I guess it has.'

They drove in silence for a moment. River's place—or rather, his parents' place, an actual farm that serviced fancy city restaurants with meat from a niche-breed cattle herd—came into view. 'Boy or girl?'

'A girl.'

'Nice.' Abi signalled, pulled into the driveway to the farm. 'You weren't... going to go up there, were you, Arden?'

It was Arden's time to snort again. She unwrapped her arms from around herself and reached for her backpack, down on the car floor. 'No way, Mum. That bitch is crazy.'

'Ha!' Abi felt a flood of relief. 'And don't say "bitch".'

Arden jumped out of the car. 'Mum, I'm sorry I didn't tell you,' she said through the open door before she turned towards the house. 'I think I knew you wouldn't... like it.'

'Sure.' *I might have just dodged a bullet*, Abi thought. 'Love you, Arden.'

'Shut up, Mum.' And her daughter smiled and slammed the car door shut, pulled on her backpack and walked towards the house to have sex.

***

After Abi got home that night, she and Grace sat down at the kitchen table together, drank some tea and wrote an email.

> Elle. It's Abi.

'She knows it's you, babe. It's from your address,' Grace said with a laugh.

> You're probably surprised to hear from me. Although, since I hear you've been emailing my daughter, maybe not.

'That's a bit aggressive, Abi.'

Abi hit Delete.

> You're probably a bit surprised to hear from me. But I need to talk to you. It's about Teddy and Freddie. And, I guess, Adrian.

'Sure you want to mention Adrian?'

'Well, he is kind of central to this story...'

> They've been staying with us at the farm for a long time now. Something you would know if you'd been talking to their father.

'*DELETE* that!'

Please call me, I think it's time we worked some stuff out. Maybe even plan a visit.

'A visit? Is that what we're doing now?'

For you to come and see them and we could all talk about their future.

'Jesus. Okay.'

My number's at the bottom of this email. Hope to talk to you soon.
Abi Black
PS: Congratulations on the baby.

'Big of you, babe. I'm proud.'
Abi hit Send.

CHAPTER 9

FRANCES

Frances had been dreading going back to work. In the foggy mess of her Denny-filled mind, the idea of returning to the ward, back to the world of Dr Darling and the treatment room plunged her into a chest-tightening panic.

But the morning Troy confronted her about the deliveries left her with no doubt it had to happen, and soon.

'Frank,' he'd said calmly, as he walked into the living room where she was doing some squats with Denny in his sling, 'what is *aloe juice*?'

'It's *juice*, Troy. And, like, a super food. I have it in smoothies, or, you know... like juice.'

'It's *juice*? And it's forty dollars?'

The significance of the original question suddenly occurred to Frances. What was Troy doing? She straightened up, looked at him. He was standing in front of her, holding his work laptop.

'What are you doing?' she asked.

'Well, I'm trying to do a budget, Frank, because we're on the bones of our arse right now.'

'Oh.'

'And so when I started looking through the account, it looks like a fair chunk of our money is going at WholeHealth on bloody aloe juice...'

'Don't exaggerate.' Denny had started whingeing, so Frances resumed her squats. But her stomach had begun to flip-flap, her forehead to sweat.

'I'm not exaggerating, Frank.' She very rarely saw Troy angry, but he was struggling to stay calm. 'We spent more than two hundred dollars last week on a WholeHealth delivery that...' Frances watched him click between tabs, 'included something called vanilla mushroom powder, and... and... I can't even say this one... ash-wagand-ha? What is this shit?'

'It's *MY* shit, okay, Troy? It's about me feeling better.' Frances shot him a look she knew would bring the guilt. 'You don't want me to feel better?'

Troy sat down on the lounge, laptop still open. 'Frank. You're not working. I'm busting my arse. How do you think we're going to pay for all this stuff?'

It was a legitimate question. Frances stopped moving again, unhooked the sling. Denny was looking sleepy, which was unlikely—his day sleeps were bullshit.

'Let me put Denny down, Troy, and we'll talk.' Holding Denny, she walked out of the living room and into the sunroom that served as his 'room'. She closed the door and leant against it for a moment, cradling Denny, 'Shhh, shhh, shhh.'

It was two p.m. and Troy had just got up after another late-night shift. He had recently taken on extra hours, managing a new bar in a state-of-the-art hotel in the city. He'd been working for the same company—Ben Bont's Bounce Group—since he left school and got his first job in a pub. He'd travelled on it for a couple of years, before he came home and met Frances.

She knew how hard he worked. She knew their new life was rough on him, when so few of his mates had babies and his body clock was completely cuckoo. She knew how much they'd saved to get 'on the property ladder' as every family member had harassed them to do. They'd always lived to the budget that Frances had crafted on colour-coded spreadsheets, back when that seemed like a fun, grown-up thing to do. She'd set aside fifty dollars each week for 'fun', and they would tease each other endlessly about what the 'fun' would be.

But since maternity leave, there had been no 'fun' budget. Not with the pram and the cot and the nappies and the clothes and the bottles and the car seat.

In fact, between the exhaustion and the worry, Frances hadn't been feeling fun at all lately. Which was the point of the potions. If a pinch of fifty-five-dollar powder in your smoothie promised a return to energy and happiness, it was money well spent, right? There still had to be some things in her life that weren't baby necessities, didn't there? She was home all the time, wasn't she, while Troy still spent most nights out at some bar with his friends? ('Working, Frank,' she could hear him saying, even as she thought this.)

While he was out in the world, she'd been the one, apparently, charged with bringing up Denny. Didn't she deserve to feel good and strong and *clean*? To do the best for their boy?

Frances tiptoed to the cot and put Denny down, ever so gently. He was getting harder to lift and lower, she noticed, a big boy now. Or maybe she was getting weaker.

How could she have been dumb enough to make that WholeHealth order on their normal bank card? What had she been thinking? Standing back at the sunroom door, she steeled herself for the argument that was coming, and where it was going to end up.

The thing was, Troy didn't know about the other credit card. Or the cupboard over the fridge.

Bugger. She really did have to go back to work.

***

Frances wasn't sure when she'd begun to feel 'dirty' on the inside, but it was around the time she'd started getting seriously into The Goddess Project, and she and six-week-old Denny had started leaving the house.

Denny wasn't an easy baby. She'd never met a mother who thought their baby was easy but, looking around, she could tell that he was particularly high-maintenance.

'Comparison is the thief of joy,' was the quote the midwife had thrown at Frances and a room full of complete strangers at mothers' group, in the Early Childhood Centre above a suburban shopping mall on a rainy Monday, five months ago. 'You are here to share stories but, remember, every baby is like a snowflake—different and special in their very own way.'

The midwife had gone on to spell out some very strict, one-size-fits-all strategies for taming these deeply individual snowflakes: 'Don't feed them to sleep. Don't rock them to sleep. Don't drive them around in your car to get them to sleep. Don't walk them around your house to get them to sleep. Don't put them in your bed with you to get them to sleep...'

Frances looked around the room and thought, *Am I the only person here who has done all of those things, many times, in the past four weeks?*

But the fact that half the women there were staring guiltily at their feet—or their baby's feet—suggested to her that no, she was not.

Frances had sought out the women who looked like they'd made a medal-worthy effort to get to the centre. They were dishevelled but, like her, they'd managed to pull a brush through their hair, find matching shoes, wear clean trackies... It was incredible how low her bar was set, already.

These were the women who were now in her WhatsApp group, pinging her about poo in the middle of the night, god bless them.

Comparison might be the thief of joy, but it was also useful. The sight of the other mums at mothers' group—there weren't any dads, her suburb wasn't hip enough for that—made her realise that some babies didn't cry incessantly after a feed, and would sometimes actually allow their mothers to put them down without screaming bloody murder.

'There's no such thing as wind,' the midwife told Frances when she asked if that might be why Denny was so unsettled after a feed. 'I think you've just got a mumma's boy on your hands.'

This wasn't helpful information.

'You've got to be tough on him,' the midwife said.

Frances looked down at Denny. This tiny little person who smelled like heaven and fitted so perfectly in the crook of her arm. She had to be tough on him?

'Babies are manipulative creatures,' the midwife went on. 'You've got to train him. Like a pup.'

But it wasn't Denny she needed to be tough on, Frances thought. It was herself. Sleep deprived, feeling too big and too sluggish, there was no way she was giving herself the best chance to get through this if she just gave in and lay on the lounge.

She went home and said to Troy, 'I have to find the energy to deal with Denny. He's a special baby and he deserves all of my attention. I'm going make sure I can be the mum he needs me to be.'

Troy shrugged and patted a teary Frances on the shoulder. For weeks, he'd been wearing the look of a man who didn't know what had happened to his world but he wasn't sure he liked it. 'Babe, whatever it takes. I want you to be happy.' And then he left for work.

Frances clicked open The Goddess Project and made a list.

***

Now Denny was almost six months old and Frances' self-discipline rarely waivered but was, she felt, often scuppered by circumstance.

Like broken blenders. And money for gold dust. And baby-free time to exercise.

She was still breastfeeding Denny, but no matter how pure her diet was, he was still a difficult, colicky baby. In a bid to soothe him, the list of things she'd given up was long. Dairy. And gluten. Eggs. Caffeine. Citrus. Seafood and anything spicy.

She wore Denny everywhere she could, because baby-wearing was meant to ease colic-inducing anxiety.

The WhatsApp group chirruped lots of other ideas for baby-settling at her, too. One mum wrote:

> Download the sound of a hairdryer, my sister-in-law said it worked like magic.

And others weighed in:

> Try warm baths and waving their legs in the air.

> A thousand pats a night fixed my Deena. Got one great bicep out of it, too.

None of it worked.

'I am in love with my life,' Frances would say, as she rocked and bounced and walked her needy baby to sleep, alone at home every night.

She'd lost some weight, but she was tired and quick to cry. Troy was always at work.

All this effort and, still, nothing was perfect.

***

So on that morning when Troy trawled the bank statements, Frances had returned to the lounge room where her husband was sitting exactly where she'd left him, on the lounge with the laptop open on his knee.

If you asked any of Troy's friends to describe him, they

would say he was 'easygoing'. It was the Irish in him, her mother said. 'They're so relaxed, they're asleep,' she'd mutter, making it clear that was A Bad Thing.

But at that moment, Troy didn't look relaxed.

Frances sat down next to him. 'Sorry, Troy, I just went a bit crazy at the health-food shop. I forget that I'm not earning sometimes. I won't do it again.'

'Frankie, we are in deep shit.'

'Stop overreacting,' she said, crossing her legs on the couch, active-wear tucked beneath active-wear.

'Seriously, when I clear these cards, the mortgage is going to put us overdrawn. Again.'

'Well, that's what the overdraft is for, right? We'll get back on top.'

'How, Frank?' Frances could tell Troy was steeling himself to say something she didn't want to hear. 'I know we wanted you at home with the baby for a year, but I think you're going to have to go back—even just a few shifts.'

Frances used to love nursing. She'd always said she was going to be a nurse, right from when she was at primary school. Looking after people, helping. Feeling important. At home, at the end of her line of brothers, she felt like no use to anyone. Like a throwaway joke. It wouldn't be like that at a hospital.

And she'd been right, it wasn't like that at hospital: patients and their loved ones needed you. But other things happened there that could make you feel pretty small, too. Things she hadn't told Troy about, because they didn't fit with the way she'd always wanted him to see her: capable, strong, happy-go-lucky.

From the perspective of six months wrangling a colicky newborn, the idea of going back to SouthLand Private had its upsides. Friends. Linley. And the patients, especially the older women, who were appreciative that anyone was caring about them so very much when they were considered an inconvenience in much of their lives now.

But then there was the Dr Darling issue. And also, how the hell could Frances stay focused on being the best for Denny if she was running off to work at crazy hours? And, she asked Troy, 'Who would have Denny if I did that?'

'Your mum. My mum. That's what grandmas are for, right? They'd do it in a heartbeat.'

'But they don't even believe he's sick.'

'He's not sick, Frank,' Troy said. 'He's just a whingey baby.'

'Come on, Troy, how would you know? You're never here.'

'Well, Frankie, isn't that what the doctors have said? And you pushing yourself so hard, well...' Frances could tell Troy was weighing up how far to go with this, since her anger was surely visible on her face, glowing red now. 'I think it would be good for you to have something else to think about than... all this.' He gestured towards the laptop screen. Towards the mushroom vanilla powder and the aloe juice. 'This is ridiculous. It's like a drug habit you're keeping secret here.' He managed a little laugh as he said it.

'As opposed to the actual drug habits of all your cool friends from the bar?'

'Ah, come on, Frank, let's not have that fight now. We're talking about you, and us.'

'Denny's six months!'

'We're talking about a few shifts a week. You're not leaving home!'

Frances could sense that the preferable option here would be to give in—before he started digging any further into her 'habit'.

'I'll call Linley,' she said darkly. 'See what's happening on the wards. Maybe I could get a few nights.'

'Good.' Troy looked generally relieved. He shut the laptop and stood up. 'And no more health-food shopping, Frank. Not now.'

Don't tell me what to do, Frances thought. But what she said was, 'Of course.'

After he'd kissed her and left for the hotel, Frances reached for her phone and typed into the WhatsApp group:

Husband making me go back to work!

There was an immediate chorus of replies:

Nooooooo!

Mine keeps hinting about that. I'm playing dumb.

Just tell him you can't get a shift.

Denny needs you too much!

Frances wrote:

I don't want to go back there. I'll think of something.

What would Elle do? Frances asked herself. Then she realised that her wages could bring her closer to Gurva.

And from the bedroom, Denny started to wail.

CHAPTER 10

BEN BONT

Ben Bont couldn't be certain, but it seemed a mini-nightclub had been built on his farm while he wasn't looking.

'So,' he said, 'the reason we need a bar with a dancefloor at a wellness spa is...?'

'The clients like to cut loose before they detox, Ben,' said the burly manager guy, Matt. 'I can't even tell you the number of people who get off that bus with the shakes, looking like death. We thought we might as well get a clip of that particular ticket.'

'Okay. Whose idea was that?' Ben thought he might already know.

'Mine,' said Elle, behind him, her hands on his back. 'We're calling it a pretox party. We'll fire it up on the first night when we have the younger groups in. It's perfect for the Bondi crowd, they like to think they're pure as the driven—'

'Yes, I get the snow reference.' Ben laughed. He had to admit, it was well done. An old sheep shed had been whitewashed within an inch of its life, its original beams painted black and running at angles across the ceiling. There were abstract fluoro murals across one wall—'We got some local kids in to do that'—and an Instagram-friendly vertical garden on the other. A large timber-topped bar ran along one side of the small dancefloor—'The numbers aren't big, so we want it to be intimate'—which boasted a one-person podium that looked like it was made from wool crates.

'The sound system is incredible!' Matt pushed a button behind the bar and the whole shed pumped for thirty seconds before he flicked it off. 'But you barely hear a thing outside.'

'Are you're thinking we're going to advertise this?' Ben asked.

'Noooo... If you're in the know, you're in the know,' said Elle, running a hand across the top of the bar. 'It's the kind of thing that starts a whisper campaign.'

'Word will get out to those who want to hear it,' said Matt. 'And, obviously, all the drinks will be pure. Sloe gin. Icelandic vodka. Organic wines—'

'And you definitely didn't build this place so the staff have somewhere to come and try to fuck each other?' Ben asked.

'Ha.' Matt shook his head. 'They don't need any help with that.'

Ben looked at Elle. She was wearing bright purple yoga tights and a floaty white top that was almost completely see-through—underneath, a tiny purple lace bra-let. Her shiny black plait swung down her back; she was grinning at him.

'Aren't I clever?' she asked. 'It's an optional extra, and I think we can charge big for it. And in non-retreat weeks, we can hire it as a venue. Small weddings, birthdays...'

The way she was smiling at him right now... it was intoxicating. But he couldn't shake the feeling that things at Gurva were slipping a little bit beyond his control.

'You are clever.' He grabbed her around the waist. 'You are very, very clever.'

'I'll leave you guys to it,' said Matt, heading for the door. 'Let me know, Ben, if there are changes you want made.'

He thinks I'm going to screw her right here, thought Ben. People had an exaggerated idea about how he behaved, he found. Based, no doubt, on their own fantasies of how they would live if they had the funds and the freedom. Or, possibly, from Elle's blog, where she frequently alluded to the fact their sex life was... potent.

Not now. Control was what was important here. Self-control and control over his farm.

He looked down at Elle, still tucked under his arm. 'You should have asked me.'

'Oh, Ben,' Elle seemed a bit surprised, 'I didn't want to bother you—you've got a lot happening in your life, in your business. And if I called you about every little thing on the farm, you'd never get anything else done.'

'Elle, you should have asked me, I need to know what's going on. Always.' He pulled her closer, and whispered, 'You are very clever. But these decisions need to be made... together.' He squeezed her a little tighter on the 'together'.

'Of course, Ben.' Elle twisted away. 'I get it. Matt and I just got carried away, I guess. Seemed like a good opportunity, and...' She pushed out her bottom lip into something like a pout. 'I thought you said I was in charge when you weren't here?'

Ben laughed shortly. 'You are, kitten—of the house, of the staff, of the guests. Not infrastructure. Come on, that's a hundred grand right there.'

He watched her eyes flash. Was it panic, at being in his bad books? Or was it anger? With Elle, it was hard to know.

One thing he knew about her for sure was that she was used to being in control, too. Which was why he had to keep surprising her. With yoga swings. With boundaries.

'It's alright,' he said, 'I'm sure it will pay for itself. Just, next time...'

Her smile came back. With one long-legged box jump, Elle was on the podium in the middle of the tiny dancefloor, moving slowly in the sudden silence.

'We could do private shows in here,' she said, swaying, her arms above her head. 'Audience of one.'

'Oh, is that why you built it?' he asked, playing along. 'Really?'

'For sure...' Elle dropped to her haunches, bum back, arms reaching towards him. 'Come on, before we go up to Alma...'

Ben took her hand.

***

Ben Bont had met Elle Campbell on a plane.

Between Sydney and Byron, Ben usually flew himself. He'd qualified as a pilot in his early twenties, and his new Cirrus SR22T was his favourite toy. A tiny little thing—he called it 'the gnat'—he buzzed it up and down the coast whenever he could. But Sydney to Melbourne, well, that was a boring work flight.

He was heading down for a few days to check on the progress of a renovation: Bounce was turning an old wool warehouse in Carlton into a twenty-room hotel with a spa, bar and restaurant. It was going to be called The Lamb. The design team needed his forensic eye for detail before they got much further from the renovated shell.

He'd planned to do what he usually did if he found himself flying commercial: work.

His assistant Ireland knew to book him two seats so he wouldn't be disturbed. When someone sat down next to him, he looked up with irritation from the plans for The Lamb on his iPad Pro.

But the woman who'd come to sit beside him said something surprising. 'Mind if I meditate?'

'Pardon?'

'Do you mind if I meditate? The plane's the best place for it when you've had a crazy week. And I have.'

'Actually, that seat is—'

Before he could finish his sentence, the woman did the weirdest thing. She put three fingers up to his lips. Actually physically touched him. 'Shhh,' she said. 'It's alright.'

Afterwards, Ben found it almost impossible to explain why he hadn't done what anyone would do if a complete stranger invaded their space on a plane: press the bloody call button and get them thrown off.

Yes, Elle was a good-looking woman, but Ben had exclusively dated models throughout his twenties. He was well aware that beauty was no indicator of stability.

She could have been a stalker—the two of them would laugh about that later because, actually, that's exactly what she was. She could have been trying to sell him something—also true, as it turned out.

So why did he do nothing but look at this strange woman and nod? Why did he let her take his hand and sit next to her in silence for twenty minutes while she whispered him through a meditation, wordlessly shooing away the flight attendants who kept trying to make sure Mr Bont had his usual hot water and lemon.

When he opened his eyes and looked at her, he asked, 'Are you a witch?'

And Elle Campbell smiled a slow smile, released his hand and said, 'Plenty of people think so.'

***

'Love doesn't make any sense,' he'd said to friends over a Melbourne dinner, two nights after that flight.

'Love?' spluttered his old school friend Gregory, almost spitting out the three-hundred-dollar pinot they'd ordered at Grizzly, Ben's newest restaurant. 'Are you serious?'

'I am. It's fucking crazy.'

He was, and it was.

He'd walked off the plane with Elle that day and put her in the car that was waiting for him. He told the driver to take her wherever she wanted to go, but to bring her back to dinner with him that night at his hotel.

In the meantime, he called his PA, Ireland. 'I'm on my

way to the meeting with the Haze brothers about the fit-out. I want you to pull absolutely everything you can on a woman called Elle Campbell.'

'That mummy blogger?' Ireland had asked. 'The crazy one?'

'Sure. Send me a briefing doc before the meeting ends, please.'

The report was confronting reading: all of these things Elle was meant to have done had only just happened. And yet, the woman he'd met on the plane already looked so different to the woman in the pictures Ireland had pulled from the *Daily Trail*. Less make-up, less hair, no fake talons, no spike-heeled shoes. The Elle Campbell he'd met looked like a pared-back version of this woman. Like her younger, fresher sister.

The thing was, and he knew it now—Ben had been searching. He was bored. He'd had fifteen years of working insanely hard and partying harder—of building things and moving on, of beautiful people in clubs with no names, of friends who liked the guest-list life. He didn't want to spend the next fifteen years chasing thrills that he'd already had. He saw what trying to constantly up that ante had done to plenty of people around him, including his father, who'd died with a pickled liver and four ex-wives on his payroll.

In short, Ben was in exactly the right frame of mind to take a chance on a strange woman with a bizarre reputation who'd looked him straight in the eyes the first time she'd met him and said, 'You need healing.' If this was a wild fling with a crazy person, then that would distract him while he was in Melbourne to deal with the fucking marble-makers for The Lamb. If it was more, well, it was time.

The other thing was that Elle hadn't come back for dinner that first night.

He'd actually sat in the restaurant like a sap, working on his iPad and getting increasingly furious until the driver called him. 'She's disappeared, sir. I went to the address she gave me and she wasn't there.'

Ben hated himself for doing it, but he looked up all of her

social feeds, right there in the restaurant. Every single one had been taken down, cleared out.

He left the restaurant, fuming, and called Gregory to have a whisky with him in the shell of The Lamb.

The next night, he was at the site until late and came back to his room to change before a late dinner meeting with a new investor.

She was just there, in his room. Sitting on the expensively covered lounge, cross-legged, like a golden Buddha. Naked.

'You really are a crazy stalker, aren't you?' he said.

'The crazy stalker of your dreams,' Elle answered.

And that was that.

***

Now Ben Bont was sitting in the bedroom yoga swing, gently rocking Baby Alma back and forth on his knee. The sun was going down and the French doors were open to the deck. Elle was sitting on a wicker chair, her laptop on her bare knees, checking images for the blog.

He looked down at Alma and thought how rare it was for a moment to feel as good, to be as good, as it looked from the outside.

He knew there was plenty on the farm that wasn't what it seemed. He'd laughed along with Elle when she'd written Alma's outdoor birth story on her blog. In reality, Alma had come into the world on the most exclusive floor of the most exclusive private hospital in Brisbane, away from the snooping Sydney society press. A C-section birth and a week in a private suite before coming home to the farm where they had two nurses—one for Alma, one for Elle—on twenty-four-hour duty.

It had been as civilised an experience as it was possible to have, he'd been told. Whether the wonder of fatherhood was lessened or heightened by that experience, he would never know, but 'wonder' was the word. And there was nothing fake about it.

He had actively avoided having children his entire adult life, shut down any woman who'd hinted at it, paid for at least two terminations. But when Elle had told him about Alma, he'd looked her right in eye and asked, 'Are you trying to trap me?'

And she had looked back at him, shrugged ever so slightly, and said, 'A little bit.'

But now Ben couldn't stop a feeling from bubbling up in him that it was actually he who needed to do the trapping—to make sure this thing wasn't only a business deal.

As he watched Elle out there on the deck, absorbed in her work, the irritation he felt was at the fact that up here, she and Alma were floating free of him.

Today's moment with the bar was one thing; really, if she wanted to keep evolving the Gurva offering, that was only going to benefit him. But more and more, he felt she was moving separately to him, moving away.

To his friends in Sydney, the set-up of having a 'family' on call for weekends and holidays was ideal. 'The only way to do this,' was how his sister Georgie had described it when he'd told her about Elle's pregnancy, 'is to keep her at Byron. If you're going to get into that with her, make sure you keep that distance, and some serious boundaries.'

Those boundaries seemed to suit Elle. She was up here, with Alma, building her little empire. And it had suited him; it was what he'd thought he wanted. But now...

He knew about her sons. Elle had never spelled it out to him, but he knew her wimp of an ex-husband was using them as a weapon against her for leaving him, after all that bullshit at the blogging awards. Ben thought that he could see the sadness of it on her face sometimes, but also that part of her felt Adrian was right, that she deserved to be exiled from her children.

She seemed to carry it with such pragmatism, and grace. Was that who she was? Could she separate herself so easily from the things that bound others together? And if so, did she not really need him at all?

Over on the deck, Elle stretched and looked over her shoulder at him, staring at her.

'You,' he called out to her, 'are the most interesting thing that has happened to me for a long time.'

For a moment, Elle looked like she might not react. Then she slid the laptop off her knee and walked to the swing, knelt down in front of it and kissed her baby's extended little foot.

'Alma and I like it when you're here, Daddy,' she said.

For a moment they stayed like that.

'I think it's time we told everyone we're getting married,' said Ben.

For the second time that day, he saw genuine surprise and confusion in her eyes, just for a moment, and it gave him a jolt of happiness. Of power, reaffirmed.

'We... are?' she said.

'We are. On New Year's Eve.'

Elle was still kneeling on the floor. He could tell she was calculating her next move. 'But Ben—'

'I know.'

'I'm still—'

'You're still married, I know.'

'Well.' She stood up, holding Alma, who was beginning to whimper just a little, up under her chin. Elle was clearly regaining her composure. 'Don't you think that's a problem?'

'No. We're going to sort that shit out.' Ben leant back on the yoga swing so that he was looking at the ceiling. 'Even if I have to go down there and tell that sad little man to his face—your divorce is overdue, we're getting married, and your boys will be at that wedding.'

It felt good, taking control. Fixing this whole bullshit situation with Adrian and her boys. It was what he should have done from the start.

He swung back, stared at Elle. 'So, what do you say?'

She looked genuinely confused. 'Say to what?'

'My proposal. Elle Campbell, will you marry me?'

CHAPTER 11

ELLE

Elle was furious that Ben had fucking proposed. Absolutely livid.

Today she was taking a new bunch of retreaters through her Elle-ness 101 class, and she could barely contain her rage.

Matt had structured the Elle-ness weeks so that 101 was the first opportunity the clients had to set eyes on her after two days of them being at the farm.

The sixteen women—they were almost always all women—got off the tasteful white-on-white, Gurva-branded shuttle bus from Ballina airport on a Sunday afternoon. It was on that first night that they were encouraged to go and have a few drinks at the newly created and named The Bar(n), where they got a briefing from Matt and the practitioners who would be working with them all week.

Elle and Matt had recruited the team carefully. As well as the young, keen hospitality crew, led by Matt's right-hand man, a clear-eyed young Canadian called Ennis, there was a mix of stunning female trainers who were young but not too young ('They need to believe they can be them,' had been

Elle's brief), who designed the clients' very own exercise program for the week. There were a few attractive young men (they did massage, the aerial yoga and Pilates reformer classes—deep voices and firm hands), and a Byron-based chef couple who ran classes and catered the first three days of the retreat with their so-called 'negative calorie' superfood regimen: an intense, mostly juice-based detox.

And then there was the Hot Home Chef. A rugged, surfie foodie who had fled to Byron from New York, he taught comfort wholefoods and catered the second half of the week when Elle-ness retreaters were allowed to eat actual food.

There were also the dermatologists, Andy and Andi, who did microdermabrasion, peels, botox and plain old facials. They would consult with all retreaters on that first evening and then schedule in treatments as needed.

There was Guru Gwendi, the meditation teacher, who called everyone 'blessed soul' and carried a teeny-tiny gong with her everywhere she went. It was meant to be a meditation cue, but Elle had noticed she tended to dong it whenever she was bored of talking to a particular client: 'Next, blessed soul.'

And finally there was Dr Jonti, a plastic surgeon who operated out of a small private clinic in Byron. For clients who wanted to roll their stay into a procedure at his place, he offered five-star service, door-to-door transfers and a discounted rate.

Dr Jonti had redone Elle's breast implants during her first month at Gurva. She—and Ben, truth be told—had wanted a slightly smaller, more 'natural' look than what she'd upgraded to after Freddie's birth three years earlier. He'd done such an excellent job that they'd asked him to be Gurva's 'breast man', and he said the referrals had transformed his business. Enquiries about Dr Jonti's services tended to peak on day three, after the group had seen Elle's keynote performance.

As Elle was limbering up in the empty studio before her class, she showed Matt her engagement ring. 'Can you believe this shit?' she said, offering up an enormous round blue diamond on an engraved platinum band.

Matt lifted her hand, twisted it from side to side. 'That's some rock. Bigger than your first?'

'Yes, but... I wanted that one.' *For my own reasons*, she thought. The jewellery that Adrian had bought her was all stashed for safe-keeping, just one of many 'insurance policies' she had hidden around the place.

'Most chicks would be stoked with that,' Matt said, letting her hand go. 'Ben Bont proposing. A permanent place in his family. A right to the fortune.'

'What it is,' Elle spat, 'is a power move.'

'Jesus, so romantic. I thought women loved huge rings and men telling them it was forever...' Matt took to shuffling the yoga mats into straighter lines.

'Women do not love being owned,' Elle replied, sticking a leg in the air and yanking it towards her for a deep stretch.

'Elle,' Matt got gruff when he was irritated, 'you have a baby and a business with the guy. It's not like you two have just been on a few dates.'

'Shut up, Matt,' she snapped. 'I just need to work out how to play this thing. Maybe you should focus on letting in the paying customers?'

'Sure,' he said, shrugging. 'But Elle, if you two are plotting some sort of big reveal, I think you should take the bauble off. The punters aren't going to miss that, and it will be all over social as soon as practice is finished.'

He was right. Elle took off her sparkly ball and chain, and pushed it deep into her bra. 'Let's do it.'

***

Elle-ness 101 had a rock-star vibe to it.

The believers, the Elle-ness retreaters, were here for this reason: Elle Campbell, in the flesh.

The guests were weak and depleted from two days of

consuming only vegetable juice with photogenic garnishes, and they'd been pulled and pushed in every direction by their yoga/Pilates/yogalates instructors, then encouraged to run around the dam at dawn.

So they were already in a highly emotional state when they came into the studio to meet their guru. This encounter was meant to bolster them, replenish them, push them into the next day and towards solid foods with a renewed enthusiasm. Sometimes, someone screamed. And more than once, someone had fainted.

After the clients were ushered in by Matt and several Gurva staffers wearing the uniform—white tunics, placid smiles—they arranged themselves on their yoga mats, glass bottles of green potion beside them, and whispered and giggled and chatted among themselves until the music started.

Today, it was 'Look What You Made Me Do' by Taylor Swift.

Elle walked out from the side of the raised platform, wearing a tiny white sports bra and tiny white shorts, tan gleaming, plait swinging, bare feet with painted toes (she was working on getting her go-to nude shade trademarked and in the online shop). And she stood there, hands clasped together at 'heart centre', while the hullaballoo of sixteen whooping women died down.

'Friends,' Elle said. 'Friends. Thank you for believing in me. There is no greater honour.'

Cue another explosion of noise.

'There's only one thing better than feeling the way I feel right now, standing here, basking in your love...'

Silence fell.

'...helping *you* to feel the way I feel right now, standing here, basking in love.'

More wild whooping.

'You have come here, to my home, on a journey to help you better understand yourself, and your potential. And today, in this practice, we are going to move, and we are going to share, and we are going to shake off the negativity that has been bringing us down...' At this point, Elle—as she always did—lowered her voice and spoke conspiratorially, 'And believe me, I know a little bit about people trying to take you down with negativity...'

Cue uproarious laughter.

'But even if you haven't been shamed on a global media stage, as I once was—' loud boos '—there's no doubt you carry your own shame around with you.

'There is no doubt that people who don't understand your gifts try to reduce you all the time... Try to make you small like them. Bitter and jealous like them... *WELL!*

'Here's my message for you, friends:

'You are not mediocre. You are not messy. You are not going to accept a second-rate version of yourself. This week, today and forever, you are going to pledge to remake your body and soul to reflect the strength within.

'You are going to leave Gurva more beautiful, less weighed down by your baggage—yes, your emotional *and* your physical baggage—we are going to throw that stuff *OUT*.

'You are going to commit to being your best self every single day!

'And when you're niggling yourself with "no" and "maybe" and "can't be bothered", what are we going to say?!'

'NO EXCUSES!' the small crowd chanted at her.

'What was that, lazybones?' she called to them.

'NO EXCUSES!'

'What was that, poor me?'

'NO EXCUSES!'

Blisteringly loud dance music came on, and Elle led her followers in a twenty-minute cardio blast that saw her leaping and squatting and running and dancing, and a room full of hungry mere mortals trying to mimic her every move, before the music changed to a chiming Zen beat, and she brought them all into a fifteen-minute wind-down of yogic Elle-ness moves and affirmations.

'You are a work in progress,' she called.
'I am a work in progress,' they replied.
'You are in love with your life.'
'I am in love with my life.'
'You will not lose.'
'I will not lose.'
'No excuses.'
'No excuses.'

The session ended with Elle sitting cross-legged on stage while each depleted disciple filed up to meet her, one by one. A staff member made sure the line moved quickly—'No photos,' they said, every five seconds.

Women cried—they always cried, and Elle would nod along and sometimes offer a comforting pat. But as she'd learnt when she'd begun doing these sessions, it was best not to listen to the women's stories: they were all the same. And most were real downers, Elle found. Stories about breast cancer, divorce and anxiety. It was a lot to take on.

'Oprah, eat your heart out,' Matt said to one of the new staff, approvingly, as Elle came off stage. He was smiling widely as he watched the women file out, dabbing themselves with their Gurva-branded sweat towels.

'You *are* pretty good at that,' the young female staff member said to Elle. 'I can't believe you've just had a baby.'

'You should have seen her do it when she was pregnant,' said Matt. 'It was really something to see her doing those kicks, in those shorts, with a belly.'

Elle caught the way the new girl looked sideways at Matt as he said that, her eyes slightly narrowed.

'He means I'm unstoppable,' Elle said to the girl. 'That's what they want to see.'

The session had been forty-five minutes, start to finish. The guests would see her again, on their last night, when she came and led them in a meditation on resilience and discipline.

In their six days at Gurva, they'd get two doses of Elle. And they'd dine out on them for months.

***

In truth, Elle was knackered when she came off stage after a 101.

She'd been a trainer and a fitness instructor in her pre-Adrian life, so she was used to leaping around in front of a class, but she'd never been a public speaker. So she had literally studied TED Talks and, yes, Oprah monologues until she'd got it down.

'I think we need to be doing this with bigger crowds,' Matt said as he walked her back up to the farmhouse. 'If you bottle the energy in that studio, it's worth a shedload if we can scale it.'

'One step at a time.' Elle was now wearing a white robe and trainers, like a prize fighter after a bout. She was happy not to have to do that again for a week or two; the neediness of those women drained her. 'Remember I'm preaching to the hardcore here, the people who are on our side. I don't think we'd fill a stadium with those people yet.'

'But we might,' Matt said quietly, 'when you're reintroduced to the world as Mrs Ben Bont.'

'I get it, Matt. Stop with the hard sell.'

And she left him outside the farmhouse door and went in to check up on the baby nurse.

Elle hadn't replied to Abi's email yet. It was another source of rage alongside how to deal with Ben's proposal.

The idea that Abi—the woman behind Elle's public humiliation last year, Adrian's sanctimonious ex-wife, Elle's enemy—was basically raising her boys was a reality she hadn't let herself entertain, until now.

Teddy and Freddie living with Adrian, she could take. She'd imagined him employing nannies and getting his tedious mother Bonnie to come in and help him look after them in the past year. But Abi's email had pushed that mental image aside: Elle now saw her beautiful boys in hemp (shudder), knee-deep in mud, roped into being hippie pageboys at Abi's big fat lesbian wedding (news of that hadn't eluded Elle's social feeds).

Her frustration was rippling on her surface, coming off her in waves. As she marched through the house to the nursery, Mauna and the housekeeper ducked out of the way.

Pushing open the double doors to Alma's bedroom, Elle saw Lucille, the baby nurse, bending over. Her little finger was hooked in Alma's mouth; Alma was smiling, kicking her legs in the air, making a gummy *maw-maw-maw* sound.

Lucille looked up at Elle. 'I think there's a tooth coming through, Mum! She's advanced, our girl,' she said cheerfully.

'Get your finger *out* of my baby's mouth!' Elle shouted. 'What the hell do you think you're doing?'

'I...' Lucille seemed scared.

This only infuriated Elle more. She dashed over to where Lucille and the baby were: Alma on a tasteful patchwork quilt on an antique-white change table, Lucille in uniform, protective hand on the baby's tummy. And Elle shoved her.

Lucille stumbled back, her head knocking the wall as she half-fell against it.

'She's not *YOUR* baby! She's not *OUR* girl!' Elle was shouting. 'She's *MY* girl. And she doesn't want your dirty fingers in her mouth.'

Alma was crying. Lucille's hand was at the back of her head, and she was looking at the floor. 'You crazy woman,' she muttered.

'*GET OUT*, you're fired!' Elle screamed.

As she felt strong arms around her, she realised she was lunging towards Lucille.

'Elle. Calm down. Stop, for fuck's sake.' It was Matt. 'Just stop.'

Lucille pushed past them both and ran out the door.

'Fuck!' said Matt, watching her go. 'That was *not* a good move.'

He'd let go of her now, and was holding something out to Elle—the blue diamond. 'You dropped your ring,' he said.

But Elle couldn't really hear him. She was looking at Alma, pushing her own little finger into her daughter's mouth, hoping to stop her crying.

'It's true,' Elle half-whispered. 'She has got a tooth.'

CHAPTER 12

ABI

The fun police

It's easy to go to war over a wedding.

I'm organising one, GDs, and I can tell you, it might sound ridiculous when I say this but I never knew it was so fucking difficult.

And I've actually done it before.

It was back in the year 2001, and honestly, I barely remember sorting anything. I bought a forgiving dress, we had some cake, and my parents controlled most of the guest list.

We probably spent too much money and created too much waste.

Now, all of us here know how that marriage worked out, but since I came out of it with my two daughters, it will always rank as one of my life's better decisions.

One thing's for certain—I didn't spend any time worrying about table settings and hashtags.

But now I'm making decisions about the craziest things. Rice, not rose petals, for throwing. One meat meal on the vegetarian menu for my dad, who's never looked sideways at a lentil. No posed photos, only a roaming reporter.

G wants me to take care of it, deal with all the details.

Except for this one: My glorious G wants our wedding to be DRY.

No booze. No booze at all.

Just a selection of refreshing, kombucha-based punches with fruit from our garden.

I KNOW. I know that's good for us, GDs. I know that here in this intentional community of like-minded souls we eschew binge-drinking and wine o'clock, and the nonsense created to make us spend our hard-earned money on drugs that keep us dulled to our own possibilities. I know, I know.

I know that in my previous life, there was much too much 'casual' drinking. It could lead, often, to 'casual' words of cruelty, 'casual' car accidents, 'casual' tears, 'casual' domestic violence, 'casual' divorce. So yes, I know, I know.

BUT—Champagne at a wedding! Tipsy dancing under the tree-tops! Fancy wine in fancy buckets on fancy tables! A drunk uncle telling you for the fourteenth time why you should have stayed married to that nice man in a suit... *That's* a WEDDING, right???

What say you, my tribe?

If the bride is always right but two brides disagree, who gets to make the call? Just how righteous do we want our righteous day to be?

I await your word.

Your QGD—Abi xx

'I can't believe you're writing about *that*,' said Grace, leaning over Abi's shoulder as she finished typing. 'I mean, slow news day.'

'You're just worried about being shown up as the wowser you are, sugar,' replied Abi, kissing Grace's hand.

'Really? I think your people will support my vision for a non-toxic celebration.' Grace pulled her hand away. 'Who wants people punching on in the bathroom and throwing up on the dancefloor?'

'Give our nearest and dearest a little more credit,' said Abi. 'They're not footballers on a bonding weekend.'

'Still, weird post,' said Grace, setting an assortment of glass bowls on the table and placing a jug of water with them. 'You running out of wars to wage?'

Grace was still home-schooling her youngest, Otto. He was nine and the most sensitive of their kids; his preferred place was at Grace's skirts, always. That's where he was right now, as Abi typed and Grace laid out a lesson plan—science experiments, today—on the kitchen table. Otto was sprawled on the floor at her feet, reading a book about worms.

'There's a war I'd like to start,' Abi said. 'But I don't think it would be good for us.'

She turned her laptop around to face Grace. It was open to The Goddess Project—and there, lying across the top of the page, was the gleaming, dark, naked body of a woman: tiny waist, defined abs, arms casually draped across her breasts, legs crossed at the thigh, glistening all over. The woman was headless, the only identifying sign a thick black plait hanging across her body.

'Who is *that*? Not your usual taste in lady sites.' Grace smiled and nudged Abi as she made this crack.

Abi didn't smile back. 'Scroll down,' she said.

Grace did, and came to the next picture: another body shot, but this time the woman was in a sports bra and very tiny shorts. She was contorted into a complex stretch, face still obscured. The heading read: *The Goddess Project. Release weight, years and negativity to remake your life.*

'Is that...?'

'Yes.'

'Wow.' Grace kept scrolling. The next picture did show Elle's face, and her round pregnant belly, in a warrior pose in front of a stunning traditional farm homestead, surrounded by green rolling hills. 'Pregnant?'

'Um, not anymore. Baby girl.'

'*O-kaaay*. So many questions, Abi.'

'Mum, are we going to start lessons soon, or is my brain going to turn to mud?' Otto piped up from the floor, holding up a picture of an earthworm in the ground.

'Any minute, now, Otto. Abi?'

'It makes me so fucking angry—'

'Swear jar!' yelled Otto.

'Which part?' Grace went on shifting the bowls around in order of size. 'At least now I know why you're distracting yourself with posts about this wedding.'

This wedding, again?

'The shit she's peddling, Grace. Take away all the stuff about Adrian and the boys and her being a lying, devious cu—'

'Swear jar!'

'It's this shit right here—I had to subscribe to this, with actual money. And people *do*. They hand over hard-earned cash, and for what? For her to show me naked pictures, share ridiculous recipes no one can follow without taking out a bank loan, and spout a lot of psycho-babble about being your best self. I mean...' Abi put her head on the table. 'It makes me... want to hit someone.'

'Don't do that.' Grace sounded irritated. 'Don't let Elle's bullshit come back into our lives any more than she needs to.'

'Well, that's another thing.' Abi lifted her head. 'She replied to the email.'

'Okay... Have you spoken to Adrian about all this

because—Sol, *ONE MINUTE!*—I think it's him, not me, you need to be talking to about Elle.'

'I'll talk to him when he gets back tonight,' Abi said. 'But, really, it involves us all.'

***

Adrian had gone down to Melbourne early that morning. A meeting with the publisher interested in Manifesting Money had tempted him into the city for the first time in eighteen months.

He came back bouncy with excitement. Bursting into dinner, where five of the six kids were eating Grace's dahl and grilled eggplant, he waved a paper bag above his head which, judging by the tasteful branding, was from Chez Burch, one of Melbourne's fanciest patisseries. 'I'm back, and I brought cake!'

'Cake? All the way from South Yarra?' Alex asked in her most unimpressed voice. 'They have cake in town, you know.'

'Not like this, they don't, my love!' He looked around. 'Where's your sister?'

'Somewhere with River,' Abi answered.

As Adrian fizzed around the kitchen getting plates, Abi thought he looked so happy he was almost rippling. She couldn't remember the last time she'd seen him look like that.

'What kind of cake?' asked Sol, who was certainly trying to gauge his mother's attitude to the dessert and whether he'd be getting any. 'And what are we celebrating?'

'Look, Sol, it's some kind of fancy chocolate ganache thing, and...' Adrian nodded to Grace. 'I'm certain it's gluten-free.'

'Ha!' Grace was trying to keep Freddie and Teddy away from the bag. 'Tell us your news.'

'They're publishing Manifesting Money, they're committing to a big marketing campaign, they think they can turn it into a podcast, possibly a TV show!' Adrian was laughing now. 'They think... they think... I'm going to be a guru.'

'Jesus, we have enough of those in the family,' Abi said, but she was laughing, too. It felt like a good night—possibly too good a night to turn sour by talking to Adrian about Elle. But, with Grace's eyes on her, she knew she couldn't put it off anymore.

The little kids were in bed and the chocolate ganache was cleared away. ('Wasted on those two,' Abi had commented, watching Freddie and Teddy smear it all over each other's faces. 'Their tastebuds have already evolved past sugar,' Grace told her smugly). And then Abi, in a possible spirit of rebellion against Grace's dry wedding demand, took a bottle of whisky over to the barn, where lights were blazing and an eternally shirtless Adrian was bashing away at his laptop.

'Woah,' he said when he saw her with the bottle in the doorway, 'where the hell did you get that from in this place?'

'There are a few secrets in that old house,' Abi said. 'People bring things, they get stashed.'

'And does Grace know you're coming over here armed with Scotch?'

'Grace knows what I'm here for, so, yes.'

Adrian turned away from the computer. 'Sounds serious.'

Abi poured a finger of liquor into a couple of teacups and then handed Adrian her phone. He looked confused and held it out at arm's length, the way people who are fifty do. Squinted a little.

It was the email.

> Abi,
> My life has been much more pleasant without you in it, so I can't say your email was welcome.
>
> But I have done a great deal of spiritual work over the last little while to be able to forgive the toxic people who have tried to ruin me. In doing that, I have realised that I must not rail against your presence in my inbox, but instead face it head on, and reply.

Adrian glanced up, recognition flickering in his eyes. Then he held out the phone to Abi as if he was trying to get rid of a smelly fish. 'You emailed her?'

'Come on, Adrian. Read it.'

> The news the boys are living with you is upsetting to me, but not surprising. With hindsight I can see that you and my sister conspired against me in a sort of jealous rage. You always wanted what I had, or what you thought I had taken from you (believe me, it wasn't hard to take!).
>
> But, if I am generous, I suppose it was Adrian who kept that from me, and not you. It is hardly your place to tell me where my boys are being held.

'Being held!' Adrian exclaimed. 'For fuck's sake, Abi, this is ridiculous.'

'Go on,' Abi urged.

> Also, in the spirit of moving forward, I am living a different life now. A more pure, deeper existence than I ever thought possible. I am a mother again.

Abi's cue that Adrian had reached that line was the colour draining from his face.

> It takes every ounce of generosity to say this, Abi, but in the state of new motherhood, I find it necessary to thank you for extending a nurturing spirit to my boys. I doubt that Adrian would be able to give them that.
>
> As for your question about making longer-term

plans: my mind is also turning to the future as I am planning a wedding for New Year's Eve.

'You're still married!' Adrian exclaimed at the phone.

'And New Year's Eve is when *I'm* getting married,' Abi pointed out.

And so taking you up on your offer to visit the boys and the farm to talk about this seems like the most mature and heart-wise thing to do.

'You invited her here?' Adrian asked Abi, who shrugged.

Let me advise you that I will be bringing my partner Ben and a cameraman to capture the occasion (and to keep a record of events).

Please talk to my assistant Matt Buchanan on the Gurva email address in my signature below in order to organise a date.

I hope life has been kind to you in this last year, Abi. The universe can be forgiving, and we can only try to follow its example.

Elle

Adrian finished the email and dropped the phone in Abi's lap. He didn't say anything.

So Abi started. 'First, Adrian, you have to think, *What has happened to her? Who talks like that?* "Let me advise you that... I have done a great deal of spiritual work..." I mean—'

'Abi,' Adrian gulped some Scotch, 'I can't believe you would *do* that. To me, or the boys.'

'Do what?'

'Contact her behind my back. It's none of your meddling business what's going on with my ex-wife and the custody of my kids.' He wasn't shouting; his voice was steady, serious.

'Well, it kind of is, since you're all living—'

'You couldn't fucking help yourself, could you? Always got to get in and control things, to get your fingers into other people's messes. Tell other people how to live!'

'Now, hang on a minute, Adrian,' Abi felt her anger rising, 'that is NOT what this is about.'

'I was having a fucking great day.' Adrian put his face in his hands, rubbing them up and down as if he was washing it. 'Even going to the city was okay. Nowhere near as bad as I thought it would be. Memories everywhere, of course, of what I'd done and what a lie I was living and what a fucking fool I'd been, but I rode through it, because I could see a glimmer of something good coming out of it.'

'Adrian, there still is!' Abi interrupted. 'But you've got to face her. You can't keep pretending that the mother of your children doesn't exist.'

'I can't?' he asked.

For a moment Abi felt genuinely sorry for him. Nothing in Adrian's upbringing had prepared him for life taking the kind of turn that now saw him hiding from the world above his ex-wife's shed. Perhaps this was a kind of penance—maybe he couldn't let himself have a proper life because he'd done something as stupid as going along with Elle Campbell's lies.

'Adrian,' Abi said softly, 'let her come here. Let her see your gorgeous boys, and how they're thriving with their dad. Let her hear about your book. Give her a divorce. Make a deal. Move the fuck on.'

'Easy for you to say,' Adrian said, reaching out with his empty teacup, gesturing for a refill.

'Actually, Adrian,' said Abi, 'it's not easy for me to say at all. None of this is easy. But I want to move on, too.'

Adrian sipped. There was silence for a moment, only cicadas.

'Um, a cameraman?' he said, after a while. 'A fucking cameraman?' And he laughed.

'Over my dead body,' said Abi. 'There is no way she is turning this shit into a reality show.'

'And who is this boyfriend, anyway?' asked Adrian. 'Which poor bastard has been suckered into this mess?'

'Well, you might need another drink for that...'

CHAPTER 13

FRANCES

'Yoga people are *so* intimidating,' Frances hissed to Linley.

The man rolling out his mat next to hers had white hair and deep laughter lines, but his body was as hard and sinewy as a twenty-three-year-old rock-climber's. Once his mat was arranged *just so*, he lay down and dropped his knees out to the sides, offering his crotch to the sky. Eyes closed, breathing deeply, he then shot one leg in the air, grabbed it and pulled it to his nose.

'What the fuck is *that*?' whispered Linley. 'He's as old as my grandad, and bendier than a baby.'

'That'll be us, soon,' Frances replied. 'We'll be flossing our teeth with our toes after a couple of weeks of this.'

As she pulled her vest down over her stomach and un-wedged her leggings from her bum, Frances tried to fight off the feeling that she really shouldn't be here. Not because this yoga centre seemed to be full of beautiful people half her size, rippling with muscle definition and a glow that possibly came from the gold dust in their smoothies, but because if

Troy knew that she had spent money signing up to this course, he would be furious.

'Don't you let that man tell you what to do!' Linley had insisted on the phone when Frances expressed her reservations about signing up for yoga. 'All that stretching on your own in the sunroom is making you more tense, not less. You're not going to rebuild your core with Denny yelling at you from the sidelines.'

Linley wasn't wrong about that, but Frances felt a pang: Troy wasn't the patriarchy, repressing her, as much as he was just the guy looking at their bank balance and wondering how the hell they were going to make it to payday.

'I'll try it,' she'd told Linley. 'But it's a secret. We're going for a *walk*, okay? He already thinks my gym membership is too exxy.'

Secret yoga classes and clandestine superfood deliveries: Frances really was cheating now.

Since Troy's intervention, two weeks ago, she had made some changes. She'd found an online delivery service that sold the supplements for her smoothies in bulk at a lower price. And she'd cleared out her locked secret cupboard, the one with all the potions and powders she'd been buying, trying and abandoning in a bid to feel more like her 'old' self. She'd stashed them—along with her supersized sack of psyllium husk—in their lock-up space in the block's shared garage.

The yoga teacher sat at the front of the room, so serene-looking and physically perfect that Frances just wanted to go over and curl up in her lap. 'Hello, there,' she said. 'I see we have some new faces in here today.' She nodded towards Linley and Frances with an extra-wide smile. 'Welcome.'

'She can tell we're new because we're wearing clothes,' whispered Linley.

Frances shushed her. But it was true—it seemed the crop tops, gym shorts and leggings became more and more revealing as your skills advanced, all the way up to the level of the teacher, who was wearing a tiny bra top and what could only be described as yoga hotpants.

Frankie looked at her own leggings and the baggy vest she'd got free as part of some pharmaceutical company promotion, and she realised she was about to do a yoga class with the word *Cialisa* emblazoned across her chest. It was a treatment for erectile dysfunction. She mentally added 'new active-wear' to her internal shopping list.

'It's time to set our intention for today's practice,' said beautiful yoga lady. 'There might be something you want to achieve, or you might want to dedicate the intention of this class to someone who needs it more than you do.'

Silently, Frances dedicated the intention of this class to Denny and Troy, who were home together surely wondering why her walk was taking so long. *I hope my stretches bring you half an hour of peace from colic and yelling and stressing about money*, she thought as she went into her first downward-facing dog pose.

The other thing that had changed was that Frances had signed up for some night shifts at the hospital.

The idea of going back to the ward full-time was too much. Every shift was busy, and Dr Darling was still there. 'Don't worry, Frank,' Linley had assured her, 'I think he's moved on to one of the younger nurses.' But Frances wasn't certain her confidence could take working with a man like that again.

She had written to her WhatsApp group at two in the morning, as Denny was refusing to sleep unless she held him, and her body was so tired she could feel a deep vein of exhaustion running through the core of her bones:

> Sometimes I feel like becoming a mother has just highlighted all the things I'm not good at.

There had been radio silence until six a.m., which Frances took as a sign all the other babies were sleeping better than Denny now. The answers were split between:

You are an amazing mum.

And:

Me, too.

But Frances felt deeply self-conscious for posting it now.

So she'd asked her old nursing supervisor for three nights a week: the money was better, and Frances would try to fit them around Troy's nights off.

'Then you'll never see him!' Linley had pointed out.

'Believe me, right now it might be better that way,' Frances had said with a laugh. But she knew that wasn't really true.

Five nights a week Troy was gone until three a.m. now that he was managing the late-licence main bar in Ben Bont's new city hotel, The Court.

Frances had distant memories of the days when she and her friends would go out to whichever bar Troy was working at. Over the past few years he'd leapfrogged between any new venue of Bont's that needed attention. Troy was known for being able to get a young crew up and running fast, making sure they lived the Bounce aesthetic and attitude—cool, friendly, with an eye for detail—and so he was often dropped in as a troubleshooter.

Those nights—Frances all dressed up, wearing actual make-up, leaning on the bar making eyes at her husband as if she was just a customer and he was just a hot barman—had been fun, even with the hangovers and the occasional jealous bust-ups when she'd seen other women doing the exact same thing.

'Is that what happens, every night?' she'd asked. 'Women flirting with you like that over the bar?'

'Well, sometimes,' he would say, smiling. 'But I always tell them I'm taken.'

And then they'd have sex.

Who *was* that person? To Frances now, it seemed like

a former life. Since Denny's birth—in fact, since she'd got pregnant—getting dressed up to go out or even just flirting with her husband seemed like something people might do in a faraway, foreign land.

Now she could barely raise a twinge of envy at the idea Troy was spending most nights a week in close proximity to good-looking reality stars and out-of-work actresses, models and WAGs.

'We should totally go check up on Troy at work,' Linley had said on the way to yoga. 'I hear The Court has got a Zen garden and all the cocktails have sprouted herbs on top.'

I'd rather eat my own hair, thought Frances. 'Sure, Lin,' she'd said, 'when Denny starts to sleep.'

Elle Campbell had written on The Goddess Project last week:

> Never forget your service to your partner in the fog of baby-raising. You chose each other, and remember, you need to stay connected to provide the safe framework for a healthy baby. It's lazy in the extreme to blame your baby for pulling away from your partner. You don't have a finite amount of love to give.

Frances wasn't so sure about that. It certainly felt like she had a finite amount of love to give right now. Her body and mind were so depleted from Denny-duty, she felt touched out, talked out, wiped out.

She and Denny were alone together a lot, on sleepless nights and in the long mornings of tiptoeing around the flat trying not to wake Daddy. Ideally, Troy would sleep until midday after a shift, but it wasn't easy to give him space to rest in their small flat with a baby who liked to wail a lot.

If she added three work nights of her own to that mix, she and Troy were going to see even less of each other. She wasn't following Elle's advice. So she was failing at being a wife, too.

'Namaste,' said the yoga teacher, and the class was over.

'What the fuck does that *mean*?' Linley hissed.

Frances just shrugged—she almost felt refreshed. Her nose hadn't got anywhere near her knees, and the bendy man next to her had kept flicking little beads of sweat her way when he tossed his silvery mop of hair, but an hour of moving without worrying about Denny wailing and Troy waking up had been as much of a break as the warrior poses. 'I feel positively Elle-like,' she told Linley as she pulled the centre-provided yoga mat back to its giant, sweaty pile.

'Oh, for fuck's sake, I thought we'd got that woman out of your head,' Linley groaned, knocking Frances softly with a foam yoga block.

'Don't diss it, Lin. She's teaching me about self-care,' Frances told her. 'And believe me, I need a bit of that.'

'Oh, I thought she was teaching you that you'd never live up to her perfect ideal and you needed to eat less to achieve worthiness.'

'You just don't get it.' Frances shook her head. 'You'll never get it.'

'Hey, didn't I just get you to do a yoga class? I'm *all* about your self-care.'

***

Later that night, with Denny finally down and Troy at work, Frances was looking at The Goddess Project's latest post, which was more cryptic than usual.

The Forgiveness Project

For the longest time, Followers, as you all know, I have been working on forgiveness. Forgiving the people in my life who have conspired to ruin my livelihood, my business, my marriage, my mothering.

Today it's me who needs to ask for forgiveness. Because lately, I have been behaving in a way—to some of the people closest to me—that makes me ashamed.

I know, shame is not helpful. Shame blocks the gaps where light can shine in. It stops us from seeing our true potential.

But I'm sure you can relate when you hear that sometimes the stresses of my life, the stresses of my past, bubble up inside me and I can be less than perfect in the way that I react. Who here has not felt that beast inside them overtaking their most pure intentions and lashing out in an unproductive way?

That has been me. And I have been on a cleanse, and I have looked inside, and I know, Followers, that there's a hole within me where my two boys used to be. Some events this week have brought that sharply into focus, made it clearer than even I was aware of. And so, some changes are coming, and I will share them with you. Changes that are a bid to heal my heart, which truly is fractured into three pieces.

Until then, I am asking for forgiveness: from myself, from our higher power, from you all.

E x

'Jesus. What's happened there?' Frances wondered aloud, sipping on her 'dinner' green smoothie and pulling a face. 'Ugh.' She went back to the fridge to poke around for another option.

After yoga, Frances had gone home to change. Then she'd driven Denny across three suburbs to drop him with her mum, so she could go to the hospital and talk to the Nursing Unit manager about her coming back to work sooner than planned.

'Why aren't you leaving him with his father?' asked Frances's mum as soon as she'd heard Frances wouldn't be staying for dinner.

'He's got to leave for work,' Frances called as she went back to her little car—a slightly beaten-up Toyota Yaris. 'And anyway, I thought you loved having him.'

'Oh, I do.'

Frances looked around to see her mum nuzzling Denny's head, but her son was staring after Frances's retreating figure, holding out a hand and beginning to wail. 'Good luck!' she yelled to her mum. 'Keep him moving, that's your best chance.'

Frances had noticed that the babysitting offers, even from family, were beginning to dry up lately. The more familiar they got with her beautiful Denny, the less likely they were to want to spend the day with him.

Well, tough, thought Frances, as she drove away. *If I have to go back to work, someone has to take care of my boy*.

Another two suburbs over, and Frances was back at the private hospital where she'd worked for three years before she'd left to have Denny. The sterile smell, the noises—phones ringing, monitors beeping, nurses laughing—it all felt at once very familiar and really intimidating to be stepping out of the lift onto her ward. She found herself looking towards the treatment room with a stab of what felt like fear.

She also felt terribly self-conscious. Frances knew from experience that when a woman came back to work from having a baby, everyone was judging how she looked. Had she lost her baby weight? Was she a dishevelled wreck?

But Frances was hugged warmly by the nurses who knew her. They cooed and clucked appropriately as they gathered around her phone for the inevitable baby pictures.

Louisa, the Nursing Unit manager, sat Frances in her office and gave her a cup of hot tea—Frances didn't have the heart to say that dairy and caffeine were the enemy, and this sweet gesture almost made her teary.

'Are you sure about nights, Frankie?' Louisa asked. 'Definitely what you want?'

Frances nodded. 'It's easier for me to leave Denny overnight. My mum could have him on Saturdays, Troy on Sundays and Mondays.'

The way Louisa was looking at her was making her feel uncomfortable. It was as if the older nurse could see through her smile—most likely, she could.

'It's a rough road,' Louisa said, 'coming back to work with a new baby, messed-up body clock, trying to sleep during the day...'

'You don't need to worry about me, Louisa. I've been taking good care of myself, doing a lot of exercise. I'm pretty sure that my energy levels will pull me through.'

Louisa smiled. 'This has nothing at all to do with wanting to avoid the doctors, does it?'

Frances swallowed, shook her head. What did Louisa know? 'You understand nights aren't any easier, don't you? There'll only be three of you on some shifts, so it can really get quite busy.' She was looking down at paperwork, marking a couple of points.

'I know that, Louisa. I'm not looking for a cushy ride.'

'Lucky.' Louisa looked up again. 'I know you're familiar with our codes of conduct, but there'll be no sleeping, no phones, no eating except on breaks.'

'Got it.'

'Start's strictly nine-thirty p.m., finish is seven-thirty a.m. You'll be expected to have all of the patients' notes up to date and meds done for the morning team—'

'I know, Louisa.' Frances was sure the woman had never been this formal with her previously. 'I *have* worked the odd night shift in the past—'

'Yes, yes, of course you have. Right then, when can you start?'

'Next week?'

'Next week! Our rosters are done three months in advance, you know that.'

'Well, look, we're just keen to get started.' Frances kicked herself: she'd sounded like an amateur. Too keen.

'I'll ask around to see if anyone's desperate to get off nights in our ward.' Louisa stood up, signalling it was time for them both to go. Then she stepped forwards and gave Frances a quick hug. 'Be kind to yourself, love,' she said. 'The first year is the hardest.'

'Is that true?' Frances asked, glancing back to the tea, a bit choked up.

'No!' Louisa laughed. 'Not when you've still got two twenty-four-year-olds at home doing god knows what till all hours of the day, night, next day...'

'Oh, Jesus.'

Frances had left the ward feeling two things: absolutely exhausted at the thought of being there for a ten-hour shift, and a little bit excited to be back in her own world.

Now she was standing at the fridge, looking for something edible that wasn't a smoothie. 'I am earning again,' she said out loud to her flat. 'How to celebrate?'

She found a slab of cheese—obviously bought in rebellion by Troy, who was refusing to observe the dairy ban. She cut off a large chunk, ate it straight and cut another.

'Yoga tomorrow,' she said, heading back to the computer and the rates for the Gurva Elle-ness retreat she'd been pouring over for twenty minutes. 'How many nights walking the ward will pay for that?' she asked the emptiness.

CHAPTER 14

MATT

Lucille the baby nurse had been a painful one to get rid of. And she hadn't been cheap either.

'Don't you think I know who she is?' Lucille had cried to Matt that day, holding an icepack to the back of her head in the staff kitchen. 'Don't you think I know what I could get for going to the press with this?'

'I think you'll find, Lucille, that you signed something that says you can't do that.' In the course of working for Elle, Matt had perfected a calm but firm voice he used when the staff got these ideas in their heads.

It was one reason he really liked to keep them as far from Elle as possible.

'I don't care what I signed,' Lucille said. 'She assaulted me!'

'She was a mother worried about her child,' Matt corrected gently.

'She has never been worried about that child in her life,' spat Lucille. 'She spends more time in the gym than with Alma. To her that baby is just an... accessory.'

'I don't think you know what you're saying, Lucille,' Matt said. 'I think we should go and start packing, don't you?'

'Packing?'

Honestly, thought Matt, *the idiocy of some women*. 'To leave. Come on, now.'

Hysterical negotiations developed, and Matt thought it was likely that even after the money they'd agreed on, he'd probably be hearing from Lucille's parents once she got back to Perth. It usually went like that.

Lucille was the third member of the domestic team Matt had needed to let go in the past six months. More and more, part of his job involved smoothing over the furious fallout from his boss's temper.

Not that he was surprised.

***

The very first time Matt had met Elle, she'd been making someone cry.

It was back in Melbourne, six years ago, and they were trainers at the same city gym. Soon she would meet that sucker Adrian, but the first time Matt had seen her, Elle had been new—and upsetting a client.

'If you're going to cheat,' she was saying to a young woman standing on the scales near the cardio room, 'you only have yourself to blame. Sitting on the couch eating biscuits is only screwing yourself over, no one else. I get paid whether you lose the weight or not.'

When Matt had questioned her later about whether this was the best approach to take, Elle had told him, 'She's a bride. They only understand deadlines and tough love.'

It was a time in his life—and Elle's—that was all about the gym. It was where they socialised, where they dated, where they gathered, even on days off, to work out and gossip and flirt and push each other harder, harder, always harder.

Elle was known, even then, as a take-no-prisoners chick.

She was also known, among the trainers and the gym regulars who wished they were trainers, as someone who did not screw the crew. This was not Matt's philosophy. For him, the hook-ups—with women, with men—were a perk of the job. There was very little as intimate as training someone, he found. You were privy to their insecurities, you knew every curve and bump and indent of their body, and you helped mould them. It was seductive, for both parties.

So of course Matt had tried it on with Elle, and of course she had told him to go jump. She had her eye on the client suits, he could see. But he and Elle became friendly, training together sometimes, sharing stories and protein shakes. Matt was from the bush too; he'd run to Melbourne from the heat and dust of western Queensland, and they bonded over the vagaries of the city—the way commuters obediently filed on and off the trains like cattle, the way there were fourteen types of coffee to choose from in every cafe but no time permitted to make a choice...

Also, like Elle, Matt was happy to have left the bush behind. To him, there was nothing romantic about the isolation he'd grown up with, the casual brutality of farm life, the endless waiting for better times. His father's moods, his mother's drinking. Nope, Matt was heady drunk on the possibilities of what and who he could be in the city.

Until he found himself facedown in the street with blood in his eyes.

***

As Matt was making sure Lucille got onto the airport shuttle bus that night, his phone buzzed—it was Ben Bont.

Hear we're looking for a new nanny.

Matt replied:

No problems. Will have someone by weekend.

Ben's response:

Maybe try not to fuck it up this time.

For fuck's sake. Matt shoved his phone back into his pocket. Bont was becoming more and more of a dickhead.

Bont had been happy to leave the running of the farm to the Byron team as they'd built it up. Happy enough to leave his missus and baby up here, flying in and out like Howard fucking Hughes. But lately, since the place was actually becoming successful, Bont seemed to want to meddle more and more. And now he was openly antagonising Matt. Clearly, the rich prick was acquiring trust issues. And really, who could blame him? This was a twisted arrangement, and he didn't know the half of it.

As the bus pulled off, another problem driving away from the farm, Matt headed back to his room. Like the other handful of staff who actually lived onsite, he slept in a tiny bunk room beyond the creek. He'd made it as least-depressing as possible, with a home for his nutrition and fitness books and somewhere for his hand weights and his tiny but sharp Bose sound system. But the irony of his cell-like home was not lost on Matt, given that a cell was very likely where he would have been sleeping had it not been for Elle.

***

It was Elle who found him the night he'd been smashed over the head by the roid-heads he was selling gear to out the back of the gym.

What he remembered most about that night was lying in the laneway, feeling incredibly alert but completely unable to move, the cold of the cobblestones against his cheek and something wet across his face. And what he was thinking about wasn't how badly he was hurt, but the fact that he'd just lost five thousand dollars, and he'd been counting on that to pay his supplier, so now he was truly in deep shit. His head was killing him, and his stomach was swashing with fear.

The other thought was how very stupid he was to be playing such an amateur fucking game in a city full of proper thugs. *This isn't the bush anymore, Matt, you dick, where you were the gangster if you'd bought a load of dodgy vials from the internet and were selling them for triple the price at the small-town weight box.*

Elle had returned to the gym that night because in the early days of her affair with Adrian, the gym was where the two of them would meet after hours to fuck. She had a key to the back door, and she would come back at eleven p.m. to meet him.

'Why wouldn't you go to a hotel?' Matt had asked her, much later, when all this became clear.

'Because it wasn't as exciting,' Elle had answered honestly.

Even then, she'd been playing the guys well, Matt thought, giving them just enough of what they needed to make them feel alive. For old, married Adrian, it was excitement and an edge of danger; for the man who had everything, Ben Bont, it was a family, a new business venture and a woman who wouldn't be owned.

But back then, that night in the laneway, Elle had just been the first person to find Matt bleeding, to help him up, clean him up and hear him out. He found himself, like the pussy he was, telling her why he was bleeding in the street, what he'd done and what they'd done, and she had asked him enough questions to make him think she was interested in his welfare. Of course, he knew now, that wasn't really why she was asking.

When the police had come two days later, tipped off by disgruntled clients who could no longer get their hands on a reliable supply, Elle had lied for him, telling them she'd seen the junkie street kids who bashed him for his wallet. And despite the cops' pointed questions, it was hard for them to argue with the only witness when she said she'd seen those kids rifling through Matt's pockets and disappearing down the lane.

At the time Matt didn't know why Elle had done that for him. His messed-up head decided maybe she was a better friend than he'd thought she was, or that maybe she really liked him after all. All the same, a week after the attack, patched up and with one last paycheque cashed, he followed her advice to get the hell out of town.

Matt moved to Sydney, kicked the steroids, danced a lot and, eventually, moved out of gyms and into travel, becoming an agent at Flight Shop. All that time, he kept an eye on Elle—who he'd have been hesitant to call his mate—as she became a trophy wife, a MILF and a social media sensation.

He wasn't a bit surprised.

What did surprise Matt was when he got a call from Elle, a year and a half ago, saying she needed a favour.

***

'Elle, I've got a girl out of Mullum who's really keen for this gig, but you have to promise me that you're going to chill the fuck out,' Matt said to her as she was stretching on the deck. He was leaning on the doorframe to the house, arms folded. 'Maybe actually breathe in one of these yoga videos you're making. Maybe actually take in a little Zen.'

'I don't appreciate your tone,' she replied, in the voice he'd come to recognise as 'lady of the house'. 'I am as Zen as they come.'

'You're about as Zen as a box of frogs,' he said with a laugh. 'But seriously, Ben is on it. You've got to cool down.'

Elle stood up and went into a one-legged tree pose. 'Then don't give me a nanny who wants to be a mum. And we'll all be happy.'

Matt wasn't even a little bit convinced that was the problem here. He knew Elle's stress levels shot up whenever she felt her control slipping, and whenever her sons with that idiot Adrian were mentioned. 'Maybe you could take Alma off the new nanny's hands a bit more often? It might make her last longer.'

'Some advice, Matt,' Elle snapped. 'Don't tell a mother how to mother! I know what I'm doing.'

'Well, it doesn't so much look that way at the moment...' Matt said, nodding towards the rock on her finger as she settled into warrior pose.

'I've got it,' she insisted. 'Did you see the latest post? I'm on my way to a little image overhaul that might just help us out of this mess.'

'Us?' Matt looked down at his finger. 'I don't think I'm engaged...'

'Us—me and my daughter,' Elle snapped at him again, but she was smiling this time. 'Your wellbeing is not really a priority for me. And anyway,' she straightened up, padded over to a glass of water, 'I think you're doing just fine up here, aren't you? You've got everything you need.'

***

When Elle had called, out of nowhere, six years after that mess in a Melbourne laneway, Matt got a little thrill. She was a celebrity now, after all. He'd seen her on TV. Of course, he was a man from the bush, and he wasn't going to gush on her.

She'd asked him if he'd seen the shit-fight about her at the blogging awards. Apparently it had been all over the media that week. Matt had to admit he'd had a bit of a big one, and *The Daily Trail* hadn't really been on his reading list.

Elle had seemed pleased and told him not to, if he could help it. Of course, as she was talking to him on the phone and he was sitting at a Flight Shop desk, he typed her name into Google and watched the drama unfold in algorithmically preferred headlines.

MUMMY FRAUD—Blogger gave her husband cancer for clicks

BLOG-ARGH—Awards show descends into farce as mummy bloggers go to war

ONE ELLE OF A SCAM—How a blogger fooled the world her husband was dying

'Woah, Elle,' he couldn't help but say as he scrolled down and down and the puns kept coming.

'Oh, you're looking. Well, okay then. Breathe it in.'

'Did you... do this?'

'Some of it,' Elle said quickly. 'But what I want to know is, can you do me a favour?'

'Well, I'm sure I can, but— '

'I'm talking about the kind of favour I did you, going back a few years. Although,' she giggled, 'you wouldn't have to lie to any cops about it.'

They both let that sink in.

'Okay...' Matt was half-intrigued, half ready to hang up.

'I need to get on a flight.'

'Well, that's easy. I do that for a job.'

'A specific flight.'

'Sure.'

'And a specific seat, next to a specific person.'

'Ohh.'

That was where it all began.

Matt had to admit, it was exciting for him to become Elle's confidant again. His new life as a Sydney travel agent was fun enough—with a young, hard-partying team across several stores, there were almost as many 'perks' as there had been at the gym—but his thrill-seeking side, once clumsily filled dealing gear to muscle-heads, was still there, niggling at him.

What he had helped Elle set in motion was a whole new

adventure, mixing old skills and new. The places to take it next were endless.

***

'Yes, I've got what I need,' he said to Elle as she threw on a robe and sipped her water.

And he did. Byron. Business. Beautiful people to fuck. The money he skimmed off the top, with the help of Elle's blind eye. A side-hustle or two, which would only be enhanced by the arrival of the party set attracted by The Bar(n).

But to keep it all going where they needed it to go, everyone had to keep their heads just a little bit longer.

'"Zen", boss,' he said as he turned to leave. 'It's the word of the week.'

CHAPTER 15

ELLE

'*Fifty Minutes* are going to do it,' Ben was telling Elle on the phone. 'Harry and I go back a long way. We'll get full approval.'

'We, or you?' asked Elle. She couldn't help it: her frustration was proving impossible to contain, even for a control freak of her high vibration.

'*WE*, Elle, I promise.' Was she imagining it, or could she hear an edge of delight in his voice at her discomfort?

'I've had experiences with Sunday night TV shows before...' Elle pointed out. 'Things can blow up.'

'Yes, but you weren't with me then, kitten. Harry's the EP and we were at school together. No one's going to try to screw me.'

'But they'll ask about—'

'Yes, there's one question in there, I've sorted it, and we'll work on exactly what that answer's going to be. I'll be up there tomorrow. The other thing we need to sort is our approach to Adrian and the boys. When we go to visit them, I think we should go lawyered-up.'

'Ben, I...'

'What, kitten?'

She knew the way to win this one was to go soft, so she let her voice drop, crack a little, held the phone closer to her mouth. 'I don't want the first time I see my sons in so long to be with a lot of scary men in suits. I think, I think, that I should go alone. Well, with Alma.'

'No way.'

'Ben, come on. Think about it. I need Adrian to agree to the divorce terms, and quick. I need him to agree to let the boys come to Byron and to appear on a television show—'

'You're their mother. You're not asking him for favours, Elle. These are your rights.'

'I am a mother who has not made any effort to see her boys in eighteen months.' This bald fact hadn't been expressed quite like this between them before; if Ben was shocked, he didn't show it. 'Ben, Adrian has lawyers too. I think our first approach should be friendly—we can tool up if that's the way it's going to go.'

There was a second or two of silence.

'Elle, you were traumatised by what happened,' Ben said firmly. But the pause had let her know she had won.

'I was.'

Tired of this conversation now that her desired outcome was achieved, Elle got up from where she'd been lying on the bed and went to her dressing room. 'I'm going to go into town, do a bit of shopping to distract myself from all this,' she said. She knew Ben liked it when she behaved as a trophy wife should, shopping and lunching and manicuring. 'I can't wait to see you tomorrow. Nor can Alma.'

'Have fun out there,' Ben said warmly. 'How's the new nanny?'

'Fine. Unlikely to make any gross breaches of hygiene standards, at least.'

'Well, that's something. I'll see you tomorrow.'

'Miss you.'

Elle punched the red button and threw her phone on the bed.

Domestic conversations with Ben Bont were making her itchy. This wasn't how she'd imagined things—like they'd just turn out to be a normal couple, talking about arrangements and shopping and the help. Not at all.

Ben Bont was meant to stay in his lane and facilitate her dreams. That was what was meant to happen. He was proving harder to manage than she'd expected.

Elle pulled out a floaty dress and sat down to do up some Jesus sandals that crisscrossed her calves with fronds of silver leather. God, she missed her heels, and her acrylic nails and her Russian hair extensions. This new look could be so... boring. But no one wore heels in Byron Bay. Tripping around the shops up here in skin-tight jeans and stilettos marked you as an outsider within seconds. The look was loose and luxe, glossy and glowing, never trying too hard.

The baby was always a very popular accessory in Byron, though, and Alma was at a perfect age for that: adorable, smiley and still happy to settle into one of those pretty wrap things that all the Zen mums wore. The Bugaboo wasn't such a good fit in town.

'Ocean!' Elle called through the house to the new nurse. 'Let's take Alma shopping!'

***

The Elle-ness guide to pure Byron

Travel guides are not my style, Followers, but some of the most frequently asked questions I get are about moving from Melbourne to Byron Bay. 'What's it really like to live there?' So I thought I would give you all a few inside tips, sister to sister.

Well, first of all, we don't live IN Byron Bay, everyone. What works for us is living the most serene and peaceful lives possible, and even Byron seems like a bustling city when you've fine-tuned your insides to the rhythm of sunrise and cicadas. No, we live in the hills behind Byron, on Gurva. But I often come down into town to connect with the energy, and to do a little shopping, or a little beautifying (I'm still a girl who likes pretty nails, after all!).

The thing you need to know about my beautiful new home town of Byron Bay, Followers, is that everything you've heard about it is wrong.

It's not full of unruly drug addicts and scruffy hippies. Far from it. It's full of people who understand the importance of aesthetics, as well as inner peace. Really, who wouldn't want to be beautiful in such a naturally stunning corner of our country? So when it comes to beauty and spa treatments, Byron has a LOT of choice.

Of course, our spa at Gurva is the best on the coast. But if you can't stretch to the time or the commitment needed to come and remake yourself here on our farm, there are lots of almost-as-good choices in town to choose from.

For example, my favourite place to get my nails done in Byron is a salon called Turtle. You'll find it tucked away inside the newest shopping complex in town: the sparkly, and decidedly non-hippie, Sunrise Strand. Here they don't use all those toxic, smelly chemicals, but instead they tint your nails with natural ocean-based dyes. And then they buff the natural dye to a state of high-shine with a piece of recycled sea-turtle shell—hence the name. Get it?

The whole process takes two hours, but you'll notice the difference immediately, in the way your nails look, feel and smell. Give them a follow on Instagram!

The other place that I love to visit for wonderful Byron-style pampering is Moanna Mask Hair. There's a wonderful lady there called Ros (I think! You know me, I'm terrible with names) who can make your hair look a million dollars, and it won't cost you a million dollars! In fact, her patented hair-mask, which is made from crushed oyster pearl and the stomach-linings of beached marine-mammals (the ultimate in recycling, right!) only costs $450 for full-service, which involves leaving it on while Ros or her girls do something for you. That might mean rubbing your feet, or your lower back. Maybe even running you an errand, like picking you up some Berry-ohm Kombucha from The Kombo Shack next door. Ros says that an act of service soaks good karma into the hair and makes the shine last longer. So, it would be rude not to!

And then to eat, of course, just like out-of-towners I love to try Byron's wholefood offerings. There are few places in the world where it's as easy to get all the supplements and potions that I have learnt let me live a better, purer life. If you told me you could get Unicorn Horn somewhere on Jonson Street, I would believe you. LOLs, obvs.

But maybe the best is a little hole-in-the-wall I like to keep to myself where two of our regular Gurva chefs—Lucienne and Loola—make incredible superfood smoothies and snacks that are actually NEGATIVE calories. Yes, I know that sounds unbelievable, but L&L did an amazing online nutrition course from Budapest that led them to the discovery that, for many of us, not every meal needs to be nourishing. Energy can be overrated. And calorie-counting is very 2000s. So pop into L&Ls to see them and try their Neggo Juice—it's much more positive than it sounds!

So I hope that gives you a few insider tips about visiting Byron, Followers. My new home town also has a very pretty beach, and some mountains around it.

The area's natural beauty can inspire you to try harder at looking great yourself, and with so many incredible

spas and shops around Byron, it's never been easier, or purer, to be drop-dead gorgeous, inside and out.
E xx

In truth, Elle wouldn't dream of going to a spa in Byron. She had private treatments at Gurva from her staff of experts; if she needed anything extra, she would go to the Gold Coast, only a forty-minute drive away and crammed with excellent cosmedical clinics.

But she did like to go to Byron for the shopping. It actually made Ben Bont happy to see a six-hundred-dollar kaftan appear on her credit card statement. She was constantly amazed by the stupidity of the people from Sydney's Paddington or Melbourne's Toorak, who would come up to Byron and buy themselves a suitcase full of designer clothes they could easily have bought back home—and for less. But still, if you were in the market for an overpriced kimono, there was no better place to be than Byron's Fletcher Street.

Which is where Elle was now, with Alma strapped to her chest and Ocean, the new nanny, pushing the Bugaboo ten steps behind.

A woman Elle had never seen before stepped out of a shop and almost straight into her.

'So sorry,' the woman said, flustered, looking in her bag. She straightened up and turned to smile a further apology when—and Elle could almost pinpoint the moment—she recognised Elle.

The woman's face changed instantly, and—as Elle stepped to the side to try to walk around her—she reached out and grabbed her arm. 'You're Elle Campbell, aren't you?' she said in a rush.

'Can I get past, please?' Elle asked, keeping her voice low and polite. She couldn't quite tell yet which way this would go. Was the woman a fan? 'I'm just having a walk with my baby.' And Elle gestured to the bundle on her chest, tucked into a tasteful wraparound sling.

'You should be ashamed to be walking down the street,' the woman said, her face twisting into a snarl. No more mystery about her intentions. 'After what you did.'

'Excuse me,' Elle pushed on. 'I really must keep going.'

Ocean the nanny had stopped behind her and seemed unsure what was happening, standing there bloody clueless as far as Elle could tell.

'My husband had cancer,' the woman said, still holding on to Elle's arm.

Oh, one of those.

'And he's gone.'

'I'm really very sorry about that, but please, let me go. I'm with my baby.'

'Baby! I didn't get a chance to have a baby with my husband...' The woman let go of Elle's arm just for a moment, and Elle walked away quickly. Ocean suddenly seemed to get the message and followed, at a pace.

'You should have gone to jail!' the woman yelled at Elle, loud enough that people began to turn around and look. 'After what you did, the lies you told. And didn't you abandon those other babies of yours?' She was screaming now, and Elle was charging on, head down, one arm tight around her bundle of Alma.

She ducked into the nearest shop, hoping the shouting woman wasn't following them, relieved when only Ocean walked in and shut the door.

Elle began to unwrap Alma to put her in the pram.

'Does that happen a lot?' asked Ocean.

'No,' said Elle, 'not a lot. Please, take the baby. Let's get her in the pram, and then if you could check that woman's not still there before we leave...' She spun around and looked at the clothes on the racks, randomly grabbing something pale blue and silky. 'I'll just go and try this on while we wait.' She waved away a confused-looking sales assistant as she pulled the curtain across the change room. 'Don't worry, I'll buy it,' she said.

Curtain closed against the shop, Elle sat on the stool and took a deep breath. Being out in the world was still so hit-and-miss. At least on the farm she knew that the people who were going to pay money to hang around her were friends, not foes.

Heading down to Victoria to see the boys was going to be nerve-racking. The thought of it nauseated her, and she rested her head in her hands. She couldn't remember why she was anxious for Ben and his entourage to stay away. Wouldn't they help protect her, keep away the crazies, make sure everyone stayed in line?

But she knew one of the reasons she needed to go alone into Abi's world: she had to be able to be herself. With Ben and the lawyer boys watching her every move, there was no way she would be able say what she needed to say to Adrian and Abi. It was getting exhausting, playing a part for Ben, even if she was beginning to let that mask slip alittle.

And her boys—what if they didn't want to know her? What she was most afraid of was that they might not run to her, hug her, even recognise her. And there was no way she could let Ben Bont see that.

Elle stood up in the change room, pulled some lip balm out of her bag and put a slick of it on. Time to get on with it.

'Has that woman gone?' she called to Ocean, who squealed back a yes.

After smoothing her floaty dress, Elle ran a hand through her hair and pushed back the curtain.

CHAPTER 16

ABI

A nude YouTube scandal had erupted in Abi's kitchen that morning. Turns out, even for a battle-hardened blogger, keeping up with what your kids were doing online was fucking exhausting.

'I'm supposed to be a pro at this,' Abi said to Grace, 'and this is what happens?'

'We have to talk to her,' Grace said. 'I think we have to make her take that down.'

Abi and Grace were on a Crisis Date.

The 'Crisis Date' was something that Grace had implemented in the overt craziness of the past year. Whenever she played that card, it meant things were getting out of hand at home, and the grown-ups needed a time-out to regroup.

This morning, Grace had quite literally pulled the card. She'd written 'CRISIS DATE' on a brown-paper lunch bag and held it up over Arden's head at the breakfast table, just as all hell was breaking loose.

Abi's eldest had arrived in the kitchen declaring her latest YouTube video a 'mad hit'.

'It's got about a hundred times what my vlogs usually get,' she said.

Boyfriend River, rubbing his head at the sink, commented, 'That's what a bit of nudity will do for you.'

And the whole kitchen reached for their phones.

A few seconds later, and Alex—fourteen and full of righteous pseudo-feminist fury—had called her sister a 'click-whore'. That tipped Arden into a rant about slut-shaming, which prompted Sol to ask loudly what a slut was.

It was around that moment—Abi standing in a corner trying to watch her daughter's 'naked' video as her phone kept buffering, two teenagers screaming about sluts, eighteen-year-old River chuckling into his homemade granola, Sol and Otto craning over their mother's shoulder for their own look—that Adrian, Teddy and Freddie came into the kitchen from the yard.

'What's all this about?' Arden's father asked cheerfully, heading to the sink to rescue bowls for the boys' granola.

'Arden's freeing the nipple!' yelled Otto.

'Or objectifying herself for cash,' Alex muttered darkly.

A moment of strained panic crossed Adrian's face, and he looked up to Abi for an explanation. Still trying to watch the clip and, at a loss for words, she shrugged and looked across to Grace, who'd just seen the clip and was now brandishing the sign: 'CRISIS DATE'.

Abso-fucking-lutely, nodded Abi.

***

'She's sixteen. She's legal, but she's not an adult. Should I be approving all her videos before they go up?'

'It's not a porno, Abi.'

On the rare occasions they went out, Abi and Grace always went to the same place: a little vegetarian restaurant near the lake. Abi had a glass of red wine; Grace drank Chinese tea. Usually, the Crisis Date rule was that the subject of the crisis was only allowed to be discussed for the first ten minutes—until the entrée arrived. Then they had to move on.

But today, it was hard to know where one crisis ended and another began.

First, there was the non-porno.

On the surface, it was a video about an all-natural fake tan infused with mineral glitter. Of course, Arden and River had decided that an excellent way to showcase this was for River to use his girlfriend's naked body as a blank canvas, painting abstract, swirling images across her torso and down her legs with a large paintbrush. The video, filmed and edited over a few days, showed the tan deepening in colour as the 'painting' darkened and shimmered, developing across her skin.

'How did we not notice that happening?' asked Abi.

'It *is* kind of beautiful, and it's not like you could *see* anything,' said Grace, lifting a forkful of zucchini noodles to her mouth.

'There was side-boob,' Abi said.

Grace smiled. 'Bum cheek.'

'Hand-bra.'

'Thigh junction.'

'Jesus. We're dissecting my daughter just like the trolls will.' Abi and Grace nodded at the same time. 'I'm sure they already are.'

And then there was Adrian's reaction.

'I don't know how helpful it is having Angry Dad around in these pivotal parenting moments,' said Abi. 'That was a little over the top, no?'

Adrian had left the three- and four-year-old to get their own granola, then he'd crossed the kitchen to look at the video over Abi's shoulder, once it was finally playing properly.

The kitchen had fallen into silence for a few seconds, as the kids around the table watched Adrian watching Arden.

Arden herself tried to keep on eating breakfast as if nothing was happening, but her hand was shaking, just a little, as she lifted her spoon. River stood behind her, hands on her shoulder, looking for all the world like he was expecting a positive review of his latest masterpiece.

There was no script, only a soundtrack and words filling the screen. *'When a beauty road test is a work of art...'* came the first lines. *'And your body is a blank canvas...'* Cue shot of Arden's body filmed by a twisting, turning camera—actually River with his iPhone on a tripod. *'Three days, one paintbrush, one bottle of tan...'*

'Are you joking?' Adrian asked. He looked up from Abi's phone, then snatched it from her hand.

'Hey, Adrian!' Abi exclaimed, reaching for her phone.

But instead of giving it to her, he actually turned the phone a little, looking at the back of it as if the video could be removed like a battery. 'Is this really... on the internet?' he asked, looking over at Arden and River. 'As in, anyone in the world could watch it right now?'

'Um, five thousand people already have,' said River.

Abi looked at him and saw him through Adrian's eyes, rather than her own: as an eighteen-year-old—a legal adult—who was encouraging a child to take her clothes off for the world. And for what? Clicks? Money? Things had worked out so well for both Adrian and Abi when they'd chased that particular dragon in the past.

Suddenly, River looked like the enemy.

Adrian was watching the rest of the video. As the camera followed the lines of the now-developed tan bands, looping around Arden's hips and thighs... *'No one will know the masterpiece that's under your clothes. No one but you.'*

Abi couldn't help herself. 'Well, this is just *bad* now.'

'MUM! That's my *art*.'

'The editing alone took us *two days*,' said River indignantly.

'Is that what's under your clothes NOW?' asked Alex. 'Ugh.'

The video closed out. Before Adrian could see the final frame, he'd handed the phone to Abi and charged across the kitchen, sending bowls flying, arms reaching out for River.

There weren't any words, there was just a strange noise coming from somewhere as Adrian grabbed River by the collar of his tatty T-shirt. Six kids watched on, mouths open as two men, separated by more than thirty years, went into an undignified, clumsy struggle—River trying to pull Adrian's hands off him, Adrian leaning into River's face with an intensity that suggested he might bite off the young man's nose, given the chance.

'Dad!' Arden stood up, started pulling on Adrian from behind. Abi, who was half willing Adrian on, half pondering how she'd come to be living in a clichéd kitchen soap opera, shook herself to go and intervene.

Grace started trying to gather the younger kids to get them out of the kitchen. They didn't want to go anywhere.

'Come on, Adrian, you're making a bit of a tit of yourself,' Abi scolded, joining her eldest daughter in trying to detach her ex-husband from the front of River's shirt.

'Me?' He let go, falling back into the women's arms somewhat dramatically. '*ME?*'

'River, I think you should go,' Abi said firmly.

'MUM!' Arden swung to her. 'This is such utter crap. You've always told me I am in charge of myself. My body, my rules, remember? And this is *ART*. What kind of hypocrite are you if you can't see that?'

'One who doesn't want blood on the floor of the kitchen right now,' Abi told her. 'I'll talk to you about this work of art later. Right now, I think River should go home, you should go upstairs and get ready for school, and we should all take a moment.'

Of course, that wasn't what happened. What happened was that Arden stomped off outside with River; Teddy and Freddie started crying loudly; Sol and Otto had wrangled Grace's phone and were watching the video on silent under the table.

Grace, giving up on the whole stressful situation, started clearing the plates. Alex was still sitting, spooning cereal into her mouth with a smug smile on her face, like a spectator shovelling popcorn.

Now, at the Crisis Date, Abi took a bite of her porcini ravioli. 'I thought he was going to pop an artery,' she said to Grace. 'There's nothing in Adrian's history or DNA that would prepare him for this. It's not how teenagers behave in Balwyn.'

'Pfft,' Grace replied. 'I bet they do.'

'Maybe. But their parents would never know. Or at least,' Abi corrected herself, imagining her former cohort of mothers from the girls' leafy Melbourne private school, 'they'd never *let on* that they knew.'

Adrian and Abi had stood across from each other in that suddenly quiet kitchen, defeated.

'This is not happening,' Adrian had said, panting slightly. 'Not my daughter, naked on the internet. This is not happening.'

'Adrian,' Abi had said, 'I know you are angry. So am I. But this *is* happening. And I have to be honest, this macho violent approach is not going to help. You have to let Grace and I handle this.'

'Macho? Violent?' Adrian snapped. 'That boy—that man—he is preying on my daughter.'

'Is he, Adrian?' Surprisingly, this had been Grace. 'Arden is a willing participant in this—in the relationship, and the video.'

'But she's a child, Grace, with all respect. She's a child.'

'Look, her judgement is off,' Grace went on, coming to stand next to Abi, a united front. 'Which is obvious from the fact she didn't anticipate this kind of reaction towards what is, clearly, a very provocative video. But... she's trying things, pushing boundaries. There's nothing actually explicit in that video—it's a young woman understanding her body, experimenting with what she can do with it.'

Abi went to grab Grace's hand behind her. She agreed with the sentiment but she needed Grace to shush, because at least one thing about that video was every bit a rebellious 'fuck you' from Arden to her parents, and her father in particular.

Luckily, Adrian hadn't noticed it yet.

But it brought Grace and Abi to the last item on the Crisis Date agenda. In the final frame of the short video, a bottle filled the screen for a moment: Elle-ness Glimmer. It was Elle's fake tan.

And Elle was coming to the farm in three days' time.

'What is she thinking?' Abi hissed, pushing the rest of her pasta aside.

'I think she's making a very strong statement about separating herself from her father,' Grace said.

'Always so smart, you are,' Abi replied. 'But really, why? Why can't she rebel without starting World War Three? How can she be helping out the woman who ruined her dad's life?' *And tried to ruin mine*, Abi added silently.

'I wonder if Elle's seen it.' Grace sipped her tea, looking at Abi.

'Of course she will have seen it. There's no way she would have *NOT* seen it. She must be really enjoying us all tearing each other apart over this.'

'Then don't give her the satisfaction,' said Grace—who, Abi was noticing, looked tired, almost... defeated. 'We'll ask Arden to take it down again, but this drama has to stop. Let's not give all of them the satisfaction.'

'*All* of them?'

'Arden, River and Adrian, of course. There's something in it for all of them, for us to be destabilised,' Grace closed her eyes. 'Sometimes, it feels like we're fighting fires on too many fronts. I'm just...'

'You're just what?' Abi picked up Grace's hand and kissed it. 'I need your wisdom, Gracey. Don't tell me you're shaky.'

'I'm just tired,' Grace said, opening her eyes and pulling her hand away. 'Tired of Crisis Dates. I want to feel calm in my own home.'

Back in the kitchen that morning, Adrian had stood

shaking, fists clenched at his sides as Grace lectured him about Arden. That's how he would have seen it, Abi knew, because she knew him well. Not telling Grace to fuck off was surely taking every last inch of discipline that Adrian had right then.

'What are we going to do about our daughter?' He pointedly turned to Abi, voice bubbling with anger. 'Can we take that fucking channel down?'

'I think you should take the boys out for the day,' Abi said. Teddy and Freddie were each holding on to one of her legs, sniffling. 'There's a lot going on here, and they need you to be calm and prepared.'

'You are patronising me, Abi. Arden is my girl. I can't ignore what's going on *here*,' he gestured around the kitchen, the house. 'We've got to deal with it.'

'One battle at a time,' Abi said, unpeeling the boys from her legs and squatting down to hug them. 'Let's just get these boys ready for what's coming.'

Or rather, *who* was coming.

CHAPTER 17

FRANCES

Carrot and turmeric juice was disgusting at three a.m.

Starting a detox cleanse the same week as going back to work after a baby might seem like a stretch—Linley and Troy certainly thought so—but Frances had Elle on her side.

The No-Excuses Spring Clean

Followers, we all need to talk.

Am I alone in feeling sluggish lately? In feeling like we've come so far together, but sometimes, it doesn't feel ENOUGH?

I have. It's important to admit our own vulnerabilities, isn't it? And right now, mine is a niggling feeling that there's more I could do to become the person I need to be.

Aren't we all in a state of BECOMING, after all? Isn't that where we're at, trying to push through the last of our toxic past, toxic secrets and, yes, our toxic insides, to live free, purely, lightly? That's why I have devised this exceptional Spring-clean Juice Cleanse, just for us.

It's true, for three days you will eat no solid food. It's true, this cleanse will work best if you have bought some of our amazing new supplement powder Elle-ness SuperGlow™ to sprinkle in your juice and smoothies (you can order it for delivery, here). But it's also true that you need to commit to see results. Always.

Let's move together towards being better, inside and out. Who's with me?

E x

Frances was with her. Sometimes, she thought, it was as if Elle was inside her head. How did she know this was exactly what Frances needed?

Frances was telling herself that going back to work this week signalled a fresh start, and nothing marked a fresh start more clearly than a renewed commitment to her pure diet. Because if she had to feel her flesh folding around itself during forward bends anymore—well, that was just disgusting, was what it was. She couldn't escape the thought that what she'd 'become' was one of those women who'd let themselves go.

Last night, with Denny finally down after a marathon hour-long shush-and-pat session, Frances had spent a couple of hours in the kitchen, chopping up all the fruit and veggies she would be living off for the next few days: mountains of kale, cucumbers, carrots, apples, lemons and oranges, and gnarly nubs of turmeric and ginger.

'Don't worry, Troy, I got them in bulk from the Asian market,' she found herself saying out loud, even though (of course) Troy wasn't there.

Elle's post about the cleanse was full of these beautiful images of an immaculately organised kitchen and fridge, all the sliced fresh fruit and veggies stored in sparkly glass jars with colour-coded lids, all the powders and supplements and herbs alongside in tiny glass bento compartments. The calm and order beaming out of that image had made Frances ache a little bit inside.

If she had a fridge like that, she knew, things would be better for her. She wouldn't be feeling so tired and nervous about going back on the ward. Her head wouldn't be so scattered, keeping her from being as organised as she needed to be to make Denny feel calm and content. Her old nurse uniform wouldn't strain and pinch around the middle, like it had when she'd tried it on. And Troy would come home every night to a spotless, well-organised home, with a nutritious 'breakfast' waiting for him when he got up at twelve.

If only.

Instead, Frances was storing all her sliced veggies in plastic freezer bags and old takeaway containers dyed slightly yellow and greasy around the edges, as old takeaway containers always were. Could she and Troy possibly have eaten that much butter chicken?

Frances had allowed herself, also at the big indoor market, to buy a whole tray of mason jars for transporting the juice. But then she'd realised she needed a special kind of pen to write on them so she knew what each juice was. And then she needed some special elastic bands to seal the jars. The hospital was a twenty-minute drive from her house, so she definitely needed a Thermabag to transport the mason jars, and cold packs to go inside.

After she made her first test juice, it was immediately apparent that making enough mush for the detox in her old blender wasn't going to cut it. So she and Denny drove to Ding Lei, and she bought herself a Nutrimullet. Frances knew she'd have to keep it hidden away in the cupboard over the fridge, only bringing it out when Troy was at work or asleep. BUT, she reasoned, it would also be good for Denny's baby mush—so it was totally worth three hundred dollars.

All in all, with the fruit and veggies, the supplements and

accessories, Frances quietly calculated that the three-day cleanse was costing her around eight hundred dollars.

Lucky I'm back at work, she thought.

None of these purchases, though, or the hours Frances spent chopping and blending, could change the fact that shaking up a separated juice for 'lunch' at three a.m. was one of the most depressing things she'd done in a while.

***

It was remarkable how quiet the ward was at night. Lights were dimmed, and if the nurses spoke at all, they whispered. On this, Frances's first night, her patients were mostly asleep.

'That patient—' One of the other night nurses gestured towards a door that was open to reveal a pair of red brogues under a roughly unmade bed. 'She'll buzz you every two hours for pain meds. And sometimes more for you to take her downstairs for a smoke.' The night nurse pointed to another door. 'That guy in there, he's a complete sweetheart but he'll talk your ear off. Only go in there in the morning if you've got twenty minutes clear.' She nodded at an elderly man making his way back to his room very slowly, gingerly holding on to the wall. 'And him,' she said to Frances, 'he looks frail, but,' she made jazz hands, 'touchy-feely.'

Frances settled into the rhythm of the night shift quickly, enjoying the sense of knowing what was expected of her. She did early rounds of her patients, introducing herself and checking charts, and remembered what she'd always liked about nursing, why she'd chosen it in the first place: the people. She enjoyed the connection. She spoke to strangers easily, felt like she was a good reader of their characters, their needs. Nights were oddly intimate, looking in on people while they were sleeping. She knew that by the end of her first week, she'd have learnt who was a sound sleeper, who was struggling to push through pain, who was lonely, who was an insomniac. Frances had always loved that side of it.

But as she sculled her juice, her head began to swim. The familiar exhaustion washed over her.

'Sometimes, we'll have a lie-down on a free bed,' said Kim, one of the two other nurses on duty. 'You look like you might need it—you're not used to this yet. Just set an alarm on your phone for an hour...'

It was when Frances's head hit the hospital pillow that she suddenly realised: she hadn't thought about Denny once since she'd dropped him off with her mother at six. What a shit mum she was. She'd been so engrossed in trying to remember what she'd done before—who she was before—she'd completely let go of her 'new' life. *Who does that?*

Frances scrambled in her pocket for her phone—contraband but, come on—and saw she had two messages, one from her mum at about ten p.m.:

> Your son is an angel, we might get a good night's sleep.

Frances's first thought: *Are you kidding me? He's going to sleep well at your place?*

And one from Troy, sent an hour ago:

> Just got home. Hope drop-off okay, and no one stole your lunch on your first day back at school. xxxx

Stupid joke, thought Frances, in her humourless three a.m. state. *I haven't GOT any lunch, and you know that*.

She didn't reply to either text. But her stomach was turning over again. A headache was starting behind her eyes.

She couldn't believe she hadn't checked on Denny. Her sisters-in-law would be talking about the fact Frances had 'dropped and run'. Of course, she'd left him with a hulking bag full of 'essentials' and an epic list of specific instructions: warm bath at six-thirty; hold him softly in a darkened room for twenty minutes, rubbing his back and singing quietly; then put him down but stay by the cot, standing quietly, and give him fifty pats... But Frances knew her mum. She would have thrown that list in the bin the moment her daughter left: 'I've had four kids of my own. You don't think I can settle a baby?'

Frances really was a shitty mother. No wonder Denny cried all the time. Jesus.

She flicked her phone to The Goddess Project and looked, for what was possibly the eighth time that day, at the page about the Gurva retreat.

> Seven days to refresh, rebuild, regroup.
> Seven days to detox, reset, revive.
> Seven days to inspire, learn, grow (and shrink!).

Frances had been looking at the different packages for weeks. She didn't think she needed the Lose 5x5 deal, where you were guaranteed to lose five kilos while also taking five years off your face, with microdermabrasion, botox, fillers...

Frances's face wasn't her problem. At least, not her main problem. What she wanted was the Purify and Release Elleness Package.

> Over six days, you will go deep inside yourself to identify the exact things that are standing between you and your best life. You will look them in the eye, and you will ditch them, one by one: toxic people, the weight of expectation, your own physical boundaries, the foods that don't nourish you, the weight that literally keeps you from soaring.
>
> Meditation, twice-daily yoga practice, detox and two sessions on resilience with Elle herself will see you leave your week lighter, stronger, more determined than ever.
>
> It is possible to release yourself from

whatever you're letting contain you. You just need to commit.

Seven nights, six brimming days. Everything you need, just $3500, excl. flights.

Reading the description again, Frances felt exactly as she did whenever she saw those brown medicine bottles in WholeHealth: the ones labelled 'DESTRESS' or 'DETOX' or 'GLOW'. It was that easy—reach out and grab one, take it home, and the solution to everything that ails you could be right there, deliberately mass-manufactured to look homemade. It probably wouldn't be, but if you never picked up the bottle, you'd never know, and then you'd have to die wondering if the answers to all your troubles were in a $29.95 bottle of murky, bin-tasting potion.

Lying there on the hospital bed, stomach rumbling, head spinning, Frances felt like maybe the key to the Better Frances—the one who had the patience for a high-maintenance baby, the one who had sex with her husband, the one who was thinner, funnier, more energetic, a better mother, daughter, friend, wife, nurse... the key to all of that really could be a week out of real life, with double yoga, some sleep and two resilience sessions with Elle Campbell.

Shit, if Elle could pull her life around after all she'd been through, Frances should be able to cope with an uncomfortable encounter with an unhinged boss, a few months of sleepless nights and a few dented expectations, right?

The alarm Frances had set for an hour pinged softly and she jumped. Shit, this was her first night and she was already slacking. She leapt off the bed, went to the tiny sink and splashed her face, looking at it in the mirror as she patted herself with a towel she'd quickly have to toss into the laundry chute. She looked so tired, pale and red around the eyes. She looked a million miles from the women she followed on Instagram, all bronzy glow and bright white smiles. Even their hair seemed to have its own bouncy energy. Frances ran her hand over her unruly head, which truly looked like it had given up.

Kim's face appeared around the door. 'Come on,' she said, 'we've got rounds and it's not long till notes.' Then she noticed Frances's face. 'You okay? You handling it?'

'Yes, all good.' Frances moved out into the hall with Kim and headed towards the front desk for her patients' notes. 'Is it hard to get these Saturday shifts?' she asked Kim. 'I would think everyone would want them, with the one-and-a-half and double-time. Good money for one shift...'

'Yeah, you'd think,' said Kim, with the air of someone who'd been pocketing that good money for a long time and was unprepared to go back to working days for some mugs' wages, even if her body clock was shot and she hadn't had a date in two years. 'But there are so many mums coming back, and none of them want this shift. What's wrong with you that you do?' She was laughing a little, half-joking, as she said this, but she looked at Frances in a way that made it clear she did want to know.

'Oh, look, I have a goal,' said Frances. 'And a very thoughtful househusband.' She added the last part carefully. 'So, I'm really happy to make these Saturday-night-Sunday-morning things regular.'

'Maybe do a few more nights before you commit to that,' said Kim, picking up her boards. 'Can really mess with your head.'

Frances nodded kindly, but she was thinking, *I'll get to Gurva in four weeks if I can keep this shift*.

'Thanks, Kim, you've been so helpful,' she said, smiling. 'I'll try to keep it together.'

Four weeks.

CHAPTER 18

ADRIAN

Every morning Adrian woke up and reached for someone who wasn't there.

The screaming birds would stir him, and his erection would have him stretching across the bed before he was fully awake. And every morning, Adrian felt the pillow rather than his wife. Or, his wives. Either Elle or Abi had been there on most mornings of his adult life, but now, when he felt that handful of emptiness, he remembered, all at once, why those birds were so loud and where he was in the world.

Moments later, his boys would land on him, quite literally, screaming 'Dadddeeee!' and 'Brekkkkkie!' and 'Nooow!' And his first physical contact of the day would be wrestling them, rather than having sex with their mother.

Every morning, this thought occurred to him, so every day started with him thinking of Elle and her absence, whether he liked it or not.

He did not.

This morning, he'd reached across the bed to touch no

one, and the very next thought in his head was, *She'll be here tomorrow*.

Immediately followed by, *She's going to see me like this*.

Adrian couldn't quite decide how he felt about that. Part of him was proud of his new minimalist existence. He was strong and lean and unencumbered by stuff for the first time since his travelling days.

But also, he lived in his ex-wife's shed.

This wasn't where Adrian had seen himself living out the first year of his sixth decade.

In his 'Before' life, he'd thought of this place—Abi's farm—as a madhouse, as hell on earth, dirty and messy and loud and full of children and women and tears and drama.

He'd been right about all that, as it turned out. But what he hadn't known until he retreated here after the Blog-ahhs was that it was also a real home, a haven. And a great place to hide out.

The converted barn was sealed from the elements, tastefully whitewashed, practically fitted out—but still, sometimes when it rained he was overwhelmingly aware of the faint smell of sheep shit that would never, ever truly leave these walls. In summer the door was always open, protected only by a hanging curtain of beads in a futile attempt to keep out flies and mozzies. In the winter, he piled on the blankets and bought a fancy Dyson heater fan that blew valiantly into the large open space, knocking the arctic edge off by a degree or two.

The boys didn't sleep here. They were in the guestroom in the 'big house', but their presence was everywhere: in dirty finger-smears and footprints, in toys and discarded clothes on the floor, in the books and the unlikely number of balls that were always underfoot. They ran through the beads and between the two dwellings at breakneck speed many, many times each day, and they ran through the veggie garden, clambered over the fences into the paddocks, raced through the long grass and along the stony paths. Freddie and Teddy had been city kids eighteen months ago, who had no idea what to do with themselves without a screen in their hands. Now, they ran and ran; Adrian could only try to keep up.

Last week, in the city for the first time in over a year, he'd tried to see a way back into his old life. But there, in the traffic and the bustle and the rush, he could imagine himself striding through it, as he used to, in his designer suits, always somewhere to be, always rushing, and it was like looking at a stranger.

The way that he'd dealt with all of this—or rather, not dealt with it—didn't make any sense to his old self, and he knew it. His and Elle's Brighton house had been standing empty—exactly as he'd left it last August when he'd gone to throw things into bags for the boys—for over a year. Just sitting there, like the giant white elephant it was, while Adrian lived off his investments.

'It's worth... millions,' Abi would say, whenever she went through a phase of pushing him to make decisions about life.

'I know,' he'd reply. 'I'll get to it.'

He'd similarly disappeared on his job, his career, his friends, his world.

If he hadn't hastily resigned via text—*Dean, I'm sorry, mate, for everything. I just can't. I'm going to make things easy for you here and disappear. Full termination, no conditions. Happy for you to say you let me go.*—the firm where he'd worked for more than ten years would have fired him anyway. After all the publicity, they would have had no choice.

His boss and his colleagues and his football buddies called and texted and mailed for a while. And then they stopped.

They'd wanted an explanation. And they'd craved all the details. And Adrian hadn't felt—still didn't feel—like he could give them what they wanted.

Sometimes, trying to drop into a meditation, he would tick off the people he'd overtly lied to—his boss, his children, his *mother*—and try to limit the damage in his head.

So I told them a lie, this internal monologue went, *but*

mostly, I just went along with Elle's story. I didn't contradict her narrative, that's true, but I didn't go on TV talking about treatment, I didn't write a story on her blog, I didn't...

But the wave of mortification would not be held at bay. The shame of it. It was lessening, but it still stopped him from leaving the farm most days.

Because also, the children.

The worst moment of Adrian's life had come on the day after the Blog-ahhs, when he'd had to sit at that kitchen table in the Daylesford farmhouse and tell his daughters he did not have cancer.

'Under different circumstances,' Abi had joked, in her brutal Abi way, as they'd all sat down, 'this would be excellent news.'

Alex, younger but lighter, somehow, sat and listened to Adrian's stumbling explanation—'There is no excuse for this, I was out of my mind'—and when he had finished, she came and hugged him. 'This is still excellent news,' she said. 'I get to keep my dad.'

He could still feel the tears on her cheek to his.

Arden had looked at him with something closer to the way he was feeling about himself: disgust. 'I thought you were *dying*. You let us think that? And you did that... for *her*?'

'I did it for money, Arden. That's the hard truth of it. Elle and I had convinced ourselves that it would lead to more success for us all...'

'It's like they were sharing a psychosis,' Abi added helpfully.

'But you already have *money*,' Arden said.

And Adrian could only lay his hands flat on the table and admit, 'There's always more money, Arden.'

'She must be...' It was hard to know where Arden's sentence was going to end '...very smart. And very evil.'

'No one is evil, Arden,' Adrian replied, as Abi rolled her eyes. 'And I have to own my part in this. It's as much up to me as anyone else.'

'That is not true!' Alex, too big for such things, was curled on his knee by then.

Arden pushed back her chair and left the table.

The fallout from that gut-wrenching conversation was another thing that kept him here, always in his girls' sight, if they ever chose to look his way. Lucky for him, the boys were too little to hate him yet.

As for his mother, well, he knew she wasn't doing so well, but he still couldn't bring himself to see her, but he'd written her a letter that skirted around the edges of the truth:

> Circumstances have changed rather a lot, Mum, and there's some happy and unhappy news out of it. The happy news is that I am no longer ill, the second is that Elle and I are separating and I will be living in the country for a while.

She'd written back, of course:

> Well, your life just gets more complicated, Adrian. Please let me know when I can see the children, and why don't you and Abi use this opportunity to reconsider a reconciliation?

Abi had taken all four kids to see Bonnie a couple of times, but he couldn't face it. Really, he knew, he had a lot to thank Abi for.

***

Adrian got out of bed. The boys hadn't been on him yet—where were they? He stretched, pulled on an old grey T-shirt and climbed downstairs. He pushed open the barn door, and there they were, about to come in, armed with the longest wobbly sticks they could find.

'We going to poke you awake, Dada!' yelled three-year-old Freddie.

'Arghhhhhh!' Adrian let the boys poke him and whack him with their bendy twigs until he was tamed and in submission on the floor, a little boy in each arm.

There are benefits to everything, he told himself. *I would never have had the time to whack my children with sticks in my old life*.

Or possibly, his next one.

To keep him sane in the first months in Daylesford, he'd started his Manifesting Money blog anonymously. And at Grace's urging, he'd started going to a meditation class in town a couple of times a week. To the Old Adrian, meditation was a lot of lazy people sitting on their arses indulging in too much navel-gazing; to the new Adrian, trying to turn his mind 'off ' from its relentless flood of negativity was immensely appealing. And it also inspired an idea that he vaguely remembered from his rebellious youth.

'Good deeds attract good deeds, right?' he'd babbled to Abi and Grace at the dinner table that night.

'Hold the phone, Adrian's discovered karma.' Abi laughed. 'Watch out, buddy, because yours will be a doozy.'

'Very funny. Why is money any different? You do good things with your money, you save wisely, you invest cautiously, you fund ideas that come from positivity. You don't fling it at terrible people or crazy-greedy schemes or massively risky ideas... and you've got good money karma, am I right?'

'What the fuck are you talking about, Adrian?'

'An idea. What do you think of: "Manifesting Money—your guide to growing wealth with excellent karma"?'

'As what? The title of a movie starring the world's most boring actors?'

'Abi!' Grace scolded her, as only Grace could. 'I think that sounds like a great idea, Adrian, and a way to ease back into things.'

'I don't know,' Abi grumbled, 'people who love money

don't care about karma, they care about tripling their monthly income at any cost.'

'Spoken like a woman who has never really had to think about money,' Adrian snapped. 'Grace is right and I'm doing it.'

That was the night Adrian started his blog. It wasn't an enormous hit as it turned out that people who are interested in money do really care about tripling their monthly income at any cost. But it was his passion project, a slow build from the shed that helped him understand what he had to offer after what he would now always refer to as 'The Crash'.

Sample post titles on Manifesting Money:

Three ways to grow your savings without being boring

Seven ethical investments to help you make bank

How positive visualisation can bring about change in your pocket

Grace had been right, it made Adrian feel useful again. And now it was going to be a book. Thinking about that put a bounce in his step as he shepherded Teddy and Freddie into the kitchen for breakfast. Seeing Arden and River at the table readjusted his mood immediately.

'Hey there,' he said, cautiously.

Arden didn't answer; River nodded hello. Since the showdown over Arden's fake-tan video—which was, by all accounts, clocking up thousands of views an hour—not enough had changed in Adrian's opinion.

'Ground her,' he'd told Abi.

'Punish her for expressing sexuality? That's not good for a young woman's head.'

'Bullshit. We're punishing her for uploading an explicit video without talking to us first.'

'Again,' Abi insisted, 'not good messaging. I want you to calm the fuck down and consider what you are really, deep-down angry about here.'

'At least take the video down.'

'We have asked her to do that. It's up to her, ultimately, Adrian—it's her body, her choice.'

Sometimes, co-parenting with crunchy lesbians was exhausting.

Ever since he'd lunged for River at breakfast, Arden had refused to speak to him—except to tell him she 'would not be lectured about morals by a man who let his family think he was dying for a few extra dollars'.

And clearly, his explosion at River hadn't scared the boy, since he was still here.

'Can we,' Adrian said, as the little boys play-scuffled around his feet, 'not have THIS,' he gestured between River and Arden as he spoke, 'tomorrow, please?'

River shrugged. Arden too.

'One shit-fight at a time,' Adrian muttered, and went to fix the boys their breakfast.

The very idea of tomorrow was making him shaky. Maybe he and Elle should have met separately first, as Grace had suggested. But truly, the only reason to breathe the same air as that woman was for their boys.

He might wake up missing her, but the way he felt about Elle wasn't complicated. He hated her for what he'd become when he was with her. She had made him feel all-powerful, but it was a huge, ugly lie. When he thought back now to those years with Elle in that shiny cube—the middle-aged banker and his young, beautiful wife, he could laugh. Their children all over Instagram, the cars and the clothes and the live-in help. Who *was* that guy?

And the Adrian before that? The upstanding middleclass Balwyn husband of his uni-girlfriend, two pigtailed girls in private school, dinner parties every weekend, squash on Saturdays, and summers at the family beach house. Who was *that* guy?

And now, in the kitchen of his gay ex-wife's farmhouse, a homeless, barefoot single dad with a daughter naked on the internet and a divorce settlement looming... Was this him? Closer, at least?

Grace came into the kitchen carrying books, Otto at her side. 'Oh, are you two going to fight again?' the nine-year-old asked loudly, eyeing off Adrian and River.

River looked up, surprised.

'No!' Adrian said sharply, but quickly tried to follow it with a smile. He started putting breakfast bowls out for the boys.

Today, after breakfast, he was going to take them to a Steiner education playgroup in town. Then he might see if Alex wanted to come with them to look for yabbies in the creek. One of the blessings of The Crash, without a shadow of a doubt, was that he now knew his boys. He wasn't a perfect parent—he was frequently overwhelmed with the slog involved in getting them through every day—but he knew them. They were, despite everything, excellent little kids.

Their mother had left them, and they were okay.

In the first few weeks after Elle had vanished, the boys looked for her. They asked, of course, but mostly they looked. At every footfall, every doorhandle turn, they would look up expectedly, and then their faces would fall. The piercing pain of that time would stay with Adrian always, in memories of his two tiny boys learning to put on brave faces, learning not to look heartbroken every time reality reasserted itself: their mother was gone.

If anything was to be gained from tomorrow, it was strengthening that. He needed to let Elle see that the boys were fine without her. That it was time to make it official that they belonged with him.

And also, he wanted the answer to one big question. He

was consumed by shame about what they had done, but she was not; she had barely broken stride. *How?*

Grace knew what today was. What tomorrow was. She came up beside Adrian and gave him a hug. 'It's all going to be fine, you know,' she said. 'I can feel it.'

CHAPTER 19

ELLE

'So, I won.'

Elle was talking to Ben Bont and looking at Lake Daylesford through the picture window of one of the town's fancier hotels.

'Adrian agreed to the divorce going through?'

'Well, no. But the boys will be visiting us really soon. Isn't that the win?'

Ben went quiet. 'I knew I should have come with you.'

Elle lay back on the cushion-piled bed, one leg in the air. She was admiring the shoes she'd bought at Melbourne airport: sky-high, cream, calfskin. The very opposite of Byron Bay shoes.

'Ben, this was about my boys, wasn't it? About me seeing them, about them coming to Gurva, about them meeting their sister— '

'Elle, we've talked about this. That shouldn't even be a matter for discussion, it should be a given.' She could hear the sound of Sydney traffic—he was driving, agitated. 'We're getting married on New Year's Eve, so the most urgent thing is to get Adrian to agree to not contesting the divorce. We can then push it through in time.'

'I know, Ben, I know.' Elle lowered her leg. Turned her head to look at the view. 'But that part was harder than I expected. I think Adrian is still—'

'You're fucking kidding me,' Ben cut in. 'Are you going to tell me that after all this time, no contact, running off with your kids, and *ALMA*, for fuck's sake, he thinks he still has a chance?'

Elle rarely heard Ben Bont rattled. Firm, yes. Angry, yes. Controlling, certainly. But knocked off kilter like this? No. Useful to know.

'I know, Ben, it's ridiculous and I told him that.'

'Just go home, I'll see you there on Friday. Meanwhile I'll do what we should have done in the first place and just get Bron and the legal team onto Adrian. He'll have to get over himself. Where are you?'

'I'm at the hotel. It's nice,' she rolled onto her stomach. 'I wish you were here.'

He audibly exhaled. 'And Alma?'

'Next door with Ocean.'

'And what was it like out there?'

Elle slipped off her new shoes, then looked at the mud-covered Hunter gumboots she'd kicked off at door. 'It was... satisfying.'

***

Abi's farm was pretty, Elle would give her that, but compared to manicured, tropical Gurva, it was a dump, the country equivalent of the house on any suburban Australian street that has the beaten-up sofa on the porch and a car with its hood up in the driveway.

Elle had arrived in the Porsche SUV that Ben had arranged to collect her at the airport. It came with a driver, and Elle came with Nanny Ocean and Baby Alma. She'd told Ocean—a sunny, slightly clueless local girl who was proving very manageable—to stay in the car, that she would call her if needed. But, of course, feral Abi Black was the first person to come barrelling out of the house, half-running down the driveway.

'Elle!' For one awful, confusing moment, Elle thought Abi might hug her. But no, she padded, moccasin-footed, at pace before stopping an arm's length away and putting her hands on her hips. 'I'd say it's a pleasure, but we both know that's bullshit.'

Elle almost smiled. There wasn't much to like about Adrian's ex-wife, but their shared enthusiasm for confrontation was to be grudgingly admired.

'Abi,' Elle nodded, 'I appreciate your honesty, as ever.'

It had been more than eighteen months since that night when Abi, along with Elle's treacherous little sister Zoe, had conspired to publicly humiliate Elle at the Blog-ahhs. One of her enduring memories of the night was standing on that stage as her reality tilted and everything swam around her, and Abi's face, beaming, from the table where her father and brother also sat.

The image came back to Elle now, threatening to toss her off course. But she had chosen to come alone into this enemy territory for a reason, and she mustn't lose sight of it.

'Where are my boys?' she asked.

'We need to talk a bit before that reunion happens, Elle,' Abi said. Then she caught sight of the car at the top of the driveway. 'Oh, you have people with you! Who are they? Do they want to come in?' And she walked straight past Elle and down towards the car, waving at them. 'Nice car,' she said, over her shoulder. 'Who's paying for that, then?'

Elle, reluctantly, followed her. 'Abi. Don't take it upon yourself to worry about my... staff. I was just going to come and say hello before getting the baby—'

'Oh!' Abi had reached the Porsche, seen the baby capsule in the back. 'Your baby! A little girl, right? Can I cuddle?'

Elle found herself almost throwing her body between Abi and the car door, as Ocean stood back, looking alarmed. 'NO! You can't *cuddle*.' Elle started to unclip sleeping Alma from the car seat, struggled with the clasp and motioned for Ocean to step in.

Infuriatingly, Abi stood back observing that little exchange with a smug look. 'Tricky things, car seats, when you're not used to them.'

'It's a *HIRE CAR*, Abi,' said Elle, as Ocean easily unbuckled Alma, gently lifted her out of the seat and handed her to Elle. 'This is Ocean, she's our nanny. She came to help me with Alma while we all talk,' Elle said, nodding towards the young woman, cradling her baby under her chin. 'I thought my boys might like to meet their sister.'

'Hi, Ocean. Come on in, and bring...' Abi spoke loudly and nodded towards the driver, who was still in his seat, looking like he'd rather be anywhere else.

'Bertram,' he said quietly.

'Bring Bertram,' said Abi. 'You guys can sit in the garden and have a cuppa while we all get reacquainted.'

As the awkward quintet walked down the driveway to the farmhouse and its open kitchen door, Elle hissed, 'I didn't come all this godforsaken way to see you, Abi. I don't even know why you're here.'

'Well,' Abi said, mock brightly, 'let's see. This is my house. And Adrian and your sons do live here with us. And, as I'm sure you can imagine, over the past eighteen months Grace and I have become pretty invested in Ted and Fred's wellbeing, since we, you know, are raising them for you.'

As they walked, Elle carrying Alma, Ocean carrying the giant nappy bag, Bertram carrying a packet of cigarettes, Elle's eyes were scanning the garden, the house's windows, the barn coming up on her left.

Where were they? Where would they come from? Where would she see them first?

Despite herself, despite the promises she'd run through

her head over and over on the flight here—*Don't cry, don't be emotional, don't be weak, this was your choice, stand in your choice*—Elle's stomach was rolling. She felt her heart banging into her ribcage. She knew that as she spoke her voice would tremble, showing her anxiety and excitement and fear. 'Abi. I just want to see them.'

Elle could have sworn she saw Abi pause for a split second when she heard that, duck her head just a touch.

'I'm their mother,' Elle added.

'Wait here, one second,' Abi said. She took Bertram the driver—who must have been wondering what the hell was going on with this bullshit soap-opera he'd wandered into—by the arm, nodded for Ocean to follow, and led them around the side of the house, presumably to settle them somewhere with homemade matcha tea. It gave Elle a moment alone near the open farmhouse door, and she took a big step closer to it, trying to peer in.

If I live to be a hundred, Elle thought later, *I will never forget that sight, that minute*.

Freddie and Teddy were sitting at a hefty wooden kitchen table; Adrian was between them. They were engrossed in a card game—it looked like Snap—and their heads were lowered.

Everything rushed at Elle at once:

Their height—even sitting, she could tell how tall her boys had grown.

Their clothes—they looked like someone had dressed them to look 'smart', in short-sleeved collared shirts you'd never wear for playing around a farm, their hair combed as flat as you could manage with their wild black curls.

Their faces—Freddie had looked up and was laughing, his tiny hand over the little pile of cards on the table, his mouth wide open.

Elle lost her balance, just for a moment, and knocked the doorframe ever so slightly. Alma let out a soft cry, and the three heads at the kitchen table lifted and stared right at Elle and her baby, all at the same time.

For a moment, no one said anything. Adrian, Elle thought, looked good. He was tanned like a man who spent a lot of time outdoors; his hair was greyer, but also a little softer, curlier on top. He looked older, with more lines around his eyes, leaner through the shoulders, but he looked good.

'Hello,' Elle said from the doorway, because someone had to break this strange silence.

The boys kept staring at her.

Then Freddie turned his head to Adrian and asked, 'Is that Mummy?'

And Adrian nodded and ruffled Freddie's hair. 'Yes.'

And Freddie looked up at her again and said, 'Hi, Mummy. Who's the baby?'

And then Teddy burst into tears: big, heaving sobs straight away, as if from nowhere, and he turned his body into Adrian and wrapped his tiny arms around his daddy's waist, burying his face in his shirt.

And then a hand was on Elle's shoulder, and Abi Black was saying, 'I told you to wait outside. We needed to get them ready for this.'

And Adrian had his arms around both the boys and was muttering into Teddy's hair, and then he looked at Freddie. Smiling, Adrian turned to Elle and said, 'Hi, Elle.'

***

The best part of the entire day had come an hour after that, when Adrian had let the boys show her around Abi's grubby little property.

'That's where the pig lived, Mummy, but he died.'

'I think someone ate him.'

'This is our vegetable garden—we get to grow whatever we want there.'

'I grow mud.'

'This is where Sol and Otto let us tie them up when we capture them.'

'This is where Arden and River film us dancing like monsters.'

And so on. Elle wasn't interested in their stories, particularly—little boys twittering on about nonsense—but she enjoyed the feel of their hands in hers as they pulled her between veggie beds and climbing trees.

It was obvious, of course, that the boys were being allowed to run completely wild under Adrian's care, which was information worth filing away, but also that they seemed happy enough in an ignorance-is-bliss way.

They were still beautiful, her boys, she thought, looking at them as they kept trying to yank open a heavy gate to the field where 'Gracey' kept two Wookiees, which Elle could clearly see were alpacas. But they were not as they were when Elle was Instagramming them daily in their achingly hip little outfits: they were bigger, much scruffier, even with today's obvious grooming, and she couldn't imagine getting them to stand still again.

Adrian stood back near the door, mug in hand, watching them. Ocean had taken Alma off for a sleep—'I'll hold her,' Abi had offered, grinning; 'Not on your life,' Elle had answered—and Elle stepped gingerly through the mud, steeling herself for the conversation that had to come next.

'Boys! Come back, hey, it's time for Mummy and me to talk.' Adrian had obviously decided it couldn't wait anymore. 'Go and look at Mummy's fancy car,' he said to them, shooing them away. 'See if you can make it go.' Then he gestured for Elle to follow him, 'Abi has an eye on them,' and they went over to the converted barn a little way from the house.

Once they were inside, Elle could immediately tell this was where Adrian slept. How pathetic. How could he have ended up here? Elle was almost literally biting her tongue, knowing she needed Adrian's cooperation for the next part of her plan, but her disgust at how easily he had folded without her was hard to contain.

'So,' she said, looking up the wooden ladder where she

saw the edge of a bed on a high platform, 'this whole living situation is... interesting.'

'It's temporary,' Adrian replied, gesturing for her to sit at the table. 'Good for the boys to have family around at the moment.'

'Hm.'

Who's going to break the skin of this tension first? Elle wondered.

There were a million fights to be had here, so much poison to pour out once the veneer of politeness was pierced. He was furious with her, she knew, from the emails and texts he had sent in the early months of their separation. Furious that she'd publicly blamed him for their lie. Furious that she'd abandoned him so easily. Furious about the boys. Furious that she'd vanished and left him with so much mess to clean up. She could see all that—but really, just like those bawling, emotional messages, his fury was impotent. Because, she knew, he would never stoop to what he considered to be her level.

'So, where to start?' Adrian was going to go first. 'I see you have quite the new life. New business. New... partner.'

'New baby,' she added.

'New ring.' He nodded at her blue rock.

She touched it, twisting it inwards. 'And you?' she asked.

'I have a new business sprouting. It's taken me a while to work out where I want to go next, it's true, but the road has been built...'

'And a partner?'

Adrian laughed a little. 'No. Not interested. Been there, done that.'

'I doubt you're going to be a monk,' Elle said. 'Not your style.'

'Let's not go there, Elle.' He was steeling himself against her, she could tell. 'Let me know what you want to do about the boys.'

Elle breathed in, looked down at the table and then up at Adrian directly. 'You can keep them.'

Adrian seemed genuinely surprised. 'What?'

'They're obviously happy with you. I'm not an idiot, I know I walked away. That would go in your favour if we took it to court. Mind you,' she looked around pointedly, 'I think your living situation would go in mine.'

'So?' Shock had transitioned to suspicion. 'You're just going to... let it all go?'

'I want access,' Elle said. 'I want the boys to come visit me. I want the first time to be soon, and I want you to sign a clearance for them to appear on television with me, and in a magazine shoot.'

Adrian was shaking his head.

'Your name won't be mentioned in any of that,' she said. 'I want to be able to tell them we share custody, but in reality,' she twisted her ring again, 'I'll sign whatever your lawyer draws up so that you have full, uncontested custody, and I have visitation.'

'What else, Elle? It seems unlikely to me that you came here just to tell me that, knowing you as I do.' He was struggling to stay calm, Elle could tell, although her offer had definitely thrown him off balance.

'I want the house,' she said. 'That's it, financially. Just the Brighton house.'

Her tone told him she hadn't finished, and he knew it.

'And?'

'I want you to refuse to give me a divorce.'

Silence. Then, 'I'm sorry?'

'Between us, I want you to stall.' She gazed down at her ring. 'Not forever, but I need you to say you're going to contest it, say you're going to keep it tied up. Another six months, at least.'

'No, Elle,' Adrian stood up, 'I want this done. I need to be... free.' She could tell from his face he knew how trite that sounded.

'Free?' she asked. 'I thought you weren't seeing anyone.'

'This just needs to be over,' he said grimly. 'For me, for the boys, for all of us. We need it gone, sorted. We need to move on. You know, we've been separated long enough that we could be divorced in a month.'

Elle stood up too. 'Adrian, those are my terms. You want me to be gone, I'll be gone. I'll sign anything you want to make the property and the custody official, but I need you to do this one thing before I walk away from my sons. You know,' she motioned around the barn, 'it's not a lot to ask, stacked up against that. Another six months.'

A familiar look played around Adrian's eyes. Elle recognised it as defeat—the look he got when he saw she was right. She always was.

***

Abi Black turned up again as Elle was heading back to the car.

'Everything sorted?' she asked.

'Not that it's any of your business,' Elle said. 'But yes.'

'You said goodbye to the boys?'

'Again, not your business. But yes, I'm going to see them again in the morning before I fly.'

'Not here you're not,' Abi said gruffly. 'Today was enough.'

'No, not here—Adrian's bringing them to me.' Then Elle stopped on the driveway and turned to Abi to say what she'd been dying to say to her since she arrived. 'How's Arden? She's not here for me to say hi to? I really wanted to congratulate her on her streaming video going so well. So good for sales.'

Abi looked like Elle had slapped her. 'Stay away from Arden,' she said, walking towards Elle. 'I don't understand why you're in her life but get the fuck out.'

'Why would I?' Elle said, standing her ground. 'Your daughter wants me in. And who could be surprised? Who would want to be limited to... this hole.' She gave herself an internal high-five for the rattled look on Feral Abi's face in that moment, then wondered what she'd do if Abi didn't back down first. *Let's see*, she thought. 'No wonder Arden wants career guidance from someone more... professional than her mother.'

'Really, Elle?' asked Abi, her voice rising. 'Is this about professional advice? Not about you trying to market your crappy products using someone who isn't tainted by poisonous lies? Someone younger, cleaner, fresher?'

'Fresh isn't the word I'd use to describe anyone who lives here.' Something else occurred to Elle. 'Does Adrian know about Arden and me?'

The look on Abi's face let Elle know the answer was no.

'Well, that's very interesting,' Elle said, opening the car door and looking across to where Ocean was struggling to wheel the pram over the uneven path. 'But I think Arden might be the perfect person to accompany the boys up to Byron for their visit, don't you? And I think she would completely love to come.'

'That is *NOT* happening,' Abi spat.

'I think it is,' said Elle. 'I think the whole reason you emailed me is because you need to get Adrian out of your house—and maybe your big wedding depends on it?'

Again, Abi's face told her this was close to accurate. Jesus, Feral Abi would make the world's worst poker player.

'Thought so.' Elle twisted her blue diamond back around the right way. 'My wedding's meant to be the same day as yours. New Year's Eve is such a romantic date, isn't it? Of course, if that happens, it means Adrian has screwed up, and you're very probably stuck with him.'

Abi's confused expression gave Elle a lovely warm feeling. 'What the fuck are you talking about?'

'I'll tell you what—' Elle leant in and gave Abi an air kiss on the cheek, something that she knew would make Abi absolutely livid while she was powerless to fight, with Adrian and the boys watching on from the house. 'You mind your own business. And as for Arden's visit to Byron, we'll talk about it. Just us girls, doing the best by our kids, right?'

And with a big 'hurry up' wave to Ocean and Bertram, Elle got in the car and pulled the door shut.

Yes, 'satisfying' had definitely been the right word for the visit.

CHAPTER 20

ABI

Sydney might be the worst place in the world.

There was nothing Abi liked about it. The harbour and the beaches were all very nice for tourists, she thought, but the city seemed to have complete contempt for everyone who actually lived there, or anyone just trying to get from A to B.

Case in point: it had taken Abi an hour to cross town in an Uber that kept spiralling around the one-way city streets further and further from where she was going—the offices of the Surry Hills 'influencer marketing' agency where Elle's sister Zoe Wright worked. Now, according to Google Maps, Abi was there, but the building she was standing in front of offered no clue of that. Clearly, cool young people could just intuit that this was the right place to be. Well, Abi was forty-three and had six kids in her house; she didn't have time to be this kind of cool.

She banged into Twitter:

> Sydney can bite me. How does anyone live in this place? #takemebacktothefarm #lost

After the tweet, she texted Zoe, who immediately replied:

Saw your tweet, am on my way down, laughing.

Abi got a legitimate surge of joy at the sight of Zoe pushing through the giant wooden door onto the street. *There's my girl*, she thought to herself as she swept her into a bear hug, wrapping her in the layers of her floaty ethnic prints. 'There you fucking are, you little shit—I can't believe you left me for this dump!' she yelled, squeezing Zoe hard.

After the Blog-ahhs, Zoe had come back to the farm with Abi and Grace, Adrian and the boys, the whole crazy circus. She'd worked for Abi, managing her social media and rebranding The GD for several months before—from Abi's perspective—she abandoned her, moving to Sydney and taking a 'proper' job. If convincing Instagram-famous idiots to take cash-for-comment from a warehouse hot desk was indeed a proper job.

'I miss you! The kids all miss you! You need to come for Christmas. Grace will *die* if you're not at the wedding,' Abi was babbling as she held Zoe at arm's length and got a good look at her.

The country kid was gone, as far as Abi could see. Zoe had lost weight and learnt how to put on the kind of multi-layered, matte make-up Arden was always trying to perfect on YouTube, and she was wearing a baggy denim onesie, with... was that... socks and sandals?

'What are you wearing?' Abi asked. 'You could wear that to clean out the chook shed, if you lost the white socks.'

'Oh.' Zoe laughed. 'So this is what it's like to have a mother. Let's go and get a coffee.'

The first time Abi had met Zoe, she'd been responding to an intriguing email that offered up some damaging intel on Elle. They'd met at a coffee shop in a country town, where Zoe chain-smoked and explained her motives for wanting to knock her sister down a few pegs. Then they had eaten cake and hatched a plan.

Now, Zoe took Abi to a hole-in-the-wall cafe in a back alley of Surry Hills dominated by a complicated test-tube-and-beaker-style cold-drip coffee contraption and a blackboard that boasted kombucha brewed on the premises.

'They've taken everything from us,' Abi said, rolling her eyes at the sign. 'The hipsters have even stolen the mouldy bin-juice from us hippies. We have nothing left but the matcha.' When Zoe pointed to the matcha tea on the menu, Abi faked a swoon. 'Is nothing sacred?'

Zoe ordered Abi a chai and herself a green tea, and guided them to a dark booth at the back of the cave-like cafe. 'So why are you in Sydney, Abi? I thought you hated the place.'

'I have some meetings,' she lied. 'And I wanted to see you.' She took Zoe's hands across the table. 'Tell me everything.'

So Zoe told her about life in Sydney. How she was paying half her salary to live in a sunroom in a top-floor Bondi apartment with two other young women, how she worked ten-hour days and more from home, how it took her an hour to get to work most days because of the perpetual roadworks. How expensive it was to even go out for a beer, not that she drank beer anymore, no one did, and how dating was brutal here and she was on the verge of deleting all her hook-up apps because they made her depressed every time she opened them.

'I fucking love it,' she said. 'I'm having the time of my little life.'

'Sounds like it,' said Abi with a laugh. 'Tell me about the family.'

Zoe told her about how she'd been doing since her dad's death. The last time Abi had seen Zoe had been at the funeral—'I will never forget you were there, Abi,' she said—and how she was in sporadic touch with her dad's girlfriend, Pam—'She calls me every now and then to offer me something of Dad's, like his stubby-holder collection'—but how she could never see herself back in Thalwyn, the tiny country town she'd run away from as a teenager.

'The best thing to come out of all of *that*,' she said to Abi, and Abi instinctively knew she meant the furore around the Blog-ahhs, 'has been Liam. I have a brother now, one who isn't a dropkick. He's been living up in Newcastle with his partner and their kids, and he comes down to see me. Like, he might actually care. So, I feel like I have family there. It's... nice.'

'You have family in Daylesford too, you dickhead,' Abi said. 'Don't forget us.'

'As if I would,' Zoe assured her. 'Now, your turn, tell *me* everything.'

Abi struggled to know where to begin, so she started in the now: Elle's visit.

In the months since they'd seen each other, Abi and Zoe had communicated as everyone does, via social media. They were across each other's lives from Instagram posts and Facebook updates. Occasionally, Zoe would text to tell Abi when one of her posts missed the mark, or when something one of Abi's editorial team did was particularly good or bad: 'That would never have happened with the dream team.' Abi would respond with scathing commentary and often WhatsApp Zoe with cute photos of the kids.

So they were familiar with the milestones and the highlights of each other's lives, but not the events no one would have boasted about. Like when your ex-husband's evil ex-wife came to your house and hijacked your daughter.

Zoe was spluttering into her teeny-tiny coffee. 'You *saw* Elle?'

'Saw, spoke to, argued with, managed not to assault...'

'Jesus.'

'You've known what's been going on with her, haven't you? I can't believe that you, of all people, didn't tell me she was *back*.'

Zoe grimaced a little. 'I'm sorry. Really, I've been trying

to ignore her. Trying not to get sucked up by the negativity, because if I let myself...' And Zoe pulled her phone out of her onesie pocket, tap-tapped the screen a few times and turned it to Abi. An Insta account that, as far as Abi could see, was just a stream of screenshots. She took the phone from Zoe.

The account was called The Horrib-ELLE Truth, and Abi scrolled through screenshot after screenshot of comments, stories about Elle, and images of her content behind the paywall of The Goddess Project.

> Elle Campbell thinks that taking her name off the site that peddles her poisonous shit will fool us. We are not that dumb, Elle. Wherever you go, we'll hunt you down...
>
> That skinny slut has obviously moved on to someone else's husband now. Looks like she just pops out some babies to tie some poor sucker down every time she needs dollars.
>
> This $50 gold-dust powder she's flogging on her site is 95 per cent psyllium. Go get it from the health food shop for $10 and stop making this idiot rich.

'Woah.'

'You hadn't seen this? There are lots of them. Facebook too. And a Twitter account or two.'

'Are you... doing that?' Abi asked.

Abi didn't mind a bit of trolling argy-bargy; she'd been on both sides of that experience plenty of times. But since Arden had started putting herself out there, she'd become much more conservative about what to say online. Her followers and Elle's had gone hell for leather attacking each other before the Blog-ahhs, but these days Abi was all for a kinder, gentler internet, much to Grace's amusement.

'I'm mellowing on the trolling front myself,' she told Zoe.

'No, it's not me. And these accounts keep springing up, and getting closed down, but,' Zoe took her phone back, shut it off, 'I can lose hours on them if I'm having a bad day. Seriously, I get this kind of sick pleasure out of seeing these guys attack her, and then I feel disgusted with myself and kind of defensive about the fact she's my sister. And then I remember I might be her biggest troll of all... and—look, it's complicated.'

'It is, Zoe.' Abi patted her hand. 'She's an evil drain on the universe,' she said, trying to make her tone light, comic. 'But she's *your* evil drain on the universe.'

'Ha. So, how was she?'

'Well,' said Abi, taking a glug of her chai, 'you have a new niece, I assume you know that? She's pretty cute.'

'I've seen her hair on Instagram,' Zoe said, also trying for a smile. 'I guess that's the modern definition of "we're not close".'

'Elle has a super-rich boyfriend and a giant engagement ring,' Abi went on. 'Adrian isn't telling me much about what they talked about, but apparently there's a wedding planned and,' she paused again, 'Elle's happy for Adrian to have custody of the boys.'

Zoe looked like she was deciding whether or not she was shocked by that. She glanced up at Abi quickly, then shook her head and stared back at her coffee. 'That's not on Instagram.'

'And Adrian's pretty happy about that,' Abi told her. 'He's come a long way since you left. Has become a pretty good dad, really, even I have to admit. Mind you, he's had *a lot* of help.'

'Let's get out of here,' Zoe said suddenly. 'I want a cigarette.'

'So you haven't given that shit up yet?'

'Not yet.'

They got up, paid and went outside. Abi knew they must look like a weird couple in the hipster streets of Surry Hills as they walked towards a tiny triangular park squeezed between warehouses. It was already home to a small posse of smokers. Clearly it was where the exiled went to indulge in their poison.

'Anyway, Zoe, I didn't come here to tell you about that bit of it, really. Can we have dinner tonight? My shout. Will save you from your early twenties diet of cocktails and instant noodles.'

'Of course,' said Zoe, 'I'd fucking love that. Can we talk about stuff other than my insane sister?'

'Well.' Abi paused at the edge of the park. Zoe lit up her smoke under Abi's disapproving eye. *Actually, they wouldn't think we were a weird pair*, Abi thought. *They would just think I'm her mum*. 'Yes, but I need your help with one more Elle-related matter.'

'Ugh.' Zoe took a drag, and for a minute Abi could see, underneath the make-up and the ironic grey-blonde hair, that kid she'd met in Bendigo, the one who'd dragged herself out of more shitty situations than Abi had thought of yet, at twice her age. 'Go on.'

'It's Arden,' said Abi. 'I have no idea why, but she's working with Elle.'

'You mean, on her beauty vlog?'

'Sure, if that's what we're calling it. Her "vlog".'

'Why would she do that?'

'I don't know?' Abi rubbed her hands through her hair. 'Because she's sixteen and she hates me? To get back at her dad, who she's still furious with? Because she thinks that Elle is more help boosting her followers than her crusty mummy-blogger mum?'

'All interesting theories,' Zoe agreed, taking another drag.

'It could be all of the above, I don't know. But what I do know is that with teenagers, the more I tell her something's a bad idea, the more she thinks it's great. But she might listen to you. She always really liked you.'

'Okay, Abi, I'll talk to Arden.' Zoe stubbed out her cigarette on the edge of a rubbish bin. 'But just don't ask me to deep-dive too much on my crazy sister. She messes with my head.'

'Stay away from the hate-groups, idiot.' Abi hugged her—then as an afterthought said, 'Hey, do I have those too?'

'Really got to go, Abi!' said Zoe, laughing and returning the hug. 'I'll see you tonight. You owe me a giant ramen.'

'With healthy vegetables,' Abi insisted.

And she watched Zoe walk back to her warehouse office, bag swinging, looking like a confident young woman with her shit sorted out. Just as she did on her Instagram account.

CHAPTER 21
FRANCES

I cried at J's six-month injections yesterday and the doctor told me to toughen up!

That's terrible, you should report him. I bet it was a him.

It was. He said it wasn't about me! Thanks a lot, Doc. 😡

Well, I took Mavis for hers and I told the nurse that M liked me to play her music on the iPhone to distract her and she said they couldn't let babies watch iPhones on their premises—against state health guidelines!

Whaaaat?? Who are the parents around here?

Anyone else popping into clinic today for six-month check? Lulu's not 6m until next week but

I thought I'd get in early in case there's anything to worry about. 😔

I feel you. A mother's worrying is never done...

Frances's WhatsApp group was going nuts at seven on a Monday morning and she was still at work.

Her contraband phone kept vibrating in her pocket. She'd turned off the ringtone but needed to know if her mum might be calling about Denny, so kept the notifications on. And this morning the *buzz, buzz, buzz* just felt like someone was tapping on her shoulder and continually shouting in her face, 'YOUR BABY NEEDS YOU. YOU'RE DOING A SHIT JOB.'

'You okay, Frankie?' asked Kim, the more senior nurse, as she passed Frances at the computer station where she was updating notes on her overnight patients.

Unfortunately, there wasn't a box to tick for 'Irritating requests for snacks at three a.m., toilet trip needed at four a.m.'

'Yes, I'm good—just keen to get home to Denny today,' she said, as brightly as she could manage.

'Shit, I forgot to ask you. Dr Darling is doing his specialist rounds early today. He'll be here by eight a.m. and he put in a request with the unit manager on Friday that you stay around an extra half-hour? I think it's about Handsy Harry in room fifteen—he's one of Darling's.'

At the computer station, Frances's stomach plunged. 'Oh Kim, if I'd have known... Of course, but I have to pick up Denny right on time today, because my mum's got to visit her sister down in Jannali.'

'Oh, look, I'm sure it will keep,' said Kim. 'If there's something urgent Darling wants to know, I'm sure he can email you and you can update him tonight. It will all be in your notes anyway, right?'

'Yes, of course,' Frances answered quickly. 'I'll make sure Harry's notes are up to date.'

She couldn't log out of her shift fast enough.

It was her third week back on the job, and driving to her mum's place after her shift was still always a challenge. She was exhausted, her eyes swam and her head hurt. One morning, during the juice cleanse, she'd had to keep biting the insides of her cheek to stop herself from falling asleep at the wheel. Her mum had taken one look at her and instructed, 'Go and lie down. You're not putting baby in the car like that,' and Frances could have kissed her.

Now this was a little ritual. A cuddle with Denny and then an hour's lie-down for her before she took him home. There, she and Troy would sleep in shifts. She'd get home around ten a.m., he'd get up around twelve p.m. and then she'd crawl into bed and try to sleep until six p.m. when she'd get back in the car and drive Denny to her mother's in time for his bedtime and her 'breakfast'. Three days a week, she was barely seeing Denny, never seeing Troy and craving carbs at very odd hours.

Troy didn't work on Monday nights, though, so tonight she wouldn't have to make the dash back to her mum's. A slightly less crazy day to finish off her working week. A slightly less messed-up day for Denny. A day that presented a different problem for Frances: dinner with Troy.

She knew he wanted to talk about the budget. He knew that not all of her wages were going into their joint account. She'd been avoiding the issue, pleading ignorance, but today he was going to ask her right out, she just knew it.

But seriously, why the hell did Dr Darling want to see her?

Just the thought of him, now she was back at the hospital, made her feel nauseated and shaky. In her three weeks back, she'd avoided seeing a single specialist. They did their rounds with the patients during the day, of course, and emergency doctors were on-call if they were needed during the graveyard shift. For Frances, this was part of the appeal.

***

The last time she'd seen Dr Darling, Frances had been heavily pregnant.

Generally, nurses shared information about doctors: who was lovely, who was patronising, who was a downright bully. But Darling was new to the hospital and no such intel was available when he started working Frances's ward on her morning shift.

Immediately, he made her uncomfortable. He was friendly but always an inch too close. His eye contact always stayed a beat too long. Young for a specialist and reasonable-looking, he didn't fit the mould of a dirty old man, but there was something about him that unnerved her.

'Is his vibe off?' she asked Linley, not long after Darling had started.

'I haven't noticed. Maybe you've got a little married-lady crush on him?'

'Please!' Frances shook her head. 'That's gross.' But the comment made her self-conscious—certainly self-conscious enough to help shut her up.

It started when he made a comment about her weight. She was pregnant, but not so pregnant it was public knowledge. She was bringing Darling some notes for an elderly lady under his care, and it had taken her a minute longer than usual to print them out.

'That weight you've put on is slowing you down,' he said as she handed them to him.

Only they and the patient were in earshot at the time, and the woman hooted. 'Naughty, doctor! Young ladies don't care to be talked to like that these days!' But she was laughing, as Frances stood there, flushed, nauseated, mortified. Darling continued with the patient's consultation as if nothing had happened.

But it did, and it did again.

As her pregnancy became difficult to ignore, he passed her in the corridor one day and muttered, 'Nice udders you're growing.'

Another time, coming up behind her in the storage room, he leant in and whispered, 'Pregnant women are repulsive. You should be at home, so we don't have to look at you.'

What is it about me, Frances asked herself, *that lets him know he can get away with it?* What had signalled to him that despite the prominent harassment policies pinned on the inside of every door and the interminable annual training sessions, she wasn't going to report him?

I'm not someone who is rattled by idiots, Frances told herself. 'Feisty' was the word most often employed by her family, by friends, by Troy, to describe her, but the way Dr Darling made her feel—huge yet insignificant, conspicuously disgusting—gave her no space to be that person. Somehow he knew that with every word, every look, he pushed her deeper into a place she couldn't climb out of.

Frances had become very good at avoiding situations where she might be close to Darling. Linley thought her new 'clinginess' was to do with being pregnant. And perhaps it was—her body might be doing something powerful, but she had never felt so vulnerable.

However, the last time she'd seen Darling, Frances had let her guard down. She was in the tiny admin office, alone, waiting for the copier to print some records for a patient she was discharging. Suddenly he was in the room with her. But this time it wasn't words, it was hands. His hands were inside her uniform shirt, across her pregnant belly, trying to reach up to her breasts. His head was leaning into her neck, whispering, 'Those juicy hormones will mean you're enjoying this even more than usual, Graham.'

And then he was gone. It must have been seconds. And Frances stood there feeling his hands across her bare stomach, touching her *baby*. She could still feel the spot where his breath had hit her neck as if it had left a stain.

And all she could think was, *Why did I just stand here? Why did I let him do that?*

And then she vomited in the recycling-paper bin.

A few days later, Frances went on maternity leave. She hadn't seen him since. She told herself she was putting the whole thing down to a shitty work experience.

One she still hadn't told anyone—including her husband—about.

***

In the driver's seat on her way to collect Denny, she felt the nausea come back. The idea of Dr Darling even mentioning her name to Louisa, her supervisor, was tightening her chest. An image of him coming into the ward at night flashed into her head—his pale face peering around the storeroom door when she was alone, the whole floor silent, just the soft beeping of the machines and whispers of the other nurses at the far end of the corridor.

'STOP,' she said out loud to herself, banging her hands on the steering wheel. That wasn't going to happen.

She needed to bring her mind back to totting up the money she was hiding away for her trip to meet Elle. She'd managed, due to a last-minute cancellation, to join a group who were already heading to Gurva in the first week of December.

With flights, it all came to five thousand dollars. She didn't have anything near that yet, but she did have her secret credit card.

What she hadn't yet done was break the news to Troy. She ran through the conversation starters in her head:

'So, you know how you've been wondering where my new wages are going? Well, I have a surprise for you...'

'Troy, I think you might need to take a week off work...'

'Troy, I've made a big decision that I think is going to be the best thing for our family, and I need you to support me...'

That was it. That was the one.

She pulled into her mum's driveway.

Buzz. Buzz. Buzz.

Anyone else just crying at the idea their baby is six months old? Where did the time go?

I know! A lady at the park today told me Harry looked much older than six months, tho. Talk about fat-shaming a baby!

Frances picked up her phone and typed:

This group is making me anxious. I feel like I don't belong here anymore.

But she didn't send it. She deleted it and went with:

Is anyone else back at work yet? It's kicking my arse, I can tell you.

Silence. Not yet, obviously.
Typing bubbles popped up, then:

I'm going back next week! Just two days, terrified everything will fall apart.

Frances typed:

It will.

Then she felt a pang of guilt and added a winking emoji.
Suddenly her mum was at the car window. 'You want to come in and see this baby, or you going to sit there on your phone all morning?'
'Hi, Mum. I'm coming.' Frances got out and found herself hugging her mum, tight. 'Thanks so much, Mum, for being here for Denny.'
'What's the matter with you today? You have a bad night?'
'Yeah, little bit, Mum.'

'That's because you're trying to do too much,' her mum said. 'Always rushing somewhere. Gym, yoga, work... Come in for pastries.'

'Not eating pastry, Mum! You know that.' But she followed her mum into the house, the idea of holding little Denny putting some speed in her step. 'Mum, if I went away for a few days, would you be able to help Troy with Denny for a couple of extra nights?' she asked as they walked into a house full of the noise of grandchildren, the smells of baking, the morning chatter of her sisters-in-law.

'Ha!' her mum let out a short, fast laugh. 'And where are you off to?'

'You'd be surprised, Mum. Really.'

***

Surprised was *not* the word for Troy's reaction to the news that his wife was running away to Byron Bay for a week. Furious was closer.

'Frank. No.'

It was the other end of the day. They'd eaten a meal together (chicken breast and steamed veg) for the first and last time in a week, Denny was down, and Frances was about to pull on her uniform to go back to the hospital.

'Troy. You don't understand—I need this.'

'You don't need this, Frankie. No one needs this. It's what rich people do when they're tired of taking drugs. Believe me, I know. It's my boss's place—' He gestured at the open laptop where Frances had just shown him the Gurva site.

'Of course it is!' And before she could stop herself, she asked, 'Have you ever met Elle?' Looking at Troy's exasperated expression, she quickly realised this wasn't the moment.

'For fuck's sake, Frankie. These people are not *us*. They can afford to spend four thousand dollars on a week of yoga as if it's nothing. I don't know how many different ways to tell you this, but we can't—we work *for* those people.'

Five thousand, Frances thought. But what she said was, 'I just need it, Troy.'

Frances was so tired. She knew the night ahead of her would be tainted by whatever message Dr Darling had left; she knew when she got home in the morning she faced the task of resetting her body clock for the rest of the week. She knew that she would be parenting Denny alone for days while Troy worked and slept and recovered on the couch.

How was she here—like so many women she knew—standing on a sliding scale of never feeling enough or looking enough, of never being light and fun enough, or dark and interesting enough, of never having the hours in the day needed to be an excellent employee, perfect mum, sexy wife, skinny friend, wonderful nurse. How was she up to her neck in maternal drudgery and other people's shit?

She didn't understand why Troy couldn't see how much she needed to go away and try—just try—to uncover a side of herself that could be happy and carefree and healthy and caring. There was a reality of how a woman—a mother—could be that was just sitting on her Instagram account. Like Elle, like all those other women she was following. They were lithe and hot and smiling, and they were mothers and businesswomen and friends.

They had their shit together. Those women would have broken Dr Darling's arm, she knew it. She wanted to have her shit together too.

'Troy. I am going. I have to go. And seriously, while we're at it, two words: staff discount.'

'I am *not* getting you a discount to go and be brainwashed by some phoney guru!' Troy was shouting now. 'I just want you back.' Troy, who was always capable, always moving, always making something happen for someone, looked almost as broken as she did in this moment. 'I just want you back to being Frankie who was fun, who was funny. The one who wasn't always trying to change everything, the one who wasn't exhausted and crying. And the one who was responsible! Who understood we were trying to build something. I want that Frankie back.'

'She's not coming back, Troy,' Frances said. 'I've changed. You have to come with me, because I'm not coming back.'

CHAPTER 22

ELLE

Hunter gumboots and a white bikini seemed like the right kind of outfit for today's post.

> BIG ANNOUNCEMENT coming your way, Goddesses! It's the kind of news that makes a girl feel empowered, beautiful and loved, which is how you all deserve to feel. #blessed #gurva #farmlife #summerscoming

Elle's social media profile was bursting out of its shell. For more than a year now, she'd fed the beast purely behind her The Goddess Project paywall and via a private Insta account followed by twenty thousand loyal fans.

She and Matt and a couple of young retreat staff policed the comments obsessively. When she'd first come to Gurva, days after meeting Ben, and started putting her comeback plan into action, Elle knew that the scale of The Stylish Mumma was not an option. That site had closed down a week after the Blog-ahhs. On Facebook, after a few days of being flooded with abuse, its fifty thousand followers could no longer find it; on Instagram, it was gone.

But her database—drawn from loyal visitors to her blog who'd signed up so they could comment, and from her weekly newsletter—was the seed from which she grew The Goddess Project. She'd printed out the very first email she'd sent to all those people and put it in a little frame on her dressing table at Gurva. It reminded her that rebuilding was in her DNA.

Sender: goddess@goddessproject.com
Subject line: A word from Elle

Believers, I told you I would return.

I told you I would evolve past the people who tried to destroy me and my family. I told you I would get revenge.

I was wrong.

What has happened to me in the few months since our last word has been beyond evolution, beyond retribution. Beyond my wildest dreams.

It's been an awakening, a love story and a new beginning. And I want to share it with you.

Because what I've learnt since that dark night is that I have a mission—it's to live as the best version of myself, and to help you all to do the same.

I've made some changes, Believers, and they won't be for everyone. Not all of you who loved the inspiration of The Stylish Mumma will connect with the destination I've travelled to, or have the desire or the ability to tread the path I took to get here. It means letting go of a lot of what you cling to.

But if you are bold, and you want to look inside yourself and walk through this next chapter with me, I have made a place for us to meet.

It's not a place for strangers. It's a village. In my village there is only space for those who come with love and purpose.

So come and join me, true Believers, and help me build What Happens Next.

www.ProjectGoddess.com
Insta: ProjectGoddess
Snap: ProjectGoddess

This email went out to about fifty thousand people, and thirty thousand of them visited Project Goddess in the first hour. Plenty of them saw a paywall and pissed off. Ten thousand of them paid their dues.

The growth was slow but, as she told Matt, it didn't matter that the numbers were small, it mattered that these were her people—the people who would put their hands in their pockets and buy her merch, her goddess powders and her power-braid and her Glimmer tan. They were the rusted-on Goddesses.

The other advantage of the paywall and private accounts was that the extra barrier kept the trolls at bay. Even the journos at *The Daily Trail* were put off reporting daily on the antics of 'One Elle of a Liar' if they had to subscribe in order to rip off her latest blog post. For a little while, this lifted Elle out of the swamp of the digital news cycle.

But that was all about to change. As determined as Elle was not to become Mrs Ben Bont, she knew that going public with him at her side, with the protection of all his media friends, his armies of lawyers and his corporate clout, was the best possible way to do it.

So, today she was serving the world a full bikini shot and a view of her stunning farm.

Because Ben was not letting this wedding thing go.

'It doesn't matter what Adrian says, kitten, we are getting

married on New Year's Eve,' were his first words to her when he arrived at the farm after her trip to Daylesford.

Now when Elle heard the sound of Ben's plane circling, it sparked a pang of irritation, even as she and the staff were hurrying to make sure everything was in its perfect place. His arrival signalled her plunge in status from being the person who everyone asked things of—from menu choices to staff decisions to what the exact shade of the new yoga mats should be—to being another person checking that Mr Bont's needs were being met. And in her particular role, those needs were many.

Elle thought that Ben reasserting himself as the Lord of Gurva every time he landed had become more pronounced since he'd proposed. Her strong instinct was that if and when this wedding went ahead, her transition to 'the little woman' would be complete.

And Ben was determined it would. 'Legally, he doesn't have a leg to stand on. You guys have been separated over twelve months and you're not asking for a settlement, right?'

'I told him I wanted the house in Brighton,' Elle said. 'I pretty much built that house. It's mine.'

'Forget that,' Ben waved his hand dismissively. 'You don't need it.'

They were lying in bed, it was late, and their terrace doors were open to the valley and a stretch of starry sky. Ben had landed and come straight to the house to cuddle Alma and to fuck Elle, and then insisted on having their raw, organic dinner brought to the bedroom, where he instructed Mauna to light what seemed like a hundred candles.

Now it was just them, and Elle felt a pulse of exhaustion at the effort it took to constantly work out how to play every conversation. A lot was at stake now, and she couldn't let him wear her down.

She chose a professional angle. 'Ben, I need assets of my own. I'm not a child. It's money I made in my business that helped build that house. It's fair that it's mine.'

'You have assets of your own, kitten,' Ben said, turning her face to his and talking slowly, like she really was a child. 'Half of the retreat, that's how we set it up. And anyway...'

That's not enough, thought Elle. W*hat the hell have you done for the retreat?*

'I am going to look after you. The wedding agreement Bron is working on is more than generous, and I have houses, you know. And I want you in them with me.' He began kissing her again. 'I want my wife with me.'

That's the problem, thought Elle.

'Let Adrian keep the house. He just has to let you go.'

Elle changed tack. Pushing Ben off her, she slid on top of him and began stroking his face and shoulders. 'Adrian is blinded by jealousy,' she said, beginning to rock back and forth. 'He is not going to make anything easier for me to marry you. I don't think he's ready for me not to be his wife.'

'Tough.' Ben started to move too, his hands on her hips.

'Why don't we,' she kissed his neck, 'postpone the date, just by a couple of months, to give this thing space to breathe? I'm sure he'll come around.'

Ben Bont's face changed. From Elle's position above him, she saw irritation suddenly ripple across it. He bucked his body to toss her off, pulled himself above her and, with his face very close to hers, said, 'What I don't get is why you're not more upset about it.'

'What do you mean?' Elle tried to keep her tone light but she was surprised—Ben had never used his size and strength to intimidate her before. Is that what he was doing, or was he still playing? Why couldn't she read this moment?

'I mean,' said Ben, and his face wasn't playful, 'I don't want to wait for us to be married. New Year's Eve is perfect, we get to start the year truly fresh. Why don't you?'

'I do! Babe,' she hoped her laugh suggested this idea was ridiculous, 'of course I do. I just... I'm worried about what Adrian might do. He might stop me seeing the boys. And we've only just reconnected.' She came up onto her elbows, forcing a little distance, and looked at him. 'Ben, I want to be your wife so badly. The idea gives me butterflies. But my life is... complicated, and you know that, and I just wonder if it will be even more special if we wait and make sure everything is resolved and perfect.'

Elle could see he was trying to read her face, just as she was trying to read him.

He seemed to exhale a little, lying back flat on the bed next to her. 'Adrian is dragging his feet. Bron is calling him today. We'll see if we can't shake his tree a little, and then we'll regroup.'

The one hundred candles flickered, and the smell of jasmine drifted in from the deck.

Elle needed another eighteen months out of Ben Bont. It was beginning to look like a long time.

***

Everything was in motion for Ben and Elle's big reveal. The white bikini and Hunter gumboots were the first big hint.

They'd made a TV and magazine package deal with the publishing company owned by the Bont family's great friends the Hardlies, and it was guaranteed to be a friendly affair. After all, this was the first time Elle had subjected herself to any kind of questioning since the Blog-ahhs—since her stint as Australia's Most Talked About Woman.

The negotiations with *Fifty Minutes* had been robust, by all accounts. Ben and his legal team had got them to agree in the contract that there would be one question only about Elle's past: *Elle, what would you like to say to Australia about the allegations that you not only lied about your ex-husband's health, but also about your own father's death?*

Ben had given her a script of what to say in response, but Elle had no intention of following it. She knew better than he did how to present her brand.

In preparation for the shoot, the farm was getting a

touch-up. Floral arrangements were being ordered, the deck was being polished and Matt had organised for some hot-housed frangipanis to be dug into the beds behind the deck in order to create the perfect backdrop for the interview.

Elle's outfit—a floaty, virginal-looking white dress, bare feet, enormous rock—had been camera-tested. There was a slight panic that Baby Alma was developing a rash which might hang around for the shoot, so Ocean was applying an hourly derma-potion recommended by the Gurva skin gurus.

A new group of retreaters would be arriving the night before the film crew. The idea was that as well as conducting the interview, they would film Elle in action: leading her class, meeting with the people. *Laying on hands*, she thought.

Since the night they'd last discussed the wedding, Ben was being extra attentive to Elle, touching her every time they passed each other.

Planning the shoot reminded Elle that the first time she'd seen Ben Bont was in a feature story in *Winning* magazine, a since-defunct glossy newspaper supplement that specialised in obsessively styled shoots with Australia's most aspirational characters.

She'd been in the waiting room of her cosmetic dentist in Melbourne, which before the Blog-ahhs she'd visited every six weeks to top up her whitening. She could barely remember what had caused her to put down her phone to pick up *Winning*, but she remembered the photos of Ben in his office in Sydney with its harbour view, its standing desk and its balance board: *'I'm engaging my core while I do emails—it's an efficient use of my time.'*

She remembered the shots of a beautiful green getaway: *'My happy place, I only take very special people there.'*

She'd scanned the story for any useful business tips, finding very little original material: *'"Adapt or die" is the motto I live by. I need to be constantly moving something, growing something, changing something, smashing something.'*

And she remembered thinking that he sounded like a

whiny private schoolboy when he said: *'The thing is, money and success don't excite me so much these days. I've achieved everything I wanted to, really, with the hotels and the bars. What I'm craving now is a deeper connection with success—a personal challenge that will rock me. I'm up for change.'*

Clearly, that magazine story had stuck with her enough that, months later, in that beige western Sydney motel room, she'd googled his name. The very beginning of her new, big idea.

And now she was going to be on glossy pages next to him, pushing her business baby to the next level.

Don't get caught up in the negative here, Elle, she told herself sternly as she clicked Order on the outfits she'd chosen for the boys and Alma. *There is a reason you chose him. A reason you're here*.

Eyes on the prize. Adapt or die, indeed.

CHAPTER 23

ABI

'Well, Zoe, I love you, but clearly, whatever you said was an enormous fucking disaster.' Abi slapped the red button and threw her phone into the veggie garden. 'Fuck. Fuck. Fuck.'

'Abi, you know no one listens to voice messages anymore, right? You really should have texted that to Zoe.' It was eleven-year-old Sol at her elbow.

'I didn't know you were there,' Abi grumbled, putting a hand out to his head. 'Don't tell your mum about the "fucks".'

'I think she knows.' Sol smiled at her. 'She *has* met you before.'

'That's cute, Sol.' Abi mussed his hair and gently pushed him away. 'Now, can you go and find me some kids? The wedding woman's coming and we need to talk together.'

As Sol ran into the house, Abi returned to her fucks. 'Fuuuuuck!'

'Okay, I'm biting, what is it?' This time it was Adrian, from over at the door to the shed.

'Could you put a fucking shirt on once in a while?' Abi yelled at him. 'For fuck's sake.'

'I was trying to write,' Adrian said, apparently by way of explanation for his shirtless state. 'Is it our eldest daughter who's causing all this loud profanity?'

Abi looked at Adrian and thought how much, despite her avowed position as a pacifist, she would like to punch him in the face. 'This is all your fault,' she said, walking over to the shed. 'And I am going to kill you.'

'That seems extreme.'

'You have no idea what you did when you brought that fucking woman into our lives, do you?'

'Ah, I see.' Adrian's smile disappeared. 'I'll go and get a shirt on.'

'No, you fucking won't, because I have to tell you, Adrian, that I really need to yell at someone right now, and I think it's you. So you'd better stand there and take it and then tell me what the fuck we are going to do about our daughter being in cahoots with that... I'm not even going to call her a cunt. Cunts are powerful. She is just—'

'Abi—'

'It doesn't matter what you're going to say, Adrian. I know that woman did a fucking number on you. I know your heart is broken and your confidence is shattered and your dick is shrivelled and all the rest of it.' Shouting was already making Abi feel better. 'I know all that. And you are broken and we've all been fucking tiptoeing around you, trying to put you back together.'

'Abi. I'm not going to stand here—'

'Yes, you are. Because in half an hour the wedding woman is coming and she's going to talk to this fucking family about making our perfect day of joy and peace, and I am so full of rage right now that I could...' Abi looked around for something to smash. The only thing to hand was a homemade dreamcatcher Grace had been working on with Otto; a little pile of feathers and beads lying in the garden, soggy from the dew. Abi grabbed it and threw it at Adrian. The effect was less than dramatic, but the stringy feathers left a pleasing trail of watery mulch down his face. 'You're lucky that wasn't a bottle.'

Adrian wiped his face with his arm. 'Alright, Abi, is that it?'

'No, it's not fucking *IT*. Did you know that your wife has invited Arden to take the boys up to Byron for this fucking magazine shoot? And that Arden said *YES*? You are those boys' legal guardian—how are you not taking them?'

'I am not taking them,' Adrian answered quickly. 'I have no desire to see her, and anyway... you know it would become the story if I was there.'

'Then hire a fucking professional! Or get Her Highness to come down here and pick them up! It's bad enough that she's using your sons to peddle that fucking fake hippie shit that makes me want to stab myself in the eye with a spiraliser, but now she's dragging our daughter into all this? You know Arden thinks Elle's kind of cool, don't you?'

'How could Arden think that? After what she did—'

'To you, remember. What she did to *you*. Arden is fucking furious with you, in case you haven't noticed. And hating your parents and doing things to make them crazy is what you do when you're sixteen!' Abi looked around again, as if the answer to this mess was lying in the mud somewhere. Maybe she'd made a massive mistake not giving her girls more to rebel against; maybe all this 'anything-goes, actual real-life hippie stuff' hadn't given them enough to push back on.

'It's not actually my fault,' Adrian seemed to have found his voice, 'that Arden is obsessed with becoming famous on the internet. I mean, A, what sixteen-year-old doesn't want that, and B, her primary role model has built a life around it.'

'Are you talking about me?'

'Well, of course I am, Abi. None of this might have happened if you hadn't been so fixated on winning that award.'

How Adrian could say that with a straight face was completely beyond Abi, and her rage was pouring over into a maniacal laugh. 'Are you SHITTING ME?' she screamed. 'Are you?'

'*ABI!*' It was Grace, striding towards Adrian and Abi. 'Please stop yelling and swearing in the garden. Just stop. Whatever's going on, I don't think this is the way to solve it, do you?'

'What's going on is that this... dickhead, is packing up and getting out of our house. Right, Adrian? I'm sick of the sight of you. We broke up, remember? And now you're just dragging your depressing midlife-crisis drama around our home like a stinking dead dog.'

That was it—why hadn't she thought of it before? She could just throw Adrian out.

'Abi,' Grace put two hands on one of Abi's arms, 'stop it.'

Abi shook Grace off. 'He's happy for Arden to be marching off up to Elle's place on her own. He's practically pushing our daughter into her lap.'

Adrian rolled his eyes and turned to Grace. 'Don't you get sick of always being the adult in the room, Grace?'

She didn't say anything. She kept eye contact with Abi, shook her head.

'Don't you want him to leave, too?' Abi asked. 'Don't you want our life back to how it was?'

Grace still didn't say anything and, for a moment, she didn't move a muscle either. Then she shook her head again. 'No, Abi, I don't. Adrian is not our problem.'

'We have a problem?' Abi took a beat to decide if Grace was saying what she thought she was saying. 'We don't have a problem. Apart from him and all his shit.'

'I don't want to talk about this now,' said Grace. 'We'll talk later, when the celebrant's gone. But Abi, you are kidding yourself if you think the person addicted to drama around here is Adrian.'

***

The celebrant was already driving away by the time Arden returned from wherever she'd been hiding all day.

Abi immediately wrapped her daughter in a bear hug.

'Sorry I missed the celebrant, Mum,' Arden said. 'I thought you were mad with me.'

'I am,' said Abi. 'But everyone's mad at me, too, so you know...'

It had been Abi's idea to involve the whole family in the meeting with the celebrant to discuss their vows. She'd thought it would be a beautiful thing for everyone to have their say about the wedding—how it ran, what the vows were going to be. The kids had all been asked to write a suggested promise for Abi and Grace to make to each other in front of their 'village'—their family and friends.

'I think you should promise Abi that you will never, ever stop her from giving your sons chocolate again,' said Otto to his mum.

'No way,' said Grace.

'I think you should promise to stop locking yourselves away in your room on Sunday afternoons—it's getting embarrassing,' Alex offered.

'Not a chance,' returned Abi.

This was not how Abi had imagined this process. For starters, she hadn't expected that, an hour before their appointment, she and Grace would have a row so rare it had all the kids rattled.

She hadn't really imagined that Adrian and the boys would be sitting in, at Grace's insistence. 'They are as much a part of this family right now as anyone else,' she'd said, glaring at Abi to dare challenge her.

'I didn't write a vow,' Adrian offered to the table. 'But my suggestion would be "Try not to get divorced".'

And Abi hadn't planned that her eldest daughter, her 'best woman' on the day, would be AWOL, staging a mini-protest at her mother's ferocious disapproval of her travel plans.

So this is how it is, Abi thought, as she hugged Arden and watched Grace disappear into the house without a backwards look. *This is where the wedding turns to shit*.

'Mum. You know I love you, right?' Arden was speaking from Abi's armpit, where the bear hug had her pinned.

'Uh-oh,' Abi said. 'Nothing good comes after that as a start to a sentence. That's an historical fact.'

'It's just, I've been talking to River and we think...' Abi hoped her eye roll wasn't audible over Arden's head, 'that maybe you're feeling insecure. You know, about Elle, and me going up there, and you worrying that maybe I'm trying to replace you, or something...'

So much of parenting, Abi thought, was the particular pain of resisting the urge to slap your children. It starts when they're little, and they are insisting that shoes do, in fact, go on their hands, not their feet, and there are two minutes until you need to leave the house, and it's raining. And it evolves through the teenage years to a place like this—where your teenage daughter has been psychoanalysing you with her teenage boyfriend, and she presents you with a list of your shortcomings.

I didn't read this in fucking What to Expect When You're Expecting, thought Abi.

But also, you want your teenager to like you, because you suddenly have a keen sense that they have options if they decide they don't. Plus you know that if you push back on them, the ensuing argument will see you all shouting things that would really be better left unsaid.

'Well, that's interesting, darling, but I don't think I feel insecure. I think I feel angry at that woman for trying to destroy your dad.'

'But, like, isn't it maybe time to get past that?'

'Arden, it was kind of a big deal,' Abi said. But she was thinking, *Don't start a fight, don't start a fight*.

'Doesn't Grace always say we can never find peace without forgiveness? She used to tell me that all the time when Alex had done something heinous, like use my earbuds.'

'Well, look, maybe, but we all know...'

'We all know what?' Arden asked.

'That Grace is a better person than us.' Abi laughed, trying to make light of a statement that could have been taken in many ways.

'Are you two okay?' Arden asked. 'Please tell me you are.'

Abi's hug got tighter. 'We are. We're fine.'

She loosened her grip on her daughter and put an arm around her. 'Let's get Alex and go find something contraband to eat—like some spaghetti at the pub.'

'Are you going to keep trying to talk me out of going to Elle's?' Arden asked, as they walked towards the house.

'No,' Abi said, 'but there's going to be a very long list of conditions.'

And, she thought, *a little more company than you're expecting*.

***

Later, Abi was lying on her bed, her stomach full of complex carbs and regret. She was typing.

> My Dear GDs,
>
> I am growing. This last year has been a time of reinvention for me, and if that sounds familiar from a million aspirational blogs, those pale pink memes cluttering up your Instagram feed and every ad for a fad diet on your Facebook page, bear with me.
>
> I am not growing in a direction of acceptance and joy. No, as I get further into my fifth decade, I am growing in my intolerance of bullshit behaviour, of shitty charlatans, and of fake fame.
>
> I am growing in anger and righteousness.
>
> No one told me this would be the case but, as you get older, you have to put up with more (for example, my daughter is naked on the internet, but enough about that), and your ability to just keep smiling through it is actually diminished.

Women our age should be running the fucking world, because we just wouldn't put up with its shit.

BUT—I am also growing in where to put all that fury. I've been yelling at you guys for years to fuck the rules, live your life, tell your boss to stick it, do things your way. And I have grown to realise that yelling at everyone around me is not making them or me any happier, any more right or solving everyone's problems.

The hardest lesson that parenthood is teaching me right now is to swallow my instinct to lock my daughter in a bunker. I have wanted to do that since she was born. To keep her safe from every fucking thing in the entire world that might hurt, harm, limit or humiliate her.

But then I have to wrestle with that and ask, What am I protecting her for? What use is she if entirely unblemished but hidden away? Don't we need our kids—our girls, in particular—to be fucking OUT THERE, fixing things, doing things, building things, solving things, running, jumping, screwing, laughing? Isn't that what we made them for?

So, tonight, as I write this, I am growing. But also, I am asking, if I can't push all this righteous anger onto these people all around me, what do I do with it?

GDs? What do you do with it?

Yours in the very opposite of an inspirational meme,

ABI—THE GD

Abi closed her laptop and stretched back on the bed. She did have one idea of what to do with this pent-up passion. 'Gracey!' she yelled.

'Don't summon me like that.' Grace pushed through the door; she must have been right outside. *Perfect timing*, Abi thought. Although, Grace still seemed pissed. 'The boys are asleep and I'm not a dog.'

'We need to talk, don't we?' Abi reached out an arm for Grace. 'You look beautiful. Come here.'

'Abi, you can't flip straight from fight mode to seduction. We're not teenagers.'

'You make me feel like a teenager,' said Abi, rolling onto her belly. 'You always do. Look, I've made peace with Arden. Let's just forget it and get back to being us?'

'I'm happy that you and Arden are better,' Grace said. 'But how I'm feeling at the moment—like I'm at the very end of the list of all the people you're trying to "manage" right now—it's not very sexy, Abi. And it might take longer than fifteen minutes to fix.'

'Fifteen minutes? We've got all night...'

And then Abi's phone vibrated. And without thinking she reached for it.

'Finally, it's Zoe. What has she got to say for herself...?'

ABI—Arden's further gone that you think. We have a bigger problem. Call me when you can.

'Well, fuck, what now?' Abi asked Grace.

But when she looked up, Grace was gone.

CHAPTER 24
FRANCES

'That's not Elle,' Frances whispered to the young woman closest to her as they climbed off the white Gurva bus.

It certainly wasn't. The person waiting for them wasn't Ben Bont, either. He was a tall, good-looking, exceptionally buff trainer guy, wearing a sleeveless white tunic just like the driver's. He had tribal tatts from shoulder to wrist and looked for all the world like a resting Rugby League player.

'Hi, I'm Matt,' the guy said when all twelve of the people who'd been driven from the airport to the farm were standing in front of him expectantly, their hand luggage at their feet. A small posse of dreadlocked backpackers were unloading the big bags from the trailer—like a gaggle of crunchy Oompa Loompas, Frances thought.

Where was Elle?

'If you're wondering where Elle is,' Matt said, as if hearing her thoughts, 'you are going to be meeting with our Elle-ness guru a couple of times during your stay, but she isn't going to be looking after you the whole time you're here. As I'm sure you can all appreciate, she is a busy woman with a new baby, and she needs to protect her energy for planning the workshops you've come here to do, and for presenting the classes where she feels she can add the most value to your Gurva experience.'

There was an affirmative ripple across the group. 'It did say that in the fine print,' whispered the woman next to Frances pointedly. She was tall and blonde, wearing drop-crotch yoga pants, a crop top and a long, soft grey shawl. *Imagine flying in a crop top*, Frances had thought when she saw her at departures, *planes are so cold!* The blonde woman seemed to belong to the group of chattering, stretching young hipster women and two guys who clearly all knew each other. Her arms were covered in teeny-tiny triangular and circle tattoos that Frances had been trying to decode all the way from the airport.

These are Bondi people, thought Frances.

'So, the job of looking after you beautiful gurvis falls to me, and to our incredible retreat team here at Gurva,' Matt went on.

He speaks really well for such a boofhead-looking guy, Frances thought. He also smiled a lot more than most tattooed trainers she'd come across in her life.

'I'm going to leave it to these guys,' Matt motioned to the smiling Oompa Loompas, 'to get you checked in and take you to your cabins. Get sorted out, enjoy the little organic treats you'll find waiting there on your deck, and we will see you all this evening at the village hall for a quick tour, dinner and then at the barn, where you'll meet all the incredible gurus who'll guide you through Purify and Release retreat.' There were smiles and nods from the group. 'And if you fancy a sneaky pretox before your detox, we can push on with a few getting-to-know-you drinks tonight before things get serious tomorrow. Who knows, you might want to loosen up a little bit?'

A little 'whoop' ran through the crowd. Frances fumbled in her pocket for her phone—she needed to check on Denny.

'Excuse me, beautiful,' Matt cut in, immediately irritating Frances. Of all the people in this group, she was not the one to call 'beautiful'. 'No phones outside your cabin. There are dedicated social media times throughout the week when photos are allowed, but generally we encourage you to be in the now while you're at Gurva.'

Matt's perma-smile was getting a bit annoying already, but Frances just said, 'Sure, fine.' And put her phone away. Troy would be in no hurry to hear from her anyway.

***

'If you're absolutely determined to go, I'm going to make sure it doesn't bankrupt us,' Troy had finally said after several days of silent avoidance.

He'd called in a favour from one of Ben Bont's right-hand men, and a space was miraculously found for Frances on a week that was running even earlier than she'd planned, and at a discounted rate.

'This is *IT*, Frankie. The last of it. Come back fixed,' was how Troy had put it, as he booked the flights.

He didn't know, of course, that the money saved on the discount was almost entirely negated when, faced with the idea of meeting Elle Campbell in her baggy old work-out clothes, Frances bought a whole new yoga wardrobe on the secret credit card. *I'll worry about that later*, she thought.

'I need three nights off,' she'd told Louisa the unit manager. 'I know I've just started back, but it's for health reasons. And I can get someone to cover my shifts!'

To an unimpressed Linley she'd said, 'This is a once-in–a-lifetime chance for your stressed-out friend to do some self-care. Will you cover my shifts, will you, will you, will you? I'll love you forever. Will you? Will you?'

To her nonplussed mother she'd said, 'Mum, Troy is going to need your help. I know you won't understand why I need to go, but I need to go. Yes, I know you think I'm a terrible parent.'

To Denny, she'd whispered, 'I'm going to come back a better mum. I swear it. You just hold on until I'm home.'

And in response to a message left on her notes at the hospital from Dr Elliot Darling, she'd typed:

> *Apologies, Dr Darling, I can't help you with your enquiry about Mr Harcott, or any other patients. I am only the night cover and I suggest that you look at the detailed notes left on his and all other patients' files. Thank you.*

And she had got on a plane for a week off from her life.

***

Frances hadn't really known what to expect from Gurva. She'd never been to the north coast before. When she was a kid, family holidays were camping with all the aunts and uncles somewhere an easy drive from Sydney—down at Kiama or up at The Entrance. And back when she and Troy could afford a break they'd gone to Bali; for the honeymoon, they'd splurged on Fiji.

It was so green up here, and so hot. The 'hinterland', as she'd heard it was called, was inland but you could smell the ocean, sense it in the damp air. The cabins for retreaters looked like they'd been lifted from a desert island, complete with thatched rooves and decks that came with a Gurva yoga mat and a 'meditation' lounger. She had her hut all to herself; inside, the bed was big and white and spotless. The sight of it made her long for sleep, which would be a holiday in itself. That and a bed she didn't have to make, food she didn't have to cook.

On the bed was a thick matte folder with an introductory letter from Elle— '*Welcome to our home, where I hope some of the magic of the hinterland will seep into your bones... By the end of this week you will understand how this place healed me, how it made me whole again'*—a class timetable, a map, booking forms for the spa, a rundown of all the merchandise available for sale at the gift shop, and a full menu of the food they would (and wouldn't) be eating this week.

There was also a white cotton robe, and bamboo slippers, and a glass juice-and-water bottle with its own copper straw—'Bring me with you,' read a cute little handwritten tag around its neck.

To Frances it all felt overwhelmingly luxurious, and for the first time in a long while she felt hopeful, excited, positive. And knackered. She pulled on her robe, set an alarm for five-thirty p.m. and curled into the bed's stiff sheets.

***

Later, when she looked back at that disastrous first night at Gurva, Frances decided things started to go wrong when she was late to dinner.

She was so deep in the unfamiliar ocean of uninterrupted sleep that when her phone alarm beeped, she rolled over, turned it off and slept some more.

It was seven p.m. when she burst into the 'village hall' to see all the retreaters—the twelve Bondi people from her flight plus a handful of others she hadn't seen before—tucking into the vegan buffet. The hall was a big white barn with a stage at one end and an open kitchen area at the other, where some of the Oompa Loompas were busy chopping and steaming. The food was laid out on a white wooden table down one wall. It all looked as though Frances's Instagram feed had come to life and spread itself out in front of her.

'Did I miss the tour?' Frances asked the startlingly young-looking girl she'd sat next to at the first empty spot she found, in the middle of one of the long communal tables.

'Yes,' the girl said, 'but there's not much to it—you'll get the gist. It's beautiful, but quite a lot of it's closed off to people on the retreat.'

'Oh,' Frances said, confused. 'Aren't you on the retreat?'

'Oh no, I'm just visiting,' said the girl. 'I'm joining in with a few things while I'm here.'

'Are you on your own?' Frances asked.

But before the girl could answer, that Matt guy had come into the hall. 'Hello, again, everyone,' he said loudly. 'Hope you're enjoying the feed.'

Frances looked around for where she could get a plate. She'd feel like such a dick walking up there so long after everyone else.

'Remember, your detox starts tomorrow, and there'll be no solids for three days. THREE DAYS, guys. Three days to set you free, three days to wake you up. So, make the most of this vegan feast while you can!'

A lot of the retreaters cheered. Who were all these people? Frances wasn't used to going places alone; she'd never had to. The visibility of being a solo traveller was new to her, but also, she hadn't expected that Elle's disciples would be these women—so assured, so confident, so celebratory. Out of their Lululemon and into their floaty boho dresses for dinner, they didn't look like they needed purifying and releasing—they looked like they were ready to party.

Frances had tried to go back to her conversation with the young girl next to her, but she was already deep in conversation with the woman on her other side. 'Yes, I'm a vlogger,' Frances heard the girl saying. 'I'm hoping I might get a little series out of this trip.'

Frances self-consciously lifted herself out of her chair and approached the buffet table in search of a plate and some food to put on it.

'You on your own?' The woman who tapped her elbow looked familiar from the flight: dark and petite with a hairstyle that was shaved underneath and clipped back on top—she was definitely one of the Bondi people.

Frances nodded. 'You?'

'Oh no, I'm with these guys,' said the woman, waving

towards the long table. 'We're on a hens. We thought we would probably be on our own at Gurva but I guess they can always squeeze in a few more, right?' She laughed, tapping Frances on the arm, an indication that she was one of the people being squeezed in. Which was, in fact, true.

'Um, a... hens'?' *Who the hell goes on a juice-cleanse yoga retreat for a hens' party?* Linley and Frances's sisters-in-law had made her go on a cruise with strippers. No juice had been consumed, at least not without vodka in it.

'You know how it is,' the woman said, taking a plate from where they were stacked on a shelf below the table—of course! 'We're all so sick of partying. It's been ten years of *that* kind of girls' do, it feels so tragic these days. We thought we'd have something for Sal that reflects where we're at now. She's a mad Elle fan. Mind you,' she gave Frances a wink, 'tonight doesn't count, right?'

'And those... boys?' Frances looked at the two men in the Bondi party, who were deep in conversation with the bride and another woman, all laughing uproariously.

'Oh, they're the happiest of hens, believe me. Bigger girls than the rest of us, really.' The woman glanced up from stacking her plate with sweet potato wedges to wink at Frances again. 'Better to line the stomach, am I right?'

With hindsight, that was the second sign.

After dinner, Matt rounded up the retreaters and took them to meet the experts in the 'barn' he'd mentioned on their arrival. This just turned out to be a bar, where organic vodka was served over giant, singular ice cubes.

Frances hadn't had a drink in more than a year. *This trip is too important to fuck up with a hangover*, she told herself. *There's too much at stake here*. But she found herself agreeing to at least hold one of the heavy glasses, so she didn't look too out of place. An older woman was walking around in floaty robes with the smallest gong Frances had ever seen. Matt introduced her as Guru Gwendi, the meditation teacher. He was walking his team between different guests while loud music played and shots began to flow.

'I'm Frances,' she said to gong lady. 'I've never done meditation and I absolutely can't wait.'

Guru Gwendi tapped her teeny gong. 'So sorry, blessed soul, got to move along, but I *sooo* look forward to having your sweet face in my class.'

Next Frances found herself getting the hard sell for microdermabrasion on her face by his-and-hers dermatologists from Byron. 'It would really wake you up,' said one.

'It would just get rid of all this—' And the woman actually rubbed her finger hard in between Frances's eyebrows, as if erasing her frown wrinkle.

'And some of this,' said her partner, pinching loose skin at Frances's jawline.

'Oh, thank you, I'll think about it,' Frances said.

By now, the music was too loud for any kind of conversation. She could see that the experts were leaving and some of the young Oompa Loompas were coming in.

She was feeling sorry for herself and thinking about leaving to go back to her cabin, sit on her deck and call her mum to check on Denny. Somehow, that seemed sadder than staying here.

Frances looked at the melting ice cube in her glass—a puddle of vodka being watered down. She took a sip. Looking around, she saw the Bondi bride and her friends were far beyond their first sip of booze. They were leaning over the bar, talking and laughing with the young Swedish backpacker serving the drinks. The other staff—all handsome young men—had joined them. The place was getting louder, the laughter competing with the music.

Why couldn't Frances feel like that anymore? And what were all these happy, skinny, party-animal bitches doing at the peaceful retreat she'd coveted for so long?

She took another glug of her drink, and its impact felt almost immediate. After the burning sensation in her throat, a warmth spread through her chest. *Pull yourself together, Frankie. You can have a couple of drinks and talk to some strangers—this is your holiday from life, remember?*

Looking around for someone to approach for a chat, she saw the young girl from dinner in the corner. Matt was talking to her, and the way their heads were tilted together it looked like an intense, serious conversation. Maybe he was hassling her? Just as Frances went over to see, the girl threw her head back to laugh, and something about her eyes as she did that told Frances she'd been drinking. Surely she was way too young to be drinking with that guy?

'Dance with me!' It was the dark-haired woman from the buffet. She was grabbing Frances by the waist from behind, pulling her to the tiny dancefloor as old-school Madonna pumped out of the speakers. 'We don't like seeing you on your own. You can dance with me!'

Frances noticed, with a touch of alarm, that the bride was up on what looked like a podium, pumping her arms madly.

'Pretox! Pretox! Pretox!' the women were chanting, and the young men were laughing, and someone was handing out shots.

And Frances took one and threw it down. *Jesus*. That had been a long time.

Her next clear snapshot of the night was of the dark-haired woman—Frances thought she was probably called Jess. Or Jesh? That's what it sounded like over the music. Jesh was a fucking excellent dancer, and Frances was remembering how much she'd loved to dance too. Wow. Another thing that had been gone too long.

'You're a mum, aren't you?' Jesh yelled at her, eyes wide and wild. 'I can tell. Mums are always the fucking craziest when you're out.' And she nodded towards the bride friend who was still manning the podium, her floaty white dress undone to the waist, expensive lacy bra showing as she twisted, a young male Oompa Loompa precariously dancing alongside her.

Frances didn't think she was *that* crazy, but Jesh's comment made her self-conscious about her dancing.

She looked around the room and saw that Matt was standing by the door, water bottle in hand, watching everyone. She looked for the young girl but couldn't see her anywhere.

'Loo!' she yelled at Jesh. 'Going to the loo!'

'It's outside!' Jesh yelled back, grinning madly.

It was so hot in there now, and Frances was pushing through the bodies in the tiny space towards the door. 'You okay?' Matt asked when she got there.

'Yes, just need some air.' She was hot, sweating, a little bit dizzy.

'You're the one with the husband who works for Bont, right?' Matt shouted over the noise, as she reached for the doorhandle.

Oh. He knew who she was. Frances smiled broadly, pushed a sweaty strand of hair off her forehead. 'Yes!' she yelled. 'I'm France... Frankie.'

'Hi, Frankie. Hey,' Matt turned his back to the room and pulled her in, so there was only him and her in the space before the door, 'since you're a friend of the family, you can have one of these on the house. These girls have spent plenty.' Matt turned his palm up to show Frances a little plastic bag, like the ones she froze Denny's baby mush in when she ranoutof containers. In the plastic bag were capsules, like paracetamols, but with a browny-grey powder inside. She knew they weren't paracetamols.

Jesus.

'No thanks, Matt,' Frances said. She knew enough about being around these kinds of guys—some of Troy's dickhead workmates—not to betray any shock. She banged him on the arm with her fist as if they were mates. 'I really am here for the detox.'

He looked at her, shrugged, put the baggie back in his pocket and turned back towards the room, the dancing, the noise, the heat.

Frances put her hand on the doorhandle again, ready to push into the cool air outside. Then she paused. 'Where's the kid?' she yelled.

'What kid?' Matt glanced down at her, a moment of irritation on his face.

'The young girl you were talking to?'

'Oh, Arden.' He shrugged again. 'Don't know. Probably went to the dunny.'

Frances pushed through to the outside.

She took three steps and it was incredible, the noise had disappeared almost entirely. She was outside, in the dark, in the country. Just cicadas and the odd frog croaking. The air was gorgeous. Her head was clearing. No more drinks.

This was really *not* what she'd been expecting from her first night at a health retreat.

Frances looked around for a sign to the toilets, and then remembered they were fifty metres away, in the village hall building. A rough path led down to it. She looked up as she walked and saw, for the first time, the big veranda-wrapped farmhouse perched on top of the hill, lights blazing. It was beautiful, even from here.

Elle's in there, Frances thought, and she wondered if the boss knew about the carnage going on down here in the bar. Surely not—it wasn't very 'Elle-ness'. *I should dob that Matt guy in to Ben Bont*, Frances was thinking as she followed the path down to the hall, only a tiny bit unsteady on her feet. *I bet he wouldn't want Gurva's reputation damaged by a dodgy employee.*

As she got closer to the building, the sensor light on top of the hall flicked on. Something was blocking the path just a few steps up ahead. Another few steps forwards, and there was no doubt it wasn't a 'something'—it was a 'someone'.

Nurse mode, nurse mode, Frances told herself. 'Help!' she yelled as loudly as she could into the quiet country night as she ran towards the body. 'Help!'

As soon as she crouched down to reach for the pulse of

the person on the path, it was obvious who it was. She was tiny, with a mess of dyed black hair, shorty denim overalls and clumpy black boots.

It was the teenager. It was Arden.

CHAPTER 25

ZOE

'They're not going to open their wallet for ten thousand followers, friend, no matter how good your bum is.'

'We can put the kitchen brief out to a hundred mums, but you know there are only two who are really going to deliver. Most of their houses are much too relatable.'

'Does the client want "healthy skinny" or "people are worried about you" skinny?'

Zoe was getting used to the way people talked at her new job, but today she was finding it hard to concentrate.

She was meant to be finishing a roll-out plan for a campaign to sell dry shampoo for dogs, via the country's fifteen top animal influencers—many of whom made more money than their human owners did in their day jobs—but she kept being distracted by The Horrib-ELLE Truth Facebook page, which was pinging every few minutes with a new entry. It was a busy day in Elle Campbell-hating land.

> So Elle Idiot is going to be featured on *Fifty Minutes* on Sunday night? Did she learn nothing the last time she lied her arse off on national TV?

Word is that Evil Elle is going to be announcing she's marrying a millionaire playboy. I assume his life insurance has just been renewed.

Surely there should be a law against that f-ing criminal making money on a TV deal? I feel a boycott coming on...

Zoe knew she had to turn these notifications off. *My sister's like a fucking sickness*, she thought.

For the first time, with her new life in Sydney, Zoe felt kind of normal. Frequently overwhelmed with anxiety that she wasn't cool enough to be working where she worked, living where she lived, drinking where she drank, but normal. The more time she spent with the seemingly cool kids she'd met in Sydney, she discovered that mostly they felt that way too, even if they were born here.

Really, Zoe couldn't fathom being from a place like Sydney. What must that feel like, how different must your personality be, if you were born in the middle of everything, rather than constantly suspecting you were missing out, that you were in the wrong place? But then, what did these people know about how it felt to grow up where she had, how she had, with neither money nor a mother? And basically to have to hope that some loser boyfriend was your ticket out, as Zoe had until she'd found a better way.

A better way thanks to Abi Black. And also, she had to grudgingly admit, thanks to her awful sister. Elle, after all, had been the test case for escape—she'd got out of Thalwyn and away from Dad and their brothers as soon as she was physically able. And Elle had taught Zoe the basics of what was now her full-time job: social media and influence.

I can't help myself, I'm going to hate-watch that shit. The trailer's dropping tomorrow and

I shouldn't admit it but—I'm addicted. I've almost missed seeing the psycho on my TV.

I've lost three family members to cancer and I will NEVER forgive EE (Evil Elle) for lying about the disease. Cancer is not something to fuck about with. #burninhell

I wonder if she's sticking to her story about her ex-hubby lying to her? Why else would some other poor sucker want to marry that?

Zoe closed the feed on her phone; considered putting it away in a drawer. But that was deviant behaviour in a workplace like hers. This was not somewhere you'd ever be frowned upon for being on your phone—being on your phone was your job.

Double-tap, Like, Share.

After she'd spent more than six months working on The Green Diva with Abi in Daylesford, when Zoe had packed her duffle bag for Sydney and a proper role in an actual office, Abi had been indignant. 'What the fuck is Influencer Marketing? What does an Influencer Marketing Agency actually do?' Abi sounded exactly like a petulant child who didn't want her friend to go and play with the kids next door.

'They match up influencers—like you, Abi, but probably a bit less... controversial—with companies who want them to promote stuff.'

'Ugh. Don't call me an... influencer,' said Abi, with an exaggerated shudder. 'Also, we do that all the time.' Since the awards and the rebrand of The GD, thanks in large part to Zoe, brands that wanted to reach a certain 'ethically concerned mother' demographic had been doing plenty of deals with Abi.

Abi was a business now, strange as that seemed.

She was also still completely crazy. Over ramen the other night, she'd ranted and raved about trying to get Adrian out of her shed, trying to get Arden off YouTube, trying to get Grace to agree to a TV deal for the wedding, and all the while Zoe had sat there slurping her free noodles and knowing that Abi lived for this kind of chaos.

Still, the stuff with Arden was really fucking weird. As Zoe had told Abi on the phone last night, it seemed like Elle and Arden had more planned together than that first naked fake tan clip. On her site, Elle was talking about a partnership with a very exciting and risqué protégé of hers who was going to help bring The Goddess Project to a new market.

And now Zoe knew Abi hadn't talked Arden out of going to Byron. She knew—because tomorrow, Zoe and Abi were going up there after her.

Into the fucking lioness's den.

As much as Zoe loathed what her sister had done to her family, she couldn't help feeling guilt for a lot of the shit that had come after. She, after all, had convinced her father and brother to travel to Sydney to expose Elle in the most public way possible. And now, with the prospect of driving back into her orbit, Zoe felt genuinely nauseated, her stomach awash with an acidic mixture of guilt, fear and a pang of pleasure.

The pleasure at how it had felt to show her sister: *Don't you dismiss me, us. Don't you treat us like we don't fucking matter*. And guilt because, really, what had this achieved? Their dad was dead, two out of three brothers didn't speak to her, and her sister seemed to be gathering strength up there on bullshit hippie millionaire's row. And fear because, well, Elle was terrifying.

Yeah, Zoe, that worked out great.

She looked around her office warehouse for a moment, wondering how many of these earnest young people, plugging away at making popularity pay, had these kinds of problems knocking around their brains.

***

Eighteen months ago, Zoe had to twist a lot of arms to get her father to agree to come to Sydney and humiliate his eldest daughter.

Bill Wright, in the late stages of cancer and confined to a threadbare couch at his girlfriend's place on the far fringes of Thalwyn, hadn't seen Zoe for a couple of weeks when she turned up and asked him to come on a nine-hour drive with her.

Pam, the girlfriend, had tried to throw Zoe out when she heard the plan. 'Elle has helped this family,' she'd hissed at Zoe.

They were in the kitchen 'making tea', a ritual Pam still observed daily, despite the fact that Bill, sick to his bones, sat in the same spot every day chain-smoking, barely touching the succession of white-bread sandwiches and Iced VoVos Pam brought him.

'Money was tight around here until she came back,' Pam told Zoe, whose eye roll was barely concealed.

After a ten-year absence, Elle had arrived in town with a film crew, and she'd chosen to pay off her brothers and Pam to say that Bill was dead, rather than have her father expose her cancer lie by daring to be actually, genuinely sick on national television.

'Pam, you have got to be joking,' Zoe said. 'A few grand is nothing to her. Nothing.'

'Well, it's not nothing to us. I would have thought you'd know that. Or have you forgotten where you came from?'

Zoe had to stifle a laugh. At that point, she wasn't very far from where she'd come from—unlike her mansion-dwelling sister, who was living a life so foreign it could have been on another planet.

'Pam, I understand you're embarrassed about taking the money.' *Or you should be*, Zoe added silently. 'But fuck that. Elle went on television and told everyone that Dad is *DEAD*! The man who brought her up. She's written him out of her life because it's inconvenient and because she's LYING ABOUT HER HUSBAND HAVING CANCER TO MAKE MONEY!'

Zoe couldn't help but shout the last sentence. Really, she barely knew Pam, the devoted woman nursing Zoe's dad through his last days. Zoe, like Elle, had left Thalwyn as soon as she was able, and although she hadn't travelled as far—figuratively or literally—as her sister, she hadn't come back too often. Too many shitty memories in the town where her mother's death had screwed up her life too soon after it had begun. Then she'd heard about her dad's cancer.

And Pam was a good woman. It wasn't like Dad was a walk in the park, and here was someone who was making him happy in his last weeks and months. Someone who, despite having fuck-all herself, was happy to share it with an old man who had run out of everything, including time. Who was Zoe to judge her for taking some cash to turn a blind eye to a lie?

'Well, I'm not so sure about that—' Pam started.

'Who's dead around here?'

It was Bill. Zoe hadn't seen him upright at any time during his visit, but now he was intervening in the kitchen row between his daughter and his missus, holding on to the doorframe, wheezing slightly, but with a sly grin coming around his mouth.

'I'm not dead yet. Tell me again—what is it you need me to do so bloody much you're screaming in the kitchen?'

And that's how Zoe had found herself convincing her dying dad to come to Sydney and pull off the awards show stunt that was still clocking up YouTube views worldwide.

'Will one of the boys come with us?' she'd wondered out loud, once she realised he'd said yes and she pictured the endless drive with Bill asleep in the back.

'Liam might,' Pam said quietly from the kitchen doorway.

It was Zoe's turn to be shocked. Liam, the eldest of her four siblings, had been presumed dead or in jail by everyone in the family. As far as Zoe was concerned, no one had heard from him in ten years or more.

Bill had gone back to the lounge, staring at the telly. He took Zoe's hand as Pam said, 'Liam's back. He's been coming over to visit your dad lately. He's much better, by all accounts, and he's another one who's not too keen on your sister.'

Pam dried her hands on a tea towel as she said this, as if to wipe away the ethical mess this family of Bill's had dragged her into. 'God knows what you two have done to be so much bloody better than everyone, but there you go.'

'Shush, Pam,' Bill said, still holding on to Zoe's hand. 'That's it, love. Liam will come with us. He'd like to help. He's been doing a whole lot of apologising lately. When you're dying, everyone needs to tell you all the shitty things they've done.'

As it turned out, it was Liam who ended up not just by Zoe's side throughout the Elle controversy, but also by her side when, six months ago, they did lose Bill.

At the hospital in Swan Hill, her eldest brother was holding her hand next to the bed when her father opened his eyes for the last time, looking momentarily terrified as he took his last conscious breath. *Elle wasn't there—didn't even send a message, or flowers, or a flying fucking monkey*, thought Zoe. *Not that I'm bitter, but come on, Elle, he was your dad*. Elle was god-knows-where, and her two other brothers were in the pub down the road. There was just Liam and Zoe. And Pam, of course, with a packet of biscuits in her handbag—just in case Bill had finally fancied one.

It was strange, Zoe thought now, as she looked around at all the bearded boys and androgynous girls who populated her new workplace, how your family could grow and shift.

Now it included a middle-aged lesbian greenie, two little nephews who were being raised in a shed, and an almost silent giant of a big brother.

Her family must be so ashamed of her. I'll bet they're wishing the ground would swallow them up.

> Typical privileged skinny white girl bullshit. The world owes her fame and fortune, guys, don't you know?
>
> Remember that video from the awards? Can we post it again? I just love seeing Psycho Bitch's face fall off a cliff when she sees that dead dad guy!

Gah, fuck off the lot of you, thought Zoe, this time really throwing her phone into her bag.

Five days off from dogs' dry shampoo. She lifted her head and rolled her shoulders in the universal signal of 'Step back, I've totally got this'.

Tomorrow, Zoe and Abi would ride again.

CHAPTER 26

ELLE

Elle woke up to find a man standing over her bed. He wasn't Ben Bont.

It was ink-black in the bedroom. And for one jolting second, Elle thought, *This is how I'm going to die*.

'Adrian?' she said thickly, as she started sitting up.

'We've got an issue,' said Matt, and he bent down to snap on the bedside light. 'Sorry to wake you.'

'What the...?' Things were clicking into place in Elle's head. 'What time is it?'

'It's late.'

She could see Matt now. And he didn't look good.

'The boys?'

That night, for the first time, three children were sleeping in the perfect farmhouse. Teddy and Freddie had sat at the kitchen counter as Mauna fed them line-caught salmon fish fingers for dinner, with broccoli mash and a tahini dip. Elle had taken so many pictures her thumb was sore.

'No,' said Matt. 'It's Arden.'

'Arden?' What the hell could be wrong with Arden? 'Matt, tell me what's happened.'

He threw her a white kimono from a nearby chair. 'Get up, come and see. We've got a bit of a situation down at the hall.'

'Come with you?' Elle's next thought was the film shoot. Wasn't that today, or tomorrow? Ben was flying in early. 'Who's down there?'

'Just come, Elle, we're going to need all your persuasive powers.'

Matt turned his back as she got out of bed and pulled on the kimono.

His action flashed something into Elle's head. 'You didn't fuck her, did you?'

'God, no, come on. She's a kid.'

'So? What is it?'

'I gave her a pill.'

'Oh, Jesus.' The new flash in Elle's head was of Abi's face, and Adrian's. And then finally it occurred to Elle to ask, 'Is she okay?'

'Well, that's why I need you.'

In one of Gurva's electric-white golf buggies, Matt drove Elle down the hill to the hall. It was the middle of the night, the air had a tiny, sharp chill, and the lights in the hall were visible from the farmhouse.

On the way, he spoke fast. 'We've managed to handle the rest of the guests. Only a couple of staff know what happened, but—'

'Well, I'm glad someone does because I've still got no idea.'

'I got the guys to round up the others and take them for a chill-out near the dam. They should be delivering them all back to their cabins soon. The problem is the woman who found Arden.'

They were nearly at the hall. 'Just tell me what happened.'

'One minute the barn was rolling. Those hen girls were really into it. Arden was there, talking to me, dancing a bit.

And then she wasn't. Ennis was finishing off breakfast prep in the hall and heard screaming, went out the front, and Arden was on the path. Collapsed, fallen over, something—'

'Which one? Collapsed or fallen over?'

'Whichever one's not as bad,' Matt almost snapped, 'that's what you need to know.'

'Matt. You are in a world of pain if this *is* bad. It would be better not to get shitty with me.'

He pulled up outside the door, rubbing his shaved head in agitation. 'The girl who found her is a nurse,' he said. 'And they got her into sick bay, cooled her down, all the rest. She came around.'

'Thank fuck.'

'Ennis came and got me. The thing is,' Matt turned and looked at Elle, 'the nurse chick really wants to take Arden to hospital. Says we have to. And Elle, I don't need to tell you—'

'That would be bad.'

'Yes. Very bad. She's a big fan of yours, this nurse. Really big fan. Her husband works for Ben.'

'Oh, great.' The idea of Ben finding out about this, with his whole attitude towards Matt and the bar idea was... 'That's perfect.'

'Not one of the big guys. Trusty soldier, I think, bar manager or something. Anyway, when the word came through about her wanting to come on retreat, it was that it was her life's dream or some shit, so—'

'You think I can talk her out of the hospital visit?' Elle fastened her kimono tight, smoothed down her hair.

'Yes, boss.'

The way Matt called Elle 'boss' usually had a sarcastic, flirtatious edge to it. Not tonight. Tonight he sounded a little like he was begging. *And he should be*, thought Elle. She'd turned a blind eye to his side hustle, facilitated it for him even, but this...

She climbed out of the golf cart and started towards the

glowing hall. 'Wait for me here,' she said. 'And make sure none of those hens goes wandering off the path.'

Elle took a deep breath and pushed open the door. The sick bay was a small, sterile room off the main space, once an old storage cupboard. The most they usually dealt with in there were women overheating in Pilates, weak after days of a juice-only diet.

As soon as her bare feet touched the wooden floor of the hall, she began to run towards the sick-bay door. She knew that the *slap-slap-slap* of her feet on the floor needed to sound urgent.

She pushed the door open and saw Arden on the slightly raised bed, tiny and pale. Her eyes were closed, but her breathing was fast. A small, dark-haired woman was standing over her. Elle quickly took in her outfit—one of those cheap imitation sequinned kaftan dresses. The kind of thing *other* people would think locals wore on a night out in Byron Bay.

'Arden!' Elle half-shouted.

The teenager opened her eyes and looked so absolutely terrified, Elle felt a spike of panic in her own chest.

'Arden! My god, are you okay?'

The dark-haired woman's head had turned at the sound of the door. Elle could see, in the way her eyes widened a little and—most likely despite herself—a smile touched her lips for just a second, she was impressed to see Elle.

In the corner of the room stood Ennis, one of Matt's most trusted retreat workers. He was Canadian, unflappable, more or less silent. He nodded at Elle.

'Elle!' Arden let go of the stranger's hand and reached out to Elle. 'Don't tell Mum, please don't tell Mum.'

Elle had been in Arden's life for six years. While she and Adrian were together, they'd tolerated each other when they'd had to. Elle had always resented Abi's girls' sulky, judgemental presence in her beautiful home. She knew how they'd felt about her: the interloper, the homewrecker. The friendliest she and Arden had ever been was recently, over email, making a plan of mutual benefit. Elle had to admit that Arden had proved smarter than she'd given her credit for, putting aside family feelings to get ahead.

But not that smart, obviously.

'I'm scared, I'm really scared,' Arden was whispering. Her chest was still heaving; her wide eyes were darting around the small room.

Elle held Arden's hand and leant over her, ever-so-slightly edging out the nurse. She laid her other hand on the icepack, then stroked Arden's face. 'You're safe, darling,' she said in her most soothing tone. 'You're safe. Don't worry, you're going to be fine.'

'You won't tell Mum, will you?'

'Shhhh, Arden.'

'I keep telling her,' the stranger said, 'that she's not going to get in any trouble. That we just need to check that everything's okay, that no one's going to judge her.'

Obviously a nurse. This young woman had a kind, firm tone and a smooth line in bullshit that Elle recognised as common to do-gooders.

'Keep your eyes closed,' Elle said to Arden.

'And breathe,' said the nurse. 'Focus on breathing.'

Elle turned to her. 'You must be the woman who found my stepdaughter. I can't thank you enough. Really. I'm Elle. I'd shake your hand, but...' She gestured down to where Arden was gripping hers like her life depended on it.

'I'm Frances,' said the woman. 'And I know who you are.' Again, seemingly despite herself, the woman smiled.

'Is Arden going to be okay?' Elle asked.

'Yes,' Frances said firmly, flicking her eyes towards Arden to signal to Elle that she wanted the girl to hear her. 'Yes, she's going to be fine. But we need to get her checked out. We need to go to the hospital. You'll be safe there, Arden, I promise.'

'No!' Arden's eyes were open again, tears spilling. 'No! Don't tell my mum!'

'Shh, Arden, you're fine.' Elle stroked her face again.

'Frances, we need to talk, outside. I need you to tell me absolutely everything.'

'Don't leave me!' Arden grabbed Elle's arm with the other hand too, clinging to her, pleading. *Jesus, she must be spinning if she's so keen to hold on to the evil stepmother*.

'Arden, darling, I need to talk to the nurse privately, just for a second. We will be right outside the door. I want you to close your eyes and focus on breathing. In... and out... Am I right, Frances?' She turned to the nurse with an encouraging nod.

Frances hesitated, then nodded. 'Yes. I'll put this blanket on you, Arden, and you need to just breathe, breathe—'

'But him!' Arden pointed a shaky finger at Ennis in the corner.

He shrugged and raised his hands in a gesture that said, *I didn't do anything, just hanging right here, man*.

'Don't leave me with him.'

'Ennis will come out with us, too.'

'But then I'll be alone.' Arden started to cry great, gulping sobs. To Elle, she suddenly looked like the ten-year-old girl she'd first met, not a teenage YouTuber who was old enough to pop molly and get naked on the internet.

***

The previous morning, Elle had waited on the deck like a love-sick teenager, scanning the horizon for a sign of the Gurva bus heading up the long, winding driveway to the farmhouse.

She knew Arden was going to be on it, but to Elle her presence was entirely incidental to the visitors she was bringing: Teddy and Freddie.

Elle tried not to examine her excitement too closely—she really didn't want to know what it was trying to tell her—but whether it was the thrill of knowing how pissed off Adrian and Abi were, or whether Elle just genuinely wanted to be with her boys, she was feeling actual delight.

'They're here!' she called to Ocean the nanny, as Matt drove the bus up to the house.

And Arden clumped off the minibus, ushering the two little mop-haired boys ahead of her. They looked scared, and confused, and didn't want to let go of Arden's legs.

'Hello, darlings!' Elle rushed to them, and they recoiled further into Arden's skirt.

'They probs just need a minute,' said Arden, looking around at the house. 'They were pretty hectic on the plane. Woah. This place is...'

Elle straightened up, trying not to look disappointed. 'I know. Isn't it? Come in, the chef 's made some sugar-free sweet treats.'

'Wouldn't you know it,' Elle heard Arden whisper to the boys, as she untangled them from her legs and pushed them towards the house, 'there's no sugar here, either.'

It had taken a while, but slowly Teddy and Freddie began to unfurl. Elle showed them to the guestroom, which she'd had fitted out with two single beds and as many little-boy toys as her assistant could find down in Byron. And she got them changed, chucking out the 'rags' they'd arrived in—'Mum will not be happy about that,' Arden warned; 'Your mum's happiness isn't my priority,' Elle replied—and talking them into cute short-sleeved shirts and shorts and boat shoes.

Standing back and watching them fight over a giant plush dinosaur—her perfect little dudes in her perfect house—Elle allowed herself a moment of indulgence. 'I miss dressing them,' she said to Arden, who mostly seemed to look at Elle like she was a strange and exotic creature, worth studying.

'That's... weird,' Arden replied.

Ocean brought Alma out from her sleep, prompting Arden to ask where Elle's 'rich boyfriend' was. 'He's coming tomorrow,' Elle said, irritated by the question. 'I hope you won't be recounting every tiny thing that happens here to your dad... and mum.'

'Hey, I'm only here because you begged me,' Arden said, in a tone that belied her age completely.

'I don't beg,' Elle corrected. 'I thought you coming here and seeing how things are done would be mutually beneficial, that's all. Killed a couple of birds with one stone.'

'Where am I sleeping?' Arden began to shuffle from foot to foot, looking uncomfortable. Maybe, thought Elle, the reality of being away from home was kicking in. She was still a child, after all.

'I've got Matt to save you a cabin all of your own. We've got a group coming in for the retreat this afternoon, but a lot of them are sharing so I've got you a special spot. You'll have your own space, just down the hill.'

'But...' Arden didn't look as happy about this news as Elle had predicted. 'The boys, they might wake up and be scared.'

'I'll be here,' Elle snapped. 'I'm their mother. I'm going to have some time with them. And you,' she switched tack, smiling a little, 'are going to have some *fun*.'

'Oh yeah?' Arden's teenage bravado was back. 'What kind of fun?'

***

'She's okay,' the small nurse woman was saying to Elle, 'but she needs to be checked out. There's no telling what's really in those pills, and your equipment here is limited.' She blushed. 'No offence.'

Elle and the nurse had compromised with Arden—they were standing just outside the open sick-bay door, out of earshot but in sight. Ennis was banished to guarding the hall door.

'Well, I'm just delighted to hear she's going to be okay.' Elle looked in at Arden lying there, her leg pulsing, her eyes staring at the ceiling, her chest still pumping. 'You're sure?'

'She's not showing any signs of hypothermia, or any of the

serious overheating or bleeding or any of the things we look for in an MDMA overdose.'

Elle widened her eyes. 'MDMA. Jesus. How did that... I can't imagine how that even got onto Gurva?'

The nurse looked like she was about to say something, then stopped. How much did she know? She clearly thought better of spilling the beans. 'That's a question for tomorrow,' she said firmly.

'I'm just so pleased she's alright. You see, she's my ex-husband's daughter and I—'

Even as she cut Elle off, the nurse, Frances—that was it, that was her name!—looked like she could hardly believe she was doing it. 'Look, I think she's going to be alright. As I said, there are no worsening signs here. What most likely happened is that she fainted in the rush of the drug taking effect. She's vomited a couple of times but that appears to have stopped. But really, a kid her age, we should be taking her to the hospital. We don't even have sedatives here, or any means of doing a blood test, or the means to evacuate her stomach, or—'

'Frances,' Elle intervened, deciding to take a little risk, 'I know this sounds like a strange thing to ask at a time like this, and please, please forgive me for how it's going to sound but... do you know who I am?'

Frances laughed a little, rubbing her hands over her face where the traces of make-up were long since in the wrong place. 'Of course. Of course I know who you are.' For a moment, the woman looked like she was going to cry. 'Elle, I've been following you online for years. You have helped me in lots of ways, I... I came here to meet you.'

Ah, say no more, thought Elle, although Frances the nurse looked like she was gearing up to say much, much more.

'Oh, that's so lovely of you to say at a time like this.' Elle put a hand on Frances's arm, turning them both a bit from the doorway and Arden's anxious eyes, as if about to confide something significant. 'Then, Frances, you're probably familiar with the... troubles, between me and my ex-husband.'

'Well,' Frances exhaled a little, 'yes, I mean... I was a bit shocked when you said that was who she was. I mean, I thought you guys were—'

'Estranged. We are. We are.' It was Elle's turn to look as though she might cry. 'Losing touch with my stepdaughters has been one of my biggest regrets of this whole mess. Today was the first time I've seen Arden in eighteen months.'

At least that last bit is true.

'Oh, wow.'

'And, Frances, you see, if anything had happened to her—if anything *does* happen to her, well, I would never, ever forgive myself. And as you can imagine, her father, who isn't exactly my biggest fan,' she allowed a sad little chuckle, 'if he found out, well, you can imagine how that would go.'

Some people's faces were entirely incapable of keeping secrets. Clearly, Frances was one of those people. The struggle she was having, deciding which side of herself to come down on—the nurse whose mission was to take care of people, or the woman face-to-face with her idol asking for a favour—was manifesting in a crumpled forehead, speedy blinking, and a hand constantly shooting up to push her hair back.

'If you told me you seriously thought that Arden was in any grave danger, we would be halfway to the hospital already. But if you think she just needs monitoring through this... thing, I have a doctor, he's not far away, who can come over right now, with whatever supplies you think we need. We can all sit with Arden tonight. Keep an eye on her through this. And tomorrow, take her to my GP, or my shaman healer, or whoever you think would be best.'

Elle had both hands on Frances's forearm, holding her in place, stopping her fidgeting. Making her focus.

'Quiet will be better for all of us,' she said, 'especially Arden.' Elle let a tear fall. 'I don't need to tell you what my enemies would do with this. It would be hell for her. It's the price anyone close to me pays.'

Too much? Elle wondered. But Frances was crying, too.

Another beat, and then the nurse said, 'No one can know about this. That I did this.'

Another beat, another bubbling sob.

'But fine. Call your doctor.'

CHAPTER 27

ABI

'Shouldn't this place be your wet dream?'

Zoe and Abi were walking down Byron Bay's Jonson Street. Every second shop had a flabby batch of kombucha brewing in the window or a promise of a chakra reading upstairs, or was displaying a pair of two-hundred-dollar hemp culottes.

'Fuck, no.' Abi's stomp was getting heavier with every footfall. 'All this bullshit makes me want to smash a window.'

'Are you feeling possessive over your aesthetic?' Zoe teased. 'Don't want to let any new hippies in the club?'

Abi thought that Zoe should have been able to tell this wasn't the moment for banter. Arden had left with the boys the previous day. She had texted to say she'd arrived at lunchtime—*Here, and oh my god this place is next level perfect*—but Abi had heard nothing since, despite texting Arden three times.

All okay, pudding?

Two-hour gap.

Boys alright, love?

Overnight gap.

Just text me back to let me know you haven't been brainwashed and sold into fitness-model slavery, Arden.

So far, still no word. Abi was deciding how many more minutes she could let tick by before she climbed into the hire car and headed for the hills herself.

'Zoe, these people aren't hippies. Hippies don't spend four hundred dollars on a sequinned kaftan. Hippies don't turn their noses up at good honest food to buy some miracle-powder bullshit to sprinkle in their chai. And hippies certainly don't shoot their faces full of dubiously sourced chemical jelly to stop them getting wrinkles—look at that woman!' Abi realised she was speaking too loudly as she gestured to a tall, willowy woman of indeterminate age who was flicking through floaty dresses in a boutique called Aura.

'Okay, Abi, shhh. Inside voice with the hate-filled rant, please.' Zoe pulled Abi away from the shop window and hurried her along the street. 'Anyway, that was Adeline Billows. She's married to that action-hero movie star... and they *LIVE* here.'

'I don't care who she is, Zoe. No one should be walking barefoot with that much shit in their face. It's a fact—if you can afford filler, you can afford shoes. Fucking fake bullshit—'

'Jesus,' Zoe said. 'Okay, Abi, I know you're anxious about Arden, but let's just stick to our plan. She's a teenager. Her phone will have died, that's all. She'll sort it out.'

The plan, as far as Abi had drawn it, was to be close by if Arden or those poor little boys needed her—and to gather some intel about what the hell was going on inside Elle's mysterious retreat. She needed some new ammunition to get that woman away from her daughter. But first, she just really, really needed to talk to her.

'I have such bad vibes about all this, Zoe,' she said as they turned into the foyer of their serviced apartment.

'That is a very Byron thing to say, Abi,' Zoe said, but gently put her arm around Abi and squeezed. 'Arden's fine.'

'I'm going to try her one more time,' Abi said. 'And if she doesn't answer, we're getting in the car.'

***

The day before, Abi and Adrian had kissed Arden and the boys off at Melbourne airport.

Abi had embarrassed her daughter to within an inch of her life by quizzing the airline staffer who was helping old people through the automatic check-in process.

'It's important that she doesn't sit next to any dirty old men,' was one of Abi's lines. 'Someone on board will be keeping an eye on that, right?'

'And they're definitely together in a row of three, yes?' Adrian asked, even though he'd just been the one who had selected the seats.

'And at the other end, will someone help her off the plane with the boys?'

'We don't need help!' piped up Teddy. 'We love to fly.'

'And can someone make sure they get to the person who's meeting them...'

'DAD!' Arden had been eye-rolling, mortified. 'I think I can manage this.'

Meanwhile, three-year-old Freddie was standing on the baggage scales over at the check-in counter, enjoying the angry *beep-beep-beep* it made when it couldn't find his barcode.

Abi grabbed Arden's arm and pointed at him. 'Flying with kids is no picnic, Arden.'

'Freddie! Freddie!' She rushed off to pull him down.

'Are you sure about this, Adrian?' Abi asked her ex, who was dressed in his best new-age finance guy outfit: a crisp white linen shirt, long tapered shorts and boat shoes. The two of them were speaking again, egged on by Arden, but only just.

'She'll be okay,' Adrian said. 'It's not a long flight.'

'But the boys? With Elle? Are you sure she's not going to pull something nutty? She's not going to leave the country or hold them on the farm?' A tiny piece of Abi was hoping he might call the whole thing off, keep all the kids on the ground.

'Abi, Elle's not going to run off with the boys,' he said. 'They're serving a purpose—she's not dying to have them back. That's not her motivation.'

'I hope you're right,' Abi muttered. 'I used to be so miserable when the girls would come and visit you at the weekends. People would tell me how lucky I was to have some time without the kids around, and I used to just want to punch them in the face.'

'You are not Elle, Abi,' Adrian said. 'If that wasn't already obvious.'

There was a bit of Adrian, Abi could see, that was looking forward to the boys getting on the plane. He had two days in the city, for meetings with his publisher and an agent about Manifesting Money. In the car on the way down, he'd talked excitedly about the possibility of TV appearances and an audio book. Maybe she'd finally given him enough of a hard time, and his project seemed successful enough, that he was ready to move on—and out.

Here's hoping, she thought, picturing Grace's face.

Arden was back with Freddie, and it was time to see them all off through security. Abi hugged her hard and whispered, 'I know you hate my guts right now, but that's no reason to do anything extra just to piss me off. I'm already pissed off, right? Job done.'

'Mum, you're ridiculous.' But Arden squeezed her back.

Adrian was kneeling next to the boys and assuring them that if they felt worried, they were to stay close to their sister.

'You'll be back before you know it,' he said. 'Just stick together.'

As Abi and Adrian stood next to each other watching the kids walk off—Arden in the middle, a little boy holding each hand, all three with their backpacks on—Abi suddenly felt desperately worried. She took a strange sob-breath, and Adrian put an arm around her, something he never did. 'Don't worry, Abi,' he said. 'It's not like you're not on the next flight.'

Thank god.

***

Once you turned off the highway, all the roads up into the Byron hinterland were tiny and winding.

Zoe and Abi drove past the pinpoint on their iPhone map several times before they finally clocked the sign that said, 'Gurva—PRIVATE PROPERTY—Very Bad Vibes For The Uninvited'. Ten metres behind the sign was an elegant white wooden farm gate, which was at the start of a long rugged driveway. From the road, you couldn't see the farmhouse or any of the other main buildings. And the gate was locked.

'Have you got mobile reception?' They'd pulled up next to the gate, and Abi was standing on the back bumper of the hire car, waving her phone in the air.

'Come ON.' Zoe laughed, climbing out herself. 'There has to be reception. Elle can hardly be running an alt-culture empire off the grid.'

'Then a satellite or some shit had better kick in soon, because I've got nothing and I'm getting beyond anxious.'

Abi's stomach hadn't stopped churning since she'd finally got a text from Arden.

> Sorry, Mum, got a bit sick last night. Food poisoning! Slept it off, all good now.

Food poisoning! The Gurva website insisted all food was vegan and prepared by the best chefs on the coast. Who the hell got food poisoning from a fancy vegan dinner? Also, that exclamation mark was a very, very suspicious move from Arden.

'This is bullshit, Zoe. We're going,' Abi had announced, moments after the message pinged into her phone.

And now here they were, and true to Grace's description of Abi and Zoe as the 'least subtle private-eye team on the planet', they had no idea what to do.

'We could climb the fence and walk in,' Zoe suggested.

'And what, disguise ourselves as cows and spy from the field?' Abi spat back.

'Give me a better idea, then?'

'Let's just buzz the intercom.'

And that's exactly what Abi was about to do when the skinny road rattled a little and a hefty van pulled to a stop beside them at the gate. Its logo told them it was from Channel Eleven—the film crew for Elle's big shoot.

'We're with them,' Abi said to Zoe. 'We're in.'

CHAPTER 28

FRANCES

Frances had never felt more disgusted with herself. And she'd never been more excited.

Elle Campbell had invited her up into her beautiful farmhouse to sit in on today's big TV shoot. And Frances couldn't quite believe it.

She'd last seen Elle at two a.m., after Dr Jonti had arrived from Byron, helped Frances and Elle guide an anxiously wired Arden back to her cabin and given her some sedatives.

'I know this is a lot,' Elle had said to Frances, hand on her arm, 'but I have left the boys up at the farmhouse with a nanny they don't really know. I'm worried they might wake up and be afraid. Would you...?'

'Stay with Arden?' Frances had asked. 'Of course.'

And Frances, who'd been fantasising for weeks about the uninterrupted sleep she would get on her first night at Gurva, had lain down on a double bed next to a teenager she'd never really met and stroked Arden's hair as she fell asleep.

Then Frances settled into an armchair in Arden's cabin,

set twenty-minute alarms on her phone and faded into a fitful rest, waking periodically to check on Arden until the morning.

At eight a.m., Frances was still keeping watch, keenly aware she had already missed the first yoga class of her Purify and Release retreat. Were all those Bondi women really there, with their jittery hangovers? What about Matt?

She woke her phone and flicked through Elle's private Instagram account. Gurva looked like heaven itself: china bowls overflowing with photogenic persimmons, twenty women all pulling the perfect warrior pose in the sun-drenched yoga studio, Elle's six-pack gleaming against a pale green waterhole. So far, that wasn't how Frances's Gurva experience was going.

Just as her resentment was blooming in her sleep-deprived brain, there was a knock at the cabin door. She looked quickly over at Arden, still sleeping, and opened the door. It was Elle.

Frances felt deeply strange to be face-to-face in broad daylight with someone she'd only ever seen on Instagram, Snapchat and Facebook. Without filters, Elle was almost as lineless and every bit as glamorous. After the night they'd had, here she was in skin-tight white yoga pants, a white crop top and a flowing cashmere cardi. How did someone with a tiny baby and two preschoolers in the house keep her clothes so white? Her trademark braid was perfectly twisted and as glossy as a horse's mane, swinging down her back. Her make-up was flawless.

Elle was beaming, and she was holding out a picnic basket. 'Frances, hello. I know you're missing your first retreat morning today, so I'm bringing it to you.'

How had all this come together by eight a.m.? Frances was still in her skimpy sparkly kaftan from the night before, a blanket around her shoulders as a shawl. Her mouth felt disgusting. She wasn't going to breathe anywhere near Elle, that was for sure.

Elle shimmied past her, walked towards the bed. 'How's our patient?'

‘Still sleeping.’ Frances set the basket down. ‘I’d say she’ll be waking up soon—those benzos that Dr Jonti gave her will have lost their kick by now.’

Dr Jonti asked surprisingly few questions, Frances thought. *Maybe that’s how country doctors are*. Maybe he would follow up with Elle today. He’d just kind of arrived, apparently with all the information, checked Arden’s vitals, given the pills and vanished again. Another thing to add to the list of strange goings-on at Gurva.

‘Oh, I’m sure she’ll have a sore head,’ Elle said, perching on the edge of the bed. She looked like she was going to reach out and stroke Arden’s hair, then appeared to think better of it, putting her hands together in her lap.

Frances peeked inside the picnic basket: glass bottles of smoothies and juices, labelled with her name and neatly dated. There was also a pair of Elle’s signature yoga pants, she could see, a stretch mat, some miracle powder and some kind of voucher.

‘Frances,’ Elle said, ‘I think you were sent here for a reason.’

‘Me too,’ said Frances, who still found it hard to look at Elle and talk at the same time. ‘I always thought that, but the reason isn’t what I think it is.’

‘I think you’re lost, am I right?’

Arden snored a little, Elle’s tinkling voice rolling right on over the grunt.

‘Well,’ Elle said, ‘I think you were sent here to. . . yes, help my stepdaughter, who is also lost.’ Elle shrugged, a little sadly. ‘But also to alert me to something toxic in my home.’

‘Do you mean someone?’ Frances asked, and then immediately regretted it. Was that a bit rude?

‘Maybe. Don’t you worry, I will deal with that.’ Elle looked down at her hands. ‘Men have tried to take advantage of me my whole life, Frances. Do you ever feel that?’

Frances was nodding, before she realised it.

‘But today I’m telling the world that I am marrying Ben Bont. I’ve found a man who wants me to be his equal, to be his partner, and I'm going to celebrate it.' Elle looked up, smiling. 'And I think the reason you were sent here is to witness that, to see what is possible. You don't have to be tired and beaten down and lost, Frances. You don't have to be less-than.'

Despite herself, Frances felt tears in her eyes.

'I want you to spend the day up at the farmhouse with my family while we tell the world about our love. Now you have helped look after one of our own, you're family too.'

Frances really was crying now. 'Thank you, Elle, but I'm... so tired.'

Elle stood up and came over. She stopped short of a hug but put her manicured hands on Frances's cheeks. 'I know you are, darling,' she said. 'That's why you came, am I right? To recapture some of that fire.'

'Yes, but,' Frances looked down at herself, 'I mean, I'm really tired right now. I haven't slept because I've been checking on Arden all night. I would love to come up to your house, but I need some rest first.'

Elle threw her head back and laughed. It wasn't the laugh Frances had expected to come out of her mouth—it wasn't dainty, it had an edge.

'You are a literal little thing, aren't you?' Elle said, patting Frances's cheeks. 'Of course. Come up at one o'clock. I'll send one of the house staff to get you. As soon as Arden wakes up, call me and I'll have someone take over and you can go rest.'

Frances still couldn't believe that Elle Campbell was standing there, laughing and chatting with her like this. But it also sounded a lot like Elle was getting ready to go somewhere, and Frances had kind of hoped this was a handover. 'Are you leaving?' she asked, looking over at Arden.

'I am, darling, I am so busy with my boys here. But Arden's in safe hands, and she'll continue to be after you call me.'

Frances had the distinct impression she had now become a member of staff to Elle. How had that happened?

These people are not us, she heard Troy say. *We work for those people*.

But the idea of spending an afternoon with Elle, in her house, hanging out like *buddies*, was much too tempting to talk herself out of.

'I'll call you as soon as she wakes up,' said Frances—then, 'Oh, but I don't have your number.'

'Call this one.' Elle plucked the voucher from the picnic basket and wrote something on the back of it. 'They always know how to get me.'

***

Just as Frances predicted, Arden did wake up within an hour of Elle leaving.

She took one look at where she was, another at Frances, and burst into tears.

'I want my mum,' she wailed. Frances went to sit with her, as she had all night, but this time she held Arden, let her cry.

'I'm Frances, I'm a nurse. I've been here all night, making sure you're safe,' she said softly. 'You are safe. You're fine. You're safe.'

To Frances's surprise, Arden held on to her, shuddering her cries into Frances's shoulder. 'Thank you,' she managed, between hiccuppy sobs. 'Really, thank you.'

Frances couldn't believe this was Adrian Campbell's daughter. She knew more about this stranger's family than she did about some of her good friends'. There were so many questions she'd like to ask this tiny girl, but she started with one: 'How do you feel?'

'Sick,' Arden managed. 'Stupid.'

'Well, you know, both of those things are to be expected.'

'Where's Elle? Where are the boys?'

'Elle was just here,' Frances told her. 'Checking on you. She's gone back to the boys.'

Frances had been a nurse long enough to stop herself asking the question, *What the hell were you thinking?* It wasn't her place to do that—it was Elle's. Or Arden's mum's. And, of course, Arden's. But there was one question she had to ask. 'Did you ask Matt for that pill?'

Frances knew she was unlikely to get the truth out of a sixteen-year-old who had just been busted taking drugs, so she was surprised when Arden said, 'Yes. I told him I'd done it before. I hadn't. I'm a complete dickhead.'

'He should never have given it to you,' Frances said. 'This is on him.'

'Did I overdose?'

Frances shook her head and went to rummage in the bag of goodies Elle had left, pulling out something that looked like an orange juice. She shook it, peeled back the top and handed it to Arden. 'No. You fainted, and then you vomited a bit, and then you were freaked out. So we got you to rest. You'll be alright. No lasting damage apart from your stepmum— '

'She's not my stepmum anymore,' Arden said, pushing herself up to sit. 'Jesus, my mum would kill her and everyone on this farm if she knew about this.'

'I bet.' Frances smiled. 'I've heard about your mum.'

'Do you... work here?' Arden took a sip of the juice.

'No, Arden. Just visiting. I came to do the retreat. But you know... when you're a nurse and shit goes down...'

'I guess you didn't expect that this time,' Arden said. 'How many other health retreats have an ecstasy dealer onsite?'

'That, Arden, is a very, very good question.'

And then Arden looked around with complete panic. It seemed to have dawned on her that something very important—essential—was missing from this fuzzy picture.

'Where's my phone?' she asked.

***

By the time Frances made it up to the farmhouse at one p.m., she was feeling heady from lack of sleep, despite managing a thirty-minute nap and a shower.

She'd called her mum, who was still minding Denny.

'How is this retreat? You feeling healthy yet?' The sarcasm in her mother's voice wasn't disguised; as with everything in Frances's family, it was just laid out there for her to deal with.

'Mum, it's very Zen. I am feeling rested already.' Once that lie was out of the way, Frances asked her mum a million questions about Denny's eating, sleeping and even shitting habits. 'He needs to go at least once a day, Mum, so if nothing's happening, sometimes I massage his tummy while I'm changing him.'

'You are *crazy*,' her mother said. 'Why do you young mothers today just go around looking for things to worry about? It's like you're turning over rocks searching for trouble.'

Then Frances lay on the bed for twenty minutes replaying every interaction she'd had with Elle Campbell. Had she said anything really stupid? Had she said anything really smart?

Was there any universe in which it was okay not to take a teenager having an adverse drug reaction to get medical assistance? No.

Was it okay that Frances was shelving her principles—and her professional integrity—to try to impress someone she'd never met before? No.

Did she really, really want to go up to the farmhouse today and see the world she'd been looking at online for a year? Yes.

Did she really, really want Elle Campbell to like her? Yes.

I can be helpful, she told herself, *by warning Elle about Matt. She doesn't need a loose cannon like him on her team.*

So when the golf buggy came to collect her, Frances had convinced herself that spending the day with Elle Campbell, instead of cleansing and stretching, was really a good deed, both for herself and the world.

***

The homestead was as absolutely perfect as it appeared on Instagram.

Frances climbed off the golf cart, thanked the handsome,

dreadlocked guy driving it, and gingerly walked up the steps of the whitewashed deck to the open front door.

Tentatively looking in, she could see that people were everywhere: staff in their white Gurva jackets carrying trays of cold drinks to the photographer and his assistants, who were adjusting vases of peonies and plumping cushions in the living room. Someone was carrying a large TV light through to the deck; someone else had an armful of clothes on hangers. Another was polishing the glass of the abstract art on the homestead's walls.

Although this was clearly a house full of strangers, Frances couldn't bring herself to walk in unannounced, so she called out, 'Hello!' as brightly as she could manage.

The photographer looked up at her from where he was fiddling with his tripod. 'Hello?' he asked back.

'I'm here to see Elle,' Frances said, gesturing to the inside of the house as if that hallway, itself, was the guru.

'Aren't we all?' The photographer laughed a little bit, then shrugged in a way that let Frances know he had no idea where Elle was.

One of the Gurva staff, a young woman with luminous skin and a service-industry grin, came over to Frances. 'You okay?'

'My name's Frances. Elle told me to come over at one.' She still didn't set foot over the doorstep.

'Hi, Frances.' The girl's smile widened and was accompanied by a professional nod, as if she was expected. 'Elle's in hair and make-up. Why don't you go through and wait for her on the back deck?' The helpful staffer gestured widely down the hallway to the back of the house, where there were big French doors.

Frances stepped inside. She felt like she knew this house, having seen so many corners of it in vignettes from Elle's Instagram: the dark floors and the white, white walls; the way the wraparound veranda was visible from every room, bringing the green valley inside; the tasteful nude black-and-white print of Elle in the hallway.

Frances was tiptoeing through familiar scenes. The kitchen opened up to her left, where a woman with a shaved head in a spotless white uniform was placing cut-up fruit around... was that Elle's famous silent juicer? Frances paused long enough to see the woman pull out a phone from her apron pocket, snap a shot, examine it and tweak her pineapple arrangement.

Next, Frances passed the door to the nursery—oh, how she'd studied this nursery for tips about peaceful sleeping. She couldn't help but look in. There was the oversized Swedish rocking chair where Elle nursed Baby A to sleep; there was the natural sheep-skin rug for tummy time... Frances hadn't noticed, in any of the social shots, that the cot was one of those self-vibrating ones with a motion sensor that could read when your baby was crying. She supressed a stab of disapproval. Her mothers' group had discussed these—in a longing 'if only' kind of way; they were nearly two thousand dollars, after all—and their midwife had said they were bad-habit-creating sleep aids. And Frances knew that Elle was all about natural sleep patterns and waking when your baby woke, and being there for them when they needed you, so...

'Can I help you?' A young woman walked into the nursery from an internal door Frances hadn't seen. She snuck a quick glance through the open door to a room that was small and bare, with a single bed against the wall.

'Sorry, I was just looking for Elle,' Frances said, embarrassed.

'Well, you won't find her here,' the girl said, with an audible edge to her voice. Clearly hearing it herself, the girl shook her head and grimaced. 'Sorry! Not sure where she is right now, but I think she'll be out the back filming soon.'

'Are you,' Frances thought quickly, hoping to find an excuse to ask this question, 'a friend of Arden's?'

'Who's Arden?' asked the young woman. 'No, I'm the baby nurse. I live here.' And she gestured to the bed in the room attached to the nursery.

'Oh, sorry, thanks.' Frances stepped away, towards where she was actually meant to be heading—the back deck.

The wraparound veranda widened behind the house to include a lap pool, and at one end of it Frances saw Arden lying on a day bed alongside two little boys, both engrossed in matching blue-cased iPads. Frances recognised them from the days when Elle had posted fashion shots of them daily on The Stylish Mumma—her estranged sons, Teddy and Freddie.

Arden was wearing sunnies, but Frances could see she was watching the film crew setting up at the other end of the pool.

Frances waved. 'Hi! You're up!'

Arden nodded, waved back, motioned for Frances to come over.

Frances did. She perched on the edge of the day bed, gazed out at the green, gum-tree-framed view across the hills to the ocean, and couldn't help saying, 'I have never been in such a beautiful house in my entire life.' And then, remembering herself, 'How are you?'

'I'm... okay, bit shaky,' Arden said. 'Still can't find my phone, though, and I know my mum will be freaking out.'

'Use mine.' Frances dug it out of the pocket of her white shorts.

'I don't know her number—I don't know anyone's number,' said Arden darkly. 'I don't need to. I have a phone.'

'Oh, come on, I'm sure we can find it— '

A man's voice cut through the gentle hum of activity on the deck: the birds, the camera crew's banter, the muted cartoon tinkling of the boys' iPads.

'DON'T PUSH ME ON THIS!' the man's voice screamed. It was coming from the house. As far as Frances could tell, it was coming from a room along the side of the house, out of sight, around the veranda's corner.

Arden and Frances looked up at each other; the boys looked up from their iPads, to Arden.

'I AM SERIOUS,' the voice shouted. 'DO NOT *FUCKING* PUSH ME ON THIS! I TOLD YOU THIS WAS A TERRIBLE IDEA! THIS IS WHY YOU CAN'T BE HERE ALONE!'

A subdued crash made everyone—from the film crew to

the Gurva guy trimming back jasmine on the trellis—freeze for a second and turn their heads.

Frances stood up and stepped towards where the noise had come from, just as trainer Matt came around the corner.

Surprised—the yelling voice hadn't sounded like his—Frances found herself calling out, 'Everything okay?' as he walked towards the day bed, eyes on Arden and the boys.

'Yes,' he said, but his expression suggested otherwise. 'Ben Bont's home.'

CHAPTER 29

GRACE

Grace missed her sister Leisel so much it made her stomach ache. They'd lived in different cities for most of their adult lives, but they'd always, *always* been there for each other when something was going on.

And for Grace right now, something was definitely going on.

So where the hell was her big sister?

Leisel, her husband Mark and their three little kids had packed up their Sydney lives and gone on a round-Australia odyssey in a souped-up, kitted-out campervan. Leisel, whose The Working Mum blog had won a hefty cash prize at the Blog-ahh Awards, was writing from the road, but the fact that they were constantly in and out of wi-fi and phone reception made contact much too patchy for Grace's liking.

'Call me, Lee,' she was saying into her iPhone's cracked screen. 'I need to talk to someone sane. Sane and smart and married. I don't know anyone else like that.'

Grace was in Melbourne picking up her wedding dress, but she wasn't feeling any festive excitement about it. She was looking at her frock and thinking about the fight she and

Abi had had on the day of the celebrant's visit. On that day, she'd got as close as she ever came to the shouting and foot-stomping behaviour that seemed to work so well for everyone else in her house. She had told Abi that she couldn't, in all conscience, put on a happy face and participate in this great public love-in.

After Abi had got a text from Zoe and chosen to focus on that, Grace had retreated to the spot on the farm where she always went when things were getting too wild: an old bench they'd placed under her favourite tree, the angel's trumpet. Abi had come to seek her out.

'Do you know these flowers are poisonous?' she heard Abi saying, walking up behind her. 'It's the most beautiful tree in the garden, but it could kill the little ones in minutes.'

'Is that meant to be a clumsy metaphor? You tell me every time.'

Abi sat next to Grace on the bench and took her hand. 'Can we put all this shit aside and just focus on the wedding?' she asked.

'No.' Grace surprised herself with the force of her answer. 'No, we can't. I can't marry you while everything's so toxic around here. Me and you playing around in wedding dresses while Arden's melting down, and Adrian and the boys are digging in, *and* we're fighting? It's fake, Abi. And one thing we have never been is fake.'

Abi looked stricken, and Grace desperately wanted to tell her it was all going to be fine. But this time, this time, she couldn't.

And then Abi had still gone and gotten on a plane to pursue her ridiculous obsession with Elle.

'Stay,' Grace had asked. 'You need to let Arden work through this by herself.'

But Abi had gone. And here Grace was, in Melbourne, with an armful of lace.

So the timing wasn't great. But the dress was ready, and there was no way she would let it go. At least, not yet. There was also no way she was going to get it sent to Daylesford, when everything wedding-y was already costing the family way too much. That was shitting her, too, that the beautiful, odd, chaotic life that she and Abi had created for themselves was now just another gouging opportunity for the grabby capitalist market.

'You're such a communist, Grace,' she could hear Leisel saying.

The dress *was* stunning, though. It was vintage, and although the staff at the little op-shop in Collingwood's Smith Street had no idea where it had come from, Grace did. She could feel it. It had belonged to a 1970s boho rebel, someone whose mum had wanted her to wear a corseted princess dress when she married that boring guy from accounts, but who had said, 'NO, I want floating layers of chiffon and old-lady lace, bare feet and a flower in my hair.' That was exactly the vibe of this dress, and it was exactly the vibe Grace had wanted to go for... if she was going to do this thing.

This thing.

Grace pulled the precious garment bag over her shoulder and left the alterations place that had made this forty-year-old dress look like new. Otto and Sol had been with their other mum, Edie, for the weekend, and Grace was going to pick them up on the way back to the farm.

Grace and Edie had gone through an enormous amount to create these boys together a decade ago, and now Edie saw them every other weekend and on the holidays—which, even to Grace, seemed like an unbearable arrangement. But Edie was pragmatic, always had been, and had told Grace from the day she left: 'You're the mother, you decide what's best.'

Grace knew what Edie had meant by that. She was the one who had tried everything to have them. She was the one who'd stayed home to nurse and coddle and cradle them. She was the one who'd strapped them to her body and carried them everywhere. And she was the one who'd decided to leave their other mother for a weirder, wider world.

And, of course, when she and Abi had moved out of town to Daylesford, Grace had made a selfish decision. They were going with her. And so, it was weekends and holidays for Edie.

Grace found her label of 'earth mother' accurate and infuriating in equal measure. Sometimes it drove her insane, since being the 'maternal' one was generally code for 'the one who does everything'. But other times it saved her, gave her permission to be the one who put the family first. When Abi was spinning, it was Grace who grounded her. When the kids weren't thriving, it was Grace who went to the root and started watering.

But lately, it was Grace who was feeling uprooted. Although this big messy life she had craved was everything she'd wanted, the mess had become so overwhelming it was hard to tell the trash from the treasure.

Like Adrian. It made Grace furious, after everything, that man was coming between her and Abi. And here she was, pushed into being the one who defended him.

The thing about Abi, Grace knew, was that she gave courage to the weak. She was so fierce, so certain, that the faltering were drawn to her. That's how she'd managed to build such a loyal community on The Green Diva, a world of women who had a bit of what she had—conviction, guts, something to believe in.

That's what Adrian had needed after Elle did a number on him. He didn't know what to do with himself, with his boys. But Abi did. Take them in, love them. Build them back up. And now Adrian was rebuilt—on the verge, perhaps, of building something meaningful of his own again.

But his fear was still clawing at Abi, refusing to let her go. It made Grace sick. It also made her furious with her fiancée, because Abi was all caught up in it: Adrian's drama with Elle, her own fear about her daughter growing up and away. It was as if Abi didn't really know who she was if she wasn't fighting something. Or someone.

Grace, meanwhile, was all fought out. She hadn't even been

able to summon the fire Abi had mobilised to get this whole marriage thing done. She had never aspired to a respectable life—a wedding, a picket fence—so although the inequality infuriated her, the battle wasn't personal.

And yet here she was, on the tram with a wedding dress over her shoulder.

Her phone buzzed and she picked it up. 'Leisel! Where the hell are you?'

'At last, G, we are heading into Broome. I am so covered in red dirt I'll think I'm haemorrhaging every time I blow my nose for a week. It's absolutely stunning out here.'

'Well, personally,' Grace rang the bell for the tram to let her off next stop, 'I think it's very selfish of you, at this time of year, to be pretty much as far from me as you can get without leaving the country. It's nearly Christmas.'

'Oh, shush. We're flying in for the wedding, sister. Doesn't get much more festive than that.'

'Not really feeling the wedding right now.' Grace stepped off the tram and traced the familiar route to Edie's house. Once, it had been her house, too; now Edie shared it with a young and beautiful bohemian art teacher called Gaia. Edie had a type.

'Well, that doesn't sound very celebratory. What's going on?'

Grace could hear Leisel's kids in the back of the campervan, chattering and bickering. She could hear the engine chugging. She could picture the red road ahead of them, Mark's weathered hands at the wheel, flying towards a tourist town on the very edge of the desert and the continent, where the blue met red.

'I wish I was there with you, Lee,' Grace said. 'Far away from all the insanity.'

'Believe me, you don't,' Leisel said. 'The inside of a campervan smells like the bottom of a birdcage when you've had ten days between hot showers and fresh food. I think you might choose speed-reading Adrian's money manual over spending ten minutes locked in here with the Adams family.'

Grace didn't say anything as she turned into Edie's street.

'I'm in Melbourne, picking up the boys from Edie and Gaia.' She didn't mention the wedding dress.

'So that's what you're doing. But what's going on?'

'Ah, you know, Hurricane Abi is really blowing at the moment,' Grace said. 'She's up in Byron, with Zoe. Can you believe it?'

'Zoe, Elle's sister?'

'Yup. They've followed Arden to Elle's place. It's a long and weird story, Lee, but basically Elle's getting married again, and Arden's taken the boys up for the announcement shoot... and, well, you wouldn't believe it, really.'

'Hold on, hold on.' Grace could hear her sister switching ears, shushing the kids. 'Who's Elle marrying? And what are Zoe and Abi going to do up there?'

'She's marrying some money man, some guy called Ben Bont.' Grace was at Edie's door. She stopped, turned to look at the street, and kept talking. 'And god only knows what Abi and Zoe think they're doing. They act as though they're private eyes.'

'Jesus, that's a lot. Where have I been?'

'In a smelly campervan with three kids.'

'Ben Bont's an arsehole, G. A beauty editor I used to work with dated him for a while, years ago, and—'

'Takes one to know one,' Grace said, and then immediately felt horrible.

'That was *not* like you,' Leisel said. 'You're really not okay, are you?'

'The wedding is in three weeks, my fiancée is chasing some old grudge, my stepdaughter's naked on the internet, and the bloody Bare-Chested Investor is living in our shed and starting a fight every damn day.' Grace let it out, looking down at her toes in her sandals. 'So yes, I'm feeling a little unlike myself.'

'You've been here before when Abi goes on a mission,' said Leisel. 'You can always talk her down. That's what you need to do—you're so good at talking, sister, always have been.'

'That's not a compliment, is it?' asked Grace. 'I don't know. It feels like talking isn't really enough.'

'It's a place to start.' Leisel's voice softened. 'But seriously, G, I know Elle is not on top of our Christmas list, but that Ben Bont is a piece of work...'

Grace sighed. Why did everyone want to talk about Elle?

'What did he do to your friend?' asked Grace, mentally adding a dollar to the kitchen gossip jar.

'Well—'

And of course, right on cue, Sol and Otto came barrelling out of Edie's front door. '*Mama!* Edie bought us a pet mouse! Can we take it home?'

Grace's boys wrapped themselves around her and she laughed, trying to lift the wedding dress bag high out of their reach.

'Got to go, Lee. Kid invasion. Next time.'

'Of course. Kiss them for me! We'll see you all in three weeks.'

That was gossip karma, thought Grace, hanging up. *Whatever Ben Bont has done, it's not my concern*.

'A mouse? Boys, I think we have enough of those on the farm already...'

CHAPTER 30

ELLE

When she heard the film crew's car pull away, Elle locked herself in the all-white ensuite and sat on the closed toilet seat, shaking.

How did she get here? How did she let things get so out of control? How had she misjudged this man so much?

Angry men had been a feature of Elle's childhood. The men around town, furious at their livelihoods literally drying up, at wives who wouldn't do what they were told. Grown men full of frustration at the impotence of being at the will of the weather; young men confused about what their role in the world was now their broad shoulders couldn't carry the family farm. Her brothers, livid at a dead woman for being left in the hands of their feckless dad.

In adulthood, she had avoided them like they were the devil. And through her promo-girl club days, and her gym-trainer days, there had been plenty to swerve.

So, how had her radar been so off about Ben Bont? For eighteen months he'd been mostly calm, distant even. Clearly, he'd always been a man who was used to getting what he wanted, but for all this time he'd been trying to work out what she wanted from him.

And now... was it not enough?

Elle sat on the toilet seat, pulled her knees up to her chest and took a couple of deep breaths. *Get it together. You're not weak, you're not easily spooked. You can handle this. Just think.*

***

Ben Bont had got off the plane in a great mood. Elle met him on the makeshift runway, and they walked to the house, arms around each other. His mum and sister, he said, were flying up that night to celebrate the engagement. He couldn't wait to do the shoot, he said, to tell the world about them, to show off Baby Alma.

And then he saw the boys. A few minutes earlier, Elle had arranged Teddy and Freddie pleasingly next to the front door, whispering to them, 'If you don't move and you're nice to the man, you can have your new iPads this afternoon.' The poor little guys, who had no idea where they were or who was in charge, stood there with frozen smiles. It was truly remarkable what technology could buy you.

'Woah!' said Ben in the kind of large, cartoonish voice that people who aren't familiar with small children use around small children. 'This must me Teddy and Eddie!'

'Freddie,' whispered Elle, who had come to stand next to him and smile encouragingly at the boys.

'Of course, Teddy and Freddie! I've heard so much about you from your mum—I've been looking forward to hanging out all week. Wow! You guys are so big!'

'Who are you?' Teddy asked loudly.

Anger crossed Ben's face for a split second. He flicked a look back at Elle—it said, *They don't know who I am?*

She laughed, a little too loudly, and answered the unspoken question. 'Of *COURSE* they do. Boys, this is Ben. Ben's going to be...' She searched for the right words.

'Your new daddy!' Ben Bont said, in his loud 'cool kids' voice.

And both boys promptly burst into tears.

Elle thought back to the days when she was only 'managing' Adrian, a man almost twice her age who'd had a long career in finance, an ex, two kids, and all the bells and whistles of a solid middle-class life when she met him. She had known, somehow, exactly how to handle him. In hindsight, that life had been simple.

This was different. Ever since the proposal, life with Ben had become a power play without a script. Any time he appeared, Elle had no idea which version of him she was going to get. She didn't even know when he *was* going to appear; in the past few weeks he had taken to arriving at Gurva unannounced. And then, when he was around, there was the knowledge that any perceived misstep would change the temperature in any room.

It was unpredictable. It was too much.

Elle had to handle the crying boys. While a brooding Ben went to find Alma in the house full of strangers, Elle ushered her sons to the back deck with smoothies and the iPads.

Then she went back inside, and everything shifted again.

Who are all these people? Elle wondered as she moved through the house. There were familiar faces—Gurva staff with fruit trays—and there were TV people—a stylist steaming kids' clothes in the second bathroom. And there were magazine people—the photographer and his cushion-plumping crew in the lounge room.

Where was Ben?

He was in the master bedroom, holding Alma up, her face close to his. At almost four months she was ridiculously cute now, all smiles and reaching chubby fingers. She was squeezing Ben's nose, giggling. He was making goo-goo faces at her.

'Well, that went well,' he said, without looking up. 'Clearly Adrian's boys and I are going to be best friends.'

'Well,' Elle replied quickly, without really thinking, 'that "new daddy" comment was a bit much.'

Ben Bont looked from Alma to Elle. 'Really? A bit much?'

Elle moved to sit on the bed behind him. She realised her error—criticism—and knew she needed to walk things back. 'Baby,' she said, kneeling on the mattress, a knee on either side of his hips, her hands on his shoulders, 'let's return to that mood you were in when you got off the plane. We have a lot to do today—and I can't wait to do it with you.'

'You're right.' Ben went back to nuzzling Alma, who was cooing and reaching her hands up to Elle's face, which she could see above Daddy's. 'I'm alright.'

Just at the moment when it looked like the volcano wasn't going to blow, Matt walked in.

You didn't knock, you dick, Elle thought as he pushed open the door and stepped into the bedroom, where his bosses and their baby were all on the bed.

In his agitated state, it was as if Matt looked right though Ben to Elle, and just began to talk. 'Elle, we might have a problem. One of the hens has been ill this morning. She's arking up a bit, threatening to post about the—'

Whether it was the expression on Elle's face, or the sudden realisation that Ben Bont was in the room—Elle watched as reality suddenly closed in on Matt. He stopped short, but it was too late.

'About the what?' Ben stood up. He was still holding the baby, but he adjusted his grip so Alma was looking over his back shoulder, her arms reaching ahead. 'About the what?'

After Matt started muttering about food poisoning, Ben almost shoved Baby Alma at Elle.

'Mate,' Ben said to Matt, 'I am not fresh off the boat. I am not some idiot office boy. I'm not even the out-of-touch rich dick you think I am. I have been in this game since I could walk. I've been firing dodgy dickheads like you for fifteen years. I will not be even a little bit surprised to find out you're selling dodgy shit on my farm, but I *will* be furious, because a fuckwit like you should not have the power to threaten something me—and my wife—have worked so hard for.'

He's pulled me over to his side, thought Elle. *That's a good sign. For now.*

She lifted her eyes to Matt's and shook her head just a touch. *No. Walk away.*

Men were in a particular bind when the stakes were this high, Elle thought, watching Matt and Ben square up to each other. Something had to happen now.

In the silence as they all waited for what came next, Elle could hear all the activity going on around the homestead: the flower adjusting, the countertop wiping, the equipment twisting and clicking into place; the semi-hushed voices of professionals who were used to trying to pass unnoticed in another's home.

'Ben,' she said, after a moment, as Alma started to whimper—maybe *she* could break this tension. 'Ben, it's okay.'

'It's not okay, Elle. This is why,' and his voice dropped as he turned to face her, '*this* is why you can't be trusted. I should have fucking known, of course. That you were incapable of being trusted, of being... decent.'

Elle was still holding Alma, who was beginning to twist and arch, uncomfortable, tetchy. *Time to tap dance*, Elle told herself. Anything to stop these rhinos crashing into each other in a house full of cameras.

'Ben, this is not as bad as it seems. Those women, they were wild at the bar last night, and—'

'DON'T PUSH ME ON THIS!' yelled Ben Bont, at the top of his voice.

And suddenly, the thing that was about to happen, happened.

Ben didn't push Matt. He pushed Elle.

She stumbled back, Alma held close to her chest, and knocked over a lamp. It hit the glass candles on the bedside table, making a loud crash on its way to the floor.

'I AM SERIOUS. DO NOT *FUCKING* PUSH ME ON

THIS! I TOLD YOU THIS WAS A TERRIBLE IDEA! THIS IS WHY YOU CAN'T BE HERE ALONE!'

Matt took a step towards Ben, but Elle, gathering herself in a second, said, 'No. Matt. Leave, please. Leave.'

Matt waited a beat, and then he left through the French doors to the deck.

Alma started to cry, and Ben Bont just stood there looking at Elle. 'Don't push me with this shit,' he said quietly. 'I am not Adrian.'

***

'I can't quite explain it,' Ben Bont said, an hour later, 'it's like, the moment I saw her, I knew I was home. I'd never believed in love at first sight. But now I know,' he looked away from Julia Grover, the ash-blonde interviewer who'd gone to school with his mother, and over at Elle, 'that was because it hadn't happened to me yet.'

Elle beamed back at him. Alma was sleeping in her arms. Teddy and Freddie sat on either side of Ben and Elle, motionless on a promise of taking the new iPads home.

'And now,' Julia said, 'you have this family.'

'The perfect family.' Ben smiled. 'The perfect family at last.'

Julia sighed a pretty little sigh. 'Your happiness is palpable, Ben,' she said, then shifted her position to direct a question straight to the beautiful earth mother in white. 'But Elle, what would you like to say to Australia about the allegations that you not only lied about your ex-husband's health, but also about your own father's death?'

Elle's smile faded, appropriately. She looked at Freddie, sitting to her left, and then down at gently snoring Alma. 'I think it's unfortunate,' she said, 'that people choose to believe the worst in others when there's so much beauty in the world. My past has been troubled, like many other people's. My first marriage was not perfect, my upbringing was not perfect, but that doesn't make me a monster.' Elle widened her smile into a dazzling crescent. 'And I'll just be forever grateful to this man, who believes in me.' She gazed right into the camera. 'It's true, everyone, you *can* have everything. You can have the fairytale. I do.'

Julia started to say, 'But your father—'

Ben wagged his finger. 'One question, Julia, darling. I think my fiancée answered you.'

***

In the ensuite Elle stood up, washed her face. Ben's family would be here in a moment. He was all smiles after the interview. Delightedly showing off Alma to the film crew and guests, trying to rumble with Teddy and Freddie.

Frances, that funny little nurse, had looked at Elle strangely when she'd come out to the deck, ready for her close-up. *They must have heard*, Elle thought. But she just shrugged and smiled at Frances, gave the reclining Arden a little wave. She'd deal with them later.

Now she just needed to regroup, find the energy she'd expelled on camera. *No time for weakness, you idiot*, she told herself. *You can handle anything, remember. You can handle a spoilt brat like Ben Bont*.

Elle looked down at the huge blue ring. *But you cannot, must not marry him*.

She smoothed her hair back with her hands, draped her braid over one shoulder and got ready to go out and face the people.

And then she heard a familiar, but entirely unexpected, voice outside the bathroom. Shouty, female, clear as a bell. 'Where the *HELL* is my daughter?'

It was Abi Black.

CHAPTER 31

ABI

Elle's property was obscenely beautiful—a slice of wilderness pruned to within an inch of its life to give just enough rural edge for city folk. But Abi was sick of hiding in its fucking bushes.

With so many people coming and going, Abi kept thinking she might miss Arden, and had begun to imagine her daughter kidnapped and in the back of one of these hire cars, packed up with the lights and boom mics.

What Abi had found down at the cottages hadn't exactly filled her with confidence that her daughter was suffering from nothing more than a flat phone battery. She and Zoe had started at that cluster of buildings down by the water accidentally walking in on a group of greenish-looking women doing a meditation class in front of wild-haired older woman brandishing a tiny gong.

'Oops, sorry, anyone seen a teenage girl? Little? Big attitude?' Abi asked them, as Zoe pulled her away from the studio door.

'Are you *nuts*?' Zoe hissed—then added, 'Please don't try to answer that.'

They peered into a retreat villa. 'These are *nice*,' Abi said, forgetting herself for a moment. 'Maybe Grace and I could host a retreat?'

'Focus!' snapped Zoe, who'd made it clear that she was determined not to accidentally bump into her sister. 'If we can get out of here without Elle knowing we were ever around, then I'm happy.'

'As long as we find Arden...'

Abi marched off towards the big hall-like building, where a few young men in white coats were setting up tables for a liquid dinner. 'Have you guys seen a teenage girl?' Abi asked them, showing the closest boy her phone: Arden sulked from her home screen.

'Yes,' he said, taking Abi by surprise—the script in her head had kept the mystery rolling on. 'She's the girl who collapsed last night.'

'*What?*'

The backpacker boy looked sheepish, but also as though he knew exactly what he'd done.

Abi didn't like that look. 'DID YOU DO SOMETHING TO MY DAUGHTER?' she found herself shouting, grabbing his arm.

'Your daughter? Woah, no! She just had a rough night, ask Matt.' The backpacker boy shrugged off Abi's grip and stepped away.

'Who the fuck is Matt, and where is he? And WHERE is my daughter?' Abi was yelling again. The lady with the gong would definitely be able to hear her—and was probably dinging wildly.

And again, it was Zoe who pulled Abi away. 'Come on, don't be a dick to this guy. It's not his fault.'

'Up at the house,' the boy said with a shrug, clearly now keen to get rid of the crazy lady. 'I think they're up at the house.'

Abi was well and truly beside herself. *Collapsed?* She

pretty much dragged Zoe out of the hall and across the grass to where the hire car was parked near the cabins.

'I don't want to go up to the house!' Zoe protested. 'I don't want to see my sister.'

'Well look, precious, I don't want to either,' said Abi, 'but we might have no choice. Wherever Arden is, we're going.'

'Can I wait in the car?' Zoe was already slumping into the passenger seat, head down.

'Oh, for fuck's sake...'

***

Stepping through the open door in the cool, wide hall of the farmhouse, it took Abi approximately thirty seconds to sense that things were not exactly picture-perfect here, no matter how pretty the throw-rugs.

In the fancy drawing room off to the right, a glossy older woman and a young, waifish blonde were having a pre-dinner sherry with Julia Grover from *Fifty Minutes*. They looked up at Abi, in her overalls and boots, with the polite curiosity of people used to having strangers who worked for them in their homes. 'Hello?' the older woman said. *Those must be the in-laws*, thought Abi.

'Just looking for Elle Campbell,' she said, trying to smile.

'She's...' The woman motioned with her hand down the hall, seemingly perplexed. 'Is she expecting you?'

Abi just kept walking along the hall, peering through open doors. Jesus, this place was beautiful; each doorway revealed a scene more perfect than the last. A few young, uniformed people were packing away shoot props and catering trays. The sun was beginning to hang lower in the sky, glowing through the back door.

Abi was suddenly overwhelmed by the ridiculousness of this situation. She was searching Elle Campbell's house for Arden, and for Adrian's sons. She was tiptoeing through the place like a creep.

She gave up. Planted her feet. And yelled, 'Where the *HELL* is my daughter?'

And at the very same moment the words flew out of her mouth, she decided to bolt for the back doors that opened out to a deck.

Sure enough, next to the skinniest pool Abi had ever seen, there was Arden. She glanced up, confused, at the sound of her mother's voice. She was sitting on a sun lounger, looking as if she'd just been deep in conversation with a small, slight woman with black hair.

'Mum?' Arden's face was a picture of fear.

'Abi?' It was Elle, behind Abi.

'Abi!' Behind Elle stood Teddy and Freddie, in brand-new pyjamas Abi had never seen before, hair wet and neatly brushed back from their scrubbed-pink faces.

'Boys!' Behind them was a young woman in a T-shirt and shorts with a hairbrush in hand: the nanny.

'Who is this? Are we setting another plate for dinner?' Abi recognised Ben Bont from Instagram.

She turned back to Arden. 'Are you alright? I've been going crazy.' Abi went to sit next to her daughter on the sun lounger, putting an arm around her and squeezing. 'Are you?'

Arden looked teary, vulnerable. She rested her head on Abi's shoulder in a rare display of public affection. 'I'm fine, Mum,' she said. 'I'm fine.'

The small dark-haired woman reached out to give Arden's knee a reassuring pat.

'How the hell did you get up here?' Elle asked Abi.

'Elle, who the hell is this?' asked Ben.

'It's Arden's mum. Adrian's ex. Abi Black.'

'No!' The look on the dark-haired woman's face told Abi that a penny had just clanged to the ground.

'Really?' Ben crossed his arms. 'Elle, follow me, please?'

Abi hugged Arden tighter as she watched this Ben guy guide Elle back inside the house. The boys charged for Abi, but even through their tangled limbs and kisses, she thought, *That's the first time I've ever seen Elle obey anyone. This is interesting.*

'Mum, can we go home?' Arden asked, head still on Abi's shoulder as Teddy and Freddie climbed onto her knee.

'Can we?' Teddy echoed. 'And bring the iPads?'

'I need some explanations first,' Abi said. 'What the hell is happening here? And who the hell are you?' This was directed at the dark-haired woman and delivered with a glare at the hand still on her daughter's knee. Abi felt a surge of furious frustration at not knowing what was going on. It was as if everyone else was speaking a foreign language and her brain wouldn't let her catch up.

'I'm Frances—I'm a nurse. I just came for the retreat, but things went a bit wonky last night.' She smiled. 'I still haven't done any yoga.'

'Nurse?' Abi asked immediately. 'This is relevant because...?'

'We'll tell you later,' Arden said. 'When you can't get mad.'

'Oh, I can *always* get mad.'

Ben Bont came back onto the deck. 'I'd like to ask you all to stay for dinner, Abi and Arden and...?'

'Frances.'

'Fine. But my family are here to celebrate our engagement, and it's a rather private dinner. You could all get fed down at the hall, if you'd like to head down there?' He walked over and awkwardly ruffled Freddie's black curls. 'Not you, boys, of course—you're staying right here.'

Abi didn't think so: looking at Ben was making her skin feel tight. He had a veneer of perfection—the tousled hair, the slight tan, the chinos, the bare feet, the perfect, very white smile. And he was tall and lean. He looked like a man whom no one ever said no to. Which just made Abi really, really need to tell him no.

'I think the boys can come with me,' she said, standing up. Arden stood with her, shoulder tucked under her armpit, while the boys held on to her legs. 'Your little shoot's finished, hasn't it? You guys are done?'

The only person still sitting on the sun lounger was Frances, who was looking up at Abi as though still shocked she was really there.

'I don't think you get to make that decision, Abi,' said Ben. 'Our understanding is that Adrian said the boys would spend two nights with their mother.'

Freddie started to cry, softly, and pushed his face further into Abi's overall-covered leg. Teddy took Arden's hand.

Ben Bont curled a lip. 'Don't you think this is a bit cruel, Abi? The boys haven't seen their mother in over a year, and you're playing this game with them?'

'They're afraid,' Abi said. 'When Arden leaves, they won't know anyone here.'

'They are with their *mother*,' Ben Bont said, in that same tone.

'Like I said, they won't know anyone here.' *Fuck you*, she thought.

Elle appeared behind Ben Bont. She looked a little different, even more so than she had at the Daylesford farm. It was hard for Abi to pinpoint the difference—something around Elle's eyes. She looked depleted, somehow, smaller.

'Let her take them,' Elle said, remaining behind Ben.

He swung around to her. 'Are you kidding?'

'No.' Elle straightened her back, set her chin high. 'She can take them. Shoot's finished. Let's go and enjoy our engagement dinner. I know Mauna's been working really hard on it.'

She's lying, thought Abi. *This woman is lying about something*. Which would hardly be unusual in Elle's case. But what was it?

Abi looked at Arden, who seemed so tired and broken she could barely talk, and the boys, who were gazing up at Abi as if awaiting instruction. If only they were ever this quiet at home.

The nurse, Frances, was now giving Elle the incredulous stare she had fixed on Abi. *This little chicken's having her mind blown today*.

'Boys, let's go and get your bags,' Abi said. She started to walk towards the house—but moving with three other people in step is not a graceful process.

Frances was gathering her cardigan and bag, readying to follow.

'Elle,' said Ben, 'what are you doing? Why would you let this... hippie take your boys?'

'Coming from you, I'll take that as a compliment,' Abi said as she passed him. And as she passed Elle on the way into the house, she couldn't help but hiss, 'You okay?'

'Fuck off,' Elle spat, under her breath.

'Okaaay then.' Abi kept moving, all the way to the boys' suitcases.

***

Back in Byron, Abi and Zoe were sitting on the lounge of their serviced apartment. Arden was passed out asleep between them, her head on Abi's knee, her feet in Zoe's lap. The boys' snores could be heard coming from the bedroom; they'd fallen asleep in what was meant to be Abi's bed, curled around each other like speech marks.

'There *is* something going on there, Zo,' Abi said, patting Arden's hair as Zoe stroked her feet.

'Well, of course,' said Zoe, 'this is my sister we're talking about. There's bound to be something heinous going on.'

'No, it's kind of different.' Abi caught a whiff of something, bent down and smelled Arden's hair—a hint of vomit. 'I think that guy is... bad.'

'Then they deserve each other.' Zoe dropped Arden's foot. Looked away.

'I know you'd like to think that, Zo. But I also know... she's your sister.'

'What the fuck's that supposed to mean?'

'I think you know.'

'Abi, she's dumped her family, abandoned her own sons, destroyed so much—I have no sympathy for her... whatever's going on.'

'Sure, okay.'

But Abi thought, *You'll be back*.

'I'd better called Gracey,' Abi said. 'My bride. If only I can get her talking to me. We're going to be married in less than three weeks.'

'Three weeks!' Zoe shook her head. 'Shit, it's nearly Christmas.' She lifted Arden's feet and got up, going to peer into the bedroom and check that the boys were still asleep. 'What sort of Christmas are those two going to have?'

'A fucking excellent one on the farm with people who love them,' said Abi firmly. 'Zoe, it's not them I'm worried about.'

CHAPTER 32

FRANCES

It was three days until Frances saw Elle again. And, when she did, it was as if nothing had happened between them at all.

As if she'd never spent that night sitting by Arden's bedside, checking that Elle's stepdaughter was still breathing. As if she'd never been inside Elle's home. As if she had never heard Ben Bont's yelling and crashing; as if she hadn't seen him and Elle come out and turn everything on for the cameras, sparkling with shiny pretence.

And as if she hadn't seen Elle Campbell send her two tiny sons away when their work as photogenic props was done.

It was as if none of that had ever happened.

That evening, she'd seen Abi Black gather up the children and leave. Then Frances was popped into a white golf cart by a uniformed staff member and whizzed down the hill to her retreat cabin.

When she got to her room, she found a basket of complimentary Elle merchandise—including the clip-on braid and five packets of the gold dust she'd so desperately wanted to sprinkle into her broken blender—on the beautifully made bed.

A note read:

> *Thank you for all you've done for my family. I know you have missed the first day of your Purify and Release retreat, so please accept a session with our incredible derma doctors, Andy and Andi, on us. Why not go home with your outsides matching your insides? So much love and light—E x*

That night, Frances called Troy and told him she thought she was coming home.

'It's not quite what I thought it would be,' she told him as she lay on the bed, finally showered. 'I really don't think I fit in here.'

Troy's sigh was so heavy, Frances thought she felt her phone shake. 'Frankie, you told me this was what you needed more than anything. You said this was what was going to make you happy again. You can't just ditch it because it's got too tough.'

'It's not that it's tough, Troy, it's—'

'Come on, Frankie. We paid for that. And the guy did me a favour. Please, now we've gone through all this, just stick it out.'

Frances stayed silent for a moment. She looked down at herself lying on the bed. She took some of the flesh of her stomach in her hand. *I am a shitty excuse machine*, she thought. And she said, 'You're right. I'm just missing Denny. How is he?'

'I picked him up from your mum today—he's just like he always is,' Troy said, but she could hear the smile in his voice. 'Are you worried about our two nights alone together? Think I'm going to break him?'

'Not even a little bit,' Frances said.

And she stayed.

***

Three days of not-eating later, she wasn't really sure what she knew anymore.

She and the hens and a handful of other, mostly older women were neck-deep in Elle-ness now. And they were all a little bit broken.

Every morning started at five, with a dawn yoga class on a purpose-built deck in a paddock. It was startlingly beautiful, really, to be exercising in this silent space, surrounded by mist, as the valley chirped to life. But it was also slippery and damp, and made their yoga tights smell, and one morning the endlessly optimistic Brazilian instructor had to kick a dead rat off the stage.

Then they all trudged back through the wet grass to not eat breakfast in the hall. Instead, they sipped on the morning detox smoothie of some kind of berry, flaxseed, water and a whole lot of supplements that even Frances—who prided herself on a thorough knowledge of the WholeHealth catalogue—had never heard of.

After showering and changing into another set of activewear, it was off to some sort of self-improvement session. (Frances had only brought three sets, and she was easily going through that in a day, so her evenings were spent furtively washing them in her cabin ensuite and dangling them over the balcony to dry—which was optimistic in what had once been a humid rainforest.)

This morning, Frances had done 'How to Say No to Negative People' with a woman who had once talked her way out of a kidnapping situation while hiking the mountains of Pakistan. It was a remarkable story, and Frances was happy to hear it, but she wasn't completely sure of its relevance. Still, this woman—now a Byron-based mum of two—had a boutique business producing T-shirts with inspirational slogans, and you could buy them at the end of her talk. Frances lingered over 'YOU DON'T KNOW WHAT YOU'RE MADE

OF UNTIL YOU'RE REALLY IN THE SH*T' with a picture of a baby sitting in a pile of poo, but thought better of it.

Then the guests had down time until 'non-lunch', which Frances found very unhelpful as she had little to focus on other than how hungry she was, and how nice it would be to sit up in Elle's beautiful farmhouse, snacking on organic berry anti-muffins and swimming in the cobalt lap pool.

So each morning Frances went for a slow walk—she didn't have enough energy for anything more strenuous—to see if she could find someone to talk to.

On the second day she'd stumbled across some of the Bondi hens doing extended yoga practice outside their cabins. They were very bendy. One woman said hi to Frances as she walked past, and it took her a moment to work out what she was looking at—the woman's head seemed to be under her opposite arm, one leg reaching straight up behind her at an angle Frances had never witnessed before. 'Namaste,' she muttered, and hurried along.

On the third afternoon the group had their first session with Elle, and Frances had been looking forward to it.

The tired women lifted when Elle bounced onto the stage in her teeny-tiny white yoga wear. They all felt great about their hunger when she talked to them about being better than before and not giving in to their weak and pathetic inner voices. Frances heard herself whooping when Elle told them to push their physical selves into the kind of shape that would see them kicking the arses of anyone who tried to bring them down.

In her head, Dr Darling's hand was no longer up her shirt, but was dangling, helplessly, from a broken wrist she'd inflicted with one focused jab: *Take that, you pathetic creep!*

But when Elle Campbell told the enthralled audience about how hard it was to forgive the people who'd attempted to ruin her, though she tried a little more every day, Frances couldn't help think, *Bullshit*.

Frances also looked around the room and began to calculate

the money spent by each of these women: the cost of the retreat, the Goddess Project subscriptions, the powders and potions and cans of fake tan, the pay-per-view e-seminars, the sexy active-wear—and looked back at Elle and thought, *Wow*.

Was that impressive, or was it deplorable? In her hungry state, Frances couldn't be sure.

After Elle's session, all of the women—glowing, pumped, excited—lined up to meet her.

'I'll see you again on your last morning,' she said over and over to the women who shook her hand and told her how she'd changed their lives, that they were survivors, too. 'I can't wait to see what you look like then!'

When it was Frances's turn, Elle held her hand for a moment longer. 'Frances,' she said, smiling, 'what can I say? I hope you're having an important time here.'

'Well, it's improved,' Frances said, with a wry giggle, 'since that first night.'

Elle's face froze for a moment; her eyes dashed quickly to the right, as though to see who was standing nearby. 'Ha, yes, let's not dwell on that.'

'But are you okay?' Frances asked Elle, putting her hand on the guru's. 'Really?'

Elle snatched her hand away. Suddenly, Frances noticed something: Elle was wearing body make-up on her upper arms and, where she'd sweated a little, it appeared to be covering a bruise.

'You should make sure you get to Dr Andy,' Elle said. 'Use that session we booked in for you.'

'Oh, I will, but—'

A white-shirted staff member seemed to materialise from nowhere to usher Frances away from Elle, making room for her next disciple.

'I hope you're okay!' Frances heard herself yelling over her shoulder as she left the studio.

Just before she walked out, she saw a flush of irritation darken across Elle's face.

***

The next day was the one when they could all eat. The juice detox was over, and the Hot TV Chef was going to make real food for the guests. Frances was so excited at the idea of chewing something, she shook off her annoyance. There were only a couple of nights to go, and she wanted the full experience, however her feelings about Elle were changing.

That morning, the women fell on their bowls of bone broth with floating vegetables as if they were cream puffs covered in chocolate.

'OH MY GOD,' one of the Bondi hens exclaimed, 'I think I'm going to have a fucking orgasm over breakfast soup!'

'Wait till you see lunch broth,' said Hot TV Chef, who was watching proudly from the kitchen doorway. 'See, this negative calorie food tastes amazing, right?'

To be honest, Frances thought, sinking her teeth into a slice of mushroom, *week-old lettuce would taste amazing to this bunch of starving juice-heads*.

Frances had her appointment with the skin gurus after breakfast, and she was half looking forward to it, half nervous about what they'd say about her tired-lady face. But just as she was leaving to change, one of the young, dreadlocked staff members approached her with a note. 'From Elle,' he said, giving her an impressed look.

> *Dearest Frances, please come up to the house after your morning session. Ben and I would love to talk to you about something special.*

When Frances climbed onto the golf cart to be taken to the main house, she was bright red and couldn't feel half her face. Her microdermabrasion treatment had left her raw and glowing, and the filler Dr Andy had injected around her mouth 'would take a while to settle'.

She hadn't walked into the spotless white room of the

Gurva spa thinking she would come out looking different, but the doctors had told her in no uncertain terms that something had to be done.

'You're so young but you have these stress lines around your mouth,' said Andi.

'And really, if that top lip was just a little fuller, it would work so much better with that nose,' said Andy.

'A bit of botox between the brows would lift that tiredness away from your eye bags,' Andi went on.

'No,' Frances managed to say. 'No botox, thanks. I really... I really would just like a nice, relaxing facial.'

The derma doctors laughed. 'Oh darling, it's so adorable, you don't even know what you need, do you? You are going to feel so much better when your outsides match your insides.'

Those were the exact words that Elle had used, and Frances thought, *No, I am an exhausted new mum with a demanding baby and a job and a mountain of debt, my outsides absolutely match my insides*.

But what she said was, 'Well, whatever you think is best.' Frances was feeling completely overwhelmed and a bit nauseated from the unusual sensation of having food in her stomach.

Now she walked up to Elle's stunning farmhouse feeling like a peeled grape and unable to feel her teeth.

Elle came to the door. 'Oh my god, you look amazing.' She was wearing a translucent, lacy kaftan over the tiniest white bikini Frances had ever seen on a real person. Baby Alma was on her hip, drinking from a bottle.

A bottle?

'Um, thank you.' Frances doubted this was an accurate assessment, but she'd go with it.

She followed Elle through the gorgeously airy farmhouse, past the kitchen where that same crew-cutted woman was chopping kale like a demon ahead of two primed Nutrimullets.

They were heading to the deck again, Frances realised, but this time through what she assumed was a guestroom.

They walked out to where white wrought-iron chairs and a table had been set up in front of a curtain of ivy. A jug of iced water with floating berries and lemons was already on the table beside three glasses.

'How old is your son?' Elle asked Frances as she looked down at Alma.

This took Frances aback, as she didn't remember telling Elle she had a son. 'He's just a bit older—almost six months.' For a second she was overtaken by the urge to grab Alma and sniff her head, struck by an intense pang of missing her boy.

'Lovely. Such a precious time, isn't it?'

'It is,' Frances said. This was her chance to slip into some baby bonding with Elle Campbell. 'I miss him so much when I'm at work.'

'Oh, you're back at work?' Elle raised an eyebrow. 'How... brave you are to be able to leave him like that. You must be very well adjusted!' And she let out a little laugh.

Okay, now I actually want to punch you in the face, thought Frances.

Ben Bont appeared holding a tray of fruit, beautifully chopped and presented on a bed of ice. 'Ladies,' he said, all smiles and broad shoulders, and he motioned for Frances to sit as he put the platter on the table. After a brief exchange about how 'refreshed' Frances was looking, Ben said, 'There's something we all need to discuss. And it's how we can help you, Frances.'

'Help me?' Frances tentatively took a sip of water and immediately wished that she hadn't as it dribbled out the side of her numb mouth; she grabbed a cloth napkin and dabbed.

'You had such an unfortunate start to your week here,' Ben went on, 'and it brought some issues to our attention.'

'Matt has... gone,' Elle said, taking Alma's bottle and setting her on the wooden deck. 'I'm sure you won't be surprised to hear that.'

Frances nodded. 'He didn't seem like someone you'd want working for you.'

'When you run as many businesses as I do,' Ben said, crossing his arms, 'there are always a few bad apples.'

Frances nodded again, watching Alma suck the edge of Elle's doubtless extremely expensive kaftan.

'But I know that was very difficult for you,' Ben went on. 'Stressful. Unnecessary. And we want to make sure you're compensated for your trouble and inconvenience.'

'I got the sense,' Elle said, looking Frances in the eye, 'yesterday when I saw you, that you were feeling... unresolved about it all.'

'Well...' Frances wondered if her forehead was expressing her confusion at the point of this conversation—she knew it took a while for the botox to settle in.

'So,' Ben reached into his pocket, 'I spoke to a few people. You're Troy Graham's wife. Which is excellent news. Troy is one of my most valued hotel assets. He's always been exceptionally loyal.'

Frances nodded again. *And?*

'And we heard that since you've become parents, your financial situation has been... stress-inducing at times, so I thought,' Ben unfolded a piece of paper, 'we could help you. Make a bit of an offer. Compensate you for any distress, help make your life a little easier.'

And help shut me up.

Frances leant over to look at the paper on the table, without picking it up. It was a typed-up offer of fifteen thousand dollars: exactly the amount of credit card debt that she and Troy were in, mostly thanks to her.

'Are you... serious?' she asked Ben, eyebrows raised (at least, she assumed they were raised).

'Yes, very. I'm a serious guy.'

Something about the way he said that made Frances shift in her chair.

'And what do you want for it?' she asked, looking at each of them.

Elle laughed. 'Want? We want you to have benefited from

the experience of coming to Gurva. We want everyone to leave here a little more perfect. That's our goal.'

'But you're not paying off anyone else's debt?' Frances asked, with no idea where she was getting the courage to speak.

'No,' said Ben, 'because we don't have to make up for anyone else's distress. This is your chance to really change things, Frances. You take this money, and that face, and your new Gurva confidence, and you start all this over. Just like Elle did.'

'Um...' *But I haven't done anything wrong. How am I like Elle in this situation?* 'Thank you so much,' she said, then paused—what would it mean for these people to pay her off? 'But I need to think about it.'

Elle and Ben exchanged a look. A minuscule shrug.

'Okay, but obviously we need to know very soon,' said Ben.

'By tomorrow morning,' said Elle.

'Thank you so much.' Frances was suddenly overcome with an urge to get off that deck, to run screaming from this house, this farm, these people. 'I'd better go and let this settle—' She motioned her palm in a circle around her face. 'So, I'll get back to you later on.'

'Not too much later,' Ben Bont said, standing up.

Elle bent down and picked up Alma.

As they were walking back through the house, Frances suddenly thought of something she'd always wanted to say to Elle if she got the opportunity.

'You know, I'm so impressed by your wild birth story with Alma,' she said, stopping at the front door and turning around. 'I really wanted to have a no-intervention birth, and I ended up with an awful mess. I cried about it for months. Your story was so perfect, I want to do that if I have another baby. And you did it after a C-sec, too! It's so inspirational!'

Elle looked confused for a second, then she glanced at Ben and laughed. 'Oh, darling,' she said to Frances, jiggling

Alma, 'don't beat yourself up about that. The wild birth story was a bit of theatre. I took every drug I could to get this baby out, and I spent a week at the best hospital in Queensland. As if I was going to leave all that to chance!' Elle laughed again, and Ben put an arm around her shoulder, looking down at her with something like pride.

Frances stared at Elle for a moment, and then she turned and silently walked out to the golf buggy.

'Bye, Frances,' Elle called after her. 'Be your very best self, okay?'

'Okay,' Frances called back, climbing into the buggy.

All those hours of thinking about that birth. About what could possibly be wrong with her, with Frances, that she couldn't have done that, too—just got herself in the zone and pushed out her baby like a real woman.

And all those women out there who felt the same way...

Frances felt like tapping the farmhouse walls. Was anything real here?

***

When she got back to her cabin, Frances sat down and pulled out her phone. She spread Ben Bont's offer in front of her, and she began to type.

The Horrib-ELLE Truth Facebook group needed a few minutes to approve her as a member.

While she waited, she started working on her post.

> Elle Campbell hasn't changed one tiny bit. And I have proof...

CHAPTER 33

BEN BONT

Ben Bont couldn't stand the way his mother had been looking at him all week.

She had always been the only person in the world who could make him feel small—well, until recently, perhaps—and this week she was excelling at it.

Helen Bont had been his father's second wife, the mother of two of his five children. Predictably enough for a man like his dad, she'd been a model when they'd met, then a stay-at-home mother.

And then, after the marriage exploded into a mess of infidelity and boozy blow-ups, Helen had gone back to university to train as a counsellor. Her second act was as a professional and pricey relationship adviser to her Sydney Eastern Suburbs' cohort—massaging the marriages of wealthy women.

The thing she would say to him that he hated the most was, 'You're just like your father.' And she'd said it to him that first night, after Elle had let that idiot woman go home with her boys.

I am not my father, he was saying into the mirror now,

shaving in preparation for the last family dinner before his mother and sister flew out tomorrow. *I am not like my father at all*.

His sister, Georgie, also had her opinions. 'You've changed, Ben,' she'd said to him later that night, when everyone had gone to bed and she came to sit with him on the darkened deck. As was her way, she lit up a joint, took a big toke and said, 'I think she's done it to you, and I think this marriage is a big mistake.'

'Thanks, sis, for all your support, as usual.'

'You need someone in your life who'll tell you the truth,' said Georgie, before drawing in hard. 'And I'm it. That's why you love me.'

'I do?' he said, shaking his head as she offered him a toke. But he did: he valued her opinion because she wanted nothing from him. 'You have never liked any woman I've been with,' he told her.

'That's because they've all been fuckwits. But this one... well, she's a certified nut job,' Georgie looked down at her spliff, 'but you knew that.'

Ben Bont was beginning to think that perhaps *he* was the nut job. The rage that was bubbling up in him—he'd felt it before, it had always been there; it was part of what drove him and drove him and drove him. But it had never felt so close to the surface. It had never felt so accessible to him.

'I think maybe this is my fault, not hers,' he said, quietly to Georgie in the dark.

'Doesn't matter,' she replied. 'Doesn't matter whose fault it is. You just don't want to get yourself stuck here, brother.'

***

After Abi Black had left with the children, and the mousey nurse has scurried away, Ben had felt that rage surge so hard it seemed to physically move him across the deck to where Elle was standing, chin up, looking defiant.

He grabbed her by the shoulders, and he could feel her bones so close to the surface; she was such a tiny, breakable person. He could tell that he was grabbing her too hard, but in that moment he didn't care. *Good*, he thought, when he saw her defiance flip to fear. *Good*.

'You're hurting me,' she said.

'Why did you do that?' he asked. He must have been shouting, although it didn't feel like shouting to him. He felt like he might throw her, like he could throw her over the deck. His mind was crowded with images of all the things she'd done to him. He couldn't see through them. It was all rushing in too fast. 'You humiliated me in front of that... cunt,' he shouted. 'You contradicted me, and you showed strangers that you have the maternal instincts of a cat. A fucking cat. What is wrong with you?'

Elle hadn't said anything. He was shouting in her face, and she didn't say anything.

'What have you got to say? Why aren't you even trying to explain why you've let that fucking meathead risk our entire reputation and keep secrets from me? And then you let those children just... leave? Without even saying anything? WHAT IS WRONG WITH YOU?'

He was shaking her, he realised. And still, Elle didn't say anything; it was like she wasn't there. Her expression was blank, her mouth a little line.

'Ben!' It was his mother. She was standing at the French doors. His sister was standing next to her. And beside her was Julia Grover, who had interviewed them just hours before.

He looked at the three women for a moment, Elle still in his hands. What was he doing? He let Elle go suddenly, almost throwing her aside. She dropped to the deck, and he pushed past his mother, his sister and the Queen of Current Affairs television to go and shut himself away from all these women.

'You don't want to get stuck here, brother,' his stoned sister said, later.

'Georgie,' he said, getting up to go to bed, 'I already am.'

***

I'm nothing like my father, he thought, pulling on his shirt. *And Elle knows that.*

The day after that night, he'd seen the bruises on her arms, and he felt shame and disgust. Surely he hadn't done that to her?

He apologised and he meant it. He wasn't sure if he'd ever been so sorry in his life. But still, he said, as he kissed her all over in their bed that morning, she just needed to let him in. As long as he knew what was going on—what she was thinking—he wouldn't get so angry.

Couldn't she see that?

In the days since, Elle had been quiet but perfectly pleasant. They'd spent time with Alma without the nanny. They'd spoken together frankly about paying off the nurse—although they still hadn't heard from her, the little idiot. Ben had managed not to lose his temper through any of that—even though that whole mess was Elle's fucking fault and now he was going to have to pay for it.

She'd agreed to Matt being fired, immediately, and elevating Ennis to run the retreat for a while. Things had settled, and Ben Bont decided to stay up in Byron until Christmas, since the wedding planner was coming and he felt calmer when he could see Elle.

'I like to watch you,' he'd told her that morning, when she'd come back into the bedroom after her work-out.

He was lying on the bed, watching her get ready for her shower. She was pulling her hair out of its braid, peeling off her exercise clothes, picking up bottles from her dressing table. He enjoyed seeing her move around the room, the light hitting her skin.

'I know you do,' she said to him, and turned fully to face him. She just stood there, naked but with that big blue diamond. 'Do you see me?' she asked him. 'Do you see I've got nothing to hide?'

'I see you're full of secrets,' he said to her. But he wasn't angry, and he pulled her to him, and they had the kind of sex they'd had since they met.

And afterwards, everything was peaceful.

Maybe all the drama was behind them, Ben thought, as he pulled on his deck shoes. They'd have their wedding and everything would be perfect.

As long as she let him in, that could happen, right? Why not?

***

Ben Bont had taken Elle up to Gurva—not that it was called that, then, of course—only a week after they met.

He understood that she needed somewhere to lie low. And it suited him that he had her somewhere he could see her whenever he wanted but that didn't interfere with his life and business in Sydney.

She'd loved the property. Taken off her shoes and buried her toes in the earth. 'I am in heaven!' she'd told him. 'And I know exactly what you need to do with the place!'

Back then, he'd been enchanted and excited by her business ideas. She could see all this potential in rebranding Gurva: it gave her purpose; it was all investment that could easily be written off; he loved seeing it grow under her hand. He wasn't used to women like Elle, and she delighted him.

What a cliché, he thought now, *that the very things you love about someone at the beginning are the things that come between you in the end*.

He knew their relationship was advantageous to her. Early on she'd insisted that his head of legal, Bronwyn, draft up a contract saying that forty per cent of the Gurva business, excluding the existing property, was hers if she stayed and worked on it for three years. Ben had been comfortable with that—it meant forty per cent of the debt would be hers too, if it all went belly-up. And it had given them a professional framework if the relationship had fallen over.

But it hadn't, and the business was flourishing. And Alma had come along.

Recently the three-year thing had been niggling at him. They'd joked about it at the beginning—six months down, thirty to go—but now he realised he had never believed, especially after Alma, that Elle was staying for the business.

Right up until he proposed.

Now the wedding was almost here. And Elle still wasn't divorced.

Bronwyn had told him that Adrian wasn't budging on moving things along. 'I can't physically force him to sign the paperwork,' she'd said. 'We have applied pressure where we can, now it's up to him.'

Today Ben had given Adrian a personal call, and it was one of the stranger conversations he'd ever had. Adrian hadn't budged an inch, but to Ben he didn't sound like a man in love. There was no passion there, no jealousy. In fact, he said, 'Ben, mate, I've never met you, but you are absolutely crazy to marry that woman.'

'Be careful, Adrian, that's the mother of my child you're talking about,' Ben said evenly.

Adrian laughed a little. 'Yeah, mine too. Not that you would notice.'

Ben didn't reply to that. The line he'd always told himself about Elle and her boys—that Adrian was keeping them apart—didn't stand up anymore. And he hadn't yet found anything palatable to replace it with.

'Just sign the papers, Adrian,' Ben said. 'Let everyone get on with their lives.'

'I can't do that. I just can't do that.'

'Mate, she's never coming back to you. You need to understand that.'

'Oh, I do,' Adrian said. 'I'm counting on that.'

'We're getting married on New Year's Eve,' Ben said, in the voice he used when he was closing a deal, 'one way or another.'

'Well,' Adrian sounded amused again, 'that makes two of my two ex-wives who are getting married this New Year's Eve. Lucky you're not inviting me, or I'd be having a terrible clash of commitments.'

'You'll be hearing from my lawyers,' Ben said. 'Again.'

There was a pause at the other end, and then Adrian asked gently, 'Have you ever noticed, Ben, that Elle has no friends at all?'

Ben hung up.

***

'So,' Ben's mother was saying at the dinner table, 'is Hunter Billows coming to the wedding? I hear you boys are tight these days. At least, that's what the *Daily Trail* tells me.' She took a sip of wine, looked over at Ben.

'Yes, they're coming,' he said. 'Hunter will be back from filming the new *Cat Man* movie in Budapest, so they're all coming. And, Mother, please stop reading that trash.'

'Who are you inviting, Elle?' asked Georgie, who was pushing her food around the plate. She wasn't a fan of Gurva's organic vegan menu. 'Any big blogging names?'

Yes, thought Ben, *who are you inviting?*

'No,' Elle smiled into her food, 'I'm happy to leave the guest list to Ben. That's fine with me.'

'Don't leave it all to him,' said Georgie. 'He'll stack it with ex-girlfriends!' And she laughed.

Elle laughed too, but it didn't seem like her heart was in it. 'That's true!' she said. 'I hadn't thought of that. How many exes are you inviting, darling?'

'Hardly any at all,' said Ben. 'Actually, there's been a change of plan about the wedding that we all need to be across.'

'There has?' asked Elle, a little too quickly.

'We're bringing it down a notch,' he said. 'It will be a commitment ceremony, not a wedding, and it will only be close friends and family.'

'What?' Helen Bont, who had let Ben know in no uncertain terms what she thought about this match, suddenly seemed miffed it wasn't going ahead. 'But—'

'Don't worry, Mum,' Ben said. 'You can still wear a hat.'

'I don't think you should be bothering at all, then,' said Georgie, with a hopeful note in her voice.

At that comment, Ben could have sworn he saw Elle's head lift quickly, and this instantly infuriated him. He knew he was on high alert for any signs of dissent, but why didn't she know that?

'Is this the first you've heard of that plan, Elle?' asked Helen pointedly. 'Not much of a partnership, here, it seems.'

'Mother!'

'Well, come on,' said Helen imperiously, 'the first night we were here you had that terrible... incident in front of Julia. And then the whole house has been on eggshells for days, and now you tell us the wedding will be a sham, anyway. I think I might stay in Sydney for New Year's Eve after all.'

Elle looked at Ben. He looked at her. He didn't know what she was thinking, or what she was going to say, and he hated it. He absolutely hated it. His right fist was clenched under the table when Elle stood up and walked around to stand behind him.

'Helen, you don't have to come if you don't want to,' Elle said. 'Or you, Georgie.'

'Thank god for that,' mumbled Georgie into her drink.

'But I'm going to marry this man on New Year's Eve. I don't care whether it's legal in the eyes of the law or not. I just want to be his.' And she kissed him. 'Forever.'

And Ben Bont's fist unclenched.

CHAPTER 34

ABI

'I did not fucking want this!' Fourteen-year-old Alex was waving a fancy make-up palette in the air, the ribbon still dangling from the edge of the wrapping. 'She's trying to provoke me!'

'Just trying to be helpful,' said Arden from across the room, smirking as she picked away at a mountain of Grace-baked festive kale chips.

'Everyone,' Grace said, from where she was curled up with Otto and Teddy and hundreds of tiny brown blocks—a Lego alternative made from crushed coffee beans and hemp—'remember, today's about peace and love, not food and stuff.' She was laughing as she said it.

Abi felt a surge of real-deal happiness. This was exactly how she liked Christmas at the farm: all her people, a mountain of mess, a day ahead of them of nothing to do but eat and play and be forced to talk to the people in your family you'd been avoiding.

People like Adrian, whom Abi had been generally avoiding ever since their blow-up over Arden travelling to Elle's.

When Abi had brought Arden back to the farm, having heard her story of what had happened there, it took every ounce of Abi's already limited good grace not to spit, 'I told you so,' at her ex-husband. Instead, she did what she knew she had to do and focused on her family—on Arden and on Grace—rather than recriminations.

There Adrian was, over near the tree—a native cutting, of course—with Freddie on his knee, the two deep in concentration over a recycled wood 'Build a T-Rex' kit.

This would be Adrian's last Christmas as the man in the shed. He'd had his offer accepted on a cottage with small acreage just down the road.

He'd told Abi the night she and Arden had got back from Byron. 'Genuinely,' Adrian had said, 'I'm sorry it's taken me so long. I think I needed to come to the conclusion I could move on without moving backwards.'

'Wow,' Abi had joked, remarkable considering her mood that night, 'you really are growing as a human, aren't you?'

'Well, I'm trying. I appreciate what a drain I've been here, Abi, I do. But also, I don't want to be too far away. The boys need their family around them.'

'Of course, Adrian. Of course they do.'

As a peace offering, Adrian had bought Arden a brand-new vlogging camera, an 'I get you' gift that she hadn't seen coming. And, half an hour ago, Abi had watched Arden wiping something from her eye as she pulled away from her dad's long hug. Christmas spirit indeed.

Abi tapped a message into her phone:

> Happy Holidays, my GDs. May all of your people be around you. And if they are not, may you be fucking owning it. A x

But from where Abi stood, two clouds were hanging over this supposedly idyllic scene.

One was Grace. In the days since Abi had been back, full of fury and remorse and concern about her daughter, Grace had been solid but distant. She'd given her usual attention to the children—all of the children—making sure they would each feel special on Christmas, but all the while holding Abi at arm's length.

Their wedding was in less than a week, and Grace didn't want to talk about it. 'Not now, Abi,' she said, every time Abi brought it up.

Abi knew Grace's dress was hanging in the wardrobe, alongside her own, but not a word was spoken about it. As Abi's phone buzzed with arrangements—the people doing the food, the people bringing the chairs—Grace didn't ask a single question about any of it.

***

Last night, Christmas Eve, traditionally Abi and Grace hosted an open house for friends and their kids—anyone who wanted to come over for a mega-kombucha batch and a feast of honey-roasted nuts and seeds. Abi loved to ridicule Grace about the lack of edible Christmas fun, and it was always her role to break out the closely held chocolate stash at this time of year.

As the little kids put on a clumsy play and some earnest village adults broke out the carols, Abi had tried to hold Grace's hand. Grace pulled away as if she'd been shocked.

'Gracey, we need to talk about this,' Abi whispered. 'You've barely looked at me since I've been home.'

'Let's just get through Christmas, Abi,' Grace replied. 'Let's get through Christmas and see where we are.'

But Abi already knew where she was: staring at the love of her life with a heavy feeling in her gut that this time she had really, really fucked things up.

The other cloud was Arden.

On the flight between Ballina and Melbourne, she'd told Abi about the party and the pill. 'Mum, I can't explain it. I was so uncomfortable and scared there on my own, but also just kind of fucking furious at everything that had brought me there. And when the guy offered the pill to me, I thought, *Fuck it*. I wanted everything to disappear, to just have a good time. The women there...' Arden shrugged. 'They were so cool. I thought it would be fun. I am such a stupid little idiot.'

Abi could feel the anger roiling in her stomach. She looked at her smart, sensitive daughter, and let her maternal instinct wash over her: the overwhelming urge to take Arden home and wrap her up and never let her perfect, delicate skin be exposed to the harsh elements—other people who didn't love her like her mother did—ever again.

Abi dimly remembered being sixteen and hating herself with a passion, but also that the self-loathing was spiked with something else—a sense that you knew that your possibilities were endless, that the adults around you were dead inside, that their core had hardened, while you were opening and blooming and coming to life. It was a confusing fucker of a time, even if you didn't have the insanity of Arden's family to contend with.

'Arden,' Abi leant back on the headrest so her eyes were level with her daughter's, 'two things. First, those women are not cool. The people who are trying to buy a slice of what Elle's selling them are as lost as anyone. And believe me, everyone's pretty lost. There's a whole tribe out there who wouldn't use chemicals to clean their toilets, but they'll happily snort them and swallow them. You can see that level of hypocrisy, right?

'I promised myself years ago I wouldn't lie to you and your sister about drugs. I know they're going to be in your world, just like they were in mine, once. But what happened at Gurva—that was a bad decision on your part. A roomful of strangers in the middle of nowhere and a pill from an older man you'd never met before. Let's just say you were lucky, really—'

'Thanks to Frances.' Arden sniffed. 'Really.'

'Yes, thanks to Frances. And there might often be angels like her watching your back, but they might not always get to you in time.'

Arden nodded.

'And second—' Abi began.

'You're not finished?'

'Not even close.' She smiled. 'Second, you should have called me. You can call me any time, in any state, and I will move heaven and earth to get to you. You understand that? I can't promise that you won't get in trouble later, but in that moment I am always, *always* your best chance of help. Nobody cares as much as I do. Not even River.'

Arden was crying. 'I was too scared that night, Mum, but the next morning I wanted to. I'd just lost my phone.'

'But you told me a lie! Food poisoning?'

Arden looked confused for a moment, and then they landed on the same thought at the same time.

'Where did you find your phone?' Abi asked.

'Elle gave it back to me,' said Arden. 'She must have—'

'I can't! I can't deal with that woman. And you must not. She cannot be fucking trusted, and that is it. She did not have your back that night, and she lied to your mother about it. If you needed another fucking thing to convince you to stay the hell away from her—this is it.'

Elle's sons were sitting right alongside them on the plane, engrossed in the iPads they'd taken from Elle's—the ones Abi knew she'd have to confiscate and hide just before she turned the car into the farm driveway.

'I'm sorry, Mum.' Arden sobbed. 'I thought she could help me.'

'Help you what?'

'Help me get more followers, build my channel.'

For fuck's sake, Abi thought, *have we learnt nothing?* But she said, 'There are other ways, darling, that don't bond you to the devil.'

***

Now that they were home, the Arden 'cloud' had shape-shifted. Frances's post in Elle's hate group had guaranteed it. There were only three thousand people in that group, but one of them was a *Daily Trail* journo who loved nothing better than the clicks a blogger war could bring.

Abi was certain that Frances's intentions had been pure, but now Abi was dealing with calls from journalists wanting confirmation that it was Arden—Abi and Adrian's teenage daughter—who had OD'ed at Elle Campbell's wellness retreat. Abi could see how this was too good a story to pass up, but her need to protect her daughter was—unbelievably, perhaps—stronger than her desire to destroy Elle.

She hadn't yet worked out how to do both.

Her phone buzzed.

'Merry fucking Christmas, Zoe!' Abi yelled into the phone. 'Where are you? Why aren't you with us?'

'I'm still in Byron,' said Zoe, in a small voice.

'But... I left you at the airport. You were getting the Sydney flight—'

'Abi. I changed my mind.'

Abi could tell Zoe was outside; her voice sounded flat, defeated.

'What's the matter, darling? What is it? Where are you?'

'I can't really explain it, Abi. I couldn't leave, I kept thinking about what you said, about Elle—'

'Zoe, I've changed my mind about that,' Abi said. She'd walked out of the gift mayhem of the farmhouse living room and was pacing the kitchen. 'What Arden's told me about what goes on there... well, fuck Elle, to be honest.'

Silence for a moment. 'I can't,' said Zoe. 'I can't. I've been talking to people who've worked at Gurva, who know people who work at Gurva... They say Ben's controlling and...'

'And? I hardly think Elle would qualify as easygoing.' But

Abi remembered Elle following Ben Bont back into the house from the deck.

'And he pushes her around—like, literally,' Zoe finished.

'Oh,' said Abi. She hated being right about that.

'So, here's my Christmas question for you, Abi,' Zoe said, clearly making a huge effort to lighten her tone, 'if your sister's a complete C-U-N-T...'

'Are you spelling that out because it's Christ's Day?' Abi said, trying for a little joke.

'If your sister is a complete cunt, does that mean you'd happily leave her, in the middle of nowhere, with a dangerous man and a baby?'

Abi sighed. 'I guess not.'

'Okay. Well, wedding's on New Year's Eve.'

'So is ours, Zoe. I think you know—this is one you've been invited to.'

'It can't happen, Abi. It just can't.'

'Okay, Zoe. So what next?'

'That's what I'm working out, Abi.'

'Well, merry fucking Christmas, Zoe. And good luck.'

CHAPTER 35

ELLE

Dear Goddesses,

It's Christmas Eve at Gurva. I can't even tell you how stunning it is here tonight, so I'll let Instagram do that for me. Go on over there to see the magic of the solar lights in all our trees, the silver seashells hanging from our beautiful deck and the chimes that ring on every breeze.

Even more magical is that I am sitting here writing this to you in my wedding dress. You see, I had a fitting today, and I can't bear to take this creation off, it's so ethereal and other-worldly, it makes me feel like a Christmas angel. Of course I'll have to shed its beauty before BB gets home—bad luck! Just one week, and you will all see it too!

What a year we've shared, Goddesses. The arrival of my beautiful baby girl, the journey my body took to motherhood and back again, the growth of our beautiful community.

Now, I have some news to end out our year. Some good, some not so good.

Bad news first. It has been brought to my attention that there is some salacious gossip circulating about Gurva on an horrendous hate page. Our lawyers are investigating it right now (yes, even on Christmas Eve!).

It hurts my heart to be here again, almost two years after the last attempt to bring me down. Why can the world not resist trying to bring a woman of power to her knees?

It also hurts my heart to have to tell my side of this grubby story, especially since the lawyers have put so many of the real details out of bounds.

So here's what I can tell you.

A mentally unwell young woman with a grudge against me found her way onto our retreat here at Gurva. The fact she breached the trust barrier that is so necessary when you are hosting people in your own home is one of the most concerning things about this for myself, BB and Baby Alma, as you can imagine.

It seems this young woman (a new mother, can you believe it?) wanted only to invade our sacred space and discredit the business—no, the calling—I have spent more than a year building up with love.

What makes this even worse is that I—seeing that this young woman was troubled—took her into my home. She met my children. She met my partner. She even met my beloved stepdaughter, the one she is now making up such spurious claims about. How she can do that to a 16-year-old girl, I have no idea.

All I can tell you, my Goddesses, is that some

people out there have no soul. They look at their own ugliness and want to blame others for it. They look at the mess of their lives and point the finger everywhere but inwards.

This woman is one of those people. If you stumble across these words, these disgusting rumours about our home, please direct the negativity where it belongs—back at the dark heart who spread these lies.

The good news is that BB and I will not let this get us down, we will not let it damage this most precious of festive seasons. This is our baby's first Christmas and the time of our commitment ceremony.

If there are people in your life who are trying to bring you to your knees as there are in mine, just remember, where there is beauty and success, there will always be jealousy and hate.

Happy Christmas to you, Goddesses, and may your day be full of love and nourishment.

E x

PS: Oh, one more piece of good news. Just in time for the new year, I am launching a brand-new product—the inimitable 5x5 Elle-ness Program. Lose 5kg and 5 years in 55 days.

I know that because of this little world right here, many of you are ending your year in better shape than you started it, and well done you. Remember, keep yourself nice over Christmas, Goddesses—don't use it as an excuse to let yourself go. Actually, if there was ever a euphemism that needs to disappear, it's that one, am I right? There's nothing freeing about not caring about your health and appearance. Let's make our New Year's resolution to never, ever 'let ourselves go'.

Elle hit Post and turned to Ben, who was standing behind her, reading every word.

'Good enough for you?' she asked. 'It's a start,' he said.

CHAPTER 36

FRANCES

Christmas Day on the ward was fun, if you could silence the part of yourself that wished you were home with your family, watching your baby disappear under a pile of colourful wrapping.

Still, since Troy had been fired, the extra money that came from working on Christmas was not something they could refuse.

The ward was quiet—any patients who could go home had gone home, and only the most chronic cases remained. Frances had done her rounds wearing her tissue-paper crown and her best smile, and she knew that soon all the staff on today would be roped into a round of carolling. She didn't mind. She was happy to be useful.

When she'd got back from Gurva, Frances had told Troy everything. *Everything*.

She'd told him about Dr Darling's hands on her body, his words in her head.

She told him about how she couldn't love Denny more, but how she couldn't shake the idea that it was all her fault she didn't have a 'normal' baby.

She told him that sometimes she wished for more than a life of work, washing and video games.

She told him about the feeling she couldn't quite identify that was gnawing away at her that she was failing—falling and failing—every day.

And she told him about how she'd been spending money, hand over fist, to try to patch all this shit up: not with booze or drugs, but with miracle cures and gold dust and extreme diets that were only making her more anxious by the moment.

And then she told him that she was done with it all.

And *then* she told him that Ben Bont had offered them fifteen thousand in cash to pay off their debts, and she had said no.

'So, that's quite a lot to take in, Frank,' Troy had said, staring at her like she'd just landed from somewhere strange and far away—which in a way, she had, since she was straight off the plane from Byron Bay. 'I mean, some of this I knew, of course, but...'

And Frances had taken him by the hand to her private cupboard, where she'd opened up her stash and had pulled out, one by one, all the unopened packets from her WholeHealth deliveries: the spirulina and the maca powder and the green superfoods dust. The one that was going to boost her skin elasticity; the one that was going to heal her gut. The one that was going to supercharge her libido, and the one that was going to sharpen her brain. The Moringa leaf and the crushed baobab, the lucuma and the matcha and the whey.

'There's hundreds of dollars of this shit here,' she said. 'I thought every one of them might be the answer to making me feel more in control. I'm an idiot.'

Troy looked like he might cry. He ran the flat of his hand across his head. 'Frankie, you're not a fucking idiot. You've just always been a lot. And you never think you're enough. Seriously, babe, you're enough. You're more than enough for me and Denny.'

And they'd hugged and kissed, and they'd joked about

how they could sell all this stuff on Gumtree, and even Denny seemed to be gurgling happily on the floor. And for a moment Frances thought the light had shone in and that this strange, anxious chapter of her life would have a happy conclusion.

But then Troy's phone had rung.

It was Ben Bont himself.

He told Troy that he was fired, that he had betrayed Ben, the Bounce group and everyone who had worked so hard to build something beautiful up at Gurva. He told Troy that his wife was mentally unstable, and that she would be hearing from the Bounce lawyers, and that this 'mistake' of hers was going to cost them both, enormously.

Frances listened as Troy tried to defend her:

'Ben, that's not how it was...'

'Frances has never wanted to hurt anyone in her life...'

'She says you had a dodgy guy selling pills on the farm...'

'My wife doesn't tell lies, Ben.'

It moved Frances so much to hear him say those things, even as her stomach was flipping and a sense of doom was closing over her head. She'd gathered Denny up to hold him and smell him, but she held him too hard and he squealed, and Troy pulled an irritated face and put a finger in his ear to better hear the character assassination Ben Bont was flinging down the phone.

Troy was trying so hard to be decent about it, because—as Frances could see with sudden blinding clarity—that was who he was.

He hung up and looked at Frances, devastated. 'Happy Christmas, Frank. I'm out of a job and we're getting sued.'

Frances had cried, and Denny had cried, and they'd all sat on the floor of their little apartment while Frances tried to explain why she'd done what she did.

'Troy, you need to understand how vulnerable I was, how vulnerable so many women are, to hearing all this stuff about how we can be better.' She was probably crying too hard, she knew, to make any real sense. 'And how if we just ate that or tried this or did this exercise or drank this smoothie, we'd be fixed. And,' big snotty sob, 'it's not even *truuuuuue*. It's not even true for her, for Elle. Even she doesn't live like that. What hope have any of the rest of us got, without the beauty and the staff and the rich husband and the discipline... if it's not even true WITH all that? I just... I just couldn't shut up about what really happened that night.'

'It might be noble, Frank,' Troy said, 'and I'm proud of you. But man, this was a shitty time for you to discover your principles.'

And Frances laughed at that. Because he was right. 'But I am telling the truth, Troy. All that *did* happen. A teenager could have died. Elle's duty of care was nowhere. She's lying about her boys. Her fiancé's an abusive arsehole. And her whole company is built on a lie.'

'It might be true, Frank, but people like that don't get done,' Troy said. 'People like us get done.'

***

As Frances moved around the ward, watching visitors file in with presents, fetching vases for flowers, passing out mince pies ('No pastry for the heart patients!') she realised that she should be feeling much worse than she did.

Considering that they were—she and Troy—in a world of trouble, she felt better than she had in months. She'd spoken to Abi Black, who wanted to thank her for looking after Arden but also to beg her not to identify her daughter in any of the stories that might follow her post. And Abi had said something that stuck with her. 'Elle lies like other people breathe, but if you really know the truth, she can't touch you. The weakness she has is that other people know way too much about her life now, her lies. And if you can back up even half of what you claim, she won't come after you. Even Ben Bont's money can't shut down the rumours that will cause them damage they can't undo.'

Abi was right, of course.

She received a letter from Ben Bont's lawyers on the same day that the interview aired on *Fifty Minutes*.

The closest Frances came to having her own lawyer was a visit to her second cousin's husband. He was a solicitor in Camden and had given her a free assessment for the price of some of her mum's cannoli. She'd sat in his living room as her little third cousins played around them and recorded him as he told her this letter was a missive designed to scare her, but there was no real risk there. 'You posted in a Facebook group, it came down, and now real reporters are sniffing around. He's just trying to stop you from cooperating on any of their stories.'

And they *were* calling her: they were calling her all the time. Frances was letting the calls go. She was too scared to go any further, but her gut told her she'd been right to go as far as she did.

I feel good, she realised, as she went into the treatment room to restack the meds for the night-shift staff who'd be starting soon.

As soon as she walked in there, she realised she wasn't alone.

'Merry Christmas, Graham.' It was Dr Darling. He stepped to the door and closed it. They were alone in a space barely big enough for one.

This time, Frances found her voice and used it. 'Help!'

'Don't be so dramatic, Graham,' said Darling, although a flash of annoyance crossed his face. 'You don't need to be afraid of me.'

I don't?

'I only popped in to see you since you've been so studiously avoiding my requests for updates on my patients. I wanted to check you didn't have any... plans to make things difficult.'

Frances suddenly realised that he was scared. She'd been ignoring him, and he thought it was because she was going to make a complaint?

He took a small step—that was all the room there was—towards her and looked her up and down. 'You look different, now you're not breeding,' he said. His voice made her skin prickle all over.

He probably couldn't see her hands. She reached into the pocket of her uniform.

'Do I, Doctor?' She spoke loudly, clearly, face up. 'I'm very busy. How can I help you?' Suddenly she didn't feel so afraid.

'I just want to make sure there's no misunderstanding between us,' he said, his face so close to hers she could smell his breath, warm and a little boozy, as if he'd just enjoyed a Christmas lunch.

'What kind of misunderstanding? You mean about how you groped me and said awful, sexual things to me?' As Frances's voice got stronger, a sense of relief swept over her—she was managing to talk.

'That's your interpretation,' he said. 'I would say you were flirting with me, and I responded in kind. I always knew you liked me.'

Frances surprised herself. She took a step towards him, forcing him to back away so he was against the door. 'I was eight months' pregnant. You called me a sow, commented on my breasts and weight, and sexually assaulted me in the room we're in right now.'

'And you loved it, Graham,' Darling said, a sneer spreading across his face. 'You loved every minute. Just like you're loving this.'

Frances reached towards Darling as if to touch him—but really she was reaching under his arm to the doorhandle. She strongly yanked the door towards her, knocking him into her for a second before she squeezed past and out into the corridor.

Frances half-ran to where the other nurses were gathered, sharing some mince pies that had been brought in by a grateful patient's mum.

Before she reached them, she pulled her phone from her

pocket. Yes. Exactly what she'd hoped. With three strategic taps, she'd recorded the whole encounter.

She turned around to watch Darling, crumpled and glaring, emerge from the storeroom. And she waved.

First thing in the New Year, she was filing that complaint.

Come at me, Ben Bont, she thought.

Maybe this whole Elle-ness thing had helped her find her voice after all.

CHAPTER 37

THE WEDDINGS

'This is like one of those bad American mini-movies,' Arden said. She was standing behind her mum, pulling her curls up and under an arrangement of white lotus flowers.

'What are you talking about?' Abi asked. She was on her phone, poking wildly.

'When everybody's getting ready for the wedding but we don't know if it's going to happen—like, "will they, won't they".'

'Well, I'm glad it's giving you so much entertainment, Arden. It's giving me a fucking heart attack.'

No one knew where Grace was. That morning, the house had woken up full of guests and soon to be awash with people setting up chairs and a buffet and a marquee in case it rained. And one of the brides was missing.

Even Sol and Otto had no idea where Grace was. The old station wagon she drove sometimes was gone, but all of her stuff was still here. The wedding dress was still hanging in the wardrobe, next to Abi's.

'Mum, OF COURSE Grace will be here,' Arden said,

as she pulled out a comb and started trying to smooth over Abi's frizz. 'And look, if she isn't, you could always go all *Philadelphia Story* and remarry Dad at the last minute!'

'That is the most depressing sentence I've ever heard.' Abi sighed. 'Fucking hell, Gracey.'

'I'm not worried, Mum. You and Grace have a love story for the ages. You are meant to be together.' And Arden spun Abi around to look into the tarnished dressing-table mirror. 'See?'

'Darling, you have done so much more than put lipstick on a pig here,' Abi said, squeezing Arden's hand. 'But there's no such thing as a love story for the ages. That's the sixteen-year-old in you, right there.'

'There is, too,' said Arden. 'River and I have one, and so do you and Grace.'

With that, Arden pulled out her new vlogging camera and began talking to it, as though it was a friend she was *super-excited* to see. 'Mum number one's make-up DONE, guys. Now it's time for me and River to morph into woodland faeries for our places in the bridal party. For our how-tos, keep watching!' And she snapped the camera shut.

'Woodland faeries?' Abi asked. 'Do I *know* about that?'

'Sure you do.' Arden kissed her mum on top of her newly styled head. 'And stop worrying. In those will-they-won't-they movies, they nearly always *do*.'

'Great,' Abi said. 'Then I'll just sit here looking pretty until my princess comes.'

Abi waited for Arden to leave the room and then she pulled out her phone, dialled Grace again. 'Grace, talk to me, please?'

***

Elle Campbell was on a commercial flight in her wedding dress.

She knew this was a touch dramatic, but she literally had not had time to change in between making the decision to go, and going. There were, after all, a lot of buttons on this thing.

She'd grabbed a jacket. And Alma. And the nappy bag. So really, she reasoned, fellow passengers on her Gold Coast to Melbourne flight might imagine that she was simply an overdressed new mum who'd lost her tiny mind.

Not that Elle ever gave a shit about what anyone else thought. But today, her mind was swirling at a rate where she couldn't tell which thoughts were hers and which weren't.

Although after last night, there was one thought that wasn't shifting: *I can't live like this. Not for any prize. Not for any man.*

As Alma whimpered against her chest, Elle buried her nose in her baby's wispy hair. She also kept thinking, *I didn't leave you behind.*

And the other thing she thought was, *Here we go again.*

But this time, she wasn't alone. Baby Alma was snuggly secured in her lap, and in the seat next to her was her sister, Zoe.

As turbulence gave the plane a firm nudge, Zoe grabbed Elle's hand. And they stayed sitting like that.

***

Ben Bont knew he shouldn't fly in this mood. No, he really shouldn't. But he had a houseful of people at Gurva. Business associates from Sydney and Melbourne, exes and employees, old friends from Krox. A fucking movie star, for god's sake. His mother, even after all her threats. His sister. He had to get away.

Wherever Elle had gone, that's where he was going to go. Because you don't humiliate Ben Bont like that. You just don't.

He should have known. He should have known this past week, but he should also have known since the very beginning that he and Elle were going to end up here. Enough people had warned him.

He was angry at himself for that. But what he was most angry about was who he had turned into along the way.

Since Christmas, and since the decision had been made to stop pushing for Elle's divorce, to make the wedding a commitment ceremony, he had thought things had really mellowed. She seemed to relax, to stop looking at him as if she was peering from a great height. To stop jumping when he walked into a room. She was a bit more her old self. Confident. Cocky. Sexy.

But last night they'd had an argument about Sydney. After the ceremony, he'd decided, she would move there with him. That was what he'd always wanted, for her to follow him wherever he went. To have her with him. That's what a wife does.

But Elle said no. She said no because she 'hated Sydney'. She said no because she 'loved Gurva'. She said the business 'needed her', that Alma 'needed stability'. She said she 'needed independence', that this was 'always their arrangement'.

And the way she told him all of this—lying next to him in bed, heads together in apparent intimacy. So close, but pushing him so far away.

He felt that familiar rage pulsing inside him. He felt himself needing to react. He tried to step away from it, but she was right there, talking at him, in his face, sounding so sure, so reasonable. He stood up and went to the French doors for some air.

She followed him, and then...

Now he wasn't sure what had happened between them, but suddenly she'd been out on the deck, crying, and he was inside.

He had closed the doors and she was out there, naked, banging on the glass.

'You make me do this,' he remembered shouting through the glass door.

He'd known that for her, this was the worst: she was humiliated, furious, because she would have to come another way into the house, and be seen—naked, cast out—by whichever staff member let her back in.

Why did I think she was going to marry me after that? Ben Bont wondered as he climbed into his little Cirrus.

Because she'd told him she was going to.

***

Frances and Troy were setting up the bar at Abi Black's wedding.

It was an unusual gig, because there was no alcohol. Well, there was very little: Abi had instructed them to order a few bottles of excellent champagne and have them hidden—chilled, of course—waiting for a secret signal. Mostly they'd be serving four kinds of kombucha, lots of water with berries in it, and some elderflower cordial on ice.

'This will be a piece of piss,' Troy had told Frances. 'A wedding with no booze! Your biggest problem at most weddings is dealing with all the pissheads. We can do as many jobs as you like for these friends.'

Abi and Arden had asked Frances and Troy to come down and do this gig after they'd heard that Troy had lost his job over the Elle problem. 'Some money and a weekend in the country, plus Arden would love to see you,' had been Abi's gambit, and that was all Frances had needed to hear before she said, 'Absolutely.'

She and Troy and baby Denny had driven down the day before, and now Alex and Arden had absorbed Denny into the farm's crèche of what seemed like a hundred children. Since Frances couldn't hear him whingeing, he was surely happy enough.

'This year's going to be different,' Frances told Troy as they were polishing glasses.

'No more bloody resolutions,' Troy said. 'No more giving something up, taking something else on. Can we just try "being" for a while, please?'

'That's exactly it,' said Frances. 'I feel like now I've stopped trying to be better, I am actually getting better.'

She'd also found a counsellor, eased up on the restrictive diet, and prepared a submission to the hospital about the inappropriate behaviour of one Dr Darling. 'I really am.'

'Well, that's the best start to the year I could hope for,' said Troy.

They were grinning at each other like idiots.

***

Adrian had brought a date. His book was ready for publication in May, and Fran was the associate publisher. They'd been working pretty closely together, and when he'd asked her to come, he'd genuinely felt nervous.

Alex had been horrified when he told her. 'Dad! Haven't you learnt anything? She's in her thirties—she's going to want children!'

'Since when is that the kind of thing you worry about?' Adrian had asked his younger daughter. 'Leave that worrying to me. Anyway, she's already got a little boy, Thomas.'

'Even worse!' Alex pouted. 'We don't need any more children in this family.'

'Really?' Adrian asked. 'Is there a strict limit that I didn't know about? When did we cross it? After you, by any chance?'

'Dad, you're such a dick.' But he could see that Alex, just like Arden and Abi, was secretly pleased to see Adrian behave more like Adrian. It had been a long time.

He'd finally filed the divorce papers, and Elle would get the Brighton box, he'd get everything else—and that was that, he thought, as he drove Fran into the grounds of the Daylesford farm, which were buzzing with activity.

'Things must be pretty crazy,' Fran said, looking at the posse of kids playing in the paddock, 'having two ex-wives and so many children around.'

'It was,' Adrian said, 'for a while. Now, it's pretty sorted. I think next year is going to be the Year of Calm. Hopefully, it starts today.'

***

Grace was sitting by Lake Daylesford with her sister, Leisel.

They'd been walking since early in the morning, but for the past hour, tired out, they'd just been sitting, watching the water. Leisel had brought Grace up to date on everything that was going on with Mark and the kids and the campervan, and Grace had listened, and nodded, and said little.

Now, Leisel looked at her watch. 'Gracey,' she said gently, 'we've got a wedding to go to, you know. You've got a dress to put on.'

'I know.' Grace was picking apart some tufts of grass with her blunt fingers. 'Lee, do you think I should?'

'What kind of a question is that?' Leisel said, laughing. 'I can't answer it. Only you can.'

'But you have an opinion?'

'Of course I do.'

'Tell me.'

'I think it's hard to be in a relationship with a force of nature like Abi,' she said. 'I think in every relationship there's a dynamic of energy where one's steady, and one's not, and playing your part in that gets tiring sometimes, whichever side you're on.'

'You and Mark?'

'He's steady,' Leisel said. 'And often, it drives him crazy. Being the one who's always calming the waters after a storm is wearing, right?'

'Right.' Grace looked back to the water. 'I just don't know if I wanted all this. I mean, we fought so hard for it, but I'm talking about *me*—I've never aspired to it.'

'Well, to be fair, until late last year it wasn't on the menu, Grace,' Leisel said. 'You haven't had as much time to ponder this.'

'True.'

That morning, Grace had left the house at dawn. She

warmed a matcha tea and took it down to her bench, under the angel trumpets.

There, on the bench, was a little wooden box, along with an envelope addressed to *Grace*.

Inside was a pearl necklace, and a piece of paper.

She knew instantly what it was. It wasn't a gift. They were Abi's pearls, the necklace she'd worn all the time when Grace had first met her—when Grace was Arden's tutor, visiting a nice middle-class home in the suburbs to help a little girl with her maths.

The piece of paper just read:

> You freed me from these beautiful chains, Grace Adams. Never forget how powerful you are – A x

'I know you love Abi,' Leisel said now, by the shores of the lake.

'She's everything,' Grace found herself saying. 'Even with her infuriating temper, and ego, and inability to consult, and chocolate, and ex-husband baggage... Life is in colour with her.'

Leisel laughed. 'Had you already written your vows? Because I think you just did.'

'So, this is the bit in the movie when we go back to the farm and I get my dress on?' Grace asked.

'What movie?'

'Arden has a theory that we're just drawing out the drama. For a better movie.' Grace smiled. 'I fucking love that girl.'

'Then yes, we're up to that bit in the movie. Let's hustle.'

And Leisel pulled her sister up and pushed her back into her bridal station wagon.

***

The ceremony was meant to happen at sunset.

Half an hour before, Abi was posting:

You can have your happy ending, GDs. But it just might look like a new beginning. #truelove

'That,' Grace said, over her shoulder, 'is some soppy shit.'

Abi turned to face her. Her bride looked like she'd stepped out of a Pre-Raphaelite disco, all flowing wavy hair and floaty chiffon layers and glittery eyelids.

'Arden?' Abi asked, although it was obvious who was responsible.

'Arden.'

Grace held out her hand. Around her wrist, she had wrapped Abi's pearls.

'You are the most beautiful thing I have ever seen in my life, Grace,' Abi said. 'The sunset will be embarrassed showing up next to you.'

'Thank you, you look incredible. Maybe this wasn't such a bad idea.'

Abi was wearing what she called her pearly peasant dress: a simple shift but beaded to within an inch of its life. 'It's so heavy, you'll never be able to carry me over the threshold,' she said and laughed.

They just stood there, looking at each other. Almost a decade of history passing on a current between them.

'You know,' Abi said, 'this is the moment. Not out there, in front of everyone we've ever freaking met. In here, you and me. *This* is the moment.'

Abi and Grace kissed. And then a herd of children came piling through the door.

'Muuuummmm. *Euuuuw!* It's time!'

***

That morning, Elle had started with every intention of going through with this ridiculous wedding charade.

The night before, she'd tapped on Ocean's window, motioning for the confused nanny to come and let her in the front door. Wrapped in a chair cover snatched from the deck, Elle had gone and slept on the floor of Alma's nursery, right next to her cot.

There had been no sleep, really, just the familiar roll-call of rationalisations in her head of all the reasons she was still at Gurva, at the most perfect place in the most perfect part of Australia, with the perfect man and the perfect baby.

As she had showered and began to put on her exquisite wedding dress—flown up from Sydney in its own seat from a designer friend of Ben's—she listened to the rising hum of activity around the farm. She glimpsed Ben through the picture windows, directing staff to put a chair 'here where the view is just so', or move this tower of flowers 'over there, where the light will catch them'.

And Elle thought, *This is the ugliest thing I have ever seen.*

On her buffed and polished skin, Elle could still feel the grime of what had happened last night, of the effort of holding up her head while Ocean, and then Mauna, had watched her walk down the hallway with a slight limp from the force of the door hitting her as she'd tumbled through it. She felt it all over her, like a light dusting of shame.

And she thought, *I am not ashamed.*

She looked through the French doors to Ben. He had come to check on her first thing this morning, and she had kissed his cheek and apologised to him, told him she would be a better wife in this new year.

From the garden, he looked up and gave her a little wave, mimed covering his eyes to avoid seeing the dress.

'I am not fucking marrying you,' Elle suddenly said out loud, to no one. 'I'm not even pretend-marrying you.'

And right then, on the dressing table, her phone started to flash.

It was Zoe.

I'm outside. At the gates. COME.

***

'You may kiss the bride,' had just been said when all hell broke loose at Abi and Grace's wedding.

Arden would later say that she wasn't sure what happened first: the car screeching up the driveway, or the plane buzzing overhead.

But it was the car.

As soon as it came to a halt, Zoe fell out of the back door. 'Damn, I missed it!' she said, as more than a hundred heads turned towards her.

Then Elle got out—still, bizarrely, wearing a wedding dress. Over the top of the elaborate, mostly sheer designer gown she wore a baby carrier, with Alma snuggled on her chest. She looked around with something on her face that seemed like fear, and then pushed her shoulders back and put one arm around Alma.

'I'm so sorry,' Elle said to the members of the crowd who could hear her, 'I really haven't had a minute to change.'

And then a big, tattooed man climbed out of the driver's seat. It was Matt.

Faerie Arden gasped audibly, and Frances rushed out from behind the bar.

***

Abi and Grace were still in each other's arms, holding on very tight. 'I'm so sorry for all the mess,' Abi was whispering into Grace's hair. 'I promise to never lose sight of you again.'

It was Grace who became aware that the crowd's murmur had turned into a roar, and that now a small plane was flying low overhead—it looked dangerously low. She pulled away from Abi and, hand in hand, they stood and watched their crowd of nearest and dearest gazing up at the sky.

Abi had a fast thought that it might be photographers. She'd finally turned down the offer from the magazine, but surely they wouldn't be going to these lengths. She wasn't Nicole Fucking Kidman.

Then, through the crowd, she caught a glimpse of Elle, and the look on her face as she stared up at the plane—and Abi knew. It was Ben Bont.

Abi kissed Grace again quickly and stomped as best she could through the crowds to Elle and Zoe. 'What. The. Fuck?' She looked at Elle, shook her head. Looked at Zoe.

'We didn't know where else to go,' said Zoe.

'Bullshit,' said Abi. 'There are a million hotels between here and Byron Bay. Perfect places to hide out where you are not going to ruin someone's wedding. And what...' she caught proper sight of Elle now, 'are you wearing?'

'Abi, it's a long story, but I had to get away, and we just ran.' Elle was looking directly at Abi, her arm still protectively curled around the baby on her chest. Abi felt like she was seeing this woman for the first time. She looked... genuinely scared. 'Everything's been so fast, and I haven't even had time to buy something to change into. And I don't want to ruin your wedding but I *do* want to see my boys.' She looked around wildly, then up to the plane. 'And I need your help... with *him*.'

The ridiculous small plane was circling, surely looking for somewhere to land.

'Jesus Christ,' said Abi. 'Get inside. Where's Adrian? *Adrian!*'

Adrian's date was looking at him. 'Isn't that...?'

'Yes, it is, it's my ex.'

'And she's wearing a wedding dress.'

'Apparently so.'

'At your other ex's wedding.'

'Yup.'

'Okay. Year of Calm?'

'Uh-uh. Please excuse me.'

By the time Adrian got over to Elle and Abi, Arden was telling her mum that Matt was the man who'd given her the pill at Gurva, and Abi was having to be restrained by River.

'Please, Adrian, make yourself useful and punch that man,' Abi yelled.

'Can we focus, please?' asked Zoe. 'Ben's going to land in a moment.'

They all looked up. It was true: Ben Bont had obviously decided that the long paddock next to the woods would do just fine, and he'd already taken one pass. The noise from the plane was deafening.

'I'll take care of the guests,' yelled Frances, and she and Troy kicked into action, grabbing some of the local waiters to herd the crane-necked guests over to the marquee for drinks and nibbles.

Now it was Grace's turn to stand in front of Elle in her wedding dress and look her up and down. 'What are you wearing?'

Elle sighed. 'Where are my boys?'

'What do you care?' Abi asked. 'You were very happy to see the back of them when their modelling shift was over.'

'Abi,' Elle gave another sigh, 'I know you think I'm a monster, but I let you take them that night for their own protection. They've been through enough, and I didn't need them being around that man.'

'So, are we supposed to believe,' Abi said, 'that all the heinous things you've done, you did because you're dating a bully?'

'You finally met your match, right?' asked Arden.

'Arden,' Grace said evenly, 'enough. There's no pleasure in someone else's fear, no matter who it is.'

'Do you know something, Grace?' asked Adrian.

'I know a bit,' said Grace, looking over at Leisel. 'Elle, come inside.'

And two women in wedding dresses walked together into the farmhouse, one leaning over the other to peer at the cute baby.

'This is the strangest wedding!' said a woman's voice nearby. It was Grace and Leisel's mum, here from Sydney for the occasion. 'I knew a lesbian ceremony would be different, but three brides?' Leisel put an arm around her and guided her to the marquee.

The plane, with a roar, was down, and Ben Bont was climbing out.

Matt started towards him first, but Abi—surprising herself with the speed she could move in her beaded dress—managed to get to Matt before he got to Ben.

'No,' she said, looking at Matt with undisguised fury, 'no one is beating anyone up on my farm, at my wedding.'

'Then what?' said Matt. 'He's used to getting what he wants. And that baby is his baby.'

'We're going to talk.'

Ben Bont had to climb over a fence to reach the house. He looked around for a moment, taking in the scene of all these people dressed in formal wear, standing around with little glasses of fizzy kombucha, staring at him. 'Where's Elle?' he shouted.

'You won't be seeing her,' said Abi. 'Please leave.'

'You.' Ben sneered. 'As if—'

'This is my property and you will get off it before I call the police,' Abi said, and then added, 'Fuckhead.'

'Really? Well, the police might be interested in the charge of kidnapping I'm going to slap on that... woman,' Ben said, 'taking my baby—'

'To a family wedding?' asked Adrian, who was standing alongside.

'Oh. And you. And your little pill-head daughter. And... the dealer.' Ben looked at Matt.

Despite his tone, Abi could tell it was becoming apparent to him that he was very definitely on enemy territory.

'Ask Elle to come out and this will all be over,' Ben said. 'I just want to take her home.'

'That won't be happening,' said Abi.

Ben was looking around for Elle, his eyes sweeping all of the women in their best dresses, as if she might be hiding in plain sight.

'Tell her, she needs to come out, right now. She's about to lose everything that matters to her.' He spoke loudly, as if addressing the crowd or hoping that wherever Elle was, she could hear him. 'Gurva!' he almost shouted. 'And her reputation...'

At that word, Abi couldn't help it—she snorted a little.

'And me! As if I couldn't make a claim that Alma's good character was at risk, living with *that*!' He was booming now.

Every wedding guest's head was turned in the same direction. Little kids had run over to get a closer look at the plane.

'So, you're hoping to blackmail your bride into coming back?' Arden asked, from nowhere. 'That sounds like a love story for the ages.'

At being spoken to by a little woodland faerie wielding a camera, Ben Bont widened his eyes.

'What you're going to do,' Abi told him firmly, 'is get back in your stupid little plane and buzz off.'

'Why would I do that?' he asked, squaring up, hands on hips.

Abi, who had spent the morning wondering if her life was about to collapse around her like so much rubble, who had spent months watching her daughter spinning out of her orbit, who had spent years trying to piece together a life she could stand in proudly, suddenly felt everything click into place. She had this.

'Because my vlogger daughter is filming all of this,' Abi nodded at Arden, pride in her voice, 'and my journalist sister-in-law has her editor on the phone,' she nodded at Leisel, who'd left her mother at the marquee and returned, 'and this man, here, Matt, will be able to confirm that narcotics were being sold on your property. And that woman over there...' Abi nodded to Frances, who was walking towards them, 'has the actual document you gave her offering her hush money. And at least three of these people have witnessed you being physically aggressive to your partner. So, if I were you...'

Ben Bont wanted to fight them all. He was pulsing with fury and humiliation. Standing in a fucking paddock in Victoria in an undone bow tie, being lectured by a middle-aged lesbian in a wedding dress—this was *not* what happened to Ben Bont.

Frances was close enough to speak now. 'I saw the bruises,' she said. 'I heard the fight.'

Matt stepped forwards and put a hand on Ben's shoulder. 'Come on, mate.'

As the two men walked back towards the plane, Ben wrestled free of Matt's grip and made a break for the house, but River and Adrian brought him down before he got to the veggie garden.

The wedding guests were all standing, open-mouthed, watching it all.

Ben was shouting, 'I won't have enough fuel!'

'Then fly as far as you can get, mate,' Matt said, pushing him into the plane.

***

Inside the house, Elle Campbell was sitting at Abi's kitchen table, spooning some organic vegetable baby mush into Alma's mouth.

'Is this... okay? Sterile and stuff?' she asked Grace.

'I thought you were one of us these days,' Grace replied. 'All earthy and natural, not afraid of a few germs...'

Elle laughed. 'Come on, you know that's just for clicks,' she said.

And as she did, Abi, Frances and Arden came into the kitchen.

'Has he gone?' Elle asked anxiously.

Abi nodded and sat down at the table.

Elle visibly slumped, exhaling. 'Oh, thank god.'

'I want to get back to our wedding,' Abi said, looking up at Grace, and then at Elle. 'But first, I think we should write something. In fact, you should write something... with Frances.'

'I don't think I can...' said Elle, pulling herself back up. 'I have all kinds of legal things pending and—'

'Elle,' said Abi. 'It's the last part. It's a step to freedom.'

Elle looked up and through the window. Outside, Adrian seemed as if he was trying to explain something to a young blonde woman. Teddy and Freddie were playing around him, dangling off his arms, dashing through his legs to get a ball to Sol and Otto.

'What am I writing?' Elle asked.

And three women in wedding dresses and one exhausted new mum in a bartender's apron gathered around a laptop at a farm's kitchen table to work together for the first time.

Dear Goddesses and Ordinary Human Women,

I owe you all an apology.

I hope this will be the last one.

You see, through all the little lies I have told over the years, there's one that hurts the most.

It's that you're not enough.

That you're not thin enough. Friend enough. Mum enough. That you're not pure enough. Rich enough. Hot enough.

That you're not wife enough. Beautiful enough. Sharp enough.

I have told plenty of lies to sell you that lie.

I didn't push my baby out in a forest.

I don't breastfeed.

I don't start my day doing silent yoga with a baby who never cries.

I don't blend my own smoothies and live on fresh air.

I don't have smooth skin, pouty lips and great boobs because I drink a lot of water.

I don't have a perfect supportive partner who lives to please me.

I didn't bounce back to skinny just by being positive and staying out of the sun.

I don't have an amazing relationship with the little boys whose life I blew up.

My life is a mess.

Maybe yours is, too.

It's okay.

Our new project is honesty. Let's start there this year.

Yours, E x

'Happy now?' asked Elle, looking around the table.

'It's a start,' said Frances.

And the wedding party began at last.

ACKNOWLEDGEMENTS

I wrote most of this book the same way I wrote *The Mummy Bloggers*—sitting on my bed, hiding from my family. Writing is a deeply selfish pursuit—for me it's just silence and the laptop and endless tea for endless hours—but also for me, it can't be done without the support of so many others.

So first, a thank you to the family who encourage me to leave the bedroom sometimes—my partner Brent McKean, who keeps everything travelling, reads every word, named this book and whose regular offer to 'take the kids out, so you can write' is perhaps the most underrated of romantic proposals. I love you. And also those kids, our Matilda and Billy, who do not respect the boundary of the bedroom door, and whose heads have been under my arms, on my knees or right next to mine while I wrote much of this. You're just the best reason to do anything.

And then there are the people who help me get the words out of my head and onto the page—cheerleaders like Monique Bowley and Lucy Ormonde, without whose advice I'd be completely at sea. My girls Mel Ware and Rebecca Rodwell, who read early and tell me what's working and what's not. And this time, the fabulous Sam Marshall, who let me visit her hospital ward and ask her a hundred silly questions about nursing. Thank you, Sam, I won't tell your boss.

The women who do life and dinners and children and family with me—Penny Kaleta, Sally Godfrey, Angie McMenamin, Karen Graham, Miranda Herron. You're the source of much support, inspiration and relief.

Thanks to the women I work with whose crackling passion drives me to want to make things—not least of those Mia Freedman, who encourages me daily to be better, go harder and to act, not to dither. Likewise Rachel Corbett, Briony Benjamin and Lauren Joyce. I get wise counsel from my podcast partner Andrew Daddo—who is always writing two books at once—and from Elissa Ratliff, my country correspondent. And thanks to the entire Mamamia team of kick-arse, generous, smart women (and a few good men) who allowed me to disappear again to write this.

My publishers at Allen & Unwin, Claire Kingston and Kelly Fagan, who changed my life and completely 'get' these books. And to my editor Kate Goldsworthy, who dug deep and found the resolve to meet Elle again.

Many more thanks go across the oceans to my Manchester family—my Mum and Dad, Jeff and Judith Wainwright, whose visits here seem to keep coinciding with book-writing and much-appreciated extra babysitting shifts. To my brother Tom and his partner Emilie, to Lila, Louie, Poppy and Henry, all of whose support I can feel from here. And to my dearest Lindsay Frankel and Ian McLeish who are my family, too, and who crack me up even more than the idea of doing a juice cleanse.

Lastly, just a massive, fizzy bucket of thanks to everyone who loved *The Mummy Bloggers*. So many women (almost all women, sorry, Mark Brandon) who laughed and messaged me and told their friends and took it to book club. Thank you. You're an army of women who know that scrolling through Instagram shouldn't be an exercise in self-flagellation. It should just be an exercise in ignoring your children when they're crying in public. Keep going. x

We hope you enjoyed reading *How To Be Perfect* as much as we did here at Legend Press. If you haven't read *The Mummy Bloggers* yet, here's an excerpt from the first chapter.

CHAPTER ONE

ELLE

The Stylish Mumma

30,167 people know how Elle and Adrian met.

That's how many followers Elle's anonymous blog—Somebody Else's Husband—had at the height of its infamy.

More people than lived in the small brown town where Elle grew up had followed the story of a young personal trainer and the married financier she'd met at the gym.

A sample post:

> Today, Reader [she was twenty-two, after all], I tried to resist A. When he looked at me Like That, I looked away. When he touched my arm Like That (in front of Adam from Zumba!!!) I pulled away. I know what I am doing is wrong. But Reader. How do I stop myself from running towards the only thing that feels right to me???? The only thing that ever has. When I am in his arms, even though I am afraid, I feel safe. It's the strangest thing. I CAN'T FIGHT IT.

That was true—Elle couldn't fight it—because there was nothing to fight. Only a plan to follow through. One night she stayed long after her last class and walked into the deserted men's changing room and right into Adrian's shower cubicle.

Unsurprisingly, that night had inspired the blog's most clicked-on post. Ever.

Elle shut her laptop when she heard footsteps outside the kitchen. Adrian had no idea that that particular blog existed. Not then, not now. But Elle had no intention of unpublishing Somebody Else's Husband. She loved that it lived on, a vivid memento of who she once was. The kind of woman who wrote florid sentences like:

> The smell of my pussy reminds me of A. I think about him the way I used to fantasise about Ryan Gosling. OMG. A and I are living our very own Notebook!

These days Elle blogged under her own name, but about much tamer topics. Her most recent post featured freshly baked beetroot-chocolate brownies, Instagrammed with the hashtag #treatday.

The picture was perfection, of course. A high-angled selfie, it took in Elle biting into a brownie, panning down just enough to show her cropped white gym top and tanned, flat stomach. You could see the edge of the oven behind her, brand name visible, and a glimpse of her new ironbark kitchen benchtop—which, she knew, would generate as many comments as the cakes. Or her abs.

She tipped the brownies into her motion-sensor stainless steel bin, immediately followed by the Organic Annie's packet they'd arrived in. If she left them out, Adrian would be on them in a heartbeat. He couldn't afford that, in her opinion.

Elle had always had a critical eye—possibly, she thought, as the result of growing up in a house where there was much to criticise. She had always felt like she was observing and running commentary on her life from afar. Now, of course, she actually was: she and 154,158 others.

If Somebody Else's Husband had granted her blogging training wheels, The Stylish Mumma was her masterpiece—a tangle of relatable mum-confession and aspirational lifestyle porn. She had changed tack at exactly the moment Instagram had started rewarding aesthetics with armies of followers. And she knew what they wanted.

Her new kitchen, for example. When she and Adrian had begun to renovate their dream glass-and-white box in Melbourne's beachside suburb of Brighton, she'd known that the kitchen would be the heart of her home. Not for her family, but for her followers. It would be the room that made every other woman in Australia feel bad about her kitchen.

And so it was. Sophisticated from every angle, it was a white-on-white masterpiece that barely needed a filter.

Whenever Elle needed a boost, she would open her fridge—the giant, French-doored beast was stacked with shiny, labelled containers. Everything was in its place, so there was no need to rummage around: 'Kale', 'Spinach', 'Rocket', all in identical Tupperware, with lids in primary colours. Then the grains, the proteins, the sliced fruit for the boys.

The fridge was the opposite of the ones in the kitchens of her childhood. From whichever council pick-up those appliances had come, they all had blackened corners and cracked plastic shelves that sagged under the weight of her dad's half-slab. All the kids knew never to take anything from a fridge without a suspicious poke and sniff: discarded apple halves, open yoghurt pots with peeled-back lids, half-eaten cans of beans, hard-edged cheese ends. And always a curdled last-inch of milk.

Elle's own fridge had a compartment just for plucked grapes that had been washed and chilled in the crisper. Her boys—should they grow tall enough or behave well enough to be allowed—could help themselves to crunchy, fresh goodness day and night. And one day, she felt sure, they would.

Her sons wouldn't share her secret fetish for 'poor-people food', as she and her sister had called it: baked beans, packet mac and cheese, two-minute noodles, tinned spaghetti. Salt. Slop. Fat. It tempted and disgusted her in equal measure. Whereas the labelled tub of kimchi on the middle shelf? It made her feel virtuous, in control, beyond temptation. So, the brownies were in the bin.

Elle's kitchen was a reminder of how far she'd come.

'Want me to do anything else before I go?' asked Cate, from the doorway. 'I've laid out the boys' clothes for the next three days in the dressing-room, and we're scheduled through till Tuesday lunchtime.'

Cate never came into the kitchen. Elle hadn't made an explicit rule, but she knew people familiar with the house could sense the force field around her showpiece. Any interloper was bound to put something in the wrong place. Any foot aside from Elle's on the polished concrete floor felt like a child's muddy hand on a fresh white summer dress.

'I think we're good, Cate. How's it looking?'

'Reach is down a little bit, but to be honest recipes aren't going as well as the homes posts at the moment.'

Cate was Elle's social media manager and unofficial au pair. Twenty-one and vibrating with ambition, she had practically stalked Elle, working for free until she was invited to stay. A girl from Sydney's western suburbs who wanted what Elle had—influence and an expensive wardrobe—she tried to style herself on the boss, spending most of each day tapping away at the phone and laptop in her no-name active wear.

What Cate didn't know about social media hadn't been thought of yet, but as an au pair she'd had a lot to learn. Elle had made it clear to Cate that her boys were on a strict daily routine. On Day Two, she'd come home from a photoshoot to find Cate feeding them spaghetti bolognaise in front of *Canimals*. That was nipped in the bud with a printed-out hourly schedule of exactly where Freddie and Teddy should be at any given moment, along with what they should be doing and the foods they should be eating. 'Don't use your initiative when it comes to the boys,' Elle had told Cate firmly. 'Just follow the rules.'

'I'll be home before eleven,' Cate was saying now. 'I think tomorrow's outfit post is going to go gangbusters.'

Elle had recently started a daily post to showcase her sons' outfits.

At two and three, Elle's 'Irish twins' were, she recognised, at the pinnacle of their cuteness, with their overgrown black curls and their mother's green eyes. She could barely keep up with the parcels of free clothes that streamed through the door. Tiny polo shirts and hipster tees, boat shoes and cargo shorts, skinny jeans and drop-crotch leggings, hats and scarves and socks and satchels—all of which would have looked perfectly acceptable on a grown man at a creative agency in Brunswick. The only things missing on her two little #dudes were the beards.

She'd dedicated a whole room to their wardrobe, outfits chosen well in advance and recorded on a polaroid board before posting, to keep track of sponsorships and avoid double-ups. It was almost a full-time job to curate and record the boys' aesthetic—'It's Prince George meets Harry Styles,' was how Elle and Cate described it to interested PRs.

Elle knew her sons were on the edge of rebellion about the now-weekly shoot. Adrian, too, had his reservations about the boys' photos—after all, he was a 47-year-old man who had, before he'd met Elle, considered fashion to be two things: a suit in the week and a polo shirt on weekends. But the engagement was too good to lose. And anyway, planning the kids' outfits days ahead made her feel calm.

'You know why you're obsessed with order, don't you?' Adrian had said to her on one of their early dates, at that stage in a relationship when the other's neuroses are still charming puzzles to be solved.

That stage in their relationship when he was cheating on his wife.

'It's because you had none when you were growing up. You're obsessed with keeping everything in its place because you think the chaos can't get you then.'

This wasn't news to Elle, a long-time devotee of self-improvement books and life-coaching seminars. And she armchair-analysed Adrian right back—not aloud, of course—quickly diagnosing him with a rescue complex. The more vulnerable she seemed, the more invested he would be.

Elle now felt the same way about her followers. She knew how to keep them interested—she knew that they needed aspiration. They needed to know that their own messy lives were a temporary state, that a broken bird could become a beautiful swan.

Her tribe needed to live and breathe that fairytale so they could believe that one day they too would have a kitchen with a spray tap and a Thermomix, even if they'd grown up with a shitty dad and currently made do with a stick blender.

Elle made sure to reveal just enough of herself, of her story, to attach and keep her followers. She exuded enough success to have them want to see her every day, but she remained vulnerable enough that they didn't completely hate her. She spoke the language of gratitude while appearing to have it all.

As a woman who had already reinvented herself more than once, she'd never felt so well-qualified for anything in her life. After all, her kitchen proved that anything was possible.

'You go, Cate,' she said, when she realised that the girl was still standing there with a fixed smile, unable to leave without permission. 'Have fun! Adrian and I have got the boys.' Actually, iPads had got the boys—a guaranteed way to silence preschoolers.

Cate obviously had a date: she was wearing lipstick and a skirt that could have passed as a belt, and she fairly sprinted out of the house at her boss's wave. Pretty girl, thought Elle, but she could do so much more with herself.

Elle swivelled on her high-backed white leather stool and opened the laptop.

A #grateful day.

Ever had one of those days, Mummas, where you realise that maybe, just maybe, you're doing a good job at this mothering thing after all? One of those days where you can see all of the tiny sacrifices you make for your family paying off?

I feel that way today. The sunlight is coming in through my kitchen window. The washing up is done, the laundry is folded away, the kitchen smells of warm, comforting home cooking. It smells of love. I have just finished baking some #healthytreats for my family that I know will nourish them and make them smile.

It's one of those days when I'm so grateful that I made the choice to stay at home and put my energy into what matters. One of those days when I know that making the effort to prepare healthy meals for my boys was the right decision. It's a day when I'm so happy that I have been the one on the floor playing trains with them.

It's one of those days when I know that everything I have been through, I have been through so I could get to be right here today, in my beautiful home with my three beautiful men. There's nothing like a #grateful day. I hope you're having one, too. And if today's been tough, know that tomorrow can be better #loveandlight

Elle snapped another selfie to go with her post. I am grateful that my new lip filler has settled, she thought, but didn't type. I am grateful that Cate is getting paid to play trains with the boys. I'm grateful for Organic Annie's home-delivery brownies. I'm grateful it's not the day when Adrian's girls come over to sulk at me. I'm grateful I am not Feral Abi.

'Come on, boys, it's bathtime!' Elle called through the kitchen door.